First Published in Great Britain 2017
By Mills & Boon, an imprint of HarperCollins*Publishers*
1 London Bridge Street, London, SE1 9GF

HIS LITTLE SECRET © 2017 Harlequin Books S. A.

Double The Trouble, *His Lover's Little Secret* and *Baby For Keeps* were first published in Great Britain by Harlequin (UK) Limited.

Double The Trouble © 2014 Maureen Child
His Lover's Little Secret © 2014 Andrea Laurence
Baby For Keeps © 2014 Janice Maynard

ISBN: 978-0-263-92956-0

05-0317

His Little Secret

MAUREEN CHILD
ANDREA LAURENCE
JANICE MAYNARD

DOUBLE
THE TROUBLE

BY
MAUREEN CHILD

Maureen Child writes for the Mills & Boon Desire line and can't imagine a better job. Being able to indulge your love for romance, as well as being able to spin stories just the way you want them told is, in a word, perfect.

A seven-time finalist for the prestigious Romance Writers of America RITA® Award, Maureen is the author of more than one hundred romance novels. Her books regularly appear on the bestseller lists and have won several awards, including a Prism, a National Readers' Choice Award, a Colorado Romance Writers Award of excellence and a Golden Quill.

One of her books, *The Soul Collector,* was made into a CBS TV movie starring Melissa Gilbert, Bruce Greenwood and Ossie Davis. If you look closely, in the last five minutes of the movie, you'll spot Maureen, who was an extra in the last scene.

Maureen believes that laughter goes hand in hand with love, so her stories are always filled with humor. The many letters she receives assures her that her readers love to laugh as much as she does.

Maureen Child is a native Californian, but has recently moved to the mountains of Utah. She loves a new adventure, though the thought of having to deal with snow for the first time is a little intimidating.

To Harlequin Desire readers everywhere.
Thank you so much for embracing the Kings of
California—and me. You make it possible for me to do
what I most love to do. Tell stories.

One

Colton King never saw the fist that slammed into his jaw.

He shook his head to clear it, then blocked the next punch before it could land. The furious man who'd stormed into Colt's office only moments before took a step back and ground out, "You had that coming."

"What the hell?" Colt dropped his packed duffel bag to the floor. "Had it coming?"

Colt did a fast mental review and came up empty. He didn't know this man and he couldn't think of a single other person who wanted to hit him—at the moment. His always-temporary relationships with women invariably ended amicably. Heck, even he and his twin brother, Connor, hadn't had a good argument in weeks.

Yeah, he'd had angry clients show up at the Laguna Beach, California, offices of King's Extreme Adventures if they didn't find the monster waves they'd been promised. Or if the dead man's run on a mountain was closed due to avalanche.

Colton and Connor arranged adventure vacations for the wealthy adrenaline junkies of the world. So, sure, there had been more than a few times when a customer was mad enough to cause a scene. But not one of them had ever punched him. Before now.

So the question was, "Who the hell are you?"

"I called security!" A woman announced from the doorway.

Colt didn't even glance at Linda, the admin he and Connor shared. "Thanks. Go get Connor."

"On it," she said, then vanished.

"Calling security won't change anything," the guy who had just punched him said flatly. "You'll still be a selfish bastard."

"Okay," Colt muttered. Not the first time he'd heard that, either. But a little context would be helpful. "You want to tell me what's going on here?"

"That's what I'd like to know." Connor stepped into the room to take a stand beside his twin.

Colt was glad to have him there, though he could have taken the guy who'd gotten in one lucky sucker punch. But probably not good business to have a fistfight here in the office, and having Connor around would help him leash his temper. Besides, fighting wouldn't give him the answers he wanted. "You took your best shot. Now tell me *why*."

"My name is Robert Oaks."

Oaks. Long-buried memories raced through Colt's mind in a blinding rush. A ball of ice dropped into the pit of his stomach and his body went utterly still. He studied the stranger glaring at him and in those narrowed green eyes, he saw…familiarity.

Damn it.

The last time he'd looked into eyes like those had been nearly two years ago. At the end of a week in Vegas that should have been ordinary and instead had been…amazing. One specific memory rose up in his mind and Colt wished to hell he could wipe it away, but he'd never been able to pull that off. The morning after he and Penny Oaks had gotten married in a tacky chapel on the strip. The morning when he'd told her they'd be getting a divorce—right before thanking her for a fun week and then leaving her in the hotel room they'd shared.

He didn't want to think about that day. But hard to avoid that now, with the man who had to be her brother standing in front of him.

Robert Oaks nodded slowly as he saw realization dawn on Colt's face. "Good. At least you remember."

"Remember what?" Connor demanded.

"Nothing." He wasn't getting into this with Connor. Not right now, anyway.

"Oh, *nothing*. That's great." Oaks shook his head in disgust. "Just what I expected."

Anger stirred. Whatever was once between him and Penny was just that. Between the two of them. He wasn't interested in what her brother thought. "Why are you here? What do you want?"

"I want you to do the right thing," Robert snapped. "But I doubt you will." His fist bunched. "So I thought punching you would be enough. It wasn't."

Impatience stirred and twisted in the anger still balled in Colt's guts. He had a KingJet waiting to fly him to

Sicily. He had places to go. Things to do. And damned if he'd waste one more minute with Robert Oaks.

"Why don't you quit dancing around and get to it. Why are you here?"

"Because my sister's in the hospital."

"Hospital?" Something inside Colt lurched unsteadily. Instantly, memories shifted, his mind filling with images of another hospital, the cold green walls, the grim gray linoleum and the stench of fear and antiseptic flavoring every breath.

For a second or two, he felt as though there was a weight on his chest, dragging him back into a past he never wanted to visit again. Deliberately, he pushed away from the blackness at the edges of his mind and fought his way back to the present. Pushing one hand through his hair, Colt focused his gaze on Penny's brother and waited.

"My sister had an appendectomy yesterday," Robert told him.

Relief that it wasn't something more serious was a small, slim thread winding its way through the tangled mass inside him. "Is she okay?"

Robert snorted a derisive laugh. "Yeah, she's fine. Except, you know, for worrying about how she's going to pay the hospital bill. And worrying about her twins. *Your* twins."

All of the air left the room.

Colt knew that because he couldn't draw a breath.

"My—" He shook his head while he tried to get a grip on what Penny's younger brother was telling him. But how the hell did you make sense of something like *that* coming at you out of the blue? What the hell was he supposed to do? Say? Think?

Colt scrubbed both hands across his face, forced one shaky breath into his lungs and finally managed to say, "*Twins?* Penny had a baby?"

"Two," Robert corrected, and looked from Colt to Connor and back again. "Looks like twins run in your family."

"And she didn't tell him?" Connor sounded as stunned as Colt felt.

Fury rose up and nearly choked him. She had never said a damn word. She'd been pregnant and hadn't told him. She'd delivered two children and hadn't told him.

He had *children?*

That weight was back on his chest again but this time he ignored it.

"Where are they?" The demand was short and sharp.

Robert looked at him warily and Colt knew that his expression must have mirrored the anger erupting inside.

"My fiancée and I have been taking care of them."

Them. Colt was the father of twins and he knew nothing about them. How was that even possible? He'd always been careful. But apparently, his mind taunted, not careful enough.

A small voice in the back of his mind whispered that this might all be a lie. That Penny could have told her brother a lie. That the babies weren't really *his.* But even as he considered that possibility, he dismissed it. That would have been too easy, and Colt knew better than most that there was nothing *easy* about any of this.

"A boy and a girl, if you're interested."

Colt's head snapped up and his gaze narrowed on Robert. *A boy and a girl.* He had two kids. Hell, he didn't know how he was supposed to feel. The only thing he was sure of at the moment was that his children's mother had some explaining to do.

"Damn straight I'm interested. Now tell me what hospital Penny's in."

He got all the information from Robert, including the man's cell number and his address. When building security arrived, Colt sent them away. He wasn't going to press charges against Penny's brother—the guy was pissed and defending his family. Colton would have done the same. But once Robert had left, Colt released some of his fury by kicking his duffel bag across the room.

Connor leaned against the doorjamb. "So, trip to Sicily is off?"

Colt was supposed to be in the air right now, heading for Mount Etna to try out a new BASE jumping spot. It's what he did—searching out the most dangerous, most awe-inspiring sport sites for their ever-growing client list.

But now, he had a different sort of adrenaline burst waiting for him. Colt slanted his twin a hard look. "Yeah, it's off."

"And you're a father."

"Looks like it."

He sounded calm, didn't he? He wasn't, though. There were too many emotions, too many thoughts crowding his mind for him to even separate one from the other. A *father.* There were two babies in the world because of *him,* and he'd had no idea until a few minutes ago. How was that even possible? Shouldn't he have *felt* something? Shouldn't he have damn well been *told* that he was a father?

Colt shook his head, still trying to wrap his mind around it. He couldn't. Hell, no kid deserved to have him for a father. He knew that. Rubbing the center of his chest to try to ease the ache settled there, Colt blew out a breath. How was he supposed to be feeling? Anger tangled with sheer terror, then twisted into a tight knot that iced over and left him feeling cold to the bone.

"And you were gonna tell me about this when?"

Colt gaped at his twin. "Seriously? I just found out myself, remember?"

"I'm not talking about the twins—I'm talking about their mother."

"Nothing to tell." Lies, he thought. Lies. Truth was, there was plenty to tell, just nothing he wanted to talk about. It was the only time in his life Colt had kept something from his twin. He still couldn't explain why. Colt shoved one hand through his hair. "It was the convention in Vegas nearly two years ago."

"You met her there?"

Colt stalked across the room and picked up the duffel he'd packed for his now-canceled trip to Sicily. Slinging it over his shoulder, he turned to face his brother. "I don't want to talk about this now, okay?"

If he didn't get out of there in the next ten seconds, he was going to blow. Temper boiling, it was all he could do to hold it together.

"Too bad," Connor said shortly. "I just found out I'm an uncle. So tell me about this woman."

His twin wasn't going to let this go and Colt knew it. Hell, if the situation was reversed, he'd be demanding answers, too, so he couldn't really blame him. Didn't make this any easier, though.

"Not much to say," he ground out, teeth gritted. "I met her at the extreme sports convention. We spent the week together and then—"

"Then?"

Colt blew out a breath. "We got married."

If he hadn't been in such a foul mood the look on his twin's face would have made Colt laugh hysterically. He'd never seen Connor so shocked. Of course, why wouldn't he be? Colt felt pretty much as if someone had knocked him over the head with a two-by-four, himself.

"You got *married?*" Connor pushed away from the doorjamb and stalked into the room. "And you didn't bother to tell me?"

"It lasted, like, a *minute,*" Colt said. Even now he couldn't believe that he'd surrendered so deeply to the passion he'd found with Penny that he'd actually married her. He hadn't said anything to Connor because he hadn't even been able to explain to himself what he'd done.

Shaking his head, he turned and looked out the window at the ocean beyond the glass. Surfers rode their boards toward shore. Tourists strolled along the beach, snapping pictures as they went, and farther out on the water, sailboats skimmed the surface, bright sails fluttering in the wind.

The world was going on just as it always had. Everything looked completely normal. Nothing out of place. And yet…for him, nothing would ever be the same again.

"Colt, it's been nearly two years, and you never said a word?"

He glanced over his shoulder at his twin. "Never could find a way to say it. Con, I still don't know what the hell happened." Shaking his head again, he huffed out a breath and tamped down the anger still rising within him. "I came home, got a divorce and figured it was done. No point in telling you about it when it was over."

"Can't believe you were *married.*"

"You and me both," he muttered, and turned his gaze

back to the ocean, hoping for the calm that sight usually brought him. This time it didn't work. "I figured there was just nothing to tell."

"Yeah, well, you were wrong."

Understatement of the century.

"Looks that way." He had kids. Two of them. He could do the math, so he'd already worked out that they were eight months old. Eight months of their lives and he'd never even seen them. Never even guessed that they might exist. Cold fury rose up inside him again and he struggled to breathe past what felt like an iron band, tightening around his chest.

It had been close to two years since he'd seen Penny— though he'd thought about her far more often than he wanted to admit, even to himself. But at the moment, it wasn't memories driving him. Or the desire he'd once felt for her. It was cold fury, plain and simple. The kind of raw rage he'd never felt before. She'd kept his children from him and she'd done it deliberately. After all, it wasn't like he was hard to find. He was a King, for God's sake, and the Kings of California weren't exactly low profile.

"Fine. So what're you gonna do?"

Colt turned his back on the ocean and faced his twin. Steely determination fired his soul and filled his voice as he said, "I'm going to see my ex-wife. Then I'm going to get my kids."

Every time she moved, Penny felt a swift stab of pain. That didn't stop her from trying, though. Wincing, she shifted around carefully until she could reach the rolla-way table that held her laptop. Swinging it around, she then scooted up higher on the bed, moving much more slowly than she wanted to.

Penny was more accustomed to moving through life at top speed. She had a business and a home and two babies to care for, so hurrying was the only way she could keep up. Being forced to lie still in a hospital bed she couldn't afford was making her a little crazy.

Every moment she was stuck here was another dollar sign ticking up on the bill she would soon be handed. Every moment here, her babies were without her. And though Penny trusted her younger brother and his fiancée, Maria, completely, she missed the twins desperately. Since she worked out of her home, she was with them all the time. Being away from them made her feel as if she were missing a limb.

She reached out to pull the rolling table closer and gasped at the quick stab of pain slicing through her. "Ow!"

"You probably should lie still."

"Oh, God." Penny froze, hardly daring to breathe. She knew that voice. Heard it every night in her dreams. Clutching the edge of the table, only her eyes moved, tracking to the doorway where *he* stood. Colton King. The father of her children, the star of every one of her fantasies, her ex-husband and absolutely the last man on earth she wanted to see.

"Surprised?" he asked.

That word really didn't cover what she was feeling. "You could say that."

"Well then," he snapped, "you have some idea of how I feel."

Robert, she thought grimly. She was going to have to kill her little brother. Sure, she'd practically raised him and she loved him dearly. But for going to Colton and ratting her out, Robert had to pay. But dealing with her brother could come later. At the moment, she had to find a way to deal with her past.

"What're you doing here?"

He walked slowly into the room, his long legs crossing the linoleum-covered floor in a few easy strides. He moved almost lazily, but Penny wasn't fooled. She could feel the tension radiating off of him in thick waves and she braced herself for the confrontation that had been almost two years in the making.

His hands were tucked into the pockets of his black jeans. His thick-soled boots hardly made a whisper of sound as he moved. His black hair was a little too long, curling around the collar of his bloodred pullover shirt. But it was his eyes that held her. That mesmerized her as they had nearly two years ago.

They were the pale blue of an icy sky, fringed by lashes so thick and black any woman would have killed to have them. And right now, those cold eyes were fixed on her.

He was still the sexiest man she'd ever met. Still had that air about him that drew women to him like metal shavings to a magnet. Still made her want to throw both herself *and* a rock at him.

"Robert came to see me," he said lightly, as if it didn't mean a thing. But she knew better. Yes, they'd only been together for a week almost two years ago, but in those two years, Penny had relived every moment with him hundreds of times. At first, she had tried to forget him, because remembering only brought pain.

But then she'd found herself pregnant, and forgetting was impossible. So instead, she'd reveled in her memo-

ries. Kept them fresh and alive by mentally deconstruct-
ing every conversation, examining every moment spent
with him. She knew the tone of his voice. Knew the feel
of his skin, the taste of his lips.

And she knew, just by looking at him now, he was
angry.

Well then, they were a match. She didn't want him
here. Didn't *need* him here. Penny took a deep breath
and braced for the coming storm.

He stopped at the foot of her hospital bed and met her
gaze with a steely stare. "So," he said. "What's new?"

Anger flashed in those cool blue eyes and a muscle in
his jaw ticked spasmodically. One glance down to where
his hands were closed over the footboard showed that his
knuckles were white with the force of his grip.

"Robert had no right to go to you." Her fingers tugged
at the thin green blanket covering her.

Her brother had been after her since before the twins
were born to go to Colt and tell him the truth. But she'd
had her reasons for keeping her secret and nothing had
changed. Well, nothing but for the fact that her little
brother had turned traitor.

"Well," he said on a sharp, short laugh. "You're right
about *that,* anyway. *You* should have told me."

Ice coated his words as well as his eyes. No doubt he
was waiting for her to quiver and shrivel up beneath his
hard gaze. Well, Penny refused to back down or to feel
guilty about her decision. When she'd first discovered
she was pregnant, she'd gone around and around in her
mind, trying to figure out the best course of action.

She had argued with herself for weeks over what was
the right thing to do. Yes, she might have had an easier
time of it the last couple of years if she had gone to Colt

in the beginning. But she also might have spent the last two years tangled up in hard feelings, accusations and arguments. Not to mention a custody battle she wouldn't have stood a chance in. He was a *King,* for heaven's sake, and she didn't have enough money to buy lunch out!

So she'd chosen to keep the truth from him and she didn't regret it. How could she, when she knew she had done what she felt was in the best interests of her children?

With that thought firmly in mind, she got a grip on her own feelings as anger and frustration began to churn inside. "I understand how you feel but—"

"You understand *nothing.*" He cut her off as neatly as if he'd used a knife. "I just found out I'm a father. I have twins and I've never seen them." His white-knuckled grip on the foot rail of the bed tightened further and still his voice remained as cool and detached as the icy glare he had pinned on her. "I don't even know their *names.*"

She flushed. Fine. Yes. She could see how he felt. But that didn't mean what she'd done was wrong. Naturally, he wouldn't see it that way, but what Colton King thought of her really didn't matter, did it?

He never blinked. He only stared at her, with those ice-blue eyes narrowed as if he were focusing in an attempt to see into her mind and read all of her secrets. Thank heaven he couldn't.

"Their names, Penny. I've got a right to know the names of my children."

She hated this. Hated feeling as though she were setting her babies up to be let down by a father who didn't really want them. But she couldn't ignore his demand, either. Now that he knew about the twins, what was the point of trying to protect their anonymity?

"Okay. Your son's name is Reid and your daughter is Riley," she said.

He swallowed hard, took a deep breath and hissed it out again. "Reid and Riley *what?*"

She knew exactly what he meant. "Their last name is Oaks."

His mouth flattened into a grim line and it looked to Penny as if he were counting to ten. Slowly. "That'll change."

Panic shot through her, riding a lightning bolt of anger. "You think you can take over and change their names? No. You can't just walk back into my life and try to decide what's best for my children."

"Why the hell not?" he countered coldly. "You made that decision for *me* nearly two years ago."

"Colt—"

"Did you bother to list me as the father on their birth certificates?"

"Of course I did." Her twins had the right to know who their father was. And she would have told them… eventually.

"That's something at least," he muttered. "I'll have my lawyers take care of the legal name change."

"Excuse me?" She struggled to push herself upright and gasped as another sharp stab of pain hit in her abdomen. Breathless, she dropped back against her pillows.

He was at the side of the bed in an instant. "Are you all right? Do you need a nurse?"

"I'm fine," she lied tightly as the pain began to ebb into a just barely tolerable ache. "And no, I don't need a nurse." She needed pain medication. Privacy so she could cry. An eight-ounce glass of wine. "What I need is for you to leave."

"Not gonna happen," he told her.

She closed her eyes and muttered, "I could kill Robert for this."

"Yeah," Colt countered. "Someone finally being honest with me. There's a crime."

Her gaze snapped back to his. He was studying her as he would a bug under a microscope. Damn it, couldn't he have gotten fat in the last couple of years? Lost his hair? *Something?* Why did he still have to be the most gorgeous man she'd ever met? And wouldn't you just know that she'd have the conversation she had been dreading for nearly two years while trapped in a hospital bed? Wearing a god-awful gown? She was in pain, she was hungry because hospital food was appalling and God knew what her hair looked like.

Oh, that's good. Be worried about how you look, Penny.

Hard not to worry about it though, she told herself glumly. Especially when Colton King was standing right in front of her looking even better than he had two years ago. He'd taken her breath away the first time she'd seen him and apparently he had the same effect on her today.

"So when do you get out of here?" he asked, shattering her thoughts.

"Tomorrow probably." And she couldn't wait. Yes, she was in pain but she hated being in the hospital. She missed her babies. Plus, Penny didn't like having to ask Robert and Maria to watch her children. They had enough going on, with their wedding only a few weeks away.

In hindsight, she should have known that Robert would go to Colt. Should have guessed that her brother, thinking he was doing the right thing, would betray her secrets to the one man who should never have found out the truth. Oh, she was going to have plenty to say to her little brother once she was released from this antiseptic prison.

"Fine, then," Colt said flatly. "We'll continue this discussion once you're home."

Well, that caught her attention.

"No, we won't. This conversation is over, Colt."

"Not by a long shot." He stared down at her until Penny twitched uneasily, and then he warned, "You've got a hell of a lot of explaining to do."

"I don't owe you anything." But those words sounded hollow even to her.

She'd kept a huge secret from him and she'd done it deliberately. She knew that anyone standing on the outside of this relationship would call her some really descriptive names. But they wouldn't know *why* she'd done it. She hadn't even told Robert everything. Penny'd had reasons for her decisions and they were good ones. Ones she wouldn't regret, even while staring up into the cool blue eyes that still haunted her dreams.

He was angry and he had the right. But she'd had the right to do what she'd thought best for her children. And she wouldn't start second-guessing herself now.

"You're wrong about that," he told her softly, but the gentle tone of his voice did nothing to hide the fury crouched inside him.

A nurse bustled into the room, all business. "I'm sorry, you'll have to wait outside while I examine Ms. Oaks."

Penny's gaze never left Colt's and for a second or two, she thought he would argue, refuse to leave. Then he took a step back and nodded.

"Fine. I'll be back tomorrow to pick you up."

Panic shot through her. "Not necessary. Robert will pick me up."

The nurse was hovering and Penny could feel her gaze moving back and forth between the two of them.

"We don't need Robert's help. I'll be here in the morning."

"Oh," the nurse piped up, "she probably won't be released until early afternoon."

Colt paid no attention. "I'll be here tomorrow."

Then he stalked out of the room and didn't look back. Penny knew because she watched him go and continued to stare at the empty doorway long after the sound of his footsteps had faded.

"Wow," the nurse murmured. "Is that your husband?"

"No," Penny said. "He's—" What? A friend? An enemy? The father of her children? Her past come back to wreak havoc with her present? Since she couldn't say any of that, she said only, "He's my ex."

The nurse sighed. "Wow, can't believe you let that one get away."

It wasn't as if she'd had a choice. Still, to avoid more conversation, Penny closed her eyes and let the nurse get on with the examination.

But her mind wouldn't stop. Thoughts of Colt jammed up in her brain until all she could see were his eyes. Cold. Icy. Fixed.

And furious enough to make Penny wish tomorrow were years away.

Two

He didn't go to see his twins.

He wasn't up for that just yet.

Colt didn't want his children's first subconscious memory of their father to be of him furious.

So instead, he went to the beach. He needed to burn off some of the fury pumping through him. But the calm waves at Laguna weren't going to be enough to soothe the temper riding him. What he needed for that was blood-pumping action with a thread of danger. Enough to make his adrenaline high enough to swamp the anger chewing at him.

In Newport Beach, the Wedge was just at the end of the Balboa Peninsula and the waves there could reach thirty feet or more. Because of some "improvements" to the jetty in Newport Harbor sometime in the thirties, the waves here were highly unpredictable. One wave com-

bined with another and then still another until the result-
ing wave was higher than anywhere else on the coast.
Best part was, no two waves were alike, and where they
would break was anybody's guess. Inexperienced surfers avoided the Wedge if they had any brains. As for
Colt and the handful of other surfers out on this cold,
autumn day…

The danger added to the fun.

Usually, anyway. Today, as he took wave after wave,
riding the crest, being tossed into the sea and coming up
in a froth of foam, his mind was too distracted to enjoy
the rush. Images of Penny flashed through his mind on
a continual loop. Visions of babies were there, too. Crying, laughing, sleeping. He couldn't clear his brain of
the thoughts plaguing him, so he pushed himself harder,
hoping for clarity. It didn't come though, and after a few
hours in the punishing tempest of the sea, Colt had had
enough. He dragged his board onto the sand and flopped
down onto it.

Wrapping his arms around his knees, he stared out at
the water and tried to make sense of what had happened
that day. He'd never expected to see Penny Oaks again.
Colt scrubbed one hand across his face and let himself
remember her, lying in that hospital bed.

Through the anger, through the frustration and shock,
he still had felt that jolt of sexual insanity he associated
only with Penny. And *insanity* was the only word he
could use to describe what she made him feel.

Penny, with her jeans and T-shirts and her lack of
makeup or artifice of any kind, was just not the type of
woman he was usually drawn to. He liked his women
fast and sleek, with no expectations other than a great

time in bed. Penny, though, was something else again. He'd known it instantly. But from that first moment at the convention nearly two years ago, he'd had to have her. One look at her and all he'd been able to think about was her long legs, wrapped around his waist. Her mouth pressed to his. Her breath warm against his skin.

And damned if she still didn't affect him that way.

Even lying in a hospital bed, with her long, dark red hair a tangle about her head, with her green eyes shining with both pain and panic, he'd wanted her so badly he'd had a hell of a time just walking out of the hospital.

After Vegas, he'd buried her memory and lost himself in dozens of temporary women. Yet he'd never really been able to wipe Penny from his mind entirely. And now she was back—with his *children*—and he'd be damned if he'd be cut out of his kids' lives. Even if, he was forced to admit, he was hardly father material.

The beach was nearly empty and the sunset stained the white clouds varying shades of pink and orange. The waves crashed relentlessly onto the shore, and out beyond the breakers, a few remaining surfers chased the next ride.

"You're an idiot."

Colt didn't have to turn around to know who had spoken. His twin's voice was unmistakable.

"Thanks for stopping by," he said. "Go away."

"Right. That'll happen." Instead, Connor settled down on the sand beside his brother and instinctively took up the same position as Colt. Arms wrapped around his drawn-up knees, gaze fixed on the ocean. They were so alike, they generally didn't even have to speak because each knew what the other was thinking.

But today, Colt realized, even *he* didn't know what he was thinking. Sexual desire, yes. Fury, oh, yes. But there was so much more. How the hell could he figure it out? Thoughts raced through his mind, slapped up against the wall of his brain and then rushed back down again to tangle with the others. Much like the legendary surf at the Wedge, Colt's mind at the moment was a dangerous place to be.

"You don't surf the Wedge alone and you know it," Connor said.

True. Even adrenaline junkies knew what line not to cross, but today, he just hadn't given a damn. Not that he would admit it to Connor.

"I wasn't alone," Colt argued. "There are at least a dozen other guys out there."

"Yeah, all looking out for themselves. Don't suppose you noticed the riptide?"

"I noticed," he admitted grudgingly. Riptides were a danger on their own. Riptides at the Wedge were a whole new level of risky. Get caught in one of those and you could be dragged out to sea so far you wouldn't have the strength to swim back in. "And I don't need you nagging me."

"Fine. Won't nag. Just leave a note behind next time you surf here alone, okay?"

"A note?" He looked at his twin.

Connor shrugged. "You're gonna commit suicide the least you can do is leave a note—you could say, 'I should have listened to Connor.'"

Colt shook his head and returned his gaze to the churning sea. White water and spray shot into the air. A cold sea wind whipped his hair back from his forehead, and overhead, gulls shrieked like the dying.

He didn't even wonder how Connor had known to find him here. For the last ten years, Colt had spent most of his time chasing the next adventure. Always searching out danger and beating it. He just wasn't the office, suit-and-tie kind of guy.

Hell, even with floor-to-ceiling windows displaying a spectacular view of the Pacific Ocean and the California coastline, he felt trapped in the building he and Connor owned on the Pacific Coast Highway. Which was why, he reminded himself, *he* was the adventure man and his twin was in charge of paperwork.

He shuddered at the thought of being buried behind a desk. Like the clients that King's Extreme Adventures served, Colt was always looking for the next shot of adrenaline. Skydiving, BASE jumping, extreme surfing, wingsuit flying—he'd done them all and had no intention of ever stopping.

In spite of what he'd learned today.

"Have you seen the twins?"

"No." Colt narrowed his gaze on the ocean and tried to ignore the sudden, frantic beat of his heart.

"Why not?"

"Because I'm too pissed at their mother."

Connor laughed shortly. "I'm guessing their mom's not real fond of you about now, either."

He turned his head to glare at his brother. "You think that matters to me?"

"No. But I know the kids do."

Well, that took the fire out of him. "What the hell do I know about being a father?"

Connor shrugged. "We had a pretty good role model for that, I think."

"Yeah, we did." Their parents had been the best. Until… Guilt reared up inside him, shouting to be heard, but he shut it down as he always did. The past didn't have any meaning here. This was all about the now. And the future. "Doesn't mean I'll be any good at it."

"Doesn't mean you'll suck, either."

Colt laughed and pushed one hand through his still-wet hair. "Quite the pep talk."

Connor grinned and turned his gaze on the ocean. "You don't need a pep talk. Unless you don't believe they're your kids…"

"No." Colt shook his head and scowled. Naturally, he'd considered that for a split second, right after Robert Oaks had punched him. But he'd discounted it just as quickly. "One thing Penny is not is a liar. In spite of the fact that she hid them from me. Besides," he reasoned, "if she was trying to push someone else's twins off as mine, she'd have come to me for money right from the jump."

"True. Still, you should do a paternity test. Cover all your bases legally."

He would, eventually. Colt wasn't an idiot. But tests or no tests, he knew, in his gut, those twins were his. Penny had been too panicked about him finding out about them to have him doubting it for a second. And she was right to panic, he told himself. Because things were going to change. Her life as she knew it was now over.

Because Colton King would do whatever he had to to make sure his kids were taken care of.

* * *

Maybe he'd forgotten to come.

Penny laughed silently at the very idea. Colton King might look like a wild, untamed, crazy adventurer—and he was. But he was also a brilliant businessman who never forgot a detail.

So then if he hadn't forgotten, why hadn't he shown up at the hospital this morning as promised? Penny had spent a long, sleepless night, worrying about what she would say to him when he strolled into her room again. Turned out, she needn't have bothered.

All day, she'd been tied in knots, waiting for him to appear. And he never showed up. Why that should irritate her when she really wished he would just go away and stay away, she didn't know.

But then, her feelings for Colton King had always confused her. That one week with him had fueled her dreams and her fantasies for months. Even when she was pregnant with the twins he had known nothing about, her mind continued to plague her every night, with alternative endings to their time together. But every morning, she was dragged back to a reality where happily ever afters didn't exist.

"And you should remember that," she muttered, giving herself a warning. Yet even while that thought squirmed through her mind, her body bristled with nervous expectation and she couldn't quite seem to calm it down.

Penny had spent most of the day—when she wasn't torturing herself with thoughts of Colt—trying desperately to be released from the hospital. Not only couldn't she afford a lengthy stay—they probably charged a hundred dollars for an aspirin—but she needed to get home.

To be with her kids. To be back at her cottage, tucked away from everything so she could... What? *Hide?* From Colt? Not a chance. Now that he knew the twins existed, Penny would never be free of him.

Her heart rate suddenly jumped into overdrive and she groaned. For heaven's sake, would she *always* have that reaction to the man? Wasn't being tossed aside once enough of a lesson? Did she really want to let him back into her life so he could do it again?

"No way," she vowed and tossed an angry glance at the still-empty doorway.

A half an hour ago, her stupid doctor had finally arrived to give her one more check and sign her release papers. But had a nurse shown up to wheel her out? No. And every second that passed increased the chances of Colt at last deciding to make an appearance.

Which made her wonder again why he hadn't come. What was he off doing? Was he at her house, insinuating himself with two babies who wouldn't have the slightest idea how to protect their hearts? Or maybe, she thought wistfully, he'd changed his mind? Decided to ignore his children after all? Could she be that lucky?

Not a chance, and she knew it. One thing she was sure of as far as the Kings of California were concerned: family meant everything.

During their brief time together, how many stories had Colt told her about his brothers, his cousins, their wives and kids? He'd painted amazing pictures of family gatherings and weddings and christenings, and she'd been both jealous of their deep family connection and intimidated by it.

She didn't know anything about big families. All she'd

had in the world was her younger brother and for years it had been the two of them—united against all comers. Heck, she hadn't even had a social life before she'd met Colton King and tossed her heart at his feet. She hadn't exactly been a virgin, but the two encounters before Colt had left her convinced that every woman on the face of the planet was lying about the whole earth-shattering-stars-exploding-orgasm thing.

Which might explain why she'd fallen so hard and so fast for Colt. She actually had seen stars with him. She'd felt things with him she wouldn't have believed herself capable of. He'd made her feel beautiful and sexy and desirable. He'd swept her off her feet so completely, she'd obviously managed to confuse lust with love. Just look where that had gotten her.

A marriage that hadn't even been twenty-four hours old when it was dissolved.

She turned her head and looked out the window to a patch of blue sky just visible beyond an old elm tree. Leaves dipped and swayed in the wind she wished she could feel on her face. Maybe it would help clear away all the clutter in her mind.

Because now all she could think of was that last morning with Colt. The day she'd awakened as a bride and in less than ten minutes had become yesterday's news.

For the past week, they'd spent every possible moment in bed, wrapped up in each other, shutting the rest of the world out of the bubble of passion they'd created. Then on the last night of the convention, they'd been married and had spent hours making love, unable to keep their hands off each other.

But the following morning, with the first feeble rays

of sunrise creeping over the sky, Penny had opened her eyes to find Colt standing beside the bed. He was dressed and packed and the expression on his face was grim. Her heart sank and then shattered when he spoke.

"I'm not the marrying kind, Penny." He pushed one hand through his hair, huffed out an exasperated breath and continued. "Last night was…a mistake. I don't want a wife. I don't want kids. Picket fences and the family dog give me hives. This week was nice and the sex was great, but that's all we share."

When she tried to speak, he cut her off with a negligent wave of his hand. "I'll have my lawyer take care of the divorce."

Finally, one word slipped past the tight knot in her throat. "Divorce?"

"It's best. For both of us." He slung his duffel bag over his shoulder, gave her one last look and said, "I'll have the papers sent to you. Goodbye, Penny."

And he was gone.

As if their incredible week together had never happened. As if he hadn't spent every waking moment learning every square inch of her body. As if it was all… nothing.

She could hardly be expected to have warm, fuzzy feelings for him after that, right? And the hot, undulating need she felt was *not* the same thing at all.

"Oh, this is so not good."

"Ready to go?" A nurse she'd never seen before popped into the room pushing an empty wheelchair and Penny should have been delighted. But her short trip down memory lane had sort of put a damper on her emotions. Now the time was here. She was leaving the expensive-but-slightly-safer atmosphere of the hospital for her home, where Colton would be showing up, and there was no time left to hide. Nowhere she could run.

But as that thought rose up in her mind, she remembered that scene in the Vegas hotel room again and instinctively stiffened her shoulders. Why should *she* run? She'd done nothing wrong. She'd only protected her kids from the same heartache she had experienced. She wouldn't stand by and see their little hearts break when their daddy walked away from them without a backward glance.

"Yes," she said, lifting her chin, already preparing for the battle she knew was coming. "I'm ready."

Or as ready as she would ever be.

The efficient nurse pushed her down the hall to the elevator and from there down a long hall headed for the lobby and the wide front doors. As they passed the billing office, Penny turned her head to look up at the nurse. "I'm sorry, but I still have to make financial arrangements and—"

"Oh, sweetie, that's been taken care of."

"What?"

The nurse smiled down at her, clearly not registering the look of shock carved into Penny's features.

"Your husband took care of all of that this morning. He didn't want you to worry about a thing. Gotta say, you picked a good one there."

"A good one—my husband—" Dread coiled in the pit of her stomach and sent spindly threads swimming through her veins. Colt had paid her hospital bill. Colt had walked in and taken over and everyone at the hospital had simply fallen into line.

Why that should surprise her she didn't know. He had the ability to make people jump whether they wanted to or not. Colton King expected to get his own way and knew just how to maneuver people into giving it to him. He'd probably never once considered that she might not want his help. He'd simply done as he always did—steamroller over everything in his path to get what he wanted.

She fumed silently in her wheelchair. It wouldn't do the slightest bit of good to argue with the hospital. Of course they'd appreciate her bill being paid in full rather than the monthly payments she was going to arrange. Why wouldn't they take a lump sum? It wasn't as if *they* were going to be indebted to the man. But for Penny, this was just one more link to Colt. A link she didn't want. She hadn't *asked* him to ride to the rescue, had she? No. And now, if she wanted to hang on to her pride, she'd have to find a way to pay him back.

The nurse wheeled her outside and the first breath of fresh, salt air lightened Penny's mood dramatically. Until she saw him.

Colt lounged against a black luxury SUV, his arms folded over his chest, his long legs crossed at the ankle. He looked relaxed, casual, in his boots, blue jeans and dark red shirt. He wore dark glasses over his ice-blue eyes and the wind ruffled his black hair. She thought she heard the nurse behind her give a soft sigh of pure female appreciation, and Penny completely understood.

Just looking at the man was enough to send most women into orgasmic shock. And she was in a better position than most to know that no matter how good a fantasy a woman could spin around him, reality with Colt was so much better.

And in spite of her churning thoughts and suddenly heated, throbbing body, her first instinct was to ask the nurse to turn around. To take her back inside. To run and hide, she was ashamed to admit, even to herself. So she swallowed her nerves, plastered a fake smile on her face and prepared to give the performance of a lifetime.

"Here she is, all ready to go home," the nurse cooed as Colt pushed off the car and walked closer.

"Right. Thanks." He slipped one hand under Penny's arm and helped her stand. Since her knees were feeling a little weak at the moment, she was grateful for the assistance. Even though it was *his* fault her knees were weak in the first place.

"You okay?" he asked, his voice a husky whisper close to her ear.

She closed her eyes and held her breath. If she had one whiff of his scent, it might just finish her off. "I'm fine. Thanks for picking me up."

He smirked as if he knew she hadn't meant a word of that and Penny ground her teeth together. The man was irritating on so many levels. Not the least of which was his apparent ability to read her mind.

She busied herself with the seat belt, only wincing once or twice as she settled herself into the wide, extremely comfortable leather seats. An unwanted comparison to her worn-out four-door sedan jumped into her mind, but she pushed it away again. Her car might not be shiny, with leather seats—and ooh, a minitelevision in the dashboard—but it got her where she was going. So far.

Colt climbed into the driver's seat, tossed her bag of

personal items into the back, then fired up the engine. He hooked his seat belt, checked the mirrors—in fact, did everything but look directly at her. Finally, Penny couldn't stand it.

"Why are you here?"

He glanced at her briefly. "To take you home."

"Robert was supposed to pick me up."

"We came to a different arrangement."

"You *have* to stop interfering in my life."

"No, I really don't."

He steered the car down the driveway and out into traffic and she was quiet as the familiar landscape flashed past. Buildings and cars on the left, the ocean on the right as he drove down the Pacific Coast Highway. Sunlight glinted on the surface of the water and made her eyes sting. That's why they felt teary. Not because of the helpless sensation beginning to build inside her.

"You're quiet," he observed. "Unusual for you as I remember."

"People change."

"Not normally," he said. "People are who they are. But situations…*they* change."

And here we go, she thought.

"You should have told me," he said tightly and she risked a quick look at him. His profile was rugged, breathtakingly gorgeous and hard as stone.

"You didn't want to know," she said.

"I don't remember being given a choice."

"Funny," she muttered, as the memory of their last morning together rose up in her mind again, "I remember."

"I don't know what the hell you're talking about."

How could he have forgotten? He'd made his choice long before they even met. But that last morning with him, he'd shared it all with her, searing the memories into her mind. If she closed her eyes, she could still see his face, hear his voice and then finally, the receding sound of his footsteps as he walked out of her life.

"I want to know everything, Penny." He stopped for a red light and threw her a hard look. "Every damn thing that's happened over the last two years."

"Eighteen months."

"Sue me," he snapped. "I rounded up."

The light turned green and he stepped on the gas. With his gaze locked on the road, he said, "And when that conversation begins, you can start by telling me *why* you thought it was a good idea to hide my kids from me."

"We're not in hiding."

"You know what I mean."

Yeah, she did. And that's exactly what she had done, though it sounded a lot colder when he said it out loud. "I had my reasons."

"Can't wait to hear them," he assured her.

Outside the car, it was a typical fall day in Southern California. Sun shining, clear sky, about sixty-five degrees. Inside the car, however, it was midwinter in the Arctic. Penny wouldn't have been surprised to see ice forming on the dashboard. Colt burned cold when he was furious. She'd seen it firsthand at the convention when they'd met.

Their third day together, Penny was running her booth, trying to win some clients for her fledgling sports photography business. A drunk stumbled onto the convention floor from the casino and had made Penny miserable. Hanging about her booth, demanding a kiss she had no intention of giving him. Chasing away potential clients.

But she'd been handling him until he made a grab for her—and before she could take care of the situation herself, Colton had been there. Icy rage in his eyes, he'd grabbed the drunk by the collar of his shirt and half dragged, half walked him off the floor. When he came back to her, Colt's anger was gone, but concern had been flashing in his eyes and Penny could remember feeling... cherished. Say what you would about equality, it was hard *not* to feel a thrill when a man was so protective.

He'd come to her rescue and then treated her as if she were made of glass instead of treating her like the fiercely independent woman she was. And she'd loved every minute of it.

He was excitement and tenderness and sex all rolled into one. No wonder she'd fallen so hard, she told herself. No woman in the world would have been able to resist Colton King. That week with him had been the most magical of her life. In a few short days, she'd fallen so completely in love with him. She'd even married him in a sweet, shabby chapel and told herself that it was meant to be. She'd indulged in dreams and imaginings and let herself drift on a tide of the most incredible sex she'd ever experienced and thought somehow that it would all work out.

Until, of course, the world came crashing down on her and reality took a bite of her heart.

And now cold, hard reality was back to do it all again. But this time, she wouldn't let herself be vulnerable to him. This time, she wouldn't make the mistake of thinking that a man who showed such passion in bed *must* feel something for her. This time, she was ready for Colton King.

"You were never going to tell me, were you?"

"No," she said, not even bothering to give him her list of reasons. They wouldn't make a difference to him. He didn't care *why*—only that she hadn't told him.

"Well, I know now."

"It doesn't change anything, Colt," she said, turning her head to look at his gorgeous, unyielding profile.

Heat stirred inside her, despite the lingering pain of her emergency surgery. Despite the fact that she hadn't seen him in eighteen months. Even despite the fact that the morning after their spur-of-the-moment marriage, he'd walked out on her, promising that a divorce lawyer would be in contact with her.

The only reason he was back now was because of the twins. Her babies. And he wasn't going to get them. She lifted one hand to rub her forehead in a futile attempt to ease the headache making her eyes throb.

"It changes everything and you know it," he said, voice as tight as the grip he had on the steering wheel. "You should have told me. You had no right to keep my children from me."

"Rights?" Stunned, headache forgotten, she stared at him as the humiliation of the last time she'd seen him washed over her. "I absolutely had the right to do whatever I had to do to protect my kids."

"From their *father?*"

"From anyone who might hurt them."

His features went stone-still but his eyes were flashing. "And you think I'd hurt them?"

"Not physically, of course not," she snapped. "But you walked away from me, remember? You're the one who said you didn't want to hear from me again. You're the one who told me that the week we spent together was 'fun' but over. Not to mention when you added that the thought of kids gave you hives. Any of this ringing a bell?"

"All of it," he said. "But I didn't know you were pregnant, did I?"

"Neither did I."

"Yeah, but you knew soon after and you didn't *tell* me."

"It wasn't any of your business."

He laughed but there was no humor in the sound. "Not my business. I have two children and they're none of my business."

"I have two kids. *You* have nothing."

"If that's what you really think, you're in for a surprise."

He made the turn that would take him to her house and Penny frowned. "How do you know where I live?"

"Amazing what you can find out if you're motivated." He glanced at her, then shifted his gaze back to the shady, tree-lined street in front of him. "For example. I know your business is getting a slow start—switched from sports photography to babies—an interesting choice. I know you don't have health insurance. And I know that you're living in your grandmother's cottage in Laguna." He took a breath and continued. "Your brother's engaged to Maria Estrada and is a general practice intern at Huntington Beach hospital. You're living off your credit cards and your car is fifteen years old." He spared her another look. "Did I miss anything?"

No, he hadn't. In fact, Penny worried about what else

he might have found out. He'd scratched the surface of her life, but just how deeply had he continued to dig?

"What gives you the right to pry, Colt?" She didn't like the idea of her past being spread out for him to pick over. Didn't like feeling as though she'd been exposed. "We spent one week together nearly two years ago."

"And apparently," he added, "we made two babies." He pulled up in front of her house and parked. When he turned the engine off, he faced her and his eyes looked like chips of ice. "That gives me any right I want to claim."

To avoid looking at him, she stared at the house she loved. A tiny Tudor with dark shutters and beams flat against cream-colored stucco and leaded windows that winked in the last lights of the sun. Ivy climbed along the porch railings and chrysanthemums bloomed dark yellow and purple in the front flower bed. The house was small and cozy and had always, even when she was a child, signified safety and warmth to Penny.

Now she looked at it and felt a sense of peace she desperately needed steal over her.

"I'm not going anywhere, Penny. Get used to it."

Peace dissolved as a stir of heat erupted inside her again and Penny wanted to shriek with frustration. *How* could her body respond to a man her brain realized was nothing but trouble? She felt as if she'd been stripped bare in front of him. Her life was nothing more than a series of facts that he felt free to dissect in a cold, dispassionate speech.

But then, that was Colton's way, wasn't it? she reminded herself. Unemotional. Detached.

Distanced from any sort of real human contact, he

kept his heart—if he had one—locked away behind a steel door that was, as far as she could tell, impenetrable.

Her voice was barely a whisper when she looked into his eyes and asked, "What exactly do you want, Colt?"

"That's easy," he said with a shrug. "I want what's *mine.*"

A cold, tight fist closed around her heart as he got out of the car, slammed the door and walked around to her side. His? She knew he didn't mean that he wanted *her,* so he was talking about her kids. Her *babies.* Fear coiled around her heart and made breathing almost impossible. But where she might try to run and hide to protect herself—to safeguard her children she was willing to walk into hell itself.

She watched him through the car window and when he opened her door to help her out, she looked into his eyes and said, "You can't have them."

Three

"You can't have my kids, Colt." Her voice hitched higher. "I won't let you."

"You can't stop me," he told her flatly.

Colton had done a lot of thinking in the last twenty-four hours and he'd come to one conclusion. If these were his children, then he wouldn't be shut out. And frankly, even though he'd already arranged for a paternity test, he knew, deep in his gut, there wasn't a need for one. When he and Penny were together, she'd been with only two other men before him. She was honest. Straightforward. So deeply moral that she'd never try to pass off another man's child as his. Hell, her sweet-natured decency was one of the reasons he'd run from her so fast.

Colt wasn't interested in being with a woman who had romance in her eyes and a plan for the future in her heart. Normally, he didn't *do* a "future." He did "now."

And normally, he preferred women who wanted nothing more than he did out of a temporary relationship. Good sex, a few laughs and an easy exit.

There was *nothing* easy about Penny Oaks.

Colton watched a flash of fire in her eyes and knew she wouldn't surrender without a fight. On any other day, he might have admired it. But not today. Today, he was the one with the claim on fury. He was the one who'd been kept in the dark for nearly two years. No, he didn't want to be married. He'd never planned on being a father—his life was too risky for that—but now that he *was* a father, things had changed.

And, he told himself grimly, they were going to change even more, soon.

"You don't want the twins," she said softly, her gaze locked with his. "You only want to hurt me."

Hurt her? What he wanted to do at the moment was kiss her until neither of them could breathe. He wanted to reach into the car, drag her out and plaster her up against him so that he could feel every one of the curves he remembered so well. Even through the anger, through the frustration and confusion, desire was clear and simple. Unfortunately, nothing else about this situation was.

"I'm not interested in hurting you." Understatement. "But I do want answers." He planted one hand on the roof of the car and leaned in closer to her. "And you don't want to challenge me, Penny. I always find a way to win."

"Win?" Her mouth dropped open. "This isn't a game, Colt. This is about two babies."

"*My* babies," he corrected, and felt a hitch in his chest as he said those words. Since yesterday, he'd done little else but think about the bombshell that had been dropped into the middle of his world. Everything around him felt as if it were slightly off balance. As if the steady, familiar course of his life had been suddenly turned into a roller coaster ride, with dips and turns hidden around every corner.

There were two kids who deserved a father. It was just their bad luck to have gotten *him* in the genetic lottery. He couldn't give them stability. A man to count on. Everything he'd had growing up. Still, he'd do the best he could by them because he owed them that.

"What're you doing, Colt?" She stared up at him, wariness and pain shining in her eyes.

"What needs to be done," he ground out, refusing to be swayed by the naked emotion he saw on her face.

What he had to remember was that she'd kept his children from him. So much for the "honesty" he'd seen in her at the beginning, he thought cynically. Hell, maybe she was really no different from the countless other women who had tried to convince a King that she was pregnant just to be able to dip into his bank account.

But she was different, wasn't she? She'd made no effort to contact him. Hadn't asked for money. Hadn't gone to a tabloid, selling her story to make some fast cash. Hell, she'd gone out of her way to avoid telling him about the twins. Hadn't once considered him in any of the decisions she'd made in the last couple of years.

Well, all of that was going to change. She might not be interested in cashing in on the King name. Might have no desire at all for him to be a part of her world. But she was about to find out just what it was like having a King in the family picture.

"We have to talk," he ground out, keeping his voice low and his gaze locked on hers. "The question is, do you want to do it now, with your brother watching us from your front window—"

She shifted a look to the house at his words and huffed out a breath. Colt had noticed Robert the instant he'd parked in front of the cottage. The man looked just as constipated and irritated as he had the day before. But at least now, Colt could understand why he was such a pain in the ass.

"Or do you want to go inside, get rid of the audience and do this in private? Your choice."

A couple of tense seconds ticked past.

"Fine," she grumbled, unhooking her seat belt and wincing a bit as she tried to get out of the car. "But this isn't over."

"That's the first thing you've gotten right," he promised, feeling a twinge of sympathy mixed with concern when he watched her trying to move through pain that was clearly bothering her more than she wanted to admit. Irritated at her stubborn independence even in the face of real discomfort, he reached into the car and lifted her out. He should have put her down at once, of course, but he noticed that her face was so pale that the freckles across her nose and cheeks shone like flakes of gold against snow.

"You can set me down now," she said, tipping her face back to look up at him.

But he didn't want to. He liked holding her. Hell, it was feeding that need to touch her. She felt…right, cradled against his chest, and that weird thought worried him quite a bit. But at least *lust* he knew how to deal with.

"I'm perfectly capable of walking."

"Sure you are." He shook his head as he looked down at her. His body tightened further and it was his turn to camouflage a wince of pain. "And it'll take you twenty minutes to get to the front door. This is faster."

She glowered at him, but Colt paid no attention. Hard to focus on her irritation when every inch of his body was reacting to her closeness. Holding her to him stirred up feelings he'd just as soon leave buried. But it was too late. Her T-shirt and jeans were worn and soft. Her curves fit nicely against him and with every breath she took, she fired the heat already scorching him.

"Just hold still, will you?" Still shaking his head, not sure if he was angrier with her or with his own reaction, Colt took the crooked, flower-lined sidewalk up to the steps. Robert opened the door and Colt carried her across the porch and into the house.

His first impression was that the place had been built for really short people. It was like a dollhouse. Cute to look at but impossible to move around in. He had to duck his head to avoid a low-hanging beam separating the entry from the postage-stamp-sized living room. And suddenly he felt like Gulliver. All that was missing were the ropes tying him down—although there were two tiny ropes somewhere in this house, prepared to do the job.

"You okay, Penny?" Robert asked as Colt deposited her gently on the overstuffed couch.

"She's fine," Colt answered for her. "I almost never beat a woman."

Robert sneered. "Is that supposed to be funny?"

"Not really," Colton told him. "Nothing about this situation is funny."

"I'm fine," Penny said, shooting Colt a look that plainly said *I can speak for myself.* Then she turned back to her brother. "How are the twins?"

Robert threw a look over his shoulder at the hallway

behind him. "Sleeping. We took them for a long walk and the fresh air just knocked 'em out. Maria's checking on them."

"Good," she said, a smile curving her mouth. "Thanks so much for watching the babies. I can't wait to see them."

"Me, either." Colt looked from Penny to Robert and back again and had the satisfaction of seeing her squirm uncomfortably.

"For what it's worth," Robert told him, "I've been after her from the beginning to tell you about the twins."

"Too bad you weren't more successful."

"She's too stubborn for her own good," her brother argued. "Once she makes up her mind, you couldn't blow her off course with dynamite." He glanced at his sister. "And it's not like I enjoyed going behind her back to tell you the truth. I'm just tired of seeing her struggle when she shouldn't have to."

"I understand. And I remember just how stubborn she is." In fact, Colt recalled plenty about the week he and Penny had spent together what felt like a lifetime ago. He remembered her laughter. He remembered the feel of her curled against him in the middle of the night. The taste of her mouth, the scent of her skin. And he remembered seeing rainbows and promises shining in her green eyes.

It had spooked him, plain and simple. No other woman before her or since had ever gotten so close to him. No other woman had ever made him so drugged on passion that he'd proposed and married her before he could come to his senses.

And no other woman's memory had stayed with him as hers had.

God knows he'd tried to bury her memory, but it just wouldn't stay gone. He could be halfway around the world, exploring some new adventure, and hear a soft, feminine laugh—and just for a second, he'd turn and search the crowd for her familiar face. He had dreams that were so clear, so *real,* that he would wake up expecting to find her lying next to him.

She'd done that to him. One week with Penny had threatened everything in his life. Of course he'd had to leave her.

"Since you remember, you know what it's like trying to argue with her," Robert was saying.

"Oh, I don't intend to argue." Colt glanced at Penny and watched as sparks glinted in her eyes. "I'm just going to tell her how things are going to be."

"That I'd like to see," Robert murmured.

"Maybe I'll sell tickets."

"If you two are quite finished," Penny announced.

"Not even close," Colt told her.

"Not my problem anymore," Robert said, lifting both hands in gratitude at being able to hand off the responsibility of worrying about his sister. He looked at Colt. "Good luck."

"Not necessary." Colt didn't need luck. All he needed was a cold shower and then a chance to settle a few things with the mother of his children.

"Seriously?" Penny tried to get up off the couch, but Colt dropped one hand onto her shoulder to hold her in place.

"Don't move from that spot."

"You are not in charge here," she argued.

"Wanna bet?"

He met her gaze and stared, waiting for her to back off first. In a contest of wills, Penny wouldn't stand a chance. She could be as stubborn as she liked, but she hadn't been raised a King. In the King family, *everyone* wanted to be right. And no one ever backed down. So if she thought she could best him in a staring contest, she couldn't be more wrong.

Took a few seconds, but eventually, she shifted her gaze from his and slumped back into the floral cushions, muttering a steady stream of words he was probably better off not hearing. A reluctant smile twitched his lips. He had to admire her fighting spirit—even though she had no hope of winning.

A pretty, dark-haired woman with big brown eyes walked into the room, passed Robert and Colt, then took a seat on the coffee table in front of Penny. Reaching out, she took Penny's hands in hers and squeezed. "The twins are fine. They're sound asleep and since it was so late in the afternoon, we fed them their dinner, too. I know it's a little early, but with any luck, they'll sleep the night through and give you some rest."

"Thanks, Maria. I really appreciate you stepping in to help."

"We both appreciate it," Colton said.

Finally, the woman lifted her gaze to his and there was no warmth in her eyes. She looked him up and down and Colt had the distinct impression she was less than impressed. He almost smiled again. He admired loyalty, too.

"Of course we helped," she said coolly. "Penny had *no one* else."

"Maria…" Robert gave a sigh.

Colt shook his head and waved one hand, dismissing Robert's objection. Now he knew two new things about Penny. Her little brother was willing to use his fists to defend her, and her friend Maria was Penny's staunch ally.

Still, all three of them had better get used to how things were going to be. "Now she does have someone else."

"We'll see, won't we?" Maria turned her gaze back to Penny and said, "If you need anything, just call. Honestly, I can be over in minutes."

Penny laughed a little. "I will. Promise."

"Good." Nodding abruptly, Maria leaned forward, kissed Penny's cheek and said, "We'll go now. I'm sure you two have plenty to talk about."

"Oh, you don't have to leave so soon."

"Yeah, they do," Colt argued, and Penny shot him a hard glare. Didn't bode well for their "discussion" but that wouldn't have gone well in any case, he assured himself.

"Okay then," Robert announced and took Maria's hand in his, drawing her up from her perch on the edge of the table. "Remember, if you need something, call."

Then it was just the two of them. Colton didn't even know where to begin. There was a lot he wanted to know and even more he *needed* to know—things like why bother buying and using condoms if they clearly didn't work? An existential question he'd have to explore more completely later. There were plenty of other things he wanted to know, though.

But at the moment, damned if he could think of a thing to say. Instead, he stared down at the woman he'd married and divorced within the span of a week and tried not to notice just how blasted vulnerable she looked. Hard to have the kind of argument that was waiting for them when the woman was just out of the hospital.

Hospital.

That word conjured up old mental images that threatened to choke him. He had promised to be there in Penny's room that morning, but hadn't been able to do it. Couldn't force himself to walk back into that building. Into a place so filled with the scent of fear and misery, so thick with memories that Colt felt them surrounding him, burying him. Even now, his mind was opening the door to the darkness that hid deep within his past. Shadows rushed out and spilled through his body like black paint, covering everything in its path.

Shaken right down to the bone, Colt reached out blindly and grabbed hold of the anger that was his salvation. If he could just focus on the situation facing him now and shut down the past, he'd get through this. As he'd done so many times before.

"Are you okay?"

"What?" He surfaced from the tangled thoughts in his mind like a surfer trying to breathe through sea foam. "What? Oh. Yeah. I'm fine."

She didn't look convinced, but that didn't bother him. The real problem here was that he was still drawn to her. Still felt that nearly magnetic pull that he'd felt so long ago. What was it about her, he asked himself, that tugged at everything inside him? And why the hell couldn't he get rid of it?

Trying to avoid looking at Penny, he glanced around the small beach cottage and really noticed it for the first time.

The rooms were small and painted a soft yellow that looked as though sunbeams lived in the walls. An old, stone-faced fireplace stood along one side of the room, with built-in bookcases on either side.

A painting of the sea hung on the wall above the hearth, and around the room, old but comfortable-looking furniture sprawled, inviting people to come in and take it easy.

Reading lamps sat on the end tables and there was a huge plastic tub filled with toys beneath the front window.

Off the living room was a hall that probably led to the bedrooms and a dining room with a door beyond that was undoubtedly hiding the kitchen. It was a typical cottage, no doubt built in the forties for long weekends at the beach. The rooms were small, the yard tiny and if you had claustrophobia you wouldn't last out the weekend. But there were charms in these old neighborhoods, too. Close to the beach, on a quiet night, you could hear the surf. Decades-old trees lined the streets and their roots caused sidewalks to ripple like waves. And any time the city tried to pull down the trees to make the sidewalks even, the neighborhoods came out in full fight mode.

Places like this never changed.

"You hungry?" he asked suddenly, to break the silence.

"I'll make something in a minute," she said and eased back into the cushions of the couch.

"I'll make it." When she looked at him in surprise, he almost laughed. He'd been on his own for a long time and though he had a housekeeper, he'd never bothered to hire a cook. Hell, he wasn't home often enough to justify it. "I'm not completely helpless in the kitchen."

"That's not what you said—" Her voice trailed away.

"What?"

She shook her head and stared up at the ceiling. Old, smoke-stained beams divided the cream-colored plaster. "That week we were together, you told me that you and your twin once set fire to your aunt's kitchen when you were trying to make French toast."

He frowned to himself. He didn't remember telling her that, and knowing that he obviously *had* told her confused the hell out of him. Colt didn't usually share much of himself with women—hell, with anyone. He didn't want the closeness and didn't crave what women always seemed to enjoy—the baring of souls. Who the hell wanted a naked soul?

He gave her a tight smile. "Been a long time since the fire in the kitchen. I'm not bad with chicken or pasta, though I'm the first to admit I'm not a chef. But I make great phone calls for takeout."

She laughed a little, then winced, and Colt felt a twinge in response. But when she spoke, all sympathy for her drained away.

"Look, Colt, I know we have to talk but I'm just too tired to deal with you tonight." She sighed a little. "Why don't you go home and we'll talk in a day or two?"

"Go home?" He repeated it because he couldn't believe she would even suggest it. He was here now and he wasn't leaving. Not yet, anyway. "And who takes care of the twins while you sit here on the couch and chew at your lip?"

She stopped that instantly and fired a look at him. "I can manage. I always do."

"No," he corrected. "You always *have* in the past. Now that's not an option."

"You're not in charge here, Colt."

"Check again." He walked closer to her and gave her a glare designed to intimidate. From what he could tell, it didn't work. "Damn it, Penny, as mad as I am at you right now, I'd almost be willing to do just what you said and leave you here on your own just so you could see what a stupid decision that would be—"

"Bye then."

"I said *almost.*" Sinking to his heels beside the couch,

he met her eyes and said, "As much as you hate the idea, you need me. Damn it, I had to carry you into the house."

"I could have walked."

"What is bothering you the most?" he asked. "Needing help? Or needing *me?*"

"You're wrong, Colt," she said. "I don't need you. Okay, maybe I need some help, but I don't need *you.*"

"Tough." He straightened up again, looming over her and forcing her to keep her head tipped back just to meet his eyes.

"'Cause you've got me. Until we get this whole mess straightened out, I'm not going anywhere."

She huffed out an impatient breath. "Don't you have a mountain to climb? A building to jump off of?"

For one split second, thoughts of Mount Etna and his Sicilian trip floated through his mind. Then he let it go. "There's plenty of time for that. Right now, you're the only adventure in my future."

"Swell." She leaned forward, braced one hand on the arm of the couch and hissed in a breath.

"What're you doing?"

She flashed him a look of pure irritation. "I'm going to check on the twins. Then change clothes. Put on something a little less constricting than my jeans."

Frankly, he preferred her in something *more* constricting. Like a suit of armor with a chastity belt. That would be good. But since that wasn't going to happen, he took a breath and got a grip on his rampaging thoughts. What he had to do here was focus on his anger, he told himself firmly. Just remember that she'd lied to him. Hidden his children from him. That should take care of the raging need clawing at him.

"All right, let's go."

She paused and looked up at him. "I can do it myself."

"Sure you can. You're a superhero." He drew her to her feet. "So do me a favor. Stop fighting this so hard. Pretend to need my help. Make me feel manly."

She snorted a laugh. "Like you need help with that."

"I think that was a compliment," he said, following her toward the hall and presumably, her bedroom.

"You don't need a compliment, either."

"Harsh," he said, amused in spite of the conversation. Walking behind her, his gaze dropped to the curve of her behind, defined by the worn, faded denim that clung to her body like a second skin. His body stirred again and he gritted his teeth.

She walked slowly and he could sense the pain that accompanied every movement. Didn't seem to stop the sexual thoughts dancing through his mind. But a part of him admired her steely determination to keep going in spite of whatever pain was gnawing on her. She refused to surrender to it. Refused to give in to what had to be an urge to curl up somewhere and whimper.

Hell, she was stronger than him. When he broke his leg off the coast of Monaco in a car wreck during a race, Colt had bitched about the pain to anyone who would listen.

Even Connor had lost all patience with him by the time his leg had finally healed. But in his defense, Colt thought, he wasn't the kind of guy to be content sitting in a damn chair and watching TV. He needed to be moving. Doing. Chasing risk and searching for that next shot of adrenaline. Life was too short to not try to wring every last drop of pleasure out of it.

Too damn short. Those three words rippled through his mind, dragging up the past from the shadows where he'd hidden it. Smothering a tight groan, Colt shoved that past back down again, refusing to acknowledge it. Refusing to even look at it.

The past was done. What counted was now.

Of course, the past was what had brought him here, to this house, today.

He watched her quietly approach a closed door off the hallway and carefully turn the knob, making no sound as she stepped inside. Colt hesitated, knowing that his children were in there. Emotions choked him as she turned to look at him, a quizzical look on her face.

Colt knew she was expecting him to follow her in and see the twins as they slept. But he wasn't interested in seeing his kids for the first time while in front of an audience. He could wait a bit longer to see the babies who had brought him here. And he'd do it in his own time.

Hell, he realized with a start, he was actually *nervous*. He couldn't even remember the last time he'd felt the skitter of nerves racking his body. Colt had faced down volcanoes, killer surf, parachutes that didn't open and broken skis on the steep face of a so-called un-skiable mountain. Yet the thought of meeting his children for the first time had him backing away from an open doorway as if it were a gateway to some black, dangerous pit.

So he waited while she fiddled with blankets and murmured soft sounds of comfort and love. He was finding it hard to breathe past a knot of sensation that he recognized as it grew inside him. This wasn't nerves. This was a familiar, buzzing feeling settling into the pit of his stomach. He felt it every time he stood at the tip of a mountain, jumped off a cliff, rode forty-foot surf. It was that surge of adrenaline that let him know he was alive.

That he was about to risk it all. About to put his life on the line and either change it—or end it.

He didn't care which.

"Colt?"

She was back in the hall, with the babies' door closed, and she was looking at him. He stared down into those green eyes he'd never really been able to forget. "What?"

"I just thought you'd want to see the twins…"

"I do," he assured her, getting a tight rein on the runaway sensations pouring through him. "Later."

"Okay then." She walked past him slowly, heading to the end of the hall and another closed door. Looking back at him over her shoulder, she reluctantly acknowledged, "You were right before. I think I will need your help getting out of these clothes."

In different circumstances, getting her undressed would have been Colt's highest priority. But things were different now. They weren't lovers. They were…what? Enemies? Maybe. Sure weren't friends. Exes with children. He looked at Penny and saw misery in her eyes and it wasn't hard to identify the reason. Couldn't have been easy for her to admit to him that she needed help. Especially from him. Right now, things between them were strained so tight, the tension in the air between them flavored every breath.

And it wasn't only the situation with the twins that had them each walking a fine line. It was the sexual chemistry still buzzing between them. But chemistry didn't have to be acted on, did it? Nodding, he said, "Fine."

His brain was busy, racing with too many thoughts to sort out, and that was just as well. If he kept his anger burning, he'd be able to ignore the rush of desire already pulsing inside him.

He followed Penny into her bedroom and took a second or two to look around. A full-size bed on one wall, bedside tables and a tall dresser. There were framed photos on the walls—hers, he was willing to bet—of the beach, parks and two smiling babies.

They were beautiful. Both of them. His heart gave an unexpected leap that staggered him. *His* children. Yes, he'd get a paternity test, but just looking at those two faces caught forever and trapped behind glass, he knew they were his. They looked like him. They each had the King black hair and blue eyes and he could see his own features replicated in miniature.

"They look like you," she said softly.

His throat squeezed shut and he could hear his own heartbeat hammering in his ears. He kept his gaze fixed on the photos. It seemed he was going to be seeing his children for the first time in front of an audience after all. "When did you take the pictures?"

"Two weeks ago," she said. "We went to the park, which is why Reid has sand on his face. He tries to eat everything he finds."

A tight smile curved Colt's mouth as he looked at his son's mischievous face. There was a sparkle in the tiny boy's eyes that promised trouble. And his sister had that same flash of something special about her, Colt thought. *His* children. And he didn't know them. Had never heard them. Had never held them. His heart took another leap and he forced himself to turn from the framed photos to the woman sitting on the edge of the bed.

"You cheated me, Penny," he ground out tightly as a fresh surge of anger washed over him. "Nobody cheats a King and gets away with it."

Four

"Cheated you?" she countered, green eyes glittering. "*You* walked away, Colt. You cheated yourself. Out of the kids, out of what we could have had."

Shaking his head, he took a step back from her and tried to keep his voice down in spite of the raging fury inside him. Seeing his kids there on her wall, realizing just how much of their lives he'd already missed, had stoked the fire of his anger until it felt as if he were being consumed.

"Yeah, I walked. From a marriage that was a mistake," he muttered. The past came rushing forward, but he wouldn't look at it. Refused to remember the pain and shock in her eyes as he left her.

"It didn't last long enough to be classified a mistake," she countered.

She was right about that much. Colt reached up and

pushed both hands through his hair. He'd relived his decision to spontaneously get married a million times over the last eighteen months and he still couldn't explain to himself why he'd done it. But in that wild moment in the tacky little chapel, he'd known he wanted her with him for always.

"Always" had lasted about ten hours.

Dawn eventually came and shook him out of the passion-induced haze he'd been operating in. In the glare of morning, he'd remembered at last that "forever" didn't exist. That marriage just wasn't in his game plan—in spite of how amazing he and Penny were in bed together.

He'd believed then, and he still did, that walking away was the right thing to do. But he would have walked right back if she'd even once mentioned the whole pregnancy thing.

"What did you think was going to happen, Penny?" He glared down at her, refusing to be swayed by the gleam in her eyes or the tilt of her chin. "Did you really see us living the suburban dream? Is that it?"

"No," she said on a short laugh. "But—"

"But what? Would it have been better to stay married for a month? Six? And then end it? Would that have seemed kinder," he asked, "or would it just have prolonged the inevitable?"

"I don't know," she muttered, pushing her hair back from her face with an impatient gesture. "All I know is, we dated, got married and got divorced in the span of a week and now you're back claiming that I somehow cheated you."

"It always comes back to the same thing, Penny," he said, voice low and deep. "You should have told me."

She blew out a breath and glared at him. "And here we are again, on the carousel of knives where we just slash at each other and nothing is ever solved."

Colt stalked a few paces away from the bed, but he couldn't get far, since the whole room would have fit inside his walk-in closet. He felt trapped. In the small space. In this situation. But despite the invisible chains wrapping around him tighter by the moment, he knew he couldn't leave. Wouldn't leave. He had children—whether he'd planned on it or not—and he had to do right by them.

He spun around to look at her and promised, "You can't keep me from the twins."

"You'll just confuse them," she told him flatly.

"Confuse them how?" He threw both hands high then let them slap back down against his thighs. "They're babies. They don't know what's going on!"

"Keep your voice down—you'll wake them up." She glared at him and after a second or two of that heated stare, he shifted uncomfortably. "And they understand when people are happy. Or angry. And I don't want you upsetting them by shouting."

Colt took a breath and nodded. "Fine." He lowered his voice because he hadn't meant to shout in the first place. Connor was the twin with the hot temper. Which just went to show how far out of his own comfort zone Colt really was. "Confuse them how?"

"You're a stranger to them—"

He gritted his teeth.

"—and you just pop up into their lives? For how long, Colt? How long before you tell them, 'Sorry kids, but I'm just not father material. I'll have my lawyers contact you about child support.'"

"Funny." His tone was flat, his eyes narrowed and he had a very slight grip on the temper that was beginning to ice over his insides. "You can be as bitter as you want about what happened between us. But I'm not going to do that to them."

"And how do I know that?" She winced as she straightened on the bed. "You walked away from a wife. Why not your kids, too?"

"It's different and you know it."

"No, I don't. That's the problem."

The last of the daylight pearled the room in a warm, pale haze that floated through the open curtains and lay across the oak floor like gold dust. As the old house settled down for the night, it creaked and groaned like a tired old woman settling in for a nap. There was a baby monitor on her bedside table that crackled with static and then broadcast one of the babies coughing.

Colt jolted at the sound. "Are they choking?"

"No," Penny said with a sigh. "That's just Riley. When she sleeps she sucks so hard on her pacifier that she gurgles and coughs."

"Is that normal?" Frowning at the monitor, he felt completely out of his element here. How would he know what was normal for an infant or not? It wasn't as if he spent all that much time with any of the new King babies. Seeing them at family parties hadn't really prepared him for a lot of one-on-one time with two infants.

"Yes. Colt—"

He heard the fatigue in her voice. Saw it in her eyes and the pale color of her skin. They were going around and around and not gaining ground. There would be plenty of time to sort out what they were going to do. And when he argued with someone, he wanted them at full strength. Penny clearly was not. He didn't want to worry about her, but a slender thread of concern drifted through him anyway.

"Let's just get you changed, all right? We'll talk about this more tomorrow."

"Oh, boy," she murmured. "There's something to look forward to." Then she winced and tugged at the snap on her jeans. "But I'm so uncomfortable, I'm willing to risk it."

"What do you need?"

"My nightgown's in the top drawer of the dresser."

Nightgown.

And she'd be naked underneath it, of course. Even as he felt his body stir and tighten, he had to wonder how he could be so furious with a woman and want her so badly all at the same damn time. Still grinding his teeth, he moved to the dresser, opened the top drawer and discovered there actually *was* a cure for lust.

"This? Really?" he asked, holding up the most hideous nightgown he'd ever seen.

She frowned. "And what's wrong with it?"

Shaking his head, he gave her the fire-engine-red sleep shirt that was stamped with oversized, mustard-yellow flowers and hot pink ribbons.

"Other than the fact that it looks radioactive? Not a thing," he mused. "It's probably great birth control. One look at you in this thing and the guy in question runs for the hills."

"Very funny." She snatched it from him. "It was on sale."

"For how many years?" It was the ugliest thing he'd ever seen and he blessed her for having it. Maybe the truly fugly nightgown would help him to *not* think about what was under it.

"I didn't ask you to critique my wardrobe."

"You could ask me to burn your wardrobe," he offered. "Or at least that part of it."

"Could you just—" She pushed one hand through her wild, wavy fall of red hair and pushed it back over her shoulder. "Never mind. I'll do this myself. Just… go away."

"Stop being so stubborn." He wanted to get this over and done with. "I'll help you with the nightgown, but I'll close my eyes to protect my retinas."

She glared at him. "Are you going to help me or just make snide comments?"

"I can do both. Who says men can't multitask?"

"God, you're irritating."

"Nice that you noticed."

He was noticing plenty himself. Too much. Such as the fact that she was trembling—and it wasn't because she was cold, or even furious. She was feeling just what he was. That raw, nerve-scraping need that had pushed them into bed together in the first place. It was something he'd never found with anyone else. Something he'd told himself many times that he just wasn't interested in. Apparently, though, his body had missed that memo.

Frustration practically wafted off her in waves and Colt told himself he really shouldn't be enjoying giving her a hard time so much. But he was owed some payback, right? Besides, it kept his thoughts too busy to entertain *other* things.

"I changed my mind. I can get undressed myself."

"No, you can't. Not yet, anyway." He stepped up in

front of her and when she drew back, he said, "Relax, Penny. I've seen it before, remember?"

God knew *he* remembered. Every square inch of her body was burned into his brain, despite how often he had tried to erase it. "We're both grownups, and believe it or not, I do have some self-control. I'm not going to jump a woman just out of the hospital."

Probably.

She whipped her hair out of her eyes to look at him. "You wouldn't be doing that anyway."

"Is that right?" If she knew just how hard and tight his body was at the moment, she'd be sounding a lot less confident.

Meeting his gaze, she reminded him again, "You're the one who walked away from me, Colt. So why would you want to go back there?"

Why indeed?

Because, damn it, he'd wanted to go back there ever since the moment he'd walked away from her in Vegas. Hell, it's one reason he *had* walked away from her. She made him think too much. Feel too much.

To cover his thoughts he said, "Trust me, once you're wearing that very effective male-repellent nightgown, you'll be safe."

"That's a relief." She didn't sound relieved, though.

"Come on, let's get this done." He moved closer, took the hem of her T-shirt and waited while she pulled her arms from the sleeves. Then he tugged it up and over her head. Her hair fell like red silk, settling over her shoulders. And if he kept his gaze on her hair, he'd be fine. Yeah, it was touchable but not nearly as hard to resist as the lace bra cupping her generous breasts. He drew in a shallow breath and waited while she unhooked the front clasp, then shrugged the bra off.

Modestly, she crossed her arms over her breasts, but the action was pointless. The quick look he'd gotten was enough to make him hard again, and he had the feeling that he'd better get used to that particular kind of misery.

To help himself as much as her, Colt tugged the nightgown over her head and took a step back as she pushed her arms through the sleeves and drew the hideous fabric down over her body. He'd called that nightshirt a man repellent—apparently he was immune.

She toed off her sneakers, then reached under the nightgown to unsnap her jeans. Once she'd pulled the zipper down, Colt stepped in again. "Lie back. I'll get them off you."

She did, but she braced herself on her elbows and kept a wary eye on him as he drew the denim down and off her long, well-toned legs. Smothering a groan, he tried not to think about those legs wrapped around his waist, pulling him closer, deeper. Tried not to remember the sound of her sighs or the flex of her muscles as she writhed beneath him. And he was failing.

Miserably.

"Okay," he said, taking a deliberate step back. "Finished."

"Thanks." Nodding, she eased into a sitting position and tugged her nightgown down over her thighs.

Good thing, too, he told himself. Because he was on the ragged edge of control, and that edge was crumbling underneath his feet. The anger still simmering inside him didn't seem to have an effect on the pulse of desire that kicked into high gear whenever he was close to her.

Hell, the woman could still turn his body to stone without an effort.

Thankfully, his heart had turned to stone ten years ago, so that particular organ was in no danger.

"I think," Penny said, drawing him back to the moment at hand, "I'll just lie down for a minute or two."

"Yeah. Good idea. Do you still drink that disgusting green tea?"

Surprise flickered in her eyes. "Yes."

He gave a shudder but said, "I'll make you some."

Colt left her staring after him and got out of her bedroom as quickly as he could. No point in torturing himself, watching Penny stretch out across a bed he really wanted to join her in. Frowning at his own train of thought, he reminded himself that he and Penny were done. The only reason he was here now was to see the twins. To make sure they were safe. Being cared for.

When he left her room, he fully intended to go straight to the kitchen. Instead, he stopped outside the twins' bedroom. He laid one hand on the old-fashioned brass knob and felt the cool metal bite into his skin. His heartbeat jumped into a gallop and every breath came fast and shallow.

He felt the way he had the first time he'd gone paragliding in the Alps. That wild mixture of excitement, dread and sheer blind panic that made a man so grateful to be back on the ground when it was all over, he wanted to kiss the dirt. But just as on that long-ago day, there was no turning back. He had to jump off the side of that mountain. Had to take this next step into a future he never would have predicted.

Opening the door quietly, he stepped inside. Colt heard them before he saw them. Quick, soft breaths, a muffled whimper and a scooting sound as one of them shifted in their sleep. Colt scrubbed one hand across the back of his neck and walked silently across the dimly lit room. Outside, the sun was setting, casting a few last, lingering rays through a window that overlooked a tiny backyard.

Inside, there were two white cribs, angled so that the twins could see each other when they woke. There was a rocking chair in one corner of the room, shelves for toys and books, and matching dressers standing at attention against one wall. Pictures in brightly colored frames dotted the walls and at a glance, Colt could see the photos were of rainbows and parks and animals…everything that would make a baby smile.

But it was the babies he was interested in. His footsteps were quiet, and still the old wood floor creaked with his movements. But the twins didn't react; they slept on, dreaming. Taking a deep breath, Colt steadied himself, then walked up to stand between the cribs, where he could see each of his children.

Riley wore pink pajamas and slept on her stomach, arms curled, hands beneath her, tiny behind pointed skyward. He smiled and looked at twin number two. Reid's black hair was trimmed shorter than his sister's. He wore pale green pajamas and slept sprawled on his back, arms and impossibly short legs spread out as though he were making a snow angel. Both of them were so beautiful, so small, so…fragile, they stole his heart in a blink.

He didn't need a paternity test to be sure they were his. Instinctively, he knew they were his children. He *felt* it. There was a thread of connection sliding through him, binding him to each of them. Colt reached out his hands and curled a fist around the top rail of the matching cribs. His heart might be stone where women were concerned, but these babies had already stamped themselves on his soul. Each whispered breath tightened the invisible thread joining them and in a few short moments, Colt knew he would do anything for them.

But first, he had to deal with their mother.

Penny woke up, disoriented at first. A quick glance at her surroundings told her she was at home and she took a relieved breath, grateful to be out of the hospital.

"The twins!" Her eyes went wide as she realized that watery morning sunlight was creeping through her bedroom window. She'd slept all night. Hadn't seen the babies since that one quick check the night before. Hadn't heard a thing. What if they had cried out for her? How could she sleep so soundly that for the first time in eight months, she hadn't heard them?

Pushing herself out of bed, she took two hurried steps toward the door before the pain in her abdomen slowed her movements to a more cautious speed. She went to the twins' room and stopped in the doorway. The cribs were empty. Her heart pounded so hard against her ribs she could hardly breathe. Panic shot through her still-sleep-fogged mind.

Then she heard it.

A deep voice, *Colt's* voice, sounded low, gentle, and her initial bout of panic edged away to be replaced by a wary tenderness.

Penny followed his voice, moving slowly, cautiously, through the house that had been hers for the last two years. The house that was still filled with memories from her own childhood. The house where she'd made a home for her kids.

At the kitchen doorway, she paused, unnoticed by the three people in the room. The twins were in their high chairs, slapping tiny palms against trays that held gleefully mushed scrambled eggs. Their father—Colt—sat opposite them, talking, teasing, laughing when Reid threw a small fistful of egg at him. Penny's heart ached and throbbed. She used to dream about seeing Colt like this with the twins. Used to fantasize about what it would be like for the four of them to be a family.

And for one quick moment, she allowed herself the luxury of living in that fantasy. Of believing that somehow, the last eighteen months had been written differently. That Colt belonged here. With them. With *her*.

"Are you going to come in or just stand there watching?"

She jolted as he turned his head to spear her with a look. Guilt rushed through her and the fantasy died a quick, necessary death. What was the point in torturing herself, after all, when she knew that Colt didn't want her? All he wanted was her children. And the twins, he couldn't have.

"I didn't think you knew I was here."

"I can feel your disapproval from here."

She flushed again and moved into the room. When the twins spotted her, there were squeals of welcome and her heart thrilled to it. She went first to one, then the other, planting kisses and inhaling that wonderful baby scent that clung to each of them. She took a seat close by and watched as Colt continued feeding the babies, dipping a spoon into peach yogurt again and again, distributing it between the twins, who held their mouths open like baby birds.

"You got them up and dressed," she said, noting the fresh shirts and pants, the little socks on their tiny feet.

"You sound surprised," he said.

"I guess I am." In fact, she was stunned. She'd thought that Colt would be lost dealing with the twins. Instead, he had them changed and fed and was behaving as if he always started out his mornings in a three-ring circus.

He never stopped feeding the babies as he spoke. "The King family has been procreating at a phenomenal rate the last few years." He shrugged. "You can't go to any family gathering without someone handing you a baby who needs changing or feeding or both. So I've had plenty of practice. We all have. Granted, I don't spend a lot of time with the babies...but enough to know my way around a diaper."

True. He'd told her about all the children his cousins were having. She just had never once considered that he would have taken any interest in them. As he'd told her himself, Colt wasn't the family type. He was more interested in risking his life than in living it.

"Still," he mused, his voice tightening slightly, "I've never done it for my own kids before." He shot her a sideways look that was hard and cold and promised a long talk in the very near future.

"Colt..." She was too tired, too achy to deal with him.

Where Colt was concerned, nothing was easy—except the passion. That had been cataclysmic from the start. From the very first moment they'd met, their eyes had locked and a chemistry like she'd never felt before had burst into life, burning away every inhibition, every ounce of logic, even her most ingrained natural defenses.

Everything she thought she knew about herself had drained away in the face of the overwhelming pull of the magnetism drawing her and Colt together. So she'd let it go. Everything she'd ever believed. Everything she'd ever promised herself. She had surrendered completely to what her body was demanding—and when it was over, when Colt walked away, she'd paid the price.

She wouldn't make the same mistake twice. So whatever he had to say to her, she would fight him. She would stand strong against that wild feeling of raw passion because she knew that it didn't last. She'd lived it.

"I think they're finished," he said abruptly, cutting off her thoughts. He stood, got a paper towel damp and wiped two happy little faces and sets of grubby fingers. While he did, he asked, "You want to tell me about them?" He paused. "Or is that a secret, too?"

She swallowed hard and stood, unbuckling Riley and lifting the baby into her arms. The twinge of pain was worth it to feel her daughter's solid warmth pressed against her. Kissing the baby's cheek, she said, "What do you want to know?"

"Everything, Penny," he murmured, lifting Reid free of his seat. "I've discovered some things on my own in the last couple of hours with them—"

"Tell me," she said, wondering what he thought of the children he'd only just met.

"Well, for one thing, Reid's going to be left-handed. And he's already got a pretty good arm on him." Colt held the little boy easily in the crook of his arm and grinned when Reid patted both of his cheeks. "And I've figured out that Riley is the more adventurous one. She doesn't like being held for too long. She wants to be on the floor, getting into things. Reid likes cuddling, but he's more than willing to join his sister to plow through a room."

Penny laughed shortly. It was such an apt description

of the twins. Reid was thoughtful contemplation and Riley was a trailblazer. "You're right. I always thought Riley was the most like you."

One black eyebrow lifted and he shook his head. "When we were little, Con was the one off pushing envelopes. I wanted to be near my mom—and the cookie supply."

She smiled at the image of Colt as a cookie-stealing little boy, but had to ask, "Then why are you the one who flies off to adventure spots while Connor runs your business from an office?"

The light in his eyes dimmed, then went out completely as his features shuttered, effectively sealing her out of whatever he was feeling. "Things change."

Penny felt as though she'd struck a nerve, but she had no idea how. King's Extreme Adventures was so well-known that everyone was aware of which twin was the crazy one. The week they were together, Colt had told her stories about his travels for the company.

And most of those stories had terrified her. Being helicoptered in to ski down the sheer face of a mountain? Climbing to the rim of a volcano where the heat of the magma was so intense, you were forced to wear protective heat suits? Parasailing in the Alps. Chasing tornadoes. He'd done them all and more and he seemed to thrive on not only the adventure—but the risk.

And as much as she'd loved him, as much as it had pained her to watch him walk away, she'd had to admit to herself that they never would have worked out anyway. How could she love a man who thought nothing of putting his life on the line in exchange for a brief shot of adrenaline? And now, how could she allow her kids to love a father who was so careless with his own life that one day he wasn't going to come home?

"You're right." Penny carried Riley into the living room and heard Colt following after her. His footsteps were loud against the wood floor and seemed to mimic the thump of her own heart. Having him here in the home she'd made was...distracting.

She had to find a way to get him out again. "Some things do change," she said, carefully easing the baby onto the floor beside a huge plastic toy bin. She took off the lid and smiled as Riley pulled herself up to wobble unsteadily, a wide, proud smile on her face.

Penny took a seat on the nearby sofa and watched as Colt set Reid down beside his sister. But rather than sitting down with her, Colt moved to the front window and glanced outside at the morning sunlight before turning to face her again.

Judging by the expression on his face, Penny knew they were about to have that "talk" he'd been promising her. And frankly, she was ready for it. Get everything out in the open so he could go away and she and her twins could have their lives back.

"You should have told me." The words dropped into the silence like stones plunked into a well.

She took a breath and prepared for battle. "I get that you're angry."

He snorted. "You think?"

She met his gaze from across the room, refusing to be cowed or ashamed of the decision she'd made. "You made it plain, that last morning in Vegas, that you didn't want to be married and you definitely didn't want kids."

His mouth tightened into a grim line and a muscle in his jaw twitched. "Yeah, I did say that," he admitted.

"But that was hypothetical kids. Did I ever say that if you were pregnant I wouldn't want to know about it?"

"You might as well have." Penny shifted on the sofa carefully, her stitches pulling and aching, reminding her that she wasn't at her best. "I knew that you wouldn't care."

"So you're a mind reader." He nodded sagely.

"I didn't have to read your mind, Colt. You said it all. Flat out in plain English," she argued, not willing to stand there and take sole responsibility for what had happened between them. "You walked out on me, Colt. Why did I owe you anything?"

"You had my *children*." His voice lowered, emphasizing that last word without having to shout.

She stiffened and he must have noticed because he took a breath, seemed to settle himself and then said, "All right. Let's start over. Just tell me *why* you didn't tell me when you first found out you were pregnant."

"I already told you." What she didn't add was that she had also been afraid. Afraid of the King name, the King fortune. She'd worried that he might simply turn his lawyers loose and take her children from her. And he'd pretty much threatened to do just that when he first stormed back into her life. What chance would she have had against the kind of power the Kings could muster?

"I missed a hell of a lot, Penny, and I'm not forgetting that anytime soon."

"I understand." Which meant, of course, that she and Colt were on opposite sides of this battle and unless they found a way to build a bridge across the gap separating them, there would be no solution. No peace. "You know about them now, Colt. What are you going to do about it?"

He pushed one hand through his hair and she remembered that impatient gesture. "I don't know," he grumbled and shot a quick look at the twins, babbling happily at each other. "All I'm sure of is I want to know them."

She could understand that and, maybe, a small part of her warmed to him because of it. But the fact was that Penny was still exhausted, sore and not a little off her game since Colt had walked back into her life. So being cool and logical was a stretch at the moment.

Walking around the couch, he took a seat in a chair opposite her and close to the twins. His gaze shifted to them briefly and Penny watched his features soften. When he looked back to her, though, his eyes were chips of ice again. "I won't be a stranger to my own kids, Penny. I won't be shut out of their lives."

A sinking sensation swamped her as she came to grips with her new reality. Whether she liked it or not, Colt would be a part of her children's lives. Now she had to find a way to protect them from caring for him too much. Because though he insisted he wanted to be a part of their world right now, she knew that wouldn't last long. How could it? He was always traveling, wandering the world, looking for the next rush.

Taking a deep breath, she said, "And what about the next time you go wingsuit flying? Or parasailing?"

He frowned. "What're you talking about?"

"You, Colt," she said. "It's just not in your nature to be a suburban dad. You won't last a month before you'll be off running with bulls or some other crazy thing."

"Crazy?"

"Yes. You risk your life all the time and you do it because you like it." She shook her head. "I saw pictures of you in a magazine last month—standing on the rim of a volcano while magma jumped in the air around you."

"Yeah. I was in Japan scouting new sites. So?"

"So how's a quiet street in Laguna going to hold your interest, Colt?" She gave him a small smile. "This isn't your world. Never will be. Why fight so hard to be a part of something you never wanted in the first place?"

His gaze never left the twins. Reid plopped down onto his behind and Riley leaned over to pull a car from her brother's grasp. Reid's face screwed up as he prepared to howl, but Colt cut off the reaction by reaching into the plastic tub and getting another car that he handed to Reid. Immediately, the baby looked up at him and gave his father a wide enough smile that all three of his teeth were displayed.

Colt laughed a little, waited another moment or two and then shifted his gaze to hers. "Because, Penny. I'm a King. And to a King, family is everything."

Five

Penny's fists curled into the fabric of her nightgown and held on as if it meant her life. And in a way, it did. The tangible, very real feel of what Colt had called her "radioactive" nightshirt reminded her of who she was and where she was. This was her home and he was the intruder. For the moment at least, they were on her turf and she held all the cards.

How long *that* would last, she couldn't even guess.

Even from across the room, she felt the magnetic pull of him and had to fight against it. He wasn't here for her—he was here to rip apart her world.

Pain ripped through her and she hated knowing that he still had the ability to hurt her. She'd worked so hard to get past this. To get over Colton King. And she'd done a pretty good job of it, too. She hardly ever thought of him anymore—well, no more than a few times a day and all night in her dreams—but now he was here again, back in her life. This was going to reset her starting-over clock and soon she'd be going through all the misery she'd already survived once. But better to do it now, she told herself. While the kids were too little to understand. Too small to remember him. To miss him when he was gone.

But their argument was circular. He blamed her for keeping secrets. She blamed him for walking away. There was no middle ground here, so she'd have to try to create some.

"Colt, I get what you're trying to do."

"Is that right?"

"But," she said, ignoring the taunt, "you don't have to. Just because they're your family doesn't mean you have to *be* here."

Nodding slowly, he fixed his gaze on hers and she could have sworn she felt the temperature in the room drop a few degrees. "Where should I be?"

She threw her hands up, already forgetting about that calm, cool middle ground she was going to build. Panic wasn't a good breeding ground for calm and cool. "I don't know. Bali? Australia? The top of a mountain, or the bottom of the sea?"

"You're wrong. I should be right here."

"No, I'm not wrong." A short, sharp laugh escaped her. "Right now, you're doing what you think you should, Colt. Not what you want to do. And when this rush of responsibility has faded, you'll take off again. It's what you do. It's who you are."

Riley chose that moment to crawl to her father and pull herself up by grabbing tiny fistfuls of his jeans. She staggered a little and swayed more than a few times, but Colt sat perfectly still, watching his daughter grow and develop right before his eyes. Her black hair curled around her ears, her blue eyes shone with happiness and her chubby hands slapped at his legs in triumph as she finally found her feet.

He covered one tiny hand with his and stroked his thumb over Riley's smooth skin. Penny's foolish, gullible heart gave a ping of tenderness at what she was seeing and just for a second or two, she caught a glimpse of *what might have been.*

Finally, Colt looked at her again. "I'm here. Whether you like it or not, and you're just going to have to deal with my presence."

Not for long, she promised herself, determined not to be touched by the gentle way he treated the twins. Not to be swayed by the warmth in his eyes. She'd been fooled once by Colton King. She'd believed that he had felt the same way she had—swept away by a powerful and unexpected swell of love. And she'd been crushed. Devastated.

In fact, the only thing that had held her together after signing his divorce papers was finding out she was pregnant.

Knowing that she would have a child—then two—helped her to refocus her life. To concentrate the love she'd thought she'd lost onto two children who had become the very center of her life.

She wouldn't allow Colt to hurt her again. Or worse, to hurt the twins with his callous disinterest in real, honest feelings.

"I'm here. Deal with it," Colt told her, his voice steely with determination. "Besides, you're just out of the hospital and you need help, whether you want to admit it or not."

She wanted to argue, but the pain in her abdomen made that impossible. Looking up at Colt, Penny had to admit, at least to herself, that she wasn't going to win this one. And if she kept arguing, she'd only end up looking like an idiot. She was in no shape to take care of herself, let alone the twins. Colt was right. She did need help.

She just didn't want to need *him*.

Still, he was here and maybe… She nearly smiled as something occurred to her. Maybe if Colt was here, in the middle of what was Penny's normal chaotic life, if he could experience firsthand just how much work two babies could be, he would leave that much sooner.

Right now, she knew he was running on anger and regret that he was only now finding out about the twins. But sooner or later, his natural inclination to take off would kick in. He might not be able to admit it to himself, but Penny knew that even now, that itch was gnawing at him. If she let him stay, let him take care of the twins, it might be enough to push him away that much faster. And though it pained her to think of him leaving again, she knew it was for the best that it happened fast.

"Okay," she said.

"Okay what?" He looked at her, suspicion gleaming in his eyes.

"Okay, you're right. I do need help and you *are* the twins' father."

"Uh-huh." If anything, his eyes narrowed even further.

She gave him a smile that cost her some of her pride. "Don't look so surprised. You convinced me, that's all."

"Is that right?"

Penny sighed. "Colt, you wanted me to agree with you and I have."

"That's what worries me," he admitted quietly, his suspicious gaze still locked on her.

Reid crawled at top speed across the floor to join his sister. Grabbing hold of Colt's jeans, he pulled himself up, and laughed in delight as he and Riley took turns slapping their palms against Colt's thigh. For a minute or two, he simply watched them, a smile curving his mouth, and when he looked over at Penny again, that smile was still reflected in his eyes.

She felt a way-too-familiar jolt of something that she knew was dangerous. Attraction mingled with old feelings of love that were already being rekindled. But she didn't want that fire again. Didn't want to get burned by her own emotions being tossed at the feet of a man who had already made it clear that he didn't want them.

But she knew there was no way to stop what she felt for Colt. The only remedy would be to get him to leave as soon as possible. Then she could lose herself in her kids and her work and pretend that there wasn't a large, gaping wound in her heart.

The next morning, after a hideously sleepless night, thanks to red-hot dreams of Colt, Penny stood in the bathroom studying her reflection in the mirror. Right away, she really wished she had simply draped a towel over the mirror instead.

Her hair was wild, her face looked pale and she really wanted a shower but didn't think she'd be able to manage it on her own. And frankly, the thought of asking Colt for help with *that* problem was too much to consider. Just thinking about being wet and slippery with Colt's hands moving over her soap-slicked body made her want to whimper with need. Which was just enough to make her push aside the fantasy and deal with reality.

He'd stormed into her life and was so busy laying claim to everything around her that Penny felt as though she had to make a stand.

Frowning, she let her gaze drop. All right, yes, her nightgown wasn't the most attractive piece of clothing she'd ever owned, but it was *hers*. Just as this house, these kids, were *hers*. And as for the nightgown being a man repellent, maybe she should have it tattooed onto her skin. But that would only take care of keeping Colt away from her. She couldn't think of a thing to keep *her* from wanting him. Except, of course, that large dose of reality. Too bad that whenever she was around Colt she tended to do more feeling than thinking.

Shaking her head at the sad, sad woman in the mirror, Penny brushed her hair, washed her face and then got dressed. A long-sleeved green T-shirt over some comfy old jeans and she thought she was ready to face Colt.

Naturally, she couldn't have been more wrong.

"What are you *doing?*" She walked into the kitchen, a little steadier on her feet, thank heaven, than she had been the day before. But what she found in the kitchen had her swaying. In indignation. Colt sat at her small round table, her laptop open in front of him and stacks of unpaid bills laid out around him.

Humiliation was a living, breathing thing inside her. With this latest invasion of her privacy, she felt as if he'd stripped her bare and she was so furious about it, she was practically vibrating.

Colt barely glanced up from her computer. "I'm paying your bills."

"You can't do that," she managed to say through gritted teeth.

"Sure I can. All you need is money and I've got plenty."

Another verbal slap—another reminder of just how different their lives were—and she felt it right down to her bones. He was a King. He had more money than she could ever dream of and here he was, tossing it in her face. Just to make sure she knew where she stood in this particular battle.

He looked so confident, so sure of himself, sitting there in a slice of sunlight while the twins happily feasted on the Cheerios scattered across their tray tables.

"I don't care how much money you have, Colt." Lies, lies. If he were poor, she wouldn't be so worried about what he could do to her life. But no, he just *had* to be one of the richest men in California. "I pay *my* bills with *my* money."

One black eyebrow quirked. "Not lately, you haven't."

Her gaze swept the embarrassingly tall stack of bills that he slapped one big hand on top of.

"Things have been a little slow lately businesswise, but it's about to pick up." Defensively, she folded her arms across her chest. "Just butt out, Colt."

"Nope, can't do it," he said, lifting his gaze to hers at last.

His features were cold, hard, and his eyes glinted like chips of ice in the sun. He looked out of place in her bright, sage-green kitchen with its yellow cabinets and old scarred floors.

"By the looks of this mess, you're in deep and sinking fast."

Who knew there was *more* humiliation to be felt,

Penny thought. Lying awake nights worrying about how to pay her bills was her business. She hated that now he knew all about it, too. With no other choice in how to handle the situation, she stiffened her spine, lifted her chin and did what she always did when she was faced with immutable facts. She brazened her way through.

"I'm building a business," she argued. "That takes time. Something you wouldn't know about, I'm guessing, because the Kings don't have to actually *work* for a living."

Inwardly, she winced at the snide tone in her voice. She even knew that what she said wasn't true. But more than that, waving a red flag in front of an already-raging bull was never a good idea. Still, was she supposed to simply stand there and be made to feel like a failure?

As she watched, the chips of ice in his eyes grew flintier. More forbidding. "The Kings have money, yeah," he said, every word covered in frost. "But we're expected to work. To build our businesses, and we *do*. Every last damn one of us works our asses off and we're good at it."

She flushed. "I know. But you don't know what it's like to do it all *alone,* do you?"

He took a breath, scrubbed one hand across his face, then nodded. "Fine. You might have a point." His gaze fixed on hers, he added, "But that's only more reason you should have contacted me. I would've helped."

"That's what you don't get. I didn't *want* your help," she reminded him and realized that she sounded like a whiny child.

Irritated at herself as well as him, she crossed the room in a flash and grabbed for the closest pile of papers.

Colt was faster. He snatched them up and flipped

through them with a casual ease that made her even more furious.

"Electric, gas, phone, cable…" He paused and looked up at her. "Credit cards. You were behind on all of them."

"I make payments," she said, embarrassment tangling with outrage and getting lost in the shuffle.

"Does the phrase 'paid in full' mean anything to you?" he asked, voice quiet, controlled.

"Not really. I pay them what I can when I can."

"Well, now you don't owe anyone," he said flatly.

It would have been really wrong of her to actually experience a sweep of relief, so of course, she didn't allow herself to feel anything like that at all.

"Except *you*," she pointed out and felt the heavy weight of that little fact settle onto her shoulders.

She really was going to have to kill Robert, she told herself firmly. And her brother probably suspected that was her plan since he hadn't come around in a while. If he hadn't gone to Colt none of this would be happening.

"You already owe me," he said, bringing her up out of her thoughts.

"For *what*?" He'd already swept her ordinary world into oblivion. What more could he possibly expect from her?

He just stared at her as silence grew and thickened in the air between them. "Time. I lost eight months with the twins. And the nine months you were pregnant. I didn't see their birth. Didn't see their first smiles or see them crawl for the first time." He shook his head slowly, his gaze still pinning her like a bug to a board. "So don't pretend you don't know what I'm talking about. You kept my children from me, Penny. I'm not forgetting that."

"Neither am I," she said softly, as a flicker of shame

joined the tumult of emotions rattling around inside her. She still believed she'd done the right thing, but seriously, the way Colt had reacted to the news of the twins' existence had really surprised her. She hadn't thought he'd be interested enough to come and see them, let alone stay there, in the house, taking care of two babies who could bring a grown man to his knees.

But even as she thought it, she knew that his actions now didn't mean he would stay.

"That doesn't mean you get to stick your nose into every aspect of my life. How I live is none of your business, Colt."

"It is when it concerns *my* children," he countered neatly. "I looked through your bills because your brother told me you didn't have health insurance. I was worried about the twins. But it seems *they're* covered and those payments are up to date."

"Of course they are," she told him hotly, making another grab for the papers he held in his hand. "I would never take chances with the twins' health."

"But you do with your own."

"I never get sick."

One black eyebrow lifted again and his gaze dropped meaningfully to the fresh scar on her abdomen, now hidden beneath her T-shirt.

Her eyes rolled practically to the back of her head. "Appendicitis is something different. That could happen to anyone."

"Which is why we have health insurance," he said, tone so calm and patient she wanted to shriek.

"I can take care of myself, Colt. I've been doing it most of my life—" She closed her mouth fast before she said more than she wanted to about that. Her past wasn't the point here anyway. Staring at the pile of bills she still held in one tight fist, she thought of something else to throw at him, as well. "You had no right to pay off my hospital bill, either."

"Again," he pointed out, "someone had to."

"But that someone doesn't have to be *you*."

Two days, she told herself. He'd been back in her world about two days and already, things were turned upside down. She didn't want to be indebted to him and if he kept this up, she'd never be able to repay him.

"This cottage is paid for—that's good," he was saying. "But when I took the twins into the yard this morning, I noticed you need a new roof."

"Yes, it's on my list and I'll get to it as soon as I can." That list was miles long though, and the roof was much closer to the bottom of that list than the top. With any luck, rain would be scarce again this winter and she wouldn't have to worry about the roof for another year.

"The roofer will be here on Friday," he said.

Control, like a single, slippery thread, was sliding out of her hands and Penny kept grasping at it fruitlessly. Colton King was a tank. A gorgeous, sexy tank. He simply mowed over whoever or whatever stood in his way, flattening everything in his path.

And she knew that he would do the very same to her if she tried to stand between him and the twins. But what kind of mother would she be if she didn't try to protect her kids from having their little hearts broken? No. She had to hold her ground, not give him another inch, or he would completely take over her life.

"You can't buy me a new roof," she said, keeping her voice quiet and her tone even.

"Already done." He stacked the now-paid bills on

the other side of the computer, where she couldn't reach them easily. Then he leaned back in his chair, folded his arms over his chest and said, "I called my cousin Rafe. His construction crew will be out here on Friday. They're checking for termites while they're at it, since these old cottages are like an all-you-can-eat buffet for those bugs—"

"Dam— Darn it, Colt," she corrected herself quickly with a guilty glance at the babies sitting close by. They would be talking soon and she didn't want them picking up the wrong words. "I don't want you doing this."

"When the first rain hits, you'll thank me," he assured her.

When she first woke up this morning, Penny had actually felt better. Less sore, less tired. Now, she felt as though she needed to go back to bed. If she slept long enough, maybe he would be gone when she woke up again. But even as that idle wish floated through her mind, she set it free because she knew it wouldn't be that easy. Colt wouldn't leave until he was good and ready. And when he did go, there would be no stopping him.

Drawing out the chair beside him, she eased down into it and looked him dead in the eye. "You can't just come into my life and reorder it to suit yourself."

"I paid some bills," he said. "You obviously need the money and I can afford it, so what's the big deal?"

"The big deal is that I pay my own way." Silently, she gave herself a cheer for remaining very cool and logical. "I take care of myself and my family."

He looked at her through serious, cool blue eyes. "But that's the thing, isn't it? The twins are *my* family, too."

Her heart iced over and her stomach sank. This is what she'd been afraid of. That Colt would find out about the twins and immediately claim them. Brush her aside—or steamroller her—and take what he wanted.

A bank of clouds rushed across the sun, sending an intermittent mix of light and shadow into the kitchen. The twins were babbling happily to each other and for the first time, Penny didn't wonder what they were saying, or if they could understand each other. She was too busy trying to understand the subtext of what Colt was saying.

Was he laying claim to his children? Was he already laying the groundwork for pushing Penny out of her babies' lives? Fear became a knot in the center of her chest. For most of her life, she'd taken care of herself. She'd solved her own problems, made her own happiness. Now her life was suddenly out of her control and she didn't have a clue how to deal with it. The one thing she did know was that she wouldn't surrender. Not without a fight.

She kept her voice low and calm when she asked, "Colt, what is it you're after? Just tell me flat out what you expect to happen."

He leaned in toward her, flashed a quick look at the babies, then shifted his gaze back to her. Cloud shadow moved over his features, making his eyes look more distant, more…mysterious.

"I expect my kids to be well taken care of. To have what they need."

"They do," she argued in a choked whisper. Hadn't she been working herself nonstop to ensure just that? She might be a little late on her bills, but they all would have been paid. Eventually. And her kids didn't want for anything. "The twins are healthy and they're *happy*."

She reached out and laid one hand on his forearm. She let him go again instantly and regretted touching him at all, because a zing of reaction shot from her hand, up her arm, to ricochet around the inside of her chest like a ball of heat. That overpowering attraction they'd shared right from the start was obviously alive and well and now throbbing deep inside her. Ignoring her body's clamoring need, she swore, "They'll never go without."

"You're right about that," he said and leaned back in his chair again. He looked every inch a King—in name and profession—lounging comfortably as if he hadn't a care in the world. While Penny sat opposite him, her stomach churning, her mind racing.

This was what it was to be as wealthy as God, she told herself. Colt was so used to being able to command whatever he wanted done, he didn't even think about it. He'd ordered a new roof for her house as easily as she bought a gallon of milk.

Somehow, over the last eighteen months, she'd managed to forget that easy arrogance he carried with him. She'd forgotten that his way of life was so different from hers that they might as well have lived on different planets.

"Don't try to fight me on this, Penny," he warned. "You'll lose."

"Don't be so sure," she countered with more confidence than she felt. What could she possibly do in a battle with one of the Kings of California? He had a fleet of lawyers at his beck and call and a bank account that was endless. If this ended up going to court, then she didn't stand a chance against him and she knew it. So what she had to do was make sure it never went before a judge. She couldn't trust that the courts would choose a mother's love over a father who could support the twins so easily.

"Really?" he asked, clearly amused. "You think you can take me on?"

Oh, there was more than one meaning to that question. She knew, because her body started buzzing and heat sizzled in his eyes, melting the ice. Penny dropped her gaze from his because she didn't want him to see what he could do to her so easily. She only wished it was as simple to hide her reactions from herself.

"I've done something else this morning that you should probably know about," he said.

She swallowed hard, hoping her voice wouldn't sound choked when she said, "What's left?"

"You know your bills are all current now, but I've also transferred money into your bank account—"

"You what?"

He smiled. "I transferred money into your account."

Her blood pressure had to be through the roof because she could actually *hear* her heartbeat in her ears. "How much money?"

One eyebrow lifted. "Greedy?"

"Appalled," she corrected.

He shrugged. "Most women would be delighted to have a half million dollars dropped into their bank accounts."

Six

"A half—" Penny gulped noisily and then blinked as the room spun around her. Her vision narrowed, black rushing in from the edges even as little dark dots danced merrily in front of her. "Half. Half…"

"Breathe, Penny," he suggested.

She wished she could, but her lungs weren't working. Shock had her blinking furiously trying to clear her vision even as she slapped one hand to her chest as if she could somehow jump-start a heart that had clearly stopped. The man was insane. And pushy. And generous. And infuriating.

She opened and closed her mouth on words that wouldn't come. Gasping now, Penny knew she was going to end this "conversation" in a dead faint.

"Damn it," he muttered, then leaned out, put his hand on the back of her head and pushed her forward, until her head was between her knees. "Breathe before you pass out."

She drew in breath after breath and still her chest felt tight and her head was spinning. Penny felt him thread his fingers through her hair, and his touch sent new nerves skittering along her spine. Wasn't it enough that he'd sent her brain into a tailspin? Did he have to do the same to her body? His closeness wasn't making it any easier to breathe.

As if from a distance, she heard the twins laughing and she fought hard against the dizzying sensation clouding her head. Thankfully, they were too young to know just what exactly their daddy could do to their mommy.

When she was able to draw a few deep breaths, she forced herself to say, "Fine. I'm fine, let me up." Once she was sitting up again, she took another breath for good measure and met his gaze. She scowled at the humor glinting in his eyes. Of course he would be enjoying this.

"Good to know I can still make a woman faint."

"You're being *funny?*"

He shrugged casually, but his eyes remained sharp and fixed on her. "I'm not joking when I say they're my kids and I'm going to make sure they're taken care of."

"By buying off their mother?" Insult slapped at her. Did he really believe he could just walk in here, wave his money in front of her face and she'd do backflips to please him? "A half a million dollars? What were you thinking?"

"That you need the money."

"I don't want it, Colt," she said tightly.

"Want it or not, it's done," he said and closed the laptop with a soft click. "You don't have to live from month to month, Penny."

"I don't need your handouts." Okay, big lie. She did need it. She just didn't *want* to need it. A half a million dollars? That was nuts. Just insane. And served to point out once again just how different their lives were.

A flash of heat singed the ice in his eyes. "It's not a handout. It's the right thing to do."

"According to you," she snapped.

"My vote's the only one that counts."

"So typical," she muttered, shaking her head as if trying to convince herself that this was all some kind of nightmare and all she had to do was wake up.

"What's that supposed to mean?"

"It means, you're the one who decided our marriage was a mistake." Words so hard to say. She could still feel the pain of that last morning with him in Vegas. The memory of his eyes, cool, distant, staring at her as if he was watching a stranger. The clipped note in his voice. The fact that he never once looked back as he walked away from her. "Your vote was the only one that counted then, too, I remember."

His features went cold and hard. His eyes took on that same distance she recalled so well. "That was then. This is now. And the sooner you get used to this," he was saying, "the easier it'll be. On all of us."

She pushed to her feet, gave a quick look to the twins, forced a smile for their sakes, then turned back to Colt. "Why should I want to make this easy on *you?* You barged in here and took over. No matter what you think, I'm not your *duty,* Colt. I'm not your *anything.*"

His smile was tight, his eyes narrowed as he looked past her briefly to the two babies still happily babbling. "This isn't about you, Penny. It's about them. And the twins are my duty. My responsibility. And I'm going to do whatever I think is right to make sure they have everything they need."

"What they need is love and they have that."

He snorted and tapped his fingers on the thick pile of newly paid bills. "Love doesn't buy groceries or pay the electric company."

She flushed but it was as much anger as it was embarrassment. Penny hated that he knew how tight money was for her. Hated knowing that he was able, with a few clicks of a mouse, to clear away the bills that had been plaguing her. Hated that it was a relief to have that particular worry off her shoulders.

Mostly though, she hated being this close to Colton again because it reminded her that wanting what you couldn't have was just an exercise in self-torture.

"I don't need a white knight in a black SUV riding to the rescue."

"You sure as hell need something, Penny."

"Don't curse in front of the twins."

He stared at her. "They're eight months old. I don't think they're listening to us."

"You have no idea what they hear or remember."

Grumbling under his breath, he pushed back from the table, the chair legs scraping against the wood floor. When he stood up, he walked past her, across the room, heading for the coffeepot. Along the way, he trailed his fingers across the top of Riley's head. He looked back at Penny as he poured two cups of coffee. "You can hardly stand without wincing. You've got two kids to take care of. Why're you fighting my help?"

Why? Because having him here tore at her. Her emotions felt flayed. Being with Colt was too hard. Too nebulous. He was here today but he'd be gone tomorrow and she knew it. The question was, why didn't *he* know it? He was always looking for a way to risk his life. How long would he last in a beach cottage in a sleepy town where the only risk was fighting diaper rash?

"Because you don't belong here, Colt," she said, idly pushing Reid's scattered Cheerios into a pile for him. "I'm not going to count on your 'help' only to watch it disappear."

Shaking his head, he carried both cups of coffee across the room and handed one to her. "I told you. This is different." He waved his cup at the twins. "They make it different."

"For how long?"

"What?"

Her hands curled around the coffee cup, drawing the heat into her palms, sending it rushing through her veins, dispelling the chill she felt. "We were married for a single day before you ended it. You left and never looked back. I won't let you do that to my kids."

"Who says I will?"

"I do," she said, gathering together every last, ragged thread of her remaining self-control. "You live your life with risk, Colt. But I don't. And I won't let my kids live that way, either. Most especially, I won't risk my children's heartbreak on a father who will eventually turn his back and walk away."

"So where is she?"

Late that afternoon, Connor looked around the small living room as if half expecting to find Penny huddled under a throw pillow.

"She's taking a nap," Colt answered and dropped onto the couch. The overstuffed cushions felt so good, he thought he just might stay there for a year or two. "So are the twins."

Connor stuffed his hands into his slacks pockets and rocked back on his heels. "Well, wake 'em up. I want to meet my niece and nephew."

Stunned, Colt stared at his brother for a second. "Are you nuts? This is the first chance I've had to sit down in three hours." His eyes narrowed on his twin. "Wake them up and die."

Connor chuckled, walked to the nearest chair and plopped down into it. "Don't look now, but you sound like a beleaguered housewife."

He frowned at that, then shrugged. "Never again will I say the phrase 'just a housewife.' How the hell do women do it? I've been here two days and I'm beat. Cooking, cleaning, taking care of two babies…" He paused, let his head drop to the couch back and added, "women are made of *way* tougher stuff than us, Con. Trust me."

He stared unseeing up at the beam-and-plaster ceiling overhead and wondered how Penny had coped all alone for the last eight months. Hell, during her pregnancy? A stir of something that felt a lot like regret moved through him and Colt frowned to himself. Yeah, he'd missed a hell of a lot that he would never get back. But she'd been here. On her own, except for her brother—and Robert was an intern so he couldn't have been around much—so how had she done it all?

Okay, yeah, she had been behind on her bills, but the house was clean, the kids were happy and healthy, and she was building her own business. He had to admire that even while it irritated him still that she'd never contacted him. That she refused to need him.

"Was this house built by elves?" Connor muttered.

"I'm getting claustrophobia just sitting here." He glanced up at the ceiling. "Why is that so close?"

Colt sighed. "I almost knocked myself out this morning," he admitted. "I slept on the couch and when the twins cried I jumped up, ran to their room and smacked my forehead on the door frame."

Con held up one finger. "Excuse me? You slept on the couch?"

"Shut up."

"How the mighty have fallen." Con leaned forward, bracing his elbows on his thighs. "Word of this gets out, your rep is shot."

"Word of this gets out," Colt told him, "I'll know who to blame."

"Point taken." Connor leaned back in his chair again with a good-natured shrug. "So, tell me about them. What's it been like?"

Colt laughed and speared one hand through his hair. "Let's see. This morning they dropped my wallet into the toilet, pulled flowers from the pots on the back porch and threw blueberry yogurt onto the kitchen floor just to watch it splat."

Connor grinned. "Sounds normal. And crazy-making."

"You got that right," Colt said on a tired sigh. "How the hell did Penny manage on her own? Not only did she take care of the twins, but she's running a photography business, too. I don't know when she finds the time to pause long enough to take photos of other people's kids when the twins demand constant supervision."

Con laughed outright. "Since when do you start using words like supervision?"

Embarrassed, Colt said, "Since I discovered that climbing Everest is *nothing* compared to giving those two babies a bath. After the yogurt incident, I threw 'em both in the tub and wound up looking like a flood survivor by the end of it."

"And you're loving it?"

Colt's gaze snapped to his twin's. "I didn't say that."

"Didn't have to. Hell, nobody knows you better than I do and I can tell you're enjoying the hell out of this. Even with all the work and yogurt trauma."

A swell of emotion filled Colt as he thought about the twins. The snuffling sounds they made when they were sleeping, the sigh of their breathing, had become a sort of music to him now. He recognized every sound. He knew that Riley wanted to be cuddled before bedtime while Reid wanted to sprawl across his mattress, looking for the most comfortable position.

He knew that Riley loved her brown teddy bear and that Reid preferred a green alligator. He knew Riley wanted Cheerios in the morning and that Reid was interested only in bananas.

His children were real to him now. Actual people— in miniature—with distinct personalities. They had become a part of him and he couldn't have said just when that had happened. But he did know that he wasn't ready for this time with them to end.

"Okay then," Connor interrupted his thoughts abruptly. "You're living in a tiny house, taking care of tiny people and sleeping on a too-short couch. Why?"

"You know why," Colt grumbled and wished for a second he hadn't opened the door to his brother. Didn't he have enough going on at the moment without Con throwing his two cents in?

"Yeah, I do. Now tell me how it's going with Penny."

"Frustrating," Colt admitted, lifting his head to look

at his twin. "She believes she did the right thing in not telling me."

"Did she?"

His eyes narrowed on his brother. "What's that supposed to mean?"

Connor shrugged. "You haven't exactly made a secret of the fact that you don't want a family of your own."

"Whose side are you on, anyway?" Colt sat up straighter.

Lifting both hands for peace, Connor assured him, "Yours. Obviously. But you gotta admit, she had reason to do what she did."

He would have argued, but over the last couple of days, his anger had slowly been drained away until he could think clearly. Logically. And damn it, he could see her point of view. Didn't mean he agreed with it, though. "Fine. She had reason. The point is, I know now and—"

"What're you gonna do about it?"

"That's the thing," Colt muttered. "No idea. You and I both know those kids shouldn't depend on *me*."

"No, I don't know that. For God's sake, Colt, stop beating yourself up." Connor huffed out an impatient breath. "It wasn't your fault. We've all told you that countless times over the last ten years."

"Yeah," he said, staring at his brother. "You all have and it doesn't change a thing. I should've been there. I told them I would be. If I had been…"

Darkness rose up inside him and buzzed in his head like a swarm of attacking bees. Pain jolted him. Memories were thick and for a moment or two, Colt was sure he could actually feel the bite of the snow, taste the cold on the wind. Hear screams that sounded almost nightly in his dreams. He hadn't lived that day, but in his dreams, he did. Over and over again.

"What makes you think you could have stopped it?" Connor jumped up from the chair, stalked across the room and looked down at him. "You weren't responsible. Let it go already."

Colt laughed shortly. *Let it go.* If only it were that easy. But ten years after the darkest day in his life, the memories were still clear and sharp enough to draw blood. How could he forget? How could he ever forgive himself? How could he allow two defenseless infants to depend on *him?*

"You can let it go. I can't." He stood up, meeting his twin's gaze with a steely stare of his own. Didn't matter how close he and Connor were, this was something Colt had to carry on his own. Had to live with. Every. Damn. Day. And no one else would ever understand what it was like to be haunted by thoughts of *what if.*

A couple of tense seconds ticked past as the twins glared at each other. But eventually Connor shrugged, shook his head and said in disgust, "It's amazing you can grow hair on that rock you call a head."

Colt snorted. "This head is identical to yours so choose your insults more wisely."

Connor's lips twitched. "Fine. So let's talk about Sicily instead. You want me to get somebody else to check out Mount Etna for us?"

He'd considered it. There were a couple of experienced climbers they'd used before to scope out new spots when Colt was too busy to do it. But he wasn't ready for that yet. "No," he said, shaking his head firmly. "I'll do it. Might take a week or so until Penny's feeling better, but I'll get to it."

"Your call," Con said, then asked, "So if I'm quiet, can I look at your kids while they sleep?"

Colt gave his brother a quick grin. "Sure. But if you wake 'em up, you'll be here until you put 'em back to sleep."

The rest of the afternoon passed on a tide of diapers, baby food, Cheerios and crazed babies crawling all over the house—usually in two separate directions. Colt was too busy to do a lot of thinking. But he still managed to have an idea that kept swimming through his mind, refusing to be ignored. He played with possibilities as he bathed the twins and then wrestled them into pajamas. Not easy since Reid refused to lie still and Riley insisted on tearing her diaper off the minute Colt got it on her.

How in the hell had his life changed so completely, so quickly?

Colt was getting into a routine and the fact that he could actually *think* that word and not run screaming for the closest exit was almost scary. But routines were meant to be broken. This wasn't forever.

But as he looked at the babies now settling into their cribs for the night, he realized that knowing this time was going to end didn't make him as happy as it should have. He scrubbed one hand across the back of his neck and tried to sort through the splintered thoughts and emotions raging inside him.

The twins had laid siege to his heart, there was no denying it. What he felt when he looked at them, when they smiled up at him or threw their little arms around his neck, was indescribable. Sure, he'd been around his cousins and heard them all talking about how their children had affected them. But he guessed you couldn't really *understand* until you'd experienced it for yourself.

Two tiny children—not even talking yet—and they'd

changed everything for him. He just didn't know what to do to protect them, other than to keep his distance.

Problem was, he wasn't ready to leave just yet.

"Enjoying your special time with the twins?"

The voice from the doorway behind him didn't surprise him. In spite of the turmoil in his mind, Colt had *felt* Penny there watching him long before she spoke.

Glancing over his shoulder at her he said, "I don't know how you take care of them so well on your own."

She looked surprised by the compliment and a quick stab of guilt hit him. Colt realized that in the last few days he had never acknowledged just what she'd accomplished in this tiny house. She'd been on her own from the jump, yet she'd managed to care for the twins and this house and try to build a business.

Exhausted him just thinking about what her life must have been like for the last eight months.

"Well, thanks." She stiffened a little as if she'd been unprepared for flattery—and didn't quite know how to take it. She fidgeted with the short, pale blue robe she was wearing, tugging the terry cloth lapels tighter across her chest. "It isn't always easy, but—"

"Oh, I get that." He stared down at his daughter, lying in her crib. In her favorite position, with her behind pointed at the sky, the tiny girl smiled as she drifted off to sleep. Shaking his head in amazement, Colt looked over at Reid, who was already sleeping, sprawled across the mattress as if trying to claim every inch of the space as his own.

Twins, but so different. Yet both of them had carved their essences into his heart in a matter of days. It was damn humbling for a man who was used to running the world around him to admit, even to himself, that two tiny babies could bring him to his knees.

Walking to the doorway, Colt turned out the light and watched as the night-light tossed softly glowing stars onto the ceiling. Then he and Penny stepped into the hallway and he pulled the door closed behind them.

In the sudden silence, he stared down at her and lost himself for a second in the deep green of her eyes. The whole world was quiet and the tension between them flashed hot as she gathered the neck of her robe in one fist. His body went to stone when he realized she was *naked* under that robe.

And in a heartbeat, his memory provided him with a very clear image of her naked body. The curves he'd spent hours exploring. The smooth slide of his hand across her skin. The fullness of her breasts, the slick heat of her body surrounding his.

His eyes narrowed on the top of her robe, as if just by concentrating, he could make her release that death grip and give him a peek at what lay beneath. Damn, the woman was going to kill him.

"I'm, uh, going to take a shower," she said and took a step back from him.

Colt's eyes narrowed on her. "Are you steady enough to do it on your own?"

Her eyes went wide at the implication that if she wasn't, he was going to help.

"I'm fine," she insisted, taking another step backward. He could have told her that a few feet of distance wouldn't be enough to put out the flames snapping between them.

Then she was talking again, her words coming quickly, almost breathlessly, as she tried to make her escape. "I'm tired of washing up. And they said I could take a shower sooner than this, I was just nervous about it. So now I'm not and I really want a shower."

Hot water, sluicing across her body, cascading over smooth skin, soap bubbles sliding down the length of her amazing legs. Colt cursed silently. If he kept up this train of thought, he wouldn't be able to walk. He wanted her badly, but he was also worried. What if she got into the shower and needed help?

His inner cynic snorted at that one. He wanted to be in that shower with her, but it wasn't *help* he wanted to give her.

"It's not safe for you to be in there on your own," he said, a part of him actually believing the statement. "I'll help you."

"Oh, no." She shook her head hard enough for her long, dark red hair to swing out from her shoulders. "Not gonna happen."

"Don't argue." He took her arm and steered her down the short hall to the bathroom. "We're adults, Penny."

"Yeah," she murmured, "that's the problem."

He gave her a wicked wink. "Are you saying you can't trust yourself around me? Can't control your raging desire to rip off my clothes and take me? Take me hard?"

Her lips twitched and he grinned back at her.

"That's exactly right, Colt," she said, sarcasm dripping from every word. "I don't want to take advantage of you in your weakened state."

"Very thoughtful," he assured her and walked into the bathroom, also designed for people a foot shorter than Colt, keeping a firm grip on her elbow. "Look, seriously, you need a shower and I'm not going to let you risk falling or something."

"What am I, ninety? I'm not going to fall. I'm not an invalid," she told him as he turned on the water and waited impatiently for it to heat up.

He let go of her, but blocked the only exit so she couldn't sidle out of the room. "All kidding aside," he said, "you can argue and we can be here for hours, or we can just get this taken care of."

She thought about that for a long minute or two, the pitiful sound of the low-water-pressure shower in the background. "Fine. You can stay in the room, but no looking."

He snorted. "I'll try to control myself."

And it would be an effort, he thought but didn't say. The room was so small, they were practically standing in the same space. The short, narrow sink dug into his thigh as he moved aside to let her get to the shower.

"Turn around," she ordered.

He did and found himself staring into the mirror—something she clearly hadn't considered. Behind him, she was reflected in the glass as she slipped out of her robe. He gritted his teeth as his gaze followed the line of her spine right down to the curve of her truly amazing behind. Her hair danced across the top of her back as she moved and he wanted to tangle his hands in that thick, soft mass as he had before.

His body throbbing, aching, Colt held his ground, though it cost him every last ounce of his self-control. Never before had he been forced to *not* take what he wanted. To stand back and let the woman driving him insane slip through his fingers. His teeth ground together and his breath came short and fast. Still, he couldn't look away and was rewarded—or tortured—with a glimpse of her breasts, high and full, as she pulled the striped curtain back and stepped into the tub.

The water ran and he heard her blissful sigh and that was nearly enough to push him over the edge. Colt looked at the curtain and imagined her behind it, naked and wet, tipping her face up to the stingy flow of water. He couldn't help wondering what she would think of the shower at his place, with its six massaging heads and the heated seats carved into the granite enclosure. In his mind, he laid her down on that wide seat, parted her thighs and—

"Ow."

"What?" he snapped, dream dissolving instantly. "What is it?"

"Nothing," she said. "I just moved too fast and I'm still a little sore, that's all. I'm fine."

He didn't believe her. If she pulled her stitches out, they'd be back to square one.

Pulling the curtain aside, he looked at her and instantly knew it had been a mistake. His imagination had *nothing* on the reality of a slick, wet, naked Penny. Her long, dark red hair hung in thick ropes over her shoulders. Drops of water clung to the tips of her hardened nipples and her face was flush with warmth and surprise. She looked like a damn water nymph and his body's reaction was instantaneous.

The tiny window over the shower was open, allowing a cold breeze to whisper through. The sea-green paint was peeling on the ceiling and the porcelain on the ancient tub was scratched and pitted. Yet all he gave a damn about was the wet, naked woman looking at him with raw desire in her eyes.

She shook her head and chewed at her bottom lip before saying, "Go away, Colt."

"No," he said, unable to tear his gaze from her. There was no way he was leaving. If it had meant his life, he still would have stayed exactly where he was.

Raw, frantic lust pumped hot through him. Desire clutched at his throat, making breathing nearly impossible. But then, he asked himself as he reached out one hand to cup her breast, *who needed to breathe?*

She gasped at his touch, and rather than moving back, she stepped closer and licked her lips, sending a lightning bolt of need slicing through him. Then she covered his hand with hers, holding him steady against her breast. Struggling for air, she whispered brokenly, "We can't. We shouldn't. I mean, I shouldn't. I mean—"

He knew what she meant. She'd had surgery a few days before. Everything between them was a mess, with neither of them happy with the other at the moment. And yet… "We'll be careful…."

"Colt—" she gasped again as his thumb caressed her hardened nipple. "Oh, my."

He smiled to himself, then stepped back long enough to shed his clothes and toe off his shoes. Then he was joining her in the made-for-munchkins shower.

Suddenly, he was liking the small space. She couldn't have backed away from him even if she had wanted to. And one look into her eyes told him she didn't want to.

"This is so not a good idea," she whispered.

"Stop thinking," he said.

Seven

Then he kissed her.

As the trickle of water splashed over their entwined bodies, he kissed her long and deep, losing himself in the taste and feel of her. When she parted her lips under his, he took the kiss deeper, tangling his tongue with hers in a frenzied dance of need and want. *Here it is,* he thought wildly. That amazing jolt of passion that he'd never felt for anyone else. The elemental, nearly primitive need to touch and take and have.

Only with her. Only with Penny.

She wrapped her arms around his neck and leaned into him, her breasts sliding against his chest. He ran his hands up and down her body, the slick feel of her skin beneath his hands a match held to the dynamite crouched inside him. "Damn, you feel good."

"You, too," she whispered. "Blast it, you, too."

He smiled against her mouth. She didn't *want* to want him, he thought. But she did and that was good enough. Colt turned her so that her back was to the water tumbling from the narrow, outdated showerhead. She looked up at him as the hot water landed on her shoulders to roll down her body in rivulets.

"Colt—"

"Let me touch you," he whispered, sliding one hand down from her breast. His fingertips trailed along her rib cage and down over her abdomen.

She shivered, closed her eyes and hissed in a breath. "I don't know…"

"I do," he said and kissed her again as he dipped first one finger and then two into her tight, wet heat.

She gasped and clutched at him, hands grabbing at his shoulders. Her breath came fast and shallow, small puffs against his skin. He touched her deeper, stroking her intimately until she rocked into his hand, reaching for the climax he was pushing her toward. His thumb moved over the heart of her, that one nub of sensation that fueled the fire inside her until it became a raging inferno.

She spread her legs for him, welcoming his touch, his caresses. Then she slid one hand from his shoulders, down the length of his body until her long, delicate fingers closed around the hard length of him. Then it was Colt's turn to hiss in air and tremble under the onslaught of too many sensations.

"That's cheating," he said softly.

"All's fair—you know." She groaned as he stroked her again, rubbing the core of her harder while his fingers delved deeper inside her body.

He took her—and she took him. Her fingers moved on him until it was all Colt could do to keep his feet. His vision blurred as completion roared toward him. But he wouldn't do it. Wouldn't surrender to what she was making him feel. Not until he'd seen her shatter in his arms.

It didn't take much longer.

He kissed her hungrily, allowing her to feel everything he felt. He wanted her to know what she was doing to him. Her breath quickened. She tore her mouth from his. Her eyes went wide and wild and she shouted his name hoarsely as her climax slammed into her.

Colt held her close until the last of her tremors had passed. Only then did he think about himself and the fact that his body was aching for the same release she'd just experienced. Then Penny looked up into his eyes and smiled. Her grasp on him tightened and he surged into her hand. Her thumb moved over the tip of him and that sensation nearly sent him over the edge. His self-control was unraveling. Fast.

No other woman had ever affected him like Penny could. From the first moment he'd met her, there had been an electricity between them. A single touch was all it took to shower them both with sparks that they could find nowhere else. Everything about her was...more. She excited him, infuriated him and aroused him more than he would have believed possible.

But when he came, it was going to be *inside her*. He pulled away from her only long enough that she was forced to stop rubbing and stroking him, though the action cost him. Aching need clawed at him and he read new desire in Penny's eyes, too. They had always been explosive when they came together and it seemed nothing had changed since he'd last seen her.

"That's it," he muttered. "Bed. We need the bed."

"But we shouldn't—" Her mouth might be saying no but her eyes were shouting *yes*.

"Is it safe for you to have sex?" he muttered thickly, saying a silent prayer that she would say yes again.

"They said as soon as I felt ready."

"Please tell me you're ready."

"Boy howdy."

He grinned at her quick response. Dropping his forehead to hers, he muttered, "We'll be careful. You can be on top. You set the pace. That's my best offer."

"I'll take it." She swallowed hard, reached behind her to turn off the water, then allowed Colt to pick her up and carry her out of the bathroom and into her room.

The bed was narrow, but Colt didn't care. All he wanted was a damn flat surface. He flopped onto the mattress and watched as she climbed up to cover his body with hers.

She was so small-boned. So delicate. So damn sexy.

"Wait," he ground out. "Condom."

"Yeah, because it worked so well before," she said wryly.

He snorted. "Good point."

"Doesn't matter," she told him. "I'm covered."

"Best news I've heard all night." He lay back again and clamped his hands onto her hips.

As she went up onto her knees, he took a breath and held it. She looked like some warrior princess from ancient tales of Ireland. Her dark red hair streamed wetly across her shoulders to lay across the tops of her breasts. Her green eyes flashed with intent and her pale skin shone like the finest porcelain. She was damned magnificent and he wanted her more than his next breath.

* * *

Penny trembled from head to foot. This was a bad idea and she knew it. But there was no way she could stop now. She had to have Colton King inside her again. She needed to feel the thick, hard length of him filling her body completely. She'd worry about tomorrow when it reared its ugly head. For right now, she was going to live in the moment. This one, amazing, incredible moment—she was going to take everything she could from it.

"You just going to torture us all night?" he asked, his voice a low, throaty growl of contained passion.

"That's the plan," she murmured, gaze locked on his as she slowly lowered herself onto him, taking him into her body inch by glorious inch. Penny watched his ice-blue eyes flash with heat and the last lingering whisper of reason in her mind faded away.

She knew this was stupid. She knew nothing had changed. Colt still wouldn't stay. They had no future. But for this one perfect moment in time she was going to forget all of that.

She'd wanted him, needed him, *missed* him and now he was here. In her bed, looking at her as if she were the only woman in the world. Desire quickened, her breath came faster and feverish bubbles of expectation rose inside her. She moved on him, felt him catch her rhythm and move with her and she surrendered to the inevitable.

Colt King was the only man she would ever want. Damn it, the only man she would ever *love* and this might be all she ever had of him. How could she possibly deny herself what she found only with him?

She took him deep and when he was fully sheathed inside her, she sighed a little as her body stretched to accommodate his. Excitement rippled through her system, lighting fires that had been simmering for nearly two years. What she'd had with Colt would never truly be extinguished. One touch from him and those flames had erupted and consumed her in an inferno of sensations. It had been like this between them from the start.

They fit so well together it was as if they had been meant to find each other.

She rocked her body on his and heard his swift intake of breath. Penny trailed her fingers across his chest and down, loving the feel of his hard, muscular body beneath her hands. Dark hair dusted his chest and trailed down his abdomen. The muscles in his arms flexed as he reached up to cup her breasts in his palms. Sighing with the intense pleasure soaring inside her, she tipped her head back and gasped as his thumbs slid back and forth across her hardened nipples.

Penny's head tipped back and she felt the cool slap of her still-damp hair against her skin. He touched her and she spun out of control. He moved inside her and she only wanted more.

Her body ached a little as she moved on him, but that tiny pain was lost in a dizzying parade of feelings that had nothing to do with discomfort.

Darkness crouched outside the window and a soft wind rattled the tree limbs against the side of the house. Inside, though, it was all heat and magic and straining breathing and racing hearts.

Penny felt the lost time without him in her life melt away until only this one moment existed. The passion she remembered roared up stronger, sharper, more overpowering than before and she gave herself up to it. Staring down into his eyes, she moved on him, loving the feel of him sliding in and out of her body. He filled her so completely, the slightest movement created a friction that left her breathless. Again and again she moved on him, setting the pace, watching his eyes flare with heat and desire. Her blood pumped fast and furious, until it became a roaring in her ears, shutting out every other sound. An exquisite, oh so familiar tingle of expectation began to build deep inside her.

Colt's hands moved over her body, touching, exploring, tantalizing her with more and more sensations. He moved beneath her, picking up the rhythm she set and meeting her at every stroke, pushing them both faster and higher.

She groaned, braced her hands on his broad, muscled chest and raced to meet the climax that was hovering just out of reach. She climbed the peak in front of her quickly, desperate to reach the top and then tumble off the other side.

"Come for me, Penny," he whispered and his voice was a caress on every raw nerve ending. "Come for me. Let me watch you fly."

Throat tight, air strangling in her lungs, she was almost there, her body alive and simmering with want. Need. Her eyes flew open, locked with his, and when the first tremor shuddered inside her, she raced to meet it.

Colt shifted one hand to where their bodies were joined. His thumb caressed that one spectacular spot and as he watched, Penny shattered into a million jagged pieces.

Her mind was still spinning, her body still buzzing when she felt his body explode into hers. She heard his guttural shout, felt the tension in him coil and then release as, locked together, they crashed into oblivion.

* * *

A short while later, Colt rolled out of the cramped bed, pulled on his jeans and left her sleeping, curled on her side. He stared down at her, his gaze tracking the curves of her naked body, and hunger grabbed him by the throat again. She was beautiful. And amazing. And *dangerous*.

He laid the faded, flowered quilt over her, then slipped out of the room. The house was quiet. Too damn quiet, if truth be told. He wasn't used to this. The world he lived in was noisy, crowded and rushed—a place where no one got too close and he could move through crowds of people without ever being touched by any of them.

It's the way he liked it, he assured himself, as he quietly checked on the twins, then moved through the darkened house like a caged tiger looking for the easiest escape. He found it as he walked through the kitchen, opening the back door and stepping into the smartphone-size backyard.

He pulled in a deep breath of the cool night air and held it inside, hoping that it might swamp the fires still raging within. Naturally, it didn't, and he was left to burn as he took a seat on the steps and stared up at the sky.

Colt was still trying to come to grips with what had just happened. Being with Penny had rocked him right down to his bones. He was used to desire. Used to slaking that desire with whatever woman was handy. What he wasn't used to was what happened to him with Penny.

Over the last couple of years, he'd convinced himself that the memories he carried of his week with Penny were exaggerated. That no one could be that amazing. That the…connection he felt with her didn't really exist. Well, those lies had just been smashed.

His heart felt like a jackhammer in his chest and his

mind was filled with a jumble of thoughts he couldn't sort through.

Sex with Penny was staggering. No other way to put it or think of it.

Stars spilled across the blackness and a quarter moon looked like a child's teeter-totter. *Child.* The twins' features swam into his mind and he felt himself tighten up. Thoughts of sex dissolved as he considered the reason he was here. Those two kids deserved better than this cramped, too-short-for-real-people house. They were *Kings.* He could admire Penny for all she'd accomplished on her own, but now that he was in the picture, things were going to change.

He was putting his own life and business on hold to be here for Penny and the twins, but that couldn't last. He had places he had to be—Mount Etna, to be specific.

That thought quickly spiraled into another and from there, his brain raced with ideas. A slow smile spread across his face as he considered one notion in particular. Hell, he could go to Etna this week. And Penny and the kids could go to Sicily with him. The twins could see some of the world—never too young to experience different things. Then Penny could take photos of his BASE jumps to be used in advertising and that would help her business.

Smiling to himself, he nodded thoughtfully as the plan came together.

"You must be out of your mind entirely." Penny stared at him the next morning, astonished at what he'd just said.

Colt spooned more yogurt into two waiting mouths and flicked her a glance. "Not at all. This is perfect. I get my work done, you get some advertising for your business and the kids get to fly on a private jet. A win all the way around."

Shaking her head, Penny grabbed her cup of coffee and took a long drink, hoping that caffeine would give her the strength to deal with Colt. She'd awakened that morning alone in her bed, and though she was disappointed, she hadn't been surprised. Colt wasn't the snuggling kind of man and she knew it. And still there was a flicker of pain when she was forced to acknowledge that he was keeping a distance between them—even after what they'd shared.

But *this* was nuts.

"You can't really expect us to go to Sicily with you."

"Why not?" He shrugged, wiped Riley's mouth with a paper towel, then shoveled more yogurt into her. "We'll give it another week. You should be good to go by then."

Was it really so easy for him? Just make a decision and go? She had responsibilities. The twins to think of. A business to build. A house to take care of. Which she told him.

"The house will be fine. The twins will be with us," he looked at her again. "As for your business, it's at a standstill and you know it. I looked into your files this morning while you were sleeping. You're barely covering expenses."

Outrage and embarrassment tangled inside her, convulsing into tight knots that felt like balls of ice in the pit of her stomach. Not only had he delved into her bank account and her bills, he'd snooped through her business. He'd riffled through her records and all he'd seen was the bottom line. He hadn't noticed the hard work, the hopes, the dreams.

"I can't believe you did that," she murmured, then

laughed shortly at her own naïveté. Of course he'd intruded. Of course he'd stuck his nose into her business. Look what he'd done to her *life!*

The night before, she'd allowed herself to forget just how wide a gulf separated them. She'd indulged her senses and put her logical self on the back burner. But now Sensible Penny was back in charge.

Keeping her voice light so the twins wouldn't pick up on any tension, she focused a laser glare on Colt. "My business isn't any of yours."

"Wrong," he said easily. Then before she could argue, he continued. "I'm not looking for a battle here, Penny. I'm just saying, your business could use a good boost— and taking pictures for King's Extreme Adventures would give you that."

She slumped back in her kitchen chair. Sunlight fell through the windows and lay across the table and the old oak flooring. "Yes, because nothing says 'I'll take great pictures of your toddler' like doing a photo spread of an insane man jumping off a volcano."

A wry grin touched his mouth briefly and she felt the punch of it to her middle. But she wouldn't be seduced again.

"Colt, I didn't ask for your help and I don't need it."

"That's a matter of opinion."

"But mine is the only one I'm concerned with."

He sprinkled a few Cheerios onto the twins' tray tables and finally turned to meet her gaze squarely. "I'm offering you a job. It pays well. And," he added with a slow smile, "there are *other* benefits."

That swirl of something hot and wicked punched her low again and even melted a couple of the ice knots. But enough of them remained to keep her on course.

"We are *not* taking the babies on an excursion to a volcano. And no," she added, "I don't want to take pictures of you risking your safety, much less have my children witness that. Do you want them scarred for life?"

He snorted. "I don't remember you being so squeamish. When we met you were into sports photography. You wanted to travel the world, capturing danger and excitement with your camera." Shaking his head, he looked at her quizzically. "Now you're happy to take pictures of suburbia? What happened to all of the big dreams?"

"I became a mom," she said, trying to make him understand, though she doubted he ever would. "Plans change. *Dreams* change."

Her words were soft but powerful, and he acknowledged that with a brief nod for her. Then Colt looked at the twins and she watched his features soften and his eyes warm. She knew that his children had reached him in a way she'd never been able to. But she also knew that this time in her cottage was a blip on his radar screen. It didn't matter how much he cared for the twins.

Colton King, as he'd told her himself, was not the staying kind.

Friday morning, Rafe King from King Construction was at Penny's house bright and early. Colt was glad for the distraction. Since his brilliant plan had been shot down the day before by Penny, the two of them had been staying out of each other's way. Which wasn't easy in a house no bigger than a good-sized garden shed.

Carrying two cups of coffee with him, Colt strode out of the house and met his cousin as he climbed down from his truck.

"Coffee." Rafe grinned as he reached for it. "You always were my favorite cousin."

"And your wife's my favorite cousin-in-law." Colt looked past Rafe into the cab of the truck. "Did Katie take pity on me and send cookies?"

Rafe's wife, widely known as "Katie King the Cookie Queen," ran her own business out of her home while taking care of their daughter, Becca, and their newborn son, Braden. She also baked cookies for the legions of King cousins who adored her.

"Nice to see you, too," Rafe said wryly. After taking a sip of coffee, he reached into the truck and came back out with a white bakery box stamped "Cookie Queen."

Colt made a grab for it but Rafe whipped it out of reach. "Not for you," he said, and seemed to enjoy the moment. "Katie sent these to Penny. Along with her commiseration on being involved with a King."

Scowling, Colt pointed out, "Doesn't say much for you, does it?"

"Nah," Rafe said with a grin and a shrug. "She *likes* me."

"Great." His gaze locked on the pastry box. "What kind?"

"White chocolate macadamia."

"That's just mean," Colt said.

"My wife's good."

"That she is." Colt looked at Rafe and thought about it. Not that long ago, Rafe had been as determinedly single as Colt was and yet now he was happily married to a great woman and had two kids. He thought about taking a step back just in case commitment was contagious. On the other hand, he was already hip-deep in familyland, wasn't he?

"How's Katie and the new baby?"

Rafe's grin got wider. "Amazing. He's gorgeous and Katie's…even better than amazing. We're gonna have a big party for the christening. You and Con'll be there, right?"

"Absolutely." Colt had been to more christenings in the last few years than he had in all the years before. But every King birth was celebrated. Every new member to the family had to be welcomed with a barbecue and lots of food and laughs.

Which reminded him, he should talk to Penny about introducing the twins to the rest of the Kings. Not that they could have a King-size party at the cottage. They'd never be able to shoehorn everyone in. But they could hold it at his place. God knew there was plenty of room.

Funny, he'd never realized before that the house he bought three years ago was really meant for a big family. He'd thought at the time that it was a good investment. It still was, of course, but now he had to wonder how Penny and the twins would like it there. It would be better for them, he thought. More room. Big yard. Close to the beach.

He gave his head a hard shake. Seriously, he was beginning to worry about himself.

Rafe asked suddenly, "So, how's your new baby? Wait a minute. *Babies.*"

"Not exactly new," Colt said. "They're eight months old."

"Right." Rafe leaned against the truck. "Con told me. That couldn't have been easy."

"No, it wasn't." And it wasn't getting any easier, either.

He was feeling nothing but conflicted about this whole situation. He wanted those kids happy and safe. But to keep them that way, he knew that he couldn't stick around. He couldn't be here, let them learn to count on him only to risk letting them down when they most needed him. The thought of not being there to hear their first words or to watch them learning to walk tore at him. The thought of never seeing Penny again hit him much harder than he wanted to admit.

But there was no place for him here in this tiny house with a family. Because to stay would mean that they would come to depend on him. And he would, eventually, let them down. Hell, that's the one thing he could agree with Penny on. She was worried that he would disappoint his children—and so was he.

"How you doin' with all of it?"

"I'm all right." And not interested in talking about this. Even with a cousin. "Really appreciate you moving on the roof this fast."

"Not a problem. Anything for a King." Rafe shot a look at the roof on Penny's cottage and frowned. "That roof's in sad shape."

Hell, most of the house was in sad shape. He knew Penny loved it, but he had to wonder if the real reason she was living there was because it didn't cost her anything. The rooms were too small and the twins were going to outgrow it soon. There was no room for them to play and with only one bathroom, things were going to get ugly at some point.

And *why* was he suddenly thinking about things like that? When did he ever do future planning or worry about yard size or whether a roof was going to make it through another winter? What the hell was happening to him?

Scowling to himself, he muttered, "Check for termites too, will ya? I've got a feeling this place is a buffet lunch for the damn things."

"Okay, I'll get the ladder off the truck, do an inspection, then come find you."

"Like I said, I appreciate this." Colt took another sip of his coffee and tried to put aside the disturbing Suburban Dad thoughts.

Rafe grinned. "What's family for?" He handed over the box of cookies. "Here. Take these in to Penny. I'll see you both in a bit."

"Okay. How soon can you get started on the work?"

"Typical King," Rafe mused. "Why were we all born impatient?"

"Just lucky, I guess." Colt shrugged.

Nodding, Rafe said, "Let me take a look and some measurements. Check for termite damage. Once we've got that I can lay out the plan for you. But I can have a crew here by Monday if that's what you want."

"The quicker the better." He couldn't leave until he knew that Penny and the kids were going to be safe and as comfortable in this tiny dollhouse as it was possible to be. And he knew that with Rafe and his brothers' company on the job, the work would not only be done fast, but well.

With King Construction handling the work, he could assure Penny everything would be taken care of the right way. As for Rafe—he and his brothers ran such a successful construction and contracting business that they seldom had to go out on calls themselves. But the Kings were always there for family, so it didn't surprise Colt at all that Rafe had shown up personally.

So, if the Kings were always there for family and he was planning on getting out of his kids' lives as fast as possible, just what kind of King did that make him?

Eight

Of course there were termites.

And not just a few, either. No, this was a regular condo association of termites. They had community leaders, Miss California Termite pageants and apparently, never-ending appetites for the wood holding up her roof.

Penny sighed and grabbed Riley before the baby could crawl off the quilt spread on the lawn in the backyard. Reid was busily tearing apart one of his books, but Riley wasn't as easily contained. Absently, Penny handed her daughter a busy box and then looked up at the men on her roof. Rafe was a sweetie and yes, it was…nice of Colt to arrange all of this.

But at the heart of everything, Penny just kept sinking deeper and deeper into the "I owe Colton King" hole. But the worst part was, she wasn't even angry about owing him. She was just too relieved to have some of the bigger worries in her life smoothed over. So what did that make her? A hypocrite?

She accused Colt of using his money to make his own path easier. She was outraged when he interfered and paid off her credit cards just before dropping a fortune into her bank account. And she'd been furious about him arranging for a new roof. Or at least, that's how she'd acted. But the truth was, she was grateful and she hated to admit that.

She was both relieved and resentful—not exactly rational. But then she'd never been completely rational when it came to Colton King. Besides, putting her own confusing feelings aside, she knew Colt well enough to know exactly why he was doing all of this. He was taking care of everything he thought needed doing so that he could disappear with a clear conscience.

Penny took a deep breath and tried to steady herself as a wave of disappointment and dread washed through her. Two nights ago, she and Colt had come together and the passion had been staggering. What was between them was so strong, so overpowering, that even remembering what they'd shared shook her right to the bone.

But neither of them had so much as talked about it. She could almost believe it hadn't happened at all. Except for the fact that her body was in a constant state of low burn from a fire that had been reignited. Being with Colt again had not only reawakened her body, but her dreams. Nearly two years ago, when they'd first met, Penny had fallen in love so quickly, so completely, she had looked at their shared future and seen only the magic and the joy. Soon enough, reality had crashed down on her, leaving her brokenhearted and alone. It hadn't been easy to recover, to move on. And now, she knew instinctively that this time, recovery was going to be so much harder.

She'd known, of course, that she still loved Colt. Love just wasn't something that ended. At least, not for Penny. And being here with him, seeing him with the twins, had only etched him deeper into her heart than he had been before. Which was, she knew, a recipe for disaster.

She could already feel him pulling away from her. From the twins. It was as if the closer to being healed Penny became, the faster Colt was drawing back. She only wished it was that easy to turn down her feelings for him. The sad truth was, she still loved him. She'd never *stopped* loving him. But at least until this week, she'd taught herself to live without him in her life.

Now he was back and it was harder than ever to imagine going on without him. Her heart ached with the might-have-beens that rotated through her brain at all hours of the day and night. She looked at her babies and felt desolate that their father would be only a visitor in their lives. They would miss out on so much—and so would Colt. He didn't even realize it, but in leaving, he was cheating himself. She knew he didn't see it that way, though. There was something driving Colt. He was a warm, funny, intelligent man who was determined to live his life alone. Why? What was it in his past that kept him from seeing a chance at a future?

Reid turned his face up to hers at just that moment. A sweet smile curved his little mouth; his blue eyes were shining with love and trust and sheer joy. His soft black hair blew across his forehead and his chubby hands lifted his book to his mouth. Penny's aching heart melted a little and she wished suddenly that Colt could see just what he was running from. That he would discover the truth in time. But she wasn't holding her breath.

Her gaze shifted to the roofline, where one of Rafe's crews was working diligently. Colt had been up there, too, until about an hour ago. It was in his nature to take risks, even if it was only walking along a roofline as if he were on a tightrope. He was so busy keeping busy that he couldn't see what was right in front of him. The biggest adrenaline rush in the world. Love.

"Oh, this isn't good, is it?"

Penny jerked out of her daydreams and shifted her gaze to Maria as she picked her way across the yard. She wore a black skirt and a red blazer over a white silk blouse, and her three-inch heels kept sinking into the grass as she walked.

"Hi. What did you say?"

"I said, this doesn't look good." She squinted up at the crew on the roof, getting ready to spread a striped tent over the house. "Termites?"

"Only a few bazillion."

Maria shook her head and said, "If they're tenting, why're you still here? Shouldn't you be at Colt's place?"

"We will be, this afternoon," Penny said on a sigh. She wasn't looking forward to it, but she didn't have much choice, either. At the moment, Colt had a team of people inside the cottage, preparing for the termite extermination. But once the tent was up and the gas pumped in, she and the kids wouldn't be able to get back inside for at least forty-eight hours. Which meant either she try to keep the twins happy locked up in a motel room…or, she did what Colt was insisting on. Move in at his place for the duration.

It was hard enough having him here at her house.

What was it going to be like staying with him? Heck, she'd never even seen the place Colt called home. Was it a palace? A condo? A plush penthouse apartment? He hadn't eased her curiosity, either, he'd just said, "You'll see when we get there."

"You sound thrilled at the prospect," Maria said, stepping out of her heels to take a seat on the blanket. Automatically, she swept Reid up onto her lap where the baby boy chortled happily and busied himself with the gold chain Maria wore around her neck.

"Well, it's weird," Penny tried to explain. "Moving into his house is completely different than having him here."

Maria nodded sagely. "The home turf advantage you mean."

"Exactly!" Penny smiled, pulled blades of grass from Riley's hand and added, "I don't want to owe him any more, you know?"

"I'm sorry," Maria said, shaking her head. "I must have gone momentarily deaf. *You* owe *him?* You already gave him two kids. How much more could the bill be?"

Penny laughed in spite of the situation. Maria was not only Robert's fiancée, but a really good friend. And right now, Penny needed one. "Maria, he paid off my bills. He stuck his nose in and used his money to 'straighten out my life.'"

"Good for him."

"What? Aren't you on my side?"

"Absolutely. But why shouldn't he pay off your bills? Honestly, Penny, pride's a great thing. But I'd rather have electricity than sit in the dark telling myself over and over again how proud I am."

"Some help you are."

"Hey, I'm a lawyer. We're soulless, remember?"

Penny laughed again. "I keep forgetting that part. And how did you know I'd be here?"

"Colt told me."

"Told you? When did you see him?"

Maria pulled the gold chain out of Reid's mouth and said, "At the hospital. I was supposed to meet Robert for lunch today but when I got there, he and Colt were just heading to the cafeteria."

"What? Why?" Colt went to see her brother? Without bothering to mention it to her? What was going on? What was he up to now? There was just no telling. Nothing was sacred to Colt. He'd invaded every aspect of her life and there was no sign of his stopping.

Maria shrugged, and kissed the top of Reid's head. "I don't know. Rob just said he'd see me at home later. But they looked…serious."

"Great." Now she could worry about what her brother and her— Wait. Just what *was* Colt to her? Her ex? Sure, but there was more. Her baby daddy? Yep, that, too. Her lover? Everything inside her curled up into a ball and whimpered at the thought. One night with Colt had her dreaming of *more* nights with Colt and that was just piling mistakes on mistakes and she knew it.

Didn't stop the wanting, though. Didn't stop the wishing or the misery that accompanied the knowledge that wishes very rarely came true.

"God. You're still in love with him, aren't you?"

Penny's gaze snapped to Maria's and she felt a flush fill her cheeks. "Of course not. That would be completely stupid."

Maria lifted one eyebrow and gave Penny her best lawyer glare.

"Okay, fine. Yes, you're right." Penny pulled the hem of her T-shirt from Riley's mouth. "I still love him since apparently I don't learn from my own mistakes."

"And what're you going to do about it?"

"Suffer," Penny muttered. "I'm going to watch him walk away. Again. And then I'm going to ask Robert if they've got an anti-love virus inoculation."

Maria laughed. "Pitiful. Really."

"Easy for you to say," Penny whispered. "Robert's crazy about you."

"I know." Maria sighed happily. "I really love that about him. But as for you—why are you so willing to let him walk away again?"

"What am I supposed to do?" Penny asked. "Tie him to the bed?"

"Not an entirely bad idea."

"True. But eventually, he'd work his way free and then he'd leave anyway." She plucked a rock from Riley's fingers and tossed it into the closest flower bed. "Besides, if he's that anxious to get away from me and his children, why should I try to make him stay?"

"Love."

"One-sided love? Not a good time."

"You could fight for him," Maria suggested.

"No." Shaking her head, Penny said, "What would be the point? If I fight and lose, none of it mattered."

"And if you fight and win?"

"I still lose," Penny told her solemnly. "It's no use, Maria. Colt lives for risk. He likes the rush. He likes the danger. I have a feeling that he's not going to be satisfied until he's cheated death so often that he finally catches up to it." She shivered at the thought, then looked at her babies and shook her head again. "I won't watch him do that, Maria. I won't watch him chase death. I can't. And I won't let my kids watch it, either."

A Spanish language radio station blared music into the quiet neighborhood. The men on the roof spreading a green-striped tarp shouted to one another and laughed while they worked.

"So that's it?" Maria watched her. "It's just over now?"

Penny smoothed her palm over Riley's head, loving the feel of her soft curls. "No. It's not over *now*. It was over almost two years ago. It was over right after it began."

The hospital cafeteria wasn't exactly filled with ambiance. But they'd done what they could with the place. Dozens of tables and chairs dotted the gleaming linoleum floor. Windows on the walls allowed bright shafts of daylight into the room and there was a patio through a set of French doors that boasted dappled shade and neatly tended flower beds.

Still, not a place Colt would have chosen to have a lunch meeting. But when you were meeting a busy doctor with limited time, it served its purpose.

Colt looked at the man opposite him. "You did the right thing telling me about the twins."

Robert took a bite of his chicken sandwich, chewed and said, "You had a right to know. But more importantly," he added, waving his sandwich for emphasis, "Penny's been struggling long enough on her own."

"Yeah, she has." Irritation swelled. Remembering what he'd discovered when he went through her bills, her business records, Colt felt another sharp stab of guilt. Though why the hell he should feel guilty, he didn't know. He hadn't *known* about the twins, had he? No one had told him a damn thing. Not until Robert had come to him.

Disgusted, Colt took a bite of his chicken enchilada. Immediately sorry he had, Colt frowned, dropped his fork onto the bright orange food tray and reluctantly swallowed. "How can you eat this stuff?"

Robert shrugged and took another healthy bite. "It's here. I'm hungry. Case closed."

Okay, he could see that. One glance around the crowded cafeteria assured him that the hospital had a captive audience here. Most of the customers were nurses and doctors, with a handful of civilians thrown in just for good measure.

"So," Robert said as he dipped a spoon into a bowl of vegetable soup, "I've only got a half hour for lunch. What did you want to talk about?"

"Right." Colt nodded, pushed his food tray to one side and folded his arms on the table in front of him. "I understand family loyalty," he began. "So I get why you kept quiet for so long. And I know what it cost you to go against Penny's wishes to tell me the truth."

Robert sat back and pushed one hand through his hair. "It wasn't easy. Penny and I've been through a lot together. She's always been there for me and I owe her everything. But I was tired of watching her live hand to mouth."

There was something more that Robert wasn't saying. It was there in the man's eyes. He owed his sister everything? Why? What had he and Penny been through together?

"I'm not saying anything else that would betray her confidence," Robert told him. "If you want more answers, you'll have to ask her yourself. Telling you about the twins was different. You're their father. You had a right to know."

"Yeah, I did." Colt nodded tightly. He didn't like knowing that Penny had felt she couldn't come to him. Didn't like thinking about her having such a hard time. Worrying. Alone with the responsibility of raising two children.

Scrubbing one hand across the back of his neck, he pushed those thoughts aside. "Look, I came here to tell you that I'll continue to be a part of the twins' lives."

Surprise flickered across Robert's features. "Is that right? So, you're staying?"

"No," he said, the word blurting from him instinctively.

Hell, he hadn't even had to think about it. He didn't stay. Colt didn't do permanent. He always had one foot out the door because it was safer that way. Not just for him but for whoever was in his life.

"I won't be staying, but I'll be around and I'll keep in touch," Colt said flatly. "And I will see to it that your sister doesn't have to worry about money anymore."

"Uh-huh. Good to know." Robert reached for his coffee and took a long sip. "So what're you going to do about the fact that she's still in love with you?"

Colt just glared at the other man. He wasn't even going to address that statement. Mainly because he didn't know *how* to address it. He'd been avoiding even thinking about it because there was no easy answer. He knew damn well that Penny loved him. It was in her eyes every time she looked at him. And it was just another reason for him to get the hell out of her life before it was too late.

He didn't want Penny to count on him. He didn't want his kids depending on him. He'd already failed people who mattered and the aftereffects of that had nearly killed him. Ten years later, he was *still* paying for what he'd done. His dreams were still haunted by the memories that wouldn't fade. By the screams. By the thunderous roar of an avalanche and the aching wail of ambulances that were just too late.

He wouldn't chance all of that happening again. But he also wasn't going to discuss any of this with Penny's brother.

"That's none of your business," he said.

"Probably," Robert agreed. "But she's my sister."

"I get that. Family loyalty is important." Colt knew that better than most. And no matter what happened or didn't happen between him and Penny, she and the twins would always be his family. He would see that they were well taken care of. Have everything they needed. In fact, he would do anything for them.

Except stay.

Colt's house was amazing.

It sat on the tip of the bluff in Dana Point, and boasted views of the Pacific from every room in the house. Three stories of living space sprawled across the cliff side, with decks and patios jutting out at every angle. There was a grassy, tree-laden space on either side of the house, with plexiglass fences to keep people safe while still allowing for the view.

It was lush and elegant yet somehow managed to feel cozy. There were ten bedrooms, seven bathrooms and a kitchen that would bring professional chefs to tears. Everything about the place, from the architecture to its perch overlooking the ocean, was breathtaking. Yet it felt…lonely. As if it were a model home waiting to be chosen by a family. Waiting to be *lived* in.

"So," Colt asked when he joined her on the stone terrace. "What do you think?"

"It's beautiful," she said automatically, then shifted her gaze to the wide sweep of ocean stretching out in front of her. Sailboats skimmed the surface of the water, breakers churned into the shore below the house, and a handful of surfers bobbed up and down with the rhythm of the waves. "How long have you lived here?"

He leaned one hip casually against the stone railing and flicked a glance at the sea. "A few years. It's a good base for me. I like being near the ocean."

"A base," she repeated. "So, you're not here often."

"Nope." He straightened up and shoved both hands into the pockets of his jeans.

"Your housekeeper must love working for you," she murmured. "Nothing much to do really until you show up occasionally."

He grinned and she had to force her heart back down from her throat to her chest where it belonged.

"I know she's excited to have you and the twins here to take care of. It's true I'm not here much, but you know me, Penny. I keep moving."

Yes, she did know that, and it tore at her heart to admit it to herself. He was standing right beside her, tall and gorgeous, his black hair ruffled by the sea breeze, his ice-blue eyes narrowed against the sunlight, and he might as well have been in Sicily jumping off that dumb volcano. He was so far from her she felt that she would never be able to reach him.

Then she noticed that his jaw was so tight it was a wonder he didn't grind his teeth into powder. That muscle flexing in his jaw was the only outward sign that he wasn't as cool and detached as he would like her to believe.

He was on edge, too. And for some reason, that made her feel better. Good to know she wasn't in an emotional turmoil on her own.

"You get the twins settled?"

"Yes," she said with a warm smile. Remembering the nursery where she'd tucked the babies in sent shafts of tenderness for Colt dazzling through her. "I can't believe you managed to have an entire room done up for them in a few hours."

"Money can accomplish a lot of things very quickly."

Her smile deepened. He might pretend to be unmoved, even isolated, but what he'd done for his children disproved that lie. The twins' nursery here was almost an exact duplicate of their room at the cottage. Bigger, of course, with a staggering view of the ocean. But the cribs were identical, the night-light was the same, their toys and dressers, right down to stacks of new clothes and towers of diapers. All sitting there waiting for the twins to make use of them.

"Yes, your money paid for it, Colt," she said. "But it wasn't your bank account that chose the twin teddy bears or saw to it that a guardrail was installed across the window."

He frowned a little.

"That was you, Colt. You were thinking about the twins. About their safety. Their happiness."

"And that surprises you?" he asked.

"No," she said, moving closer to him, tipping her head to one side to study him. "But I think it surprised *you*.

You love them. You love your children and want the best for them."

His frown deepened a bit and he looked…uneasy.

"Don't make more of this than there is, Penny," he warned. "Of course I care about the twins. But this situation with us is temporary and you know it. Soon I'll be leaving again and—"

She didn't want to think about that. Not now. Not until she had to. Penny had been so busy trying to maintain her anger at him that letting it go now was enough to unleash the barely restrained passion she felt for this man. She knew he'd be leaving. She knew that what they had together wasn't enough to hold him. But though they didn't have a future, they did have a present. If she was bold enough to demand it.

Memories of their night together rushed into her mind and sent dizzying spirals of want and need spinning through her body. She wanted Colt King any way she could have him. And if that meant that she would later pay with pain, then she was prepared to meet the cost. What she wasn't prepared to do was waste any more time with him.

"I know."

She stopped him by laying her fingers across his mouth. She was going to lose him and she knew it. She couldn't fight his nature. She couldn't offer him the risk and the danger he seemed to crave. So instead she would accept him as he was and leave the worrying about how she would live without him for later.

"Penny…"

"The twins are napping," she said, moving in even closer, until her breasts were pressed to his chest. Until she had to tip her head back to meet the ice-blue eyes that were now burning with the kind of passion she'd only known with Colton King. "Your housekeeper is out at the store stocking your kitchen. We have the house to ourselves, Colt. Let's not waste it."

He grabbed her and pulled her tightly to him. "Do you know what you're saying?"

Watery winter sunlight spilled down around them. The sea breeze ruffled their hair and sent a chill she hardly felt down Penny's spine.

"I do. I want you, Colt. There's no point in denying it," she said, laying both hands flat against his chest. She felt the thundering gallop of his heart beneath her palm. "You want me, too. I know you do."

He didn't deny it. How could he? If anything, he held her tighter, closer, and she could feel the proof of his desire pressing into her.

"Let's enjoy what we have while we have it," she said.

"I can't stay." Colt's eyes searched hers.

"And I can't go." Penny met his gaze. "But we're both here, *now.*"

For the last few days, it had taken every ounce of Colt's self-control to keep from taking Penny back to bed. He wanted her with every breath. His entire body ached with need. He walked around in a constant state of pain and discomfort. But having sex with her again would only magnify the mistake he'd already made.

Hell, he hadn't come back into her life to claim her— she deserved a hell of a lot better than *him*. He couldn't give her what she wanted. What she needed. Stability. A husband to count on. A happy family living in her dollhouse cottage surrounded by a white picket fence. It wasn't in him and he knew she'd never be happy with

anything less. And why the hell should she have to settle for a sometimes man when she was worth so much
more? She needed to find a man who would be beside
her. Someone she could depend on.

Though the thought of another man touching her,
claiming her as his own, raising his kids, sent jagged
bolts of pure fury through Colt. But he didn't know what
the hell else he could do. If he stayed, he'd fail them. He
knew it. Felt it. And that was one risk he was unwilling to take.

"Colt," she said, fisting her hands in his T-shirt, tugging at him until he came out of his thoughts to stare
into her eyes. "We have *now*," she repeated. "Let's make
that enough."

He smiled and shook his head. "You're not an 'enough'
kind of woman," he told her. "Penny, you're the all-or-
nothing type."

"Maybe I was. But people change," she insisted.

"No, they don't." He lifted both hands to cup her face,
loving the feel of her skin beneath his palms. Wishing
things were different. "Situations change and people try
to adapt. But at the heart of it, we are who we are. Always."

"And who are you?"

"A bad risk," he told her, his insides quaking, his voice
hard.

"I'll take my chances," she said and went up on her
toes to kiss him.

For a full second, maybe two, Colt didn't respond.
His brain was warning him to step back for her sake if
not his own. To do the right thing. To make her see that
nothing good could come of this.

But her mouth was insistent. Her tongue touched his

lips and his body took over, shutting his brain down. Conscience took a backseat to need and he growled low in his throat as he returned her kiss, deepening it. His tongue tangled with hers. He tasted her breath, the sweetness of her, and swore when she wrapped her arms around his neck that he felt her soul sliding into his.

How the hell could he turn down what she suggested? She was willing to risk pain; how could he do any less? He was going to have her. Going to indulge in what she offered and then he would walk away as he knew he should. It was the only way to keep her safe. To keep their children safe.

She sighed and melted into him, breasts against his chest, mouth hungrily meeting his.

The sun continued to shine down on them with warmth, not heat, and together they built a fire between them that put that pale winter sun to shame. The sound of the waves crashing into shore hammered into the silence, sounding like a ragged heartbeat. Seagulls screeched, a soft sea breeze blew and as they remained locked together on the terrace, the world slipped past in a haze of passion.

His hands roamed up and down her body, loving the feel of her curves as he continued to plunder her mouth, taking her breath, her sighs, into himself and holding them there. She moved against him and his erection throbbed painfully against the confines of his jeans. He had to have her. There was no time for niceties. No time for subtle seduction. This was lust, pure and simple and demanding.

Breaking the kiss, he bent, swept her up into his arms and headed for the house.

"You can't carry me," she complained.

"Looks like I can," he said and never broke stride.

"God, this is romantic."

He laughed, glanced into her shining eyes and said, "Glad you think so. I think it's expedient."

"That, too." She lifted one hand to cup his face, then let it drop so she could slide one hand across his muscular chest.

Even through the fabric of his T-shirt, Colt felt the heat of her touch right down to his bones. His mind was racing, his body was on hyperdrive and all he could think was *bed*. Had to get to the closest bed.

He headed for the master bedroom and didn't stop until he'd dropped her onto the mattress. Here, the walls were glass, affording a wide, uninterrupted view of the sea. At night, he could lower electric shades that would give him privacy, but here on the bluff, they weren't really necessary. No one could see into his room unless they were in a helicopter with a pair of binoculars.

And he was suddenly grateful for that privacy. He didn't want her in darkness. He wanted her in the sunlight. He wanted to feast on the sight of Penny, to burn her image into his brain so that when he was out of her life completely, he would be able to remember this day. This moment.

Nine

She stared up at him and Colt felt as if he could drown in the green of her eyes. Her dark red hair spilled across the white pillowcase and looked like spun silk. When she sat up, he pulled her to him for another hungry kiss. When he broke it, gulping for air like a dying man, he muttered, "Clothes. Off. Now."

"Yes." Quickly, she stripped out of her clothes and lay back across the bed, arms high over her head, back arched as if offering herself to him.

His mouth went dry. He undressed faster than he ever had before. In seconds, they were tangled together on the cool, crisp sheets. Rolling together across the wide mattress, their legs entwined, flesh met flesh. Hands explored. Mouths fused. Heartbeats hammered in tandem.

Sunlight flashed in and out from behind thick gray clouds scuttling across the sky. The French doors to the patio stood open and a cool, soft wind blew into the room, caressing heated skin.

Colt pinned her to the mattress, gave her a slow, seductive smile and dipped his head to take first one, then the other nipple into his mouth. Her scent filled his mind. The soft sighs she made fed the desire licking at his insides and pushed him on, wanting more, needing more. Lips, tongue and teeth teased her, toyed with her until she was writhing beneath him, gasping his name.

Hunger pitched higher in them both and he swept one hand down the length of her body to dip his fingers into her slick, wet heat. She lifted her hips and rocked into his touch, setting a rhythm that threw Colt's control down a slippery slope. He wanted. Needed. He felt her desire as his own and let the heat consume them both. He gave himself up to the fire within, jumping eagerly into the flames.

He looked her over, head to toe, and seared the image onto his brain. Sunlight dancing on pale skin. A few golden freckles lying dark against that paleness and the thatch of dark red hair at the juncture of her thighs. Perfection. She was all. She was everything. His heart stuttered in his chest as new and unexpected realizations rose up in his mind. Deliberately, he shut his brain off, letting his body take over. He didn't want to think now. Didn't want to acknowledge anything beyond this moment.

The only thing that mattered now was feeding the beast crouched inside both their bodies. He pulled his hand from her heat and she whimpered at the loss.

"Don't stop," she said on a heaving sigh. "Don't you dare stop."

"Not stopping, trust me," he managed to grind out. He couldn't have stopped touching her if it had meant his life. The feel of her beneath his hands, the flick of her tongue over her bottom lip and the glazed passion in her eyes all came together to twist him into knots so tight they might never come undone.

He flipped her over onto her stomach and ran his hands up and down her spine, cupping the curve of her incredible behind. She parted her legs, tossed her hair out of her way to look over her shoulder at him and whispered, "Oh, yes."

As if he'd needed any encouragement.

She licked her lips again as if she knew what that action did to him and enjoyed the power of it. Then she went up on her knees, silently inviting him to take what they both wanted so badly.

Her behind was full and curvy and he smoothed both hands over her soft flesh, kneading, exploring. He slid one hand down to cup her heat and she groaned, pushing into him, wiggling hips that drove him crazy.

"Don't make me wait, Colt. Don't make *us* wait. Take me where only you can," she whispered, desire-filled, forest-green eyes fixed on him.

"Oh, yeah." His voice was scratchy, words pushing through the knot lodged in his throat. He knelt behind her, pulled her in close and entered her in one long, smooth stroke.

She gasped in pleasure and he barely heard the soft sound over his own groan of satisfaction. She was tight and hot and he had to get a grip on the lust nearly choking him or he would explode in an instant.

Penny moved into him, wriggling those hips again, pushing back against him, taking him deeper, higher, and he felt every one of her movements like a caress. He moved into her, retreating and advancing, following the frantic rhythm set by his own heartbeat. He heard her gasps, her whispered moans. He felt her passion climb with his. He held her hips in a firm grip and set a pace that she hurried to follow.

Again and again, they climbed together, reaching for the peak that awaited them. And when he felt the first tremor begin inside her, he reached around to where their bodies were joined and thumbed the sensitive spot that held so many fragmented sensations.

She turned her face into the mattress and cried out, her shriek of pleasure muted but no less rousing. And an instant later, Colt followed her, jumping into the void with her, holding her close as shards of light and shadow erupted all around them.

A few minutes later, with Penny tucked close to his side and sunlight dancing in the room, Colt's old fears rose up to gnaw on him again.

He loved her. Loved her as he'd never believed it possible to love.

He couldn't tell her. She would expect…what she had every right to expect from a man who loved her. But he couldn't give her what she wanted. Needed. He couldn't take that chance.

Panic reared its ugly head, but he fought it down. His gaze locked on the small scar from the operation she'd so recently had. She was almost healed completely. And when that happened, he would leave her. As he'd known all along that he would.

Love. He didn't even want to think the word. It left him vulnerable. Worse, having him love her made Penny vulnerable and that he couldn't stand. Instead of being the blessing that most people might consider it, Colt knew that love wasn't for him. That ephemeral feeling only fed the deep-seated guilt and shame that were never far from his thoughts.

Penny sighed, nestled her head on his chest and draped one long, shapely leg across him. And even as he drew her closer, Colt began to plan his escape.

Over the next several days, Penny and Colt fell into a routine. They tag-teamed the twins and she had to admit, at least to herself, that life with two babies was infinitely easier when you had someone who could share the work *and* the fun.

Of course, whenever that thought appeared in her mind, Penny did her best to ignore it. Love filled her, but had nowhere to go. She wanted to trust him, but she knew that Colt wouldn't stay. He'd made that clear from the beginning. So she locked her love up deep inside her where he couldn't see it. Where she wouldn't be reminded of it daily.

She tried instead to simply enjoy this time with him while she had it. And when he was gone, she'd learn to go on without him. Again.

They left Colt's spectacular house on the cliff and moved the twins back home. Penny loved the cottage, always would, but now she saw the limitations of it. Oh, it was filled with good memories and it was perfect for her and the twins—at the moment. One day, she'd have to leave because the house would be too small. It wouldn't fit her growing family. So the cottage was pretty much like her and Colt. Perfect in the present but no promise of a future.

Penny thought about Colt's place and couldn't help wondering how things might have been. At the cliff house, there had been laughter and passion and so much sky and sea and lawn—open and beautiful. But it wasn't the house she missed so much as the closeness she and Colt had found there, and she knew it. It didn't matter that they spent their nights together now, making love and exploring their passions.

Because every day, she felt him slipping further and further away from her. Soon, even though he might be standing in her tiny kitchen, he would be too far away to touch.

Knowing that broke her heart, but there was nothing she could do about it.

When the twins had been fed their lunch and put down for a much-needed afternoon nap, Penny found Colt in the living room, staring down at the small fire he'd lit only an hour before. Flames crackled over wood and sparks shot up the chimney like tiny fireworks.

Outside, the day was cold and dark, threatening rain that Southern California desperately needed. Inside, despite the fire burning merrily, the cold was creeping in to encircle them both.

"The twins asleep?" he asked without tearing his gaze from the dancing flames.

"Yes. When they take a ride in the car they're always ready to conk out when they get home." It hadn't been much of a trip, she thought. Just to the grocery store. But it was good to be getting back into her routine. Good to remind herself that even when Colt was gone, she would still have her life. Her children's lives. Everything wouldn't end when he left.

It would just be…emptier.

"You should have told me you needed to get groceries," he said, gaze still locked on the fire.

"Why would I do that?" she asked. "It was just groceries. I do it all the time."

Penny sat down on the worn sofa and stared at him. Even from the back, she could tell that he was upset. Every line of his body radiated tension. Frowning, she asked, "What's wrong?"

Finally, he turned his head and speared her with a hard look out of narrowed blue eyes. "What's *wrong?* I go to the office for two hours, then get back here just in time to find you carrying heavy grocery bags, not to mention the twins, and you want to know what's wrong?"

Confused, she said, "Who do you think does it when you're not here, Colt? Me. I also do laundry and mow lawns. What's the big deal?"

"The big deal is," he said through gritted teeth, as if he were struggling to hold on to his temper, "you've had surgery. You shouldn't be lifting anything heavy until the doctor gives you the go-ahead."

Defending herself and her own choices, she said, "I see him in a few days and by the way, I feel fine. Hardly even sore anymore."

"That's not the point."

"Well, what *is* the point then?"

He blew out a breath, pushed one hand through his hair and turned to face her. His blue eyes looked hard and remote and something inside Penny tightened. She recognized that look in his eyes. She'd seen it once before. The morning after their marriage when he'd announced that it was over and walked away from her.

So it had come, she thought sadly. He was leaving again. And she wasn't ready to lose him. She wouldn't ever be ready.

"I don't like you having to do everything yourself,"

Colt was saying. "I'm here now, you know? You could have waited for me to get back."

"Waited for you, Colt?" she whispered, her voice nearly lost in the hiss and crackle of the fire. "How long? How long should I wait?"

"What're you talking about?" he asked. "You knew I was going into the office to take care of a few things and then I'd be back."

Her heart ached and a ball of ice dropped into the pit of her stomach. "I never know if you're coming back, Colt," she admitted quietly. "Every time you go out, I wonder if this is the time that you'll just keep going."

"What? Why?"

She hunched her shoulders and blew out a breath. "Because we both know you're going to leave. The only thing I don't know is *when.*"

Colt's lips thinned into a straight, grim line. "This isn't about me, Penny. It's about you. You do too much."

"How much is too much?" she argued, feeling the need to defend the way she lived her life. "I have two babies to take care of."

"Yeah," he muttered thickly, "I know, but you should have help."

She'd had help. From him. Now he was taking that help away and wanted to replace himself with…what? "Help?"

"I can hire a nanny. Or a housekeeper," he offered quickly. "Someone to take some of the load off of your shoulders."

"You want to *hire* someone?" Penny sat up straighter and met his gaze. She could see the distance in his blue eyes. She actually *felt* him putting up a wall between them, shutting her out.

"Yeah. What's wrong with that?"

"Throwing money at a problem isn't the only answer," she said.

"Give me another one," he countered.

"Stay."

Oh, God, the moment that word left her mouth she wanted to pull it back in. Wanted to pretend she'd never said it, especially when she saw shutters drop over Colt's eyes.

"We've been over this. I can't stay."

"You say that but you don't tell me *why*." She jumped up from the sofa and faced him.

"And you won't tell me why you won't accept the help I can offer you."

"Because I don't want your money, Colt." All she wanted was his love, and she wasn't going to get that. "Or your guilt."

He shook his head, threw his hands high and let them slap down against his thighs. "What's guilt got to do with anything?"

"Do you think I can't see it?" Penny took a step closer to him. "You're getting ready to leave so you want to make sure you've covered all of your bases. It's like you have a mental list. Help for Penny, check. Nanny for the twins, check. Money in her bank account, check. And once you've completed that list, you can leave with a clear conscience. Well, forget it. If I need help I'll ask for it."

"No, you won't." He laughed shortly and gave her a look that told her he was far from amused. "You think you've got me all figured out, huh? Well, I know you just as well, Penny. You're too stubborn for your own good. You hate accepting help. Don't want to lean on anyone."

That verbal slap struck a nerve and Penny felt the

sting of tears at the backs of her eyes. She blinked hard and fast, because she wasn't about to cry. He was pulling away from her with every passing moment and had the nerve to accuse her of not wanting to depend on him?

"Why should I lean on anyone, Colt?" she asked, her voice hardly more than a whisper of old pain. "I've been taking care of myself for most of my life. I grew up taking care of myself and Robert. No one was there to help."

He frowned. "Your parents?"

Shadows in the room gathered closer. The flickering light of the fire danced on the walls and reflected in the window panes. The world slipped away until it was only Penny, Colt and the past crowded into the tiny living room.

"When my mom died ten years ago, my father just shut down. He went to work, came home, but he was like a ghost in the house." It sounded so cut-and-dried when she said it, but the memories of her childhood were still with her. Still painful. When her mother died, Penny was eighteen. She felt lost and turned to her father, but he couldn't or wouldn't give her the emotional support she needed so badly. She'd had to learn how to stand up. How to be a rock for Robert and how to take care of herself.

"I couldn't lean on my father," she said hotly. "I couldn't trust him. Sometimes he came home, sometimes he didn't. So I took care of myself and Robert. And the day I turned eighteen my dad took off for good and we haven't seen him since." She poked her index finger at the center of his chest. "So don't tell me that I'm too stubborn to ask for help. It's not stubbornness, it's survival. I don't trust easily, Colt, and I learned early that it's easier in the long run to not depend on anyone but yourself."

Her breath was coming in short, hard pants and she

kept her gaze fixed on his, so she saw the shadow of sympathy in his eyes. Penny's spine went stiff and straight and she lifted her chin defiantly. "I don't need you to feel sorry for me, either."

"I wasn't."

She folded her arms over her chest, cocked her head at a mocking tilt and studied him.

"Okay," he admitted, "maybe I was. Not for who you are now, but for the girl you were, with so much responsibility dumped on you."

"I survived."

"Yeah, but it affected you." He shook his head. "You tell me I take too many risks, but you don't take any, do you? If you don't trust people they can't let you down. Is that it?"

She shifted position uncomfortably. Maybe that was a little too close to home. "I trusted you once."

He ground his teeth together until she saw the muscle in his jaw flexing furiously.

Shaking her head, Penny said, "Our situations are different, Colt. You risk your life constantly. I don't want to risk trusting the wrong person. Big difference."

"This isn't even about trust," he countered, blowing out a breath. "Or what's between us. This is about you accepting help. You've already proven you *can* do everything on your own, Penny. That doesn't mean you *have* to."

She laughed a little but there was no humor in the sound. "You don't get it. Who is there to lean on, Colt? Robert? He and Maria are building their own lives. They don't need me hanging around being needy. You?" She sighed. "Why would I lean on you when you've made no secret of the fact that you're leaving just as fast you can?"

"You could while I'm here," he started to argue.

"Why would I get used to help from you, Colt?" She reached up and shoved both hands through her hair as frustration grabbed hold of her and refused to let go. "You arrived here with your bags packed emotionally. You've had one foot out the door for this entire time. So tell me. Should I count on you, Colt? Should I depend on you?"

"No." He cut her off abruptly and Penny was so surprised her mouth snapped shut. Briefly.

"Well, at least that was honest," she choked out as she wrapped her arms around her middle and held on.

Colt looked at her and not for the first time thought she was one of the strongest people he'd ever known. Now that he knew more of her background, he was even more impressed. No wonder Robert had said he owed Penny everything. She'd raised him. She'd kept him safe. And she'd done it on her own with no help from anyone.

Hell, he hadn't wanted her to depend on him and it should make him feel good that she had no intention of counting on Colt for anything. Instead, he felt worse than ever. He wished to hell he could just grab her, pull her close and never let her go. But that wasn't gonna happen. Couldn't happen.

Pulling back from her and the kids was the right thing to do and he knew it.

But clearly Penny believed he simply didn't want to stay. That bothered him more than he wanted to admit. So if he told her the truth, then not only would she understand, she'd agree that his leaving was the best thing for all of them.

"You think I don't want to be here."

"I think you can't wait to leave. Just like before," she said sadly.

"You're wrong."

"Then prove it," she countered. "Stay."

"No," he said tiredly, feeling old guilt and the shadows of pain he'd never allowed to die swamp him.

"This is ridiculous. You're not *telling* me anything. Just like before, you're going to walk away. And I'm supposed to believe that what? You're leaving for *my* sake? Because if that's it," Penny snapped, "then don't do me any favors."

"I'm trying to keep you and the twins alive and safe." He grabbed her upper arms and barely held back from giving her a hard shake. "You think it's easy for me to walk away? It's not. But if I stay, then somewhere down the line, everything's going to go to hell."

"What's that supposed to mean?" Her eyes were locked on his, confusion and fury glittering in those green depths. She was amazing and he wanted her more than his next breath.

Deliberately, he let her go and took a step back from her. Swiping one hand across his face, he muttered, "It was ten years ago."

"What?"

He looked away from her because how the hell could he look into her eyes while he said, "I was in Switzerland with my folks. Supposed to be a big ski trip." His voice sounded as haunted as his dreams. Colt closed his eyes briefly, but the images from the past were so clear, so sharp, they nearly killed him. So he opened his eyes again and stared down into the fire.

"We were supposed to take a helicopter to the top of a peak and then ski down. But the night before the run,

I met some blonde in a bar—" he stopped and realized "—I can't even remember her name. Point is, I blew off the ski trip in favor of spending time with the blonde. My parents died in an avalanche."

He turned to face her and realized that now it was his turn to read the sympathy in her eyes and he found he liked it no better than she had. Shoving his hands into his jeans pockets, he shook his head wearily. "I let them down. They were depending on me to show them the safe route down the mountain and I wasn't there."

"Colt, I'm so sorry but—"

He shook his head. "Don't tell me it wasn't my fault. I know it was. If I'd been there, they wouldn't have died because I could have steered them to a safer run."

"Or," Penny argued, "you would have died with them."

"Maybe." He'd thought of that, too, and sometimes wondered if he wouldn't have been better off. He pulled his hands free of his pockets and scrubbed both hands over his face. She was still watching him and the urge to hold her was so strong it rocked him. But if he touched her, then he'd lose himself in the flash of heat and passion that threatened to consume everything in its path. And it wouldn't change a damn thing.

"It was an accident, Colt," she said firmly. "Not a reason for you to run from me or your kids."

"Weren't you listening?" He shook his head. "I'm not running. It's not me I'm worried about. It's whoever depends on me. I let my folks down and they died. I won't do that to my kids. Or you. I won't live with even more of the kind of guilt that chews on a man when he fails."

Penny lifted both hands and shoved them through her hair in an impatient gesture. "So, basically," she said tightly, "instead of failing, you just don't try at all."

"You don't understand what it's like."

"Yeah, I do," she said, voice breaking until she swallowed hard and took a breath. "You know, over this last week or so, I've watched you with the twins. Seen how good you are with them. How much they love you."

His heart clenched hard in his chest.

"And I tried to figure out why, when you have so much in your life, you insist on flying off around the globe chasing death in those ridiculous extreme sports." She scrubbed her hands along her upper arms as if trying to create warmth that just wouldn't come. "Now I know. Are you trying to make it up to your parents by dying? Is that it? Do you think you've been on borrowed time or something? That you should have been the one to die on that mountain?"

"I didn't say that," he argued.

"You might as well have." Penny glared at him and Colt felt his hackles rise. Damn it, he'd expected her to get it. To finally understand why nothing could work between them. Instead, she was staring at him like he was crazy.

"Let me get this straight," she finally said, tipping her head back to meet his eyes. "You want me to lean on you and at the same time you tell me you don't want anyone to depend on you. That about cover it?"

He scrubbed one hand across his jaw, then the back of his neck. It sounded…stupid when she said it like that. Irritated and getting angrier and more defensive by the moment, Colt said, "You're deliberately twisting my words around."

"No, I'm not," she countered and stepped closer, tapping his chest with her forefinger. "I'm pointing out that what you're telling me doesn't make any sense."

"It does to me," he managed to grind out. "I'm the reason my parents died. If I'd been there—"

She cut him off. "You'll never know what might have happened if you had been there, Colt. But the point is, you didn't cause the avalanche. It was an accident. A tragic, horrible accident. But you didn't do it. You weren't even there."

"That's the point," he snapped. "I promised them I would be and I wasn't."

"And I bet your mother's last thoughts were, 'Thank God Colt isn't here.'"

He jerked his head back as if she'd slapped him.

"It's what I would have thought," she continued, her voice softer now. "What I would have been grateful for. That my child was safe. How can you believe your parents would have thought differently?"

He spun away from her, his mind racing, heart pounding. He'd lived with the guilt for so long that it was a part of him. A dark shadow that crouched inside his heart always ready to take a stab at him.

"It must have been hideous, Colt," she said, threading her arms around his waist, pressing herself against his back. "But it doesn't change the fact that it wasn't your fault."

Con had said the same thing for years. So had his other brothers. His cousins. But, "No matter what you say, it doesn't change the fact that I wasn't there when they needed me."

He turned in her arms, looked down into her eyes and vowed, "I won't risk it again. Won't let you or the twins depend on me because it'd kill me if something happened to any of you."

"And if something happens anyway? Then what?"

Tears glistened in her eyes and the light from the fire made the dampness there gleam with a red-hot glow.

Slowly, she stepped back from him and stuffed her hands into the pockets of her worn, faded jeans, as if trying to keep from reaching out to him again. "Don't you see? Nobody gets a guarantee in life, Colt. All we have is every day and the people we choose to spend our lives with—for however long that is. You're not to blame for what happened to your parents, Colt. But maybe it's easier for you to tell yourself you are."

"Easy?" Voice tight and hard, he said, "You think anything about this is easy?"

"It's always easier to walk away than to stay and make it work."

"I told you—"

"I know what you told me," she said, mouth twisting as she fought trembling lips. "But you were wrong. You didn't escape that avalanche, Colt. Something in you died that day up on the mountain."

Outrage swelled up inside him. Hell, he'd expected her to get it. To understand and see that he was doing this for her and the twins. To protect them the one sure way he knew how. But she was standing there glaring at him through eyes that had gone as cold and dark as a forest at midnight. "Penny, damn it, don't you see—"

"Are you supposed to pay penance for the rest of your life, Colt? For something that wasn't your fault?" Penny shook her head, met his gaze and held it. "Is that the price you have to pay to satisfy the ghosts in your heart? You're not allowed to be happy? Not allowed to be loved?"

"This isn't penance," he argued. "This is me trying to protect you and the twins. Why don't you see that?"

"What I see is that it's time for you to go, Colt. Just

leave." She pulled her hands free of her pockets and used them both to push back her thick mane of hair. "You would have left soon anyway, so go tonight. I don't want my children to love a father who's so busy trying to kill himself that he's forgotten how to *live*."

Ten

Colt didn't stick around. What would have been the point? He threw his stuff together and left while the twins were still sleeping because God help him, he didn't think he could walk out the door with his kids watching him go. His kids.

Those two words bounced around in his skull like maniacal rubber balls. He never had bothered to get a paternity test. He hadn't needed to. He'd known in his gut the moment he'd seen them that those babies were *his*. Just as he knew now that he had to leave.

He just hadn't expected Penny to be the one to tell him to go. Damn it, *he* was the one who left. Always. No woman before her had ever asked him to leave. Though he supposed she had reason enough.

"The problem is she doesn't get it," he muttered, and drove down the Pacific Coast Highway not even noticing the ocean on his right. "How could she? She's never failed anyone before."

He had, though. His mind spun darkly through all the memories he'd just dug up and stomped through.

"Never should have tried to explain," he told himself, pushing dark thoughts aside to concentrate on the road and the wild race of his heartbeat. "Should have just gone. Should never have stayed that long in the first damn place."

But how could he not? He had *kids*. Two tiny human beings who were alive because of him and they deserved…what?

"Better than a part-time father, that's what," he muttered as he turned his car onto the private road that led to the house on the cliff.

He slapped one hand against the steering wheel, then waved at the security guard at the gate. He drove past in a hurry and followed the narrow, winding road to his driveway. When he got there, he stopped, parked and reluctantly turned off the engine.

What he wanted to do was to keep driving. To push his car and himself to their limits. To feel that rush of speed that came when you discarded the idea of being careful. When you raced out to stay just ahead of—

He stopped that thought cold as Penny's voice echoed in his mind. *Chasing death. Forgotten how to live.*

She was wrong, though, he argued silently. He wasn't chasing death, for God's sake. He was relishing every moment of his life. He wasn't wasting time. He wasn't going to be an old man and regret not taking chances. Not living life to the fullest. That's what this was about. *Life,* not *death.*

But Penny's voice wouldn't leave his mind. Her accusatory stare seemed to drill right into his soul. And the look on her face when she told him to leave the cottage would stay with him forever.

From the moment he'd met Penny, he had known that this woman wasn't the kind you could forget. And he hadn't. Now the memories of her were thicker, richer, more deeply embedded in his soul. Somehow, she'd become a part of him and leaving her had felt as though he was carving out his own heart with a butter knife.

Hands fisted on the steering wheel, he sat in the shade of the spectacular house that hadn't become a home until Penny and the twins had arrived. He looked up at the building and felt an emptiness he'd never known before. He was being chased not only by his own past but by the futures that he wouldn't be a part of.

He already missed Penny. The scent of her. The sound of her laugh. The taste of her. Colt had never thought about falling in love. Never even considered it. But now he realized that when he'd first met her in Vegas, he'd instinctively known that she would be the one woman he would never get over.

Now he'd made that situation worse.

Then there were the twins. He didn't want to think about all he would miss with his kids, but how could he help it? First words. First steps. First day of school. First heartbreak. He'd miss them all.

His heart twisted in his chest, but he couldn't back down now. He was doing the right thing and he'd keep on doing it. Even if he suffered every day of his life because he'd walked away from the three people in the world who meant the most to him.

Grabbing his duffel bag, Colt climbed out of the car, slung the bag over one shoulder and headed inside. What he needed to do was to get back to the real world. The exciting race to find bigger and better adrenaline rushes.

The house was too quiet. Deliberately, he didn't notice a thing about the place where Penny and the twins had been so recently. They'd left themselves stamped all over the house, but he figured the memories would fade in time. And if they didn't, he'd sell the damn house.

He made a few phone calls—his brother, the airport and his lawyer—threw some clothes in another bag, then grabbed up his ski equipment and headed for John Wayne Airport. A KingJet would be waiting for him and in several hours, he'd be where he should have gone nearly two weeks ago. Sicily. Mount Etna.

He'd reclaim normalcy for himself and chalk up the last couple of weeks as a glitch on his radar. A bump in the road.

Which would be much easier to do if the memory of Penny's eyes would just leave him the hell alone.

Both of the twins were whiny and Penny knew just how they felt. They missed Colt and so did she. In a couple of short weeks, he'd become a part of their lives in the cottage, and now that he was gone, there was an aching hole in the tapestry of their family.

She still couldn't believe that she'd actually *told* him to leave the night before. After wishing so hard that he would stay, it was completely ironic that she would be the one to tell him to go.

She'd been awake all night, going over their conversation, word for word. She remembered the shadowed look in his eyes when he'd told her about the day his parents died. She'd seen the pain and the guilt glittering in his gaze despite his effort to shield his emotions from her.

Penny knew he was hurt and had been for years. She felt bad for him, living with misplaced guilt for so long, but at the same time she wanted to shriek at him. He hadn't killed his family. Why did he have to keep suffering? When would it be enough?

She'd overcome her past and moved on. Why couldn't he? Why couldn't he value her and their children more than his own fears and guilt? And why was she still torturing herself?

Her baby girl let out a snuffle and a cry and Penny immediately turned her brain back to matters at hand.

"It's okay, Riley," she soothed as she changed her daughter's T-shirt. "I know you miss your daddy, but it'll get easier, I promise."

Lies. Why did parents always lie to their children? It wasn't going to get easier. It would never be easy living without Colt. The twins were lucky, she supposed; they were too young to carry this memory with them. She knew that Colt would come back for the kids. That he would visit them and remain a part of their lives. But it was just a shadow of what they might have had together.

"I never should have told him," Robert said from the open doorway of the kids' room. "I'm really sorry, Pen. I thought he'd do the right thing."

"Don't be sorry," she said and tugged a clean shirt over Riley's head. The baby girl laughed and clapped her chubby hands in appreciation. Penny glanced at her brother. "Colt had the right to know about the twins and now he does. Let's just leave it at that."

"Sure. It's no problem at all that he's gone, is it?"

"Nope. Life marches on, or something equally as clichéd and profound." Penny told herself she should probably worry. She was getting entirely too good at the whole lying thing. Scooping her daughter up for a hug, Penny held the baby tightly, then turned to face Robert, who was watching her with an all-too-knowing gaze.

"It never would have worked," she said, because she'd been telling herself that since the afternoon before when she'd practically tossed Colt out of her house. But she hadn't had a choice, right? He as much as told her that he wouldn't love her. Told her he couldn't be depended on. So what else could she have done?

"We're too different. He takes too many risks and I—"

"Don't take any?" Robert finished for her.

Irritated, she said, "Now you sound like Colt."

"Not surprising. It's pretty obvious, Pen." He moved farther into the room, plucked Riley out of her arms and held his niece close. "Dad did a real number on you when he left. You think I was too young to notice, but I wasn't. I watched how hard you worked to pick up the slack."

Her eyes filled with tears and she used the tips of her fingers to wipe them away. Those years had been terrifying, but satisfying, too. She'd discovered that fear didn't have to hold you back. She'd found her passion for photography. She'd seen Robert get a full scholarship to college—and then she'd met Colt and it had felt, for a while, as if she had finally found some magic for herself.

But that dream had ended and a new one, she assured herself, had begun. In the middle of all this pain and misery, she had to remember that she wasn't alone. She had her children. She had Robert and Maria. And one day, maybe that would all seem like enough.

When the ache for Colt finally faded.

"I saw how badly Dad leaving hurt you. You kind of closed yourself off, Penny. To everyone but me."

Her gaze snapped to his and she felt a flush rise up and

stain her cheeks. Maybe she had, she silently conceded. But she'd opened herself up to Colt eighteen months ago. She had taken a risk with her heart and she'd lost.

"But I saw you with Colt and you were happier than I've ever known you to be. Plus," he added, after kissing the top of Riley's head, "I know he cares about you so I hoped…"

Penny's heart twisted in her chest. She'd hoped, too. In spite of everything, she had hoped. Now she missed Colt so much. It was infinitely harder to lose him now than it had been eighteen months ago. Seeing him walk out the door, not knowing if he'd ever walk back in. Knowing that her kids would be cheated out of a day-to-day relationship with their father. That the man she loved was more interested in waiting to die than he was in living with her. It was all so hard.

"I appreciate that," she said when she was sure her voice wouldn't break. Reaching out, she smoothed Riley's wispy hair and straightened the tiny pink bow lying tilted on the side of her head. "But it's over now and I just have to learn to live with the reality."

Robert put his arm around her and she gratefully went into a warm hug meant to comfort and soothe. Riley patted her face as if the baby girl knew her mommy needed the extra attention. In the living room, she could hear Reid laughing with Maria and in spite of the giant hole in her heart, Penny smiled. And she would keep smiling, for the sake of her kids if nothing else.

"If he comes back, what will you do?"

"He won't." Even her hopes weren't strong enough to convince her of that.

"He came back once," Robert reminded her. "And it wasn't just for the kids. You didn't see his face when

I told him you were in the hospital. He cares, Penny. A lot more than he knows, I think. So yeah. He might come back again if he thought you were willing to take a chance."

How could she open herself up to trusting Colt? She had taken that leap of faith once and he'd walked away from her and their newborn marriage. If she risked it again, she wouldn't be the only one to suffer. She would be putting her children's hearts on the line, too, and she didn't know if she could do that.

"No, Robert," she said firmly, trying to convince not only her brother, but herself. The sooner she accepted the hard truth, the sooner she could start dealing with the pain that was already swamping her. She wished things were different, but wishing wasn't going to change a thing. "He's not coming back. Not this time."

But if he ever did, she would gladly take that risk again.

Colt's heart felt like a stone, cold and hard in his chest.

It was as though he'd been emptied out. He'd spilled his darkest secrets and shame and Penny had dismissed it all. For some damn reason, he'd expected her at least to understand what it cost him to go.

But she hadn't.

Her words were still ringing in Colt's ears two days later. He tried to pretend she hadn't been right but how could he? He lived his life with one foot out the door at all times. More than three weeks in one place and the walls started closing in on him. He had been in constant motion for ten years. Never staying put. Never settling down. Most important, never allowing anyone to depend on him for anything.

Now it killed him to know that Penny *refused* to depend on him.

"She's right," he mumbled, "it doesn't make any sense at all."

The jet's engine was a steady, throaty roar of background noise that seemed to rumble through his brain, which was jostling already chaotic thoughts. On the way to Sicily at last, Colt realized that normally, he'd have a map of the area spread out in front of him. He'd be laying out his plans for the trip—feeling that rush of anticipation that had been his near-constant companion for the last ten years. Today, though, there was nothing.

Just the solitude inside the jet and his own misery. He couldn't bring himself to care about Mount Etna or the challenge of skiing down the wicked slopes of a very active volcano. Instead, he could only wonder what Penny and the twins were doing. Had she gone back to the doctor? Had Reid started talking? Was Riley crawling through every mud puddle in the backyard?

Did they miss him?

Colt sprawled on one of the gray leather couches and stared out the window. Travel time was long, going from Orange County, California, to Italy. First to New York, then refuel and on to Sicily. From the airport in Catania, he'd take a helicopter to Mount Etna and do what he'd come to do: ski down the sharp face of a volcano on the verge of eruption. His gaze fixed on the clouds that lay stretched out like a path across the sky. Far below was Italy, a blur of green and brown. He hardly noticed the view, though.

Instead, he was seeing Penny's face. Hearing her voice asking him why he was chasing death. Saying that his mother had no doubt been *grateful* that he wasn't on the mountain on that fateful day. And though it had pissed him off then, he'd had time enough to think about it now and reluctantly he had to admit that Penny was right. If it had been him, caught by an avalanche, in those last few minutes, he would have been grateful that his kids would still live on. That Penny was safe.

You've forgotten how to live.

He scrubbed one hand across his face, but the action did nothing to wipe away the echoes of her voice or the image of her face. Was she right about that, too? Had he been trying to die to make it up to his parents for failing them? He squirmed uncomfortably. Sounded so damned stupid. So…pointless.

By spending so much time running from life, he'd been pretty much dead already, hadn't he?

Jumping to his feet, Colt paced up and down the length of the private jet. Having the luxury of a plane to himself was something he usually enjoyed. Today, not so much. Being alone made it impossible to avoid all of the conflicting thoughts crashing in his mind. He'd been running for so long that the thought of…standing still was almost unthinkable. But what had running gotten him?

He stopped in front of the wet bar, poured a generous splash of scotch into a crystal tumbler and drained it like medicine. Liquid fire rushed through his system, momentarily chasing away the chill icing his bones. Maybe he'd been coming at this all wrong from the beginning. Maybe he'd wasted ten years of his life chasing risk, and he'd never even noticed that he wasn't running *toward* anything. Instead he was running *away* from the greatest risk of all.

Love.

Risking death was nothing, he told himself. Risking

a life with someone was the real step that took courage. And while he held himself back, Penny took that chance. She was strong in spite of what she'd gone through when she was a kid. How could he be less?

Slamming the glass down onto the bar top, he stalked to the closest window and looked down on the world below. In his mind, the image of Mount Etna rose up, snowy peaks, smoking calderas. Then right beside that image was the memory of Penny's eyes when he was inside her. The warmth, the love, the promise of everything shining in those green depths.

Life? Or death?

No contest, he realized with a jolt. He didn't need a damn volcano to challenge him. Living with a woman as strong as Penny was going to be the *real* adventure. If, he thought, he could convince her to let him prove himself to her. To let him back into her life. Their kids' lives. But he couldn't very well do that from Sicily, could he?

He strode to the cockpit and opened the door.

The copilot turned in his seat and smiled.

Colt ignored the friendly gesture. "Where exactly are we?"

"We'll be landing at Catania, Sicily, in about an hour."

"Right." Colt nodded and for the first time in ten long years, listened to his heart. He knew what he had to do. Knew what he *wanted* to do. Decision made, he said, "When we land, refuel as quickly as you can. We're going back."

After the longest plane ride of his life, Colt stormed into King's Extreme Adventures and walked into his twin's office without bothering to knock.

"I thought you were in Sicily." Con sat back in his desk chair, a surprised expression on his face.

"Yeah, change of plans," Colt said and paced to the wide window that overlooked the ocean. "Tell me something. You've always said that mom and dad's accident wasn't my fault. Did you mean it?"

"Of course I meant it." Con's voice was sharp and sure. "What's this about?"

Down below, at street level, waves rushed toward shore, cars lined the Pacific Coast Highway and pedestrians wandered up and down crowded sidewalks.

"Penny." Colt shook his head and rubbed his eyes. His twin, his brothers and his cousins had all tried to reach him over the years. Tried to make him see that accidents happen and no matter how hideous it had all been, it wasn't Colt's fault. But he'd never been willing to listen before. Now he had to know. "She's got me thinking. Wondering. And I need to know if that's really how you and all of the others feel."

Con's voice was soft, but the power behind the words reverberated in the air. "Colt, *you* didn't cause the avalanche. Even you don't have superpowers."

Smiling briefly, Colt glanced at his twin. "If I'd been there, though, I could've made sure they took a safer run."

Con laughed shortly, then shrugged. "I don't know whose parents you're remembering, but our father never took the safe route in his life."

Colt frowned as Con stood up and came toward him. "Your being with them wouldn't have changed anything. Dad was just as damned crazy adventurous as you are— where do you think you got it?"

Colt had never really thought about it like that. But now that he was…he wondered.

"The only thing that would have been different," Con added, slapping his twin on the shoulder, "is that *you* would have died, too. And I'd have missed you, you big idiot."

A small smile curved Colt's mouth. All of the Kings did go for adventure, thrived on adrenaline, he thought, as he finally began to let go of the cloak of guilt he'd been wrapped in for years. "You're right. About Dad, I mean."

Con applauded slowly, deliberately, and gave his twin a smile. "Well, at long last. And it only took ten years to convince you. I always said I was the smart one."

"Funny." Colt drew a breath and knew that it would take time to finally and completely let go of the past. But at least now he had a shot at it. "Look, I'm going out to Penny's place. But I've got a few things to do first. One of which is to talk to you about an idea I had on the flight home."

Curious, Con grinned. "I'm listening…."

Penny missed Colt more than she would have thought it possible to miss anyone. The twins did, too, she could tell. They weren't as boisterous as usual and every once in a while, one or both of them would look around an empty room as if searching for their father. Though it broke her heart, she knew that soon, the babies would get past that sensation of something being gone from their lives. They'd go on and their memories would fade and one day, when Colt dropped back into their lives, they would look at him like a stranger.

She only wished it would be that easy for her, but she knew she would never get past this. She would long for him, dream of him for the rest of her life. In the middle of the night, she reached for him. She listened for the deep rumble of his voice as he read to the twins before bedtime. She even missed hearing him curse under his breath when he hit his head on the door frame.

That stupid man had left a giant hole in her life. And what she wouldn't give to have him back.

"You're just pitiful, that's all there is to it," she muttered, and picked up her digital camera. Turning it on, she pulled up the menu and then began flipping through the photos she'd taken during the time Colt was with them.

Colt bathing the twins, more water on him than in the tub. Colt holding a sleeping Riley, stacking blocks with Reid. Colt smiling up at Penny from the bed they'd shared too briefly. Her heart didn't just ache—it throbbed. Pain was her new best friend, and she had a feeling it wasn't going to get any easier any time soon.

Thankfully, just as she was ready to sink into the self-pity party of the year, the doorbell rang, which gave her an excuse to turn off the camera and get back to her life. With the twins asleep, she didn't want to risk waking them by having that doorbell ring again. Hurrying, she opened the door to find a man with a clipboard standing on her porch.

"Penny Oaks?" He had a bald head, bushy gray eyebrows, a tanned-to-leather face and broad shoulders.

"Yes…"

"Got a delivery for you," he said and thrust the clipboard at her. "Sign here."

"Sign for what?" Automatically she glanced at the delivery receipt. A furniture store? "What's this about?"

"Bring it all in, Tommy," the guy on her porch shouted before turning back to her. "I don't know what's going on. Just sign it, lady, and let me go back to the high life, okay?"

She did and then stepped back in astonishment as two more men unloaded a chocolate-brown leather sofa and matching chair.

"I didn't order that," she argued.

"Somebody did." The first guy just waved the paper at her. "We'll haul your old stuff away. Come on guys, got a million stops to make still."

"What're you—" She broke off as the two younger men smiled, nodded and slipped past her into her house. Then they were leaving, carrying her faded, overstuffed couch and chair out to the truck and then bringing in the new leather replacements.

Before she could ask any more questions, the truck pulled away and she closed the door, staring at new furniture she hadn't ordered.

"God, it smells as good as it looks," she murmured, walking to it to stroke the butter-soft leather as she would a cat. "But who— Colt. It had to be Colt," she assured herself. "He must have ordered it before he left. He probably forgot to tell me it was coming."

She sighed, sat on the arm of the couch and frowned when she heard the roar of a lawn mower starting up. Staring through her front window, she saw a gardening crew working on her lawn. *What was going on here?*

Before she made it to the front door, she heard the babies wake up and groaned. Apparently the sounds of the mower and the edger were too loud to sleep through. So much for naptime. She detoured to pick up her kids, plopping each of them on a hip, then went out onto the front porch.

"Excuse me!" she shouted to one of the guys using

a Weed Eater around the edge of her flower bed. "Who hired you?"

Reid wailed and screwed his eyes up, preparing to launch into a real scream, and once that happened, Penny knew Riley wouldn't be far behind.

"Really," she tried again, giving the hardworking man a hopeful smile. "I need to know…"

He waved and went back to work. At a loss for what to do next, Penny went back into the house, settled both kids on the floor near their toy box and then watched out the window while her yard was tidied.

"Your daddy's behind this, too," she whispered, feeling the sting of tears burn her eyes. "He won't stay, but he'll do this long-distance. Take care of my yard. Buy me new furniture. What's next?"

The doorbell rang and Penny stiffened. She hadn't actually expected an answer to that last question. Throwing a quick glance at the twins to make sure they were all right, she opened the front door to a man in a suit holding up a set of car keys.

"Who're you?" she asked.

"I'm just the messenger, ma'am," he said and handed the keys to her. "Enjoy!"

"Enjoy what?" Penny looked past him to see her fifteen-year-old reliable clunker being backed out of her driveway. "Hey! Wait!"

Panicking a little, she raced back to the living room, picked up the twins and then headed for the porch. The gardeners were already moving on to the backyard and there was a shiny red SUV parked in her driveway. From the corner of her eye, she saw her car making its slow, deliberate way down the street. "Wait! Come back!"

"I have come back," Colt said, stepping out from behind the SUV. "If you'll have me."

All the air left her body. Her stomach did a pitch and roll, then settled for butterflies. Thousands of 'em. Stunned speechless, Penny could only stare at him as he walked closer. Her gaze locked with his and her heart tumbled in her chest. "You're supposed to be on a volcano."

He gave her a quick grin that sent whips of electricity shooting through her veins.

"Now why would I want to do that when I could be right here?"

"Here?" She nearly choked on the word.

"Nowhere else," he said, stepping up onto the porch.

Penny held the babies, one on each hip, and laughed a little when they started bouncing and shrieking their delight at seeing their daddy again. Colt laughed, too, reached out and plucked both twins from her. He held them in his arms, kissed each of their foreheads and said, "I missed you guys."

"They missed you, too," Penny told him and surreptitiously wiped away one stray tear.

"How about their mother?" he asked. "Did she miss me?"

"A lot," she admitted, because what was the point of holding back now?

"Penny." His voice dropped to that low rumble that never failed to dance along her nerve endings like a caress. "You were right about me."

"What? Right? When?"

He smiled at her and said, "Can we go inside?"

"Yes. Sure." She stepped back and Colt slipped past her. He carried both babies into the living room, set them

down with their toys, then came back to her. She couldn't
look away from him. She was half afraid that if she did,
he might disappear. That she was just having delusions or
something because her heart had ached for him so badly.

But then he was there, in front of her. He smelled so
good. His black hair fell across his forehead and his ice-
blue eyes were—not icy at all, she realized. They were
warm, like a sky in summer, and they were locked on her,
showering her with emotions too dizzying to identify.

"You were right," he said softly, "when you said that
I had been chasing death because I didn't want to risk
living."

"Colt…"

He shook his head and grinned. "Don't lose your nerve
now. Everything you said to me was right, Penny. But not
anymore. I want to live. With you. With my kids. You
guys are all I'll ever need."

Oh, God, she really wanted to believe him. But, "What
about how you love adventure? How will you be happy
living in a cottage in Laguna?"

He pulled her in for a quick hug, then set her back
again so he could watch her eyes. So that *she* could read
the truth in *his*. "Living with you and the twins and all
of our other kids will be all the adventure I could ever
need."

"All the—"

"And I know you love the cottage, but it's going to be
way too small for the bunch of kids we're going to have,
so I was thinking we could give the cottage to Robert
and Maria and we could move to the cliff house?" Another smile. "If I live here, I'll eventually kill myself, you
know, smacking my head into the low beams."

Her head was spinning. "All the kids we're going to have?"

"Caught that, huh?" His eyes were shining and his smile was wide. "We may even get another set or two of twins, who knows?"

"Another— Colt, you're moving too fast," she said. "I can't keep up." And, oh, how she wanted to.

"This isn't fast," he promised her. "I've wasted too much time already, thinking about the past instead of looking at the future."

He was right there with her. In her living room. Promising her everything. Looking at her with all the love she could have dreamed of, but he still hadn't said the words she needed to hear so badly.

"I talked to Con, too, before—"

"Before you hired a gardener, and bought me new furniture and a new car?"

"Exactly." He winked at her. "We're going to be restructuring our business. Con thinks it's a great idea. King's Extreme Adventures is going to become King's Family Adventures. We're going to find the best places for families to visit. To vacation. To experience the world. We want people to enjoy their lives, not risk them."

Her heart melted. "Oh, Colt…"

"Think about it! Way bigger customer base."

She smiled at him and could only think how happy she felt. How right it was to be here like this, with him.

"Con and I think you should take all the photos for the advertising, too.…"

"I think I need to sit down." Before she fell down. Afternoon sunlight spilled through the front windows and lay across the scarred wooden floors. Her kids were in the living room playing and giggling. And the man she loved was standing in front of her offering her the world and more.

"I'll hold you up," he promised, and wrapped his arms around her. "I swear to you, Penny, I will always be there for you. To depend on. To count on. I want you to feel like you can lean on me and let me lean on you. I won't ever let you down."

She stared up into his eyes, lifted one hand to cup his cheek and said, "I never believed you would, Colt."

He took a breath, pulled her in close and held on tightly. "We can talk about the business and the move and more kids right after I finish telling you the most important thing." He let her go, took a step back and dropped to one knee. "I'm doing it right this time."

Penny lifted one hand to the base of her throat and watched as her dreams became reality.

"I love you, Penny Oaks. I think I did from the very first moment I met you." He gave her a sad smile. "That's why I ran so far so fast. What I felt for you terrified me. Now, the only terrifying thing I can imagine is having to live without you." He pulled a jeweler's box from his pocket, flipped the velvet lid open and showed her a huge, canary-yellow diamond ring.

"Oh, Colt..."

"Marry me again, Penny. Share your life with me. I promise we'll have a great adventure."

"Yes, oh my God, yes, Colt. I will absolutely marry you!"

He jumped to his feet, swept her up into his arms and swung her in a circle before setting her down and sliding that ring onto her finger. Penny couldn't stop smiling.

"We'll have the kind of wedding you deserve this time," he said, cupping her face and pausing only long enough to kiss her senseless. "We'll have the biggest damn wedding California's ever seen. Anything you want."

She looked from the ring on her hand to the love shining in Colt's eyes and said, "All I want is to go back to the chapel where we were married the first time. Just you, me and the twins."

"God, you're amazing," he whispered and kissed her again. "I'll get the jet fueled. We can go tomorrow if your doctor says it's okay. Did you see him?"

"I did. He said I'm perfect."

Colt gave her a slow, wicked smile. "He's right about that."

Penny couldn't believe this was happening. She suddenly had everything she had ever wished for. The man she loved. Her children—

"Da!"

Penny and Colt went still and in tandem turned to look at the twins. Reid was standing on his own two feet and Riley clapped her hands and shouted again, "Da!"

He moved swiftly across the room, lifted both of the twins into his arms and just for a moment, buried his face in the sweetness of them. When he looked at Penny again, she saw *love* shining in his eyes.

"I can't believe I almost missed that," he whispered.

Penny walked to them, wrapped her arms around her family and held on. Until she heard another truck pull up out front. Pulling back, she eyed the man she loved warily. "What else did you do?"

Colt grinned and shrugged. "It's probably Rafe's crew to install a picket fence."

Laughing, Penny leaned into him and listened to the

steady beat of his heart. "I thought you hated picket fences."

"They're not so bad," he mused. "Besides, when the puppies get here, we'll need it."

"Puppies?" Shaking her head, she thought that life with Colton King would never be boring and she would always, always know what it felt like to be loved completely. Nothing could have been more perfect.

Colt bent his head, kissed her and whispered, "The adventure begins."

* * * * *

HIS LOVER'S LITTLE SECRET

BY
ANDREA LAURENCE

Andrea Laurence is an award-winning contemporary romance author who has been a lover of books and writing stories since she learned to read. She always dreamed of seeing her work in print and is thrilled to be able to share her books with the world. A dedicated West Coast girl transplanted into the Deep South, she's working on her own "happily ever after" with her boyfriend and five fur-babies. You can contact Andrea at her website: www.andrealaurence.com.

This book is dedicated to single mothers everywhere, including my own hard-working mother, Meg.

You fight the good fight every day, often at the expense of your own well-being. Thank you for everything you do. (Treat yourself to some chocolate or shoes every now and then!)

One

"You'd better get on out of here, or you'll be late to stand on your head."

Sabine Hayes looked up from the cash drawer to see her boss, fashion designer Adrienne Lockhart Taylor, standing at the counter. She had worked for Adrienne the past thirteen months as manager of her boutique. "I'm almost done."

"Give me the nightly deposit and go. I'll stay until Jill shows up for her shift and then I'll stop by the bank on my way home. You have to pick up Jared by six, don't you?"

"Yes." The day care center would price gouge her for every minute she was late. Then she had to get Jared home and fed before the babysitter got there. Sabine loved teaching yoga, but it made those evenings even more hectic than usual. Single motherhood wasn't for wimps. "You don't mind making the deposit?"

Adrienne leaned across the counter. "Go," she said.

Sabine glanced quickly at her watch. "Okay." She put the deposit into the bank pouch and handed it over. Thank goodness Adrienne had come by this afternoon to put together the new window display. The trendy boutique was known for its exciting and edgy displays that perfectly showcased Adrienne's flair for modern pinup girl fashions. Sabine couldn't have found a better place to work.

Most places wouldn't look twice at an applicant with a nose piercing and a stripe of blue in her hair. It didn't matter that it was a small, tasteful diamond stud or that her hair was dyed at a nice salon in Brooklyn. Even after she'd bitten the bullet and had the bright color removed and left the piercing at home, she'd been turned down by every store on Fifth Avenue. The businesses that paid enough for her to support her son in New York were flooded with applicants more experienced than she was.

She thanked her lucky stars for the day she spied Adrienne walking down the street and complimented her dress. She never expected her to say she'd designed it herself. Adrienne invited her to come by her new boutique one afternoon, and Sabine was enamored with the whole place. It was fun and funky, chic and stylish. High-class fashion with an edge. When Adrienne mentioned she was looking for someone to run the store so she could focus on her designs, Sabine couldn't apply fast enough. Not only was it a great job with above-average pay and benefits, Adrienne was a great boss. She didn't care what color hair Sabine had—now she had purple highlights—and she was understanding when child illness or drama kept her away from the store.

Sabine grabbed her purse and gave a quick wave to

Adrienne as she disappeared into the stockroom and out the back door. It was only a couple blocks to her son's day care, but she still had to hurry along the sidewalk, brushing past others who were leisurely making their way around town.

Finally rounding the last corner, Sabine swung open the gate to the small courtyard and leaped up the few steps to the door. She rang the buzzer at exactly three minutes to six. Not long after that, she had her toddler in her arms and was on her way to the subway.

"Hey, buddy," she said as they went down the street. "Did you have a good day?"

Jared grinned and nodded enthusiastically. He was starting to lose his chubby baby cheeks. He'd grown so much the past few months. Every day, he looked more and more like his father. The first time she'd held Jared in her arms, she looked into his dark brown eyes and saw Gavin's face staring back at her. He would grow up to be as devastatingly handsome as his father, but hopefully with Sabine's big heart. She should be able to contribute *something* to the genetic makeup of her child, and if she had her pick, that was what it would be.

"What do you want for dinner tonight?"

"A-sketti."

"Spaghetti, again? You had that last night. You're going to turn into a noodle before too long."

Jared giggled and clung to her neck. Sabine breathed in the scent of his baby shampoo and pressed a kiss against his forehead. He had changed her whole life and she wouldn't trade him for anything.

"Sabine?"

The subway entrance was nearly in sight when someone called her name from the restaurant she'd just passed. She stopped and turned to find a man in a navy suit drinking wine at one of the tables on the sidewalk. He looked familiar, but she couldn't come up with his name. Where did she know him from?

"It is you," he said, standing up and stepping toward her. He took one look at her puzzled expression and smiled. "You don't remember me, do you? I'm Clay Oliver, a friend of Gavin's. I met you at a gallery opening a couple years back."

An icy surge rushed through Sabine's veins. She smiled and nodded, trying not to show any outward signs of distress. "Oh, yes," she said. She shifted Jared in her arms so he was facing away from his father's best friend. "I think I spilled champagne on you, right?"

"Yes!" he said, pleased she remembered. "How have you been?" Clay's gaze ran curiously over the child in her arms. "Busy, I see."

"Yes, very busy." Sabine's heart began pounding loudly in her chest. She glanced over her shoulder at the subway stop, desperate for an escape. "Listen, I'm sorry I can't stay to chat longer, but I've got to meet the babysitter. It was good to see you again, Clay. Take care."

Sabine gave him a quick wave and spun on her heel. She felt as if she was fleeing the scene of a crime as she dashed down the stairs. She nervously watched the people joining her on the platform. Clay wouldn't follow her. At least she didn't think so. But she wouldn't feel better until she was deep into Brooklyn and far out of Gavin's sphere of influence.

Had Clay seen Jared closely enough? Had he noticed the resemblance? Jared was wearing his favorite monkey T-shirt with a hood and ears, so perhaps Clay hadn't been able to make out his features or how old he was. She hoped.

She leaped onto the train the moment it arrived and managed to find a seat. Clutching Jared tightly as he sat in her lap, she tried to breathe deeply, but she just couldn't do it.

Nearly three years. Jared was fewer than two months from his second birthday, and she had managed to keep their son a secret from Gavin. In all this time she'd never run into him or anyone he knew. They didn't exactly move in the same social circles. That was part of why she'd broken it off with Gavin. They were a world apart. Unsuitable in every way. After she split with him, he'd never called or texted her again. He obviously wasn't missing her too badly.

But Sabine had never allowed herself to relax. She knew that sooner or later, Gavin would find out that he had a son. If Clay didn't tell him tonight, it would be the next time she bumped into someone Gavin knew. Sitting in the park, walking down the street…somebody would see Jared and know instantly that he was Gavin's son. The bigger he got, the more of a carbon copy of his father he became.

Then it was only a matter of time before Gavin showed up, angry and demanding. That was how he worked. He always got his way. At least until now. The only thing Sabine knew for certain was that he wouldn't win this time. Jared was her son. *Hers*. Gavin was a workaholic and wouldn't have a clue what to do with a child. She wasn't about to turn him over to the stuffy nannies and boarding schools that had raised Gavin instead of his parents.

As the train approached their stop, Sabine got up and

they hurried to catch the bus that would take them the last few blocks to her apartment near Marine Park in Brooklyn, where she'd lived the past four years. It wasn't the fanciest place in the world, but it was relatively safe, clean and close to the grocery store and the park. The one-bedroom apartment was growing smaller as Jared grew older, but they were managing.

Originally, a large portion of the bedroom was used as her art studio. When her son came along, she packed up her canvases and put her artistic skills toward painting a cheerful mural over his crib. Jared had plenty of room to play, and there was a park down the street where he could run around and dig in the sandbox. Her next-door neighbor, Tina, would watch Jared when she had her evening yoga classes.

She had put together a pretty good life for her and Jared. Considering that when she moved to New York she was broke and homeless, she'd come quite a long way. Back then, she could live on meager waitressing tips and work on her paintings when she had the extra money for supplies. Now, she had to squeeze out every penny she could manage, but they had gotten by.

"A-sketti!" Jared cheered triumphantly as they came through the door.

"Okay. I'll make a-sketti." Sabine sat him down before switching the television on to his favorite show. It would mesmerize him with songs and funny dances while she cooked.

By the time Jared was done eating and Sabine was changed into her workout clothes, she had only minutes to spare before Tina arrived. If she was lucky, Tina would give Jared a bath and scrub the tomato sauce off his cheeks. Usually, she had him in his pajamas and in bed by the time Sabine got home. Sabine hated that he would be asleep when she returned, but going through his nightly routine after class would have Jared up way past his bedtime. He'd wake up at dawn no matter what, but he'd be cranky.

There was a sharp knock at the door. Tina was a little early. That was fine by her. If she could catch the earlier bus, it would give her enough time to get some good stretches in before class.

"Hey, Tina—" she said, whipping open the door and momentarily freezing when her petite, middle-aged neighbor was not standing in the hallway.

No. No, no, no. She wasn't ready to deal with this. Not yet. Not tonight.

It was Gavin.

Sabine clutched desperately at the door frame, needing its support to keep her upright as the world started tilting sharply on its axis. Her chest tightened; her stomach churned and threatened to return her dinner. At the same time, other long-ignored parts of her body immediately sparked back to life. Gavin had always been a master of her body, and the years hadn't dulled the memory of his touch.

Fear. Desire. Panic. Need. It all swirled inside her like a building maelstrom that would leave nothing but destruction in its path. She took a deep breath to clamp it all down. She couldn't let Gavin know she was freaking out. She certainly couldn't let him know she still responded to him, either. That would give him the upper hand. She plastered a wide smile across her face and choked down her emotions.

"Hello, Sabine," he said with the deep, familiar voice she remembered.

It was hard to believe the handsome and rich blast from her past was standing in front of her after all this time. His flawlessly tailored gray suit and shiny, sky-blue tie made him look every inch the powerful CEO of the BXS shipping empire. His dark eyes were trained on her, his gaze traveling down the line of his nose. He looked a little older than she remembered, with concern lining his eyes and furrowing his brow. Or maybe it was the tense, angry expression that aged him.

"Gavin!" she said with feigned surprise. "I certainly didn't expect to see you here. I thought you were my neighbor Tina. How have you—"

"Where is my son?" he demanded, interrupting her nervous twitter. His square jaw was rock hard, his sensual lips pressed into a hard line of disapproval. There had been a flash of that same expression when she'd left him all those years ago, but he'd quickly grown indifferent to it. Now he cared. But not about her. Only about their child.

Apparently news traveled fast. It had been fewer than two hours since she'd run into Clay.

"Your son?" she repeated, hoping to stall long enough to think of a plan. She'd had years to prepare for this moment and yet, when it arrived, she was thrown completely off guard. Moving quickly, Sabine rushed into the hallway and pulled the apartment door nearly closed behind her. She left just the slightest crack open so she could peek through and make sure Jared was okay. She pressed her back against the door frame and found it calmed her nerves just a little to have that barrier between Gavin and Jared. He'd have to go through her to get inside.

"Yes, Sabine," Gavin said, taking a step closer to her. "Where is the baby you've hidden from me for the last three years?"

* * *

Damn, she was still as beautiful as he remembered. A little older, a little curvier, but still the fresh, funky artist that had turned his head in that art gallery. And tonight, she was wearing some skimpy workout clothes that clung to every newly rounded curve and reminded him of what he'd been missing since she'd walked out on him.

People tended not to stay in Gavin's life very long. There had been a parade of nannies, tutors, friends and lovers his whole life as his parents hired and fired and then moved him from one private school to the next. The dark-haired beauty with the nose piercing had been no exception. She had walked out of his life without a second thought.

She'd said they weren't compatible in the long term because they had different priorities and different lives. Admittedly, they fell on opposite ends of the spectrum in most every category, but that was one of the things he'd been drawn to in Sabine. One of the reasons he thought she, of all people, might stay. She wasn't just another rich girl looking to marry well and shop often. What they had really seemed to matter. To mean something.

He'd been wrong.

He'd let her go—he'd learned early that there was no sense in chasing after someone who didn't want to be there—but she'd stayed on his mind. She'd starred in his dreams, both erotic and otherwise. She'd crept into his thoughts during the quiet moments when he had time to regret the past. More than once, Gavin had wondered what Sabine was up to and what she had done with her life.

Never in his wildest dreams did he expect the answer to be "raising his child."

Sabine straightened her spine, her sharp chin tipping up in defiance. She projected an air of confidence in any situation and had the steel backbone to stand behind it. She certainly had spunk; he'd loved that about her once. Now, he could tell it would be an annoyance.

She looked him straight in the eye and said, "He's inside. And right now, that's where he's staying."

The bold honesty of her words was like a fist to his gut. The air rushed from his lungs. It was true. He had a son. *A son!* He hadn't entirely believed Clay's story until that precise moment. He'd known his best friend since they were roommates in college, one of the few constants in his life, but he couldn't always trust Clay's version of reality. Tonight, he'd insisted that Gavin locate Sabine as soon as possible to find out about her young son.

And he'd been right. For once.

Sabine didn't deny it. He'd expected her to tell him it wasn't his child or insist she was babysitting for a friend, but she had always been honest to a fault. Instead, she'd flat-out admitted she'd hidden his child from him and made no apologies about it. She even had the audacity to start making demands about how this was going to go down. She'd been in control of this situation for far too long. He was about to be included and in a big way.

"He's really my son?" He needed to hear the words from her, although he would demand a DNA test to confirm it no matter what she said.

Sabine swallowed and nodded. "He looks just like you."

The blood started pumping furiously in Gavin's ears. He might be able to understand why she kept it a secret if she was uncertain he was the father, but there was no doubt in her mind. She simply hadn't wanted him involved. She didn't want the inconvenience of having to share him with someone else. If not for Clay seeing her, he still wouldn't know he had a child.

His jaw tightened and his teeth clenched together. "Were you ever going to tell me I had a son, Sabine?"

Her pale green gaze burrowed into him as she crossed her arms over her chest. "No."

She didn't even bother to lie about it and make herself look less like the deceitful, selfish person she was. She just stood there, looking unapologetic, while unconsciously pressing her breasts up out of the top of her sports bra. His brain flashed between thoughts like a broken television as his eyes ran over the soft curves of her body and his ears tried to process her response. Anger, desire, betrayal and a fierce need to possess her rushed through his veins, exploding out of him in words.

"What do you mean, no?" Gavin roared.

"Keep it down!" Sabine demanded between gritted teeth, glancing nervously over her shoulder into the apartment. "I don't want him to hear us, and I certainly don't want all my neighbors to hear us, either."

"Well I'm sorry to embarrass you in front of your neighbors. I just found out I have a two-year-old son that I've never met. I think that gives me the right to be angry."

Sabine took a deep breath, amazing him with her ability to appear so calm. "You have every right to be angry. But yelling won't change anything. And I won't have you raising your voice around my son."

"*Our* son," Gavin corrected.

"No," she said with a sharp point of her finger. "He's my son. According to his birth certificate, he's an immaculate conception. Right now, you have no legal claim to him and no right to tell me how to do *anything* where he's concerned. You got that?"

That situation would be remedied and soon. "For now. But don't think your selfish monopoly on our son will last for much longer."

A crimson flush rushed to her cheeks, bringing color to her flawless, porcelain skin. She had gotten far too comfortable calling the shots. He could tell she didn't like him making demands. Too bad for her. He had a vote now and it was long overdue.

She swallowed and brushed her purple-highlighted ponytail over her shoulder but didn't back down. "It's after seven-thirty on a Wednesday night, so you can safely bet that's how it's going to stay for the immediate future."

Gavin laughed at her bold naïveté. "Do you honestly think my lawyers don't answer the phone at 2:00 a.m. when I call? For what I pay them, they do what I want, when I want." He slipped his hand into his suit coat and pulled his phone out of his inner breast pocket. "Shall we call Edmund and see if he's available?"

Her eyes widened slightly at his challenge. "Go ahead, Gavin. Any lawyer worth his salt is going to insist on a DNA test. It takes no less than three days to get the results of a paternity test back from a lab. If you push me, I'll see to it that you don't set eyes on him until the results come back. If we test first thing in the morning, that would mean Monday by my estimation."

Gavin's hands curled into tight fists at his sides. She'd had years to prepare for this moment and she'd done her homework. He knew she was right. The labs probably wouldn't process the results over the weekend, so it would be Monday at the earliest before he could get his lawyer involved and start making parental demands. But once he could lay claim to his son, she had better watch out.

"I want to see my son," he said. This time his tone was less heated and demanding.

"Then calm down and take your thumb off your lawyer's speed dial."

Gavin slipped his cell phone back into his pocket. "Happy?"

Sabine didn't seem happy, but she nodded anyway. "Now, before I let you in, we need to discuss some ground rules."

He took a deep breath to choke back his rude retort. Few people had the audacity to tell him what to do, but if anyone would, it was Sabine. He would stick to her requirements for now, but before long, Gavin would be making the rules. "Yes?"

"Number one, you are not to yell when you are in my apartment or anywhere Jared might be. I don't want you upsetting him."

Jared. His son's name was Jared. This outrageous scenario was getting more and more real. "What's his middle name?" Gavin couldn't stop himself from asking. He suddenly wanted to know everything he could about his son. There was no way to gain back the time he'd lost, but he would do everything in his power to catch up on what he missed.

"Thomas. Jared Thomas Hayes."

Thomas was *his* middle name. Was that a coincidence? He couldn't remember if Sabine knew it or not. "Why Thomas?"

"For my art teacher in high school, Mr. Thomas. He's the only one that ever encouraged my painting. Since that was also your middle name, it seemed fitting. Number two," she continued. "Do not tell him you're his father. Not until it is legally confirmed and we are both comfortable with the timing. I don't want him confused and worried about what's going on."

"Who does he think his father is?"

Sabine shook her head dismissively. "He's not even two. He hasn't started asking questions about things like that yet."

"Fine," he agreed, relieved that if nothing else, his son hadn't noticed the absence of a father in his life. He knew how painful that could be. "Enough rules. I want to see Jared." His son's name felt alien on his tongue. He wanted a face to put with the name and know his son at last.

"Okay." Sabine shifted her weight against the door, slowly slinking into the apartment.

Gavin moved forward, stepping over the threshold. He'd been to her apartment before, a long time ago. He remembered a fairly sparse but eclectic space with mismatched thrift store furniture. Her paintings had dotted the walls, her portfolio and bag of supplies usually sitting near the door.

When he barely missed stepping on a chubby blue crayon instead of a paintbrush, he knew things were truly different. Looking around, he noticed a lot had changed. The furniture was newer but still a mishmash of pieces. Interspersed with it were brightly colored plastic toys like a tiny basketball hoop and a tricycle with superheroes on it. A television in the corner loudly played a children's show.

And when Sabine stepped aside, he saw the small, dark-haired boy sitting on the floor in front of it. The child didn't turn to look at him. He was immersed in bobbing his head and singing along to the song playing on the show, a toy truck clutched in his hand.

Gavin swallowed hard and took another step into the apartment so Sabine could close the door behind him. He watched her walk over to the child and crouch down.

"Jared, we have a visitor. Let's say hello."

The little boy set down his truck and crawled to his feet. When he turned to look at Gavin, he felt his heart skip a beat in his chest. The tiny boy looked exactly like he had as a child. It was as though a picture had been snatched from his baby album and brought to life. From his pink cheeks smeared with tomato sauce, to the wide, dark eyes that looked at him with curiosity, he was very much Gavin's son.

The little boy smiled, revealing tiny baby teeth. "Hi."

Gavin struggled to respond at first. His chest was tight with emotions he never expected in this moment. This morning, he woke up worried about his latest business acquisition and now he was meeting his child for the first time. "Hi, Jared," he choked out.

"Jared, this is Mommy's friend Gavin."

Gavin took a hesitant step forward and knelt down to bring himself to the child's level. "How are you doing, big guy?"

Jared responded with a flow of gibberish he couldn't understand. Gavin hadn't been around many small children, and he wasn't equipped to translate. He could pick out a few words—*school, train* and something close to *spaghetti.* The rest was lost on him, but Jared didn't seem to mind. Pausing in his tale, he picked up his favorite truck and held it out to Gavin. "My truck!" he declared.

He took the small toy from his son. "It's very nice. Thank you."

A soft knock sounded at the front door. Sabine frowned and stood up. "That's the babysitter. I've got to go."

Gavin swallowed his irritation. He'd had a whole two minutes with his son and she was trying to push him out the door. They hadn't even gotten around to discussing her actions and what they were going to do about this situation. He watched her walk to the door and let in a middle-aged woman in a sweater with cats on it.

"Hey, Tina. Come on in. He's had his dinner and he's just watching television."

"I'll get him in the bath and in bed by eight-thirty."

"Thanks, Tina. I should be home around the usual time."

Gavin handed the truck back to Jared and reluctantly stood. He wasn't going to hang around while the neighbor lady was here. He turned in time to see Sabine slip into a hoodie and tug a sling with a rolled-up exercise mat over her shoulder.

"Gavin, I've got to go. I'm teaching a class tonight."

He nodded and gave a quick look back at Jared. He'd returned to watching his show, doing a little monkey dance along with the other children and totally unaware of what was really going on around him. Gavin wanted to reach out to him again, to say goodbye or hug him, but he refrained. There would be time for all that later. For the first time in his life, he had someone who would be legally bound to him for the next sixteen years and wouldn't breeze in and out of his life like so many others. They would have more time together.

Right now, he needed to deal with the mother of his child.

Two

"I don't need you to drive me to class."

Gavin stood holding open the passenger door of his Aston Martin with a frown lining his face. Sabine knew she didn't want to get in the car with him. Getting in would mean a private tongue-lashing she wasn't ready for yet. She'd happily take the bus to avoid this.

"Just get in the car, Sabine. The longer we argue, the later you'll be."

Sabine watched the bus blow by the stop up the street and swore under her breath. She'd never make it to class in time unless she gave in and let him drive her there. Sighing in defeat, she climbed inside. Gavin closed the door and got in on his side. "Go up the block and turn right at the light," she instructed. If she could focus on directions, perhaps they'd have less time to talk about what she'd done.

She already had a miserably guilty conscience. It wasn't like she could look at Jared without thinking of Gavin. Lying to him was never something she intended to do, but the moment she found out she was pregnant, she was overcome with a fierce territorial and protective urge. She and Gavin were from different planets. He never really cared for her the way she did for him. The same would hold true for their son. Jared would be *acquired* just like any other asset of the Brooks Empire. He deserved better than that. Better than what Gavin had been given.

She did what she thought she had to do to protect her child, and she wouldn't apologize for it. "At the second light, turn left."

Gavin remained silent as they drove, unnerving her more with every minute that ticked by. She was keenly aware of the way his hands tightly gripped the leather steering wheel. The tension was evident in every muscle of his body, straining the threads of his designer suit. His smooth, square jaw was flexed as though it took everything he had to keep his emotions in check and his eyes on the road.

It was a practiced skill of Gavin's. When they were together, he always kept his feelings tamped down. The night she told him they were over, there had barely been a flicker of emotion in his eyes. Not anger. Not sadness. Not even a "don't let the door hit you on the way out." Just a solemnly resigned nod and she was dismissed from his life. He obviously never really cared for Sabine. But this might be the situation that caused him to finally blow.

When his car pulled to a stop outside the community center where she taught, he shifted into Neutral, pulled the parking brake and killed the engine. He glanced down at his Rolex. "You're early."

She was. She didn't have to be inside for another fifteen minutes. He'd driven a great deal faster than the bus and hadn't stopped every block to pick up people. It was pointless to get out of the car and stand in front of the building to wait for the previous class to end. That meant time in the car alone with Gavin. Just perfect.

After an extended silence, he spoke. "So, was I horrible to you? Did I treat you badly?" His low voice was quiet, his eyes focused not on her but on something through the windshield ahead of them.

Sabine silently groaned. Somehow she preferred the yelling to this. "Of course not."

He turned to look at her then, pinning her with his dark eyes. "Did I say or do anything while we were together to make you think I would be a bad father?"

A bad father? No. Perhaps a distracted one. A distant one. An absent one. Or worse, a reluctant one. But not a *bad* father. "No. Gavin, I—"

"Then why, Sabine? Why would you keep something so important from me? Why would you keep me from being in Jared's life? He's young now, but eventually he'd notice he didn't have a daddy like other kids. What if he thought I didn't want him? Christ, Sabine. He may not have been planned, but he's still my son."

When he said it like that, every excuse in her mind sounded ridiculous. How could she explain that she didn't want Jared to grow up spoiled, rich but unloved? That she wanted him with her, not at some expensive boarding school? That she didn't want him to become a successful, miserable shell of a man like his father? All those excuses resulted from her primary fear that she couldn't shake. "I was afraid I would lose him."

Gavin's jaw still flexed with pent-up emotions. "You thought I would take him from you?"

"Wouldn't you?" Her gaze fixed on him, a challenge in her eyes. "Wouldn't you have swooped in the minute he was born and claimed him as your own? I'm sure your fancy friends and family would be horrified that a person like me was raising the future Brooks Express Shipping heir. It wouldn't be hard to deem me an unfit mother and have some judge from your father's social club grant you full custody."

"I wouldn't have done that."

"I'm sure you only would've done what you thought was best for your son, but how was I to know what that would entail? What would happen if you decided he would be better off with you and I was just a complication? I wouldn't have enough money or connections to fight you. I couldn't risk it." Sabine felt the tears prickling her eyes, but she refused to cry in front of Gavin.

"I couldn't bear the thought of you handing him off to nannies and tutors. Buying his affection with expensive gifts because you were too busy building the family company to spend time with him. Shipping him off to some boarding school as soon as he was old enough, under the guise of getting him the best education when you really just want him out of your hair. Jared wasn't planned. He wasn't the golden child of your socially acceptable marriage. You might want him on principle, but I couldn't be certain you would love him."

Gavin sat silent for a moment, listening to her tirade. The anger seemed to have run its course. Now he just looked emotionally spent, his dark eyes tired. He looked just like Jared after a long day without a nap.

Sabine wanted to brush the dark strands of hair from his weary eyes and press her palm against the rough stubble of his cheek. She knew exactly how it would feel. Exactly how his skin would smell…an intoxicating mixture of soap, leather and male. But she wouldn't. Her attraction to Gavin was a hurdle she had to overcome to leave him the first time. The years hadn't dulled her reaction to him. Now, it would be an even larger complication she didn't need.

"I don't understand why you would think that," he said at last, his words quieter now.

"Because that's what happened to you, Gavin." She lowered her voice to a soft, conversational tone. "And it's the only way you know how to raise a child. Nannies and boarding schools are normal to you. You told me yourself how your parents were always too busy for you and your siblings. How your house cycled through nannies like some people went through tissue paper. Do you remember telling me about how miserable and lonely you were when they sent you away to school? Why would I want that for Jared? Even if it came with all the money and luxury in the world? I wasn't about to hand him over to you so he could live the same hollow life you had. I didn't want him to be groomed to be the next CEO of Brooks Express Shipping."

"What's wrong with that?" Gavin challenged with a light of anger returning to the chocolate depths of his eyes. "There are worse things than growing up wealthy and becoming the head of a Fortune 500 company founded by your great-great-grandfather. Like growing up poor. Living in a small apartment with second-hand clothes."

"His clothes aren't secondhand!" she declared, her blood rushing furiously through her veins. "They're not from Bloomingdale's, but they aren't rags, either. I know that to you we look like we live in squalor, but we don't. It's a small apartment, but it's in a quiet neighborhood near the park where he can play. He has food and toys and most importantly, all the love, stability and attention I can possibly give him. He's a happy, healthy child."

Sabine didn't want to get defensive, but she couldn't help it. She recognized the tone from back when they were dating. The people in his social circles were always quick to note her shabby-chic fashion sense and lack of experience with an overabundance of flatware. They declared it charming, but Sabine could see the mockery in their eyes. They never thought she was good enough for one of the Brooks men. She wasn't about to let Gavin tell her that the way she raised her child wasn't good enough, either.

"I have no doubt that you're doing a great job with Jared. But why would you make it so hard on yourself? You could have a nice place in Manhattan. You could send him to one of the best private preschools in the city. I could get you a nice car and someone to help you cook and clean and take care of all the little things. I would've made sure you both had everything you needed—and *without* taking him from you. There was no reason to sacrifice those comforts."

"I didn't sacrifice anything," Sabine insisted. She knew those creature comforts came with strings. She'd rather do without. "I never had those things to begin with."

"No sacrifices?" Gavin shifted in the car to face her

directly. "What about your painting? I've kept an eye out over the years and haven't noticed any showings of your work. I didn't see any supplies or canvases lying around the apartment, either. I assume your studio space gave way to Jared's things, so where did all that go?"

Sabine swallowed hard. He had her there. She'd moved to New York to follow her dream of becoming a painter. She had lived and breathed her art every moment of the day she could. Her work had even met with some moderate success. She'd had a gallery showing and sold a few pieces, but it wasn't enough to live on. And it certainly wasn't enough to raise a child on. So her priorities shifted. Children took time. And energy. And money. At the end of the day, the painting had fallen to the bottom of her list. Some days she missed the creative release of her work, but she didn't regret setting it aside.

"It's in the closet," she admitted with a frown.

"And when was the last time you painted?"

"Saturday," she replied a touch too quickly.

Gavin narrowed his gaze at her.

"Okay, it was finger paints," Sabine confessed. She turned away from Gavin's heavy stare and focused on the yoga mat in her lap. He saw more than she wanted him to. He always had. "But," she continued, "Jared and I had a great time doing it, even if it wasn't gallery-quality work. He's the most important thing in the world to me, now. More important than painting."

"You shouldn't have to give up one thing you love for another."

"Life is about compromises, Gavin. Certainly you know what it's like to set aside what you love to do for what you're obligated to do."

He stiffened in the seat beside her. It seemed they

were both guilty of putting their dreams on the back burner, although for very different reasons. Sabine had a child to raise. Gavin had family expectations to uphold and a shipping empire to run. The tight collar of his obligations had chafed back when they were dating. It had certainly rubbed him bloody and raw by now.

When he didn't respond, Sabine looked up. He was looking out the window, his thoughts as distant as his eyes.

It was surreal to be in the same car with Gavin after all this time. She could feel his gravitational pull on her when they were this close. Walking away from him the first time had been hard. They dated for about a month and a half, but every moment they spent together had been fiercely passionate. Not just sexual, either. They enjoyed everything to the fullest, from spicy ethnic foods to political debates, museum strolls to making love under the stars. They could talk for hours.

Their connection was almost enough to make her forget they wanted different things from life. And as much as he seemed enticed by the exoticness of their differences, she knew it wouldn't last long. The novelty would wear off and they would either break up, or he would expect her to change for him. That was one thing she simply wouldn't do. She wouldn't conform for her parents and the small-minded Nebraska town she grew up in, and she wouldn't do it for him. She came to New York so she could be herself, not to lose her identity and become one of the Brooks Wives. They were like Stepfords with penthouse apartments.

She had briefly met some of Gavin's family, and it had scared the hell out of her. They hadn't been dating very long when they ran into his parents at a restaurant. It was an awkward encounter that came too early in the relationship, but the impact on Sabine had been huge. His mother was a flawless, polished accessory of his father's arm. Sabine was fairly certain that even if she wanted to be, she would be neither flawless nor polished. She didn't want to fade into the background of her own life.

It didn't matter how much she loved Gavin. And she did. But she loved herself more. And she loved Jared more.

But breathing the same air as Gavin again made her resolve weaken. She had neglected her physical needs for too long and made herself vulnerable. "So what do we do now?" Sabine asked at last.

As if he'd read her thoughts, Gavin reached over to her and took her hand in his. The warmth of him enveloped her, a tingle of awareness prickling at the nape of her neck. It traveled like a gentle waterfall down her back, lighting every nerve. Her whole body seemed to be awakening from a long sleep like a princess in a fairy tale. And all it had taken was his touch. She couldn't imagine what would happen if the dashing prince actually kissed her.

Kissed her? Was she insane? He was no dashing prince, and she had run from this relationship for a good reason. He may have tracked her down and she might be obligated to allow him to have a place in Jared's life, but that didn't mean they had to pick up where they left off. Quite the contrary. She needed to keep her distance from Gavin if she knew what was good for her. He'd let her go once, proving just how much she didn't matter to him. Anything he said or did now to the contrary was because of Jared. Not her.

His thumb gently stroked the back of her hand. Her

body remembered that touch and everything it could lead to. Everything she'd denied herself since she became a mother...

He looked up at her, an expression of grave seriousness on his face. "We get married."

Gavin had never proposed to a woman before. Well, it wasn't really even a proposal since he hadn't technically asked. And even though it wasn't candlelight and diamonds, he certainly never imagined a response like this.

Sabine laughed at him. Loudly. Heartily. For an unnecessarily long period of time. She obviously had no idea how hard it had been for him to do this. How many doubts he had to set aside to ask *anyone* to be a permanent part of his life, much less someone with a track record of walking away from him.

He'd thought they were having a moment. Her glossy lips had parted softly and her pale eyes darkened when he'd touched her. It should've been the right time, the perfect moment. But he'd miscalculated. Her response to his proposal had proved as much.

"I'm serious!" he shouted over her peals of laughter, but it only made her giggle harder. Gavin sat back in his seat and waited for her to stop. It took a few minutes longer than his pride would've liked. Eventually, she quieted and wiped her damp eyes with her fingertips.

"Marry me, Sabine," he said.

"No."

He almost wished Sabine had gone back to laughing. The firm, sober rejection was worse. It reminded him of her pained, resolved expression as she broke off their relationship and walked out of his life.

"Why not?" He couldn't keep the insulted tone from

his voice. He was a great catch. She should be thrilled to get this proposal, even as spur of the moment and half-assed as it was.

Sabine smiled and patted his hand reassuringly. "Because you don't want to marry me, Gavin. You want to do the right thing and provide a stable home for your son. And that's noble. Really. I appreciate the sentiment. But I'm not going to marry someone that doesn't love me."

"We have a child together."

"That's not good enough for me."

Gavin scoffed. "Making our son legitimate isn't a good enough reason for you?"

"We're not talking about the succession to the throne of England, Gavin. It's not exactly the horrid stigma it used to be. Having you in his life is more than enough for me. That's all I want from you—quality time."

"Quality time?" Gavin frowned. Somehow legally binding themselves in marriage seemed an easier feat.

"Yes. If you're committed enough to your son to marry his mother when you don't love her, you should be committed enough to put in the time. I'm not going to introduce a 'dad' into his life just so you can work late and ignore him. He's better off without a dad than having one that doesn't make an effort. You can't miss T-ball games and birthday parties. You have to be there when you say you will. If you can't be there for him one hundred percent, don't bother."

Her words hit him hard. He didn't have bad parents, but he did have busy ones. Gavin knew how it felt to be the lowest item on someone's priority list. How many times had he sat alone on the marble staircase of his childhood home and waited for parents who never showed up? How many times had he scanned the crowd at school pageants and ball games looking for family that wasn't there?

He'd always sworn he wouldn't do that to his own children, but even after having seen his son, the idea of him wasn't quite a firm reality in Gavin's mind. He had only this primitive need to claim the child and its mother. To finally have someone in his life that couldn't walk away.

That's why he'd rushed out to Brooklyn without any sort of plan. But she was right. He didn't know what to do with a child. His reflex would be to hand him off to someone who did and focus on what he was good at—running his family business. He couldn't afford the distraction, especially so close to closing his latest business deal.

And that was exactly what she was afraid of.

She had good reason, too. He'd spent most of their relationship vacillating between ignoring her for work and ignoring work for her. He never found the balance. A child would compound the problem. Part of the reason Gavin hadn't seriously focused on settling down was because he knew his work priorities would interfere with family life. He kept waiting for the day when things at BXS would slow down enough for him to step back. But it never happened. His father hadn't stepped back until the day he handed the reins over to Gavin, and he'd missed his children growing up to do it.

Gavin didn't have a choice any longer. He had a child. He would have to find a way—a better way than his father chose—to keep the company on top and keep his promises to his son and Sabine. He wasn't sure how the hell he would do it, but he would make it happen.

"If I put in the quality time, will you let me help you?"

"Help me with what?"

"With life, Sabine. If you won't marry me, let me get you a nice apartment in the city. Wherever you want to live. Let me help pay for Jared's education. We can enroll him in the best preschool. I can get someone to help around the house. Someone that can cook and clean, even pick up Jared from school if you want to keep working."

"And why would you want to do that? What you're suggesting is incredibly expensive."

"Maybe, but it's worth it to me. It's an investment in my child. Making your life easier will make you a happier, more relaxed mother to our son. He can spend more time playing and learning than sitting on the subway. And admittedly, having you in Manhattan will make it easier for me to see Jared more often."

He could see the conflict in Sabine's pale green eyes. She was struggling. She was proud and wouldn't admit it, but raising Jared on her own had to be difficult. Kids weren't cheap. They took time and money and effort. She'd already sacrificed her art. But convincing her to accept his offering would take time.

He knew Sabine better than she wanted to admit. She didn't want to be seen as one of those women who moved up in social status by calculated breeding. Jared had been an accident, of that he was certain. Judging by the expression on Sabine's face when she opened the door to her apartment, she would've rather had any man's son but his.

"Let's take this one step at a time, please," Sabine said, echoing his thoughts. There was a pained expression on her face that made him think there was more than just pride holding her back.

"What do you mean?"

"You've gone from having no kids to having a toddler and very nearly a fiancée in two hours' time. That's a big change for you, and for both Jared and me. Let's not uproot our lives so quickly." She sighed and gripped his hand. "Let's get the DNA results in, so there are no questions or doubts. Then we can introduce the idea of you to Jared and tell our families. From there, maybe we move into the city to be closer to you. But let's make these decisions over weeks and months, not minutes."

She glanced down at the screen on her cell phone. "I've got to get inside and set up."

"Okay." Gavin got out of the car and came around to open her door and help her out.

"I have tomorrow off. If you can make an appointment for DNA testing, call or text me and we'll meet you there. My number is the same. Do you still have it?"

He did. He'd very nearly dialed it about a hundred times in the weeks after she'd left. He'd been too proud to go through with the call. A hundred people had drifted in and out of his life, but Sabine leaving had caught him by surprise and it stung. He'd wanted to fight, wanted to call her and convince her she was wrong about them. But she wanted to go and he let her.

Now he could kick himself for not manning up and telling her he wanted her and didn't care what others thought about it. That he would make the time for her. Maybe then he would've been there to hear his son's heartbeat in the doctor's office, his first cries and his first words. Maybe then the mother of his child wouldn't look at him with wary eyes and laugh off his proposal of marriage like a joke.

He made a point of pulling out his phone and confirming it so she wouldn't think he knew for certain. "I do."

Sabine nodded and slowly started walking backward across the grass. Even after all this time apart, it felt awkward to part like strangers without a hug or a kiss goodbye. They were bonded for a lifetime now, and yet he had never felt as distant from her as he did when she backed away.

"I'll see you tomorrow, then," she said.

"Tomorrow," he repeated.

He watched as she regarded him for a moment at a distance. There was a sadness in her expression that he didn't like. The Sabine he remembered was a vibrant artist with a lust for life and experience. She had jerked him out of his blah corporate existence, demanded he live his life, not just go through the motions. Sabine was nothing like what he was supposed to have but absolutely everything he needed. He'd regretted every day since she'd walked out of his life.

Now, he regretted it more than ever, and not just because of his son. The sad, weary woman walking away from him was just a shadow of the person he once knew. And he hated that.

The outdoor lights kicked on, lighting the shimmer of tears in her eyes. "I'm sorry, Gavin," she said before spinning on her heels and disappearing through the doors of the community center.

She was sorry. And so was he.

Three

Gavin arrived at the office the next morning before seven. The halls were dark and quiet as he traveled to the executive floor of the BXS offices. The large corner office had once belonged to his father and his grandfather before him. Gavin's original office was down the hallway. He'd gotten the space when he was sixteen and started learning the business and then passed it along to his younger brother, Alan, when Gavin took over as CEO.

Opening the door, he walked across the antique rug and set his laptop bag and breakfast on the large wooden desk. The heavy mahogany furniture was originally from his great-grandfather's office and was moved here when BXS upgraded their location from the small building near the shipping yards.

His great-grandfather had started the company in

1930, Depression be damned. What began as a local delivery service expanded to trains and trucks and eventually to planes that could deliver packages all over the world. The eldest Brooks son had run the company since the day it opened. Everything about Brooks Express Shipping had an air of tradition and history that made it one of the most trusted businesses in America.

Frankly, it was a bit stifling.

Despite how he'd argued to the contrary with Sabine last night, they both knew this wasn't what he wanted to do with his life. The Brooks name came with responsibilities. Gavin had been groomed from birth to one day run BXS. He'd had the best education, interned with the company, received his MBA from Harvard… Each milestone putting him one step closer to filling his father's shoes. Even if they were too tight.

Sabine had been right about some things. He had no doubt his family would assume Jared would one day be the corporate successor to his father. The difference would be that Gavin would make certain *his* son had a choice.

He settled in at his desk, firing up his computer. He immediately sent an email to his assistant, Marie, about setting up a lab appointment for their DNA testing. With it, he included a note that this was a confidential matter. No one, literally no one, was to know what was going on. He trusted Marie, but she was friendly and chatty with everyone, including his father, who she used to work for. Gavin had barely come to terms with this himself. He certainly wasn't ready for the world, and especially his family, to know what was going on.

Marie wouldn't be in until eight, but she had a corporate smartphone and a long train ride in to work. He was certain she'd have everything handled before she arrived.

That done, he turned to the steaming-hot cup of coffee and the bagel he picked up on his way in. The coffee shop on the ground floor of the building was open well before most people stumbled into BXS for the day. Gavin spread cream cheese on his toasted bagel as he watched his in-box fill with new messages. Most were unimportant, although one caught his eye.

It was from Roger Simpson, the owner of Exclusivity Jetliners.

The small, luxury jet company specialized in private transportation. Whether you were taking a few friends for a weekend in Paris, transporting your beloved poodle to your summer home or simply refused to fly coach, Exclusivity Jetliners was ready and waiting to help. At least for now.

Roger Simpson wanted to retire. The business had been his life, and he was ready to finally relax and enjoy the fruits of his labor. Unlike BXS, he didn't have a well-groomed heir to take his place at the head of the company. He had a son, Paul, but from the discussions Roger and Gavin had shared, Roger would rather sell the company than let his irresponsible son drive it into the ground.

Gavin quickly made it known that he was interested. He'd been eight years old when his father let him ride in the cockpit of one of their Airbus A310 freighters. He'd immediately been enamored with planes and flying. For his sixteenth birthday, his parents had acquiesced and got him flying lessons.

He'd even entertained the idea of joining the Air Force and becoming a fighter pilot. There, sadly, was where that dream had died a horrible death. His father had tolerated Gavin's "hobby," but he wouldn't allow his son to derail his career path for a silly dream.

Gavin swallowed the old taste of bitterness on the back of his tongue and tried to chase it with his coffee. His father had won that battle, but he wasn't in charge anymore. He clicked on the email from Roger and scanned over the message.

BXS was about to offer a new service that would push them ahead of their shipping competitors—concierge shipping. It would appeal to the elite BXS clientele. Ones who wanted their things handled carefully and expeditiously and were willing to pay for the privilege.

The fleet of small planes from Exclusivity Jetliners would be transformed into direct freight jets that would allow the rich art lover to see to it that their new Picasso bought at auction over the phone would arrive safely at their home the same day. It would allow the fashion designer to quickly transport a dozen priceless gowns to an Academy Award nominee while she filmed on set two thousand miles from Hollywood.

It was a risk, but if it worked, it would give Gavin something he'd been wanting his whole life—the chance to fly.

Sabine had encouraged him years ago to find a way to marry his obligations and his passions. It had seemed impossible at the time, but long after she was out of his life, her words had haunted him.

Just as her words had haunted him last night. He'd lain in bed for hours, his brain swirling with everything that had happened after he'd answered Clay's phone call. Sabine had always had the innate ability to cut through his crap. She called it like she saw it, as opposed to all the polite society types who danced around delicate subjects and gossiped behind your back.

She didn't see Gavin as a powerful CEO. The money and the privilege didn't register on her radar at all, and really it never had. After years of women chasing after him, Sabine was the first woman he was compelled to pursue. He'd spied her across an art gallery and instantly felt the urge to possess her. She had no idea who he was or how much he was worth at first, and when she did, she didn't care. He insisted on taking her out to nice dinners, but Sabine was more interested in making love and talking for hours in bed.

But she couldn't ignore their differences. They'd lasted as long as they had by staying inside the protective bubble of the bedroom, but he could tell it was getting harder for Sabine to overlook the huge, platinum gorilla in the room. She didn't see his power and riches as an asset. It was just one thing on a list of many that made her believe they didn't have a future together. She would rather keep her son a secret and struggle to make ends meet than to have Jared live the life Gavin had.

What had she said? …*You know what it's like to set aside what you love to do for what you're obligated to do.*

He did. Gavin had done it his whole life because of some misguided sense of duty. He could've walked away at any time. Joined the Air Force. Sacrificed his inheritance and what little relationship he had with his parents. But then what would happen to the company? His brother couldn't run it. Alan hadn't so much as sat down in his token office in months. Gavin wasn't even sure if he was in the country. His baby sister, Diana, had a freshly inked degree from Vassar and absolutely no experience. His father wouldn't come out of retirement. That meant Gavin ran BXS or a stranger did.

And no matter what, he couldn't let that happen. It was a family legacy. One of his earliest memories was of coming into this very office and visiting his grandfather. Papa Brooks would sit Gavin on his knee and tell him stories about how his great-grandfather had started the company. Tears of pride would gather in the old man's dark eyes. Gavin and his father might have their differences, but he wouldn't let his grandfather down. He'd been dead for four years now, but it didn't matter. BXS and its legacy was everything to Papa Brooks. Gavin wouldn't risk it to chase a pipe dream.

A chime sounded at his hip. Gavin reached down to his phone to find a text from Marie. She'd arranged for an appointment at 4:15 with his concierge physician on Park Avenue. Excellent.

He could've just copied the information into another window and included the location to send it to Sabine, but he found himself pressing the button to call her instead. It was a dangerous impulse that he wished he could ignore, but he wanted to hear her voice. He'd gone so long without it that he'd gladly take any excuse to hear it again. It wasn't until after the phone began to ring that he realized it was 7:30 in the morning. Sabine had always been a night owl and slept late.

"Hello?" she answered. Her voice was cheerful and not at all groggy.

"Sabine? It's Gavin. I'm sorry to call so early. Did I wake you?"

"Wake me?" Sabine laughed. "Oh, no. Jared is up with the chickens, no later than 6:00 a.m. every morning. I tease him that he's going to grow up to be a farmer like his granddaddy."

Gavin frowned for a moment before he realized she was talking about her own father. Sabine spoke very rarely of her parents. Last he'd heard they were both alive and well in Nebraska, but Sabine wasn't in contact with them. It made Gavin wonder if he wasn't the only one who didn't know about Jared.

"My assistant got us an appointment." Gavin read her the information so she could write it down, including the address of the doctor's office.

"Okay," she said. "We'll meet you there at a little before 4:15."

"I'll pick you up," he offered.

"No, we'll take the subway. Jared likes the train. There's a stop about a block from there, so it's not a problem at all."

Sabine was fiercely independent. Always had been. It had made him crazy when they were dating. She wouldn't let him do anything for her. He wanted to argue with her now, but he wouldn't. His afternoon schedule was pretty hectic, and he'd have to shuffle a few things around to drive out to Brooklyn and get them in time unless he sent a car. And yet, he wasn't ready to end the conversation, either.

"After the appointment," he said, "may I take you and Jared to an early dinner?"

"Um…" Sabine delayed her response. She was probably trying to come up with a reason why she couldn't, but was failing.

"A little quality time," he added with a smile, happily using her own words to get his way.

"Sure," she said, caving. "That would be nice."

"I'll see you this afternoon."

"Goodbye," Sabine said, disconnecting the call.

Gavin smiled as he glanced down at his phone. He was looking forward to his afternoon with Jared. And even though the rational side of his brain knew that he shouldn't, he was looking forward to seeing Sabine again, as well.

Sabine was surprised that it didn't take long at the doctor's office. The paperwork took more time than anything else. Gavin and Jared got their cheeks swabbed, and they were told the office would call with the lab results on Monday.

By four forty-five, they were standing on the sidewalk watching the traffic stack up on Park Avenue. Sabine secured Jared in the collapsible umbrella stroller she sometimes took into the city. It was too busy to let him walk, even though he was getting more independent and wanted to.

"What would you like to eat?" Gavin asked.

Sabine was pretty sure that the majority of places he was used to eating at were not equipped to feed a picky toddler. She glanced around, getting her bearings for where she was in the city. "I think there's a good burger place about two blocks from here."

Gavin's gaze narrowed at her. "A burger?"

She swallowed her laugh. "Let's wait until Jared is at least five before we take him to Le Cirque. They don't exactly have a kid's menu."

"I know."

Sabine shook her head and started walking toward the restaurant. Gavin moved quickly to fall into step beside her.

"You're used to taking people out to nice places and spending a lot of money for dinner. I suppose that's what people expect of you, but that's not how Jared and I roll. We'll probably all eat for less than what you normally pay for a bottle of wine. And that's fine by us. Right, Jared?"

The little boy smiled and gave a thumbs-up. He'd learned the gesture in day care a few weeks ago and since then, a lot of things had called for it. "Cheeburger!"

"See?" Sabine said, looking over to Gavin. "He's easy to impress."

The restaurant was already a little busy, but they were able to order and get their food before their toddler started to revolt. Sabine tried to keep her focus on Jared, making sure he was eating small bites and not getting ketchup everywhere. It was easier than looking at Gavin and trying to guess what he was thinking.

Things were still very up in the air between them. He was being nice to her. More polite than she expected, under the circumstances. But once the test results came back, Sabine was certain that things would start to change. Gavin had sworn he wasn't about to snatch her baby from her arms, but she was more concerned about it happening slowly. A new apartment in the city. A new school for Jared. New clothes. New toys. Even if he gave up the idea of marrying for their child's sake, things would change for her, too. He'd insist she stop working. He'd give her spending money. Suggest they just move in with him.

And when the time came that she decided to move out, she was certain he'd see to it that Jared stayed behind in the stable home they'd created for him there. She'd be unemployed and homeless with no money of her own to fight him for custody.

These were the thoughts that had kept her quiet throughout her pregnancy. The same fears that made her hide Jared from his father. And yet, she found herself smiling as she watched Jared and Gavin color on the kid's menu together. There was a hamburger with legs dancing on one side. Jared was scribbling green across the bun. Gavin was more cautious, making the meat brown and the cheese orange as he stayed between the lines.

That was Gavin for you. No matter what he did, he always stayed between the lines. He never got dirty. Or screwed up anything.

Opposites attracted, but they were polar to the point of near incompatibility. A lot of Sabine's clothes had paint splattered on them from her art. She embraced that life was messy. You had to eat a little dirt before you died. Gavin was polished. Tailored. You couldn't find a speck of dirt beneath his fingernails.

How had she ever thought that dating Gavin was a good idea?

Her eyes drifted over his sharp features and thick, dark hair. His broad shoulders and strong jaw. In truth, that was why she'd let herself indulge. Gavin was a handsome, commanding specimen of a man. Every inch of him, from his large hands attempting to clutch a tiny crayon, to his muscular but trim frame, radiated health and power. He was interesting and thoughtful. Honorable and loyal to a fault.

If she'd *had* to get pregnant, her instincts had sought out a superior male to help her propagate the species.

Somehow, even that most scientific of thoughts spoke straight to her core. Her appraisal of Gavin had shot up her pulse. She felt a flush rise to her cheeks and chest.

The heat spread throughout her body, focusing low in her belly. She closed her eyes, hoping to take a private moment to wish away her desire and regain control.

"Do you need to do anything else in the city before I take you back to your place?"

No such luck. Sabine's eyes flew open to see Gavin looking at her with a curious gaze. "You don't have to take us back," she snapped. She wasn't certain she could take being so close to him in the car. At least not at the moment. "We'll take the subway."

"No, I insist." Gavin paid the check and handed his crayon over to Jared.

"Gavin, you have a two-passenger roadster with no car seat. You can't drive us home."

He smiled and fished into his pocket, pulling out the ticket for the garage attendant. "Not today. Today I have a four-door Mercedes sedan…"

Sabine opened her mouth to reiterate the lack of car seat when Gavin continued, "…with a newly installed combination car seat that Jared can use until he's eighty-five pounds."

Her mouth snapped shut. He was determined to undermine any arguments she might make. Sure, it was harmless when it came to rides home from dinner, but what about when the decisions were important? Would Gavin find a way to make sure he got his way then, too? He'd always seemed to win when they were dating, so she wouldn't be surprised.

Tonight, Sabine didn't feel like arguing. She waited with Jared while Gavin had the attendant retrieve his car. Admittedly, it was nice to just sit in the soft leather seats and let Gavin worry about the stressful exodus of traffic into Brooklyn. No running down stairs to the train platforms…no crowded, B.O.-smelling subway cars…

And when he pulled up right in front of her building and parked, trimming several blocks from her walk, she said, "Thank you."

"For what?"

"Driving us home."

Gavin frowned slightly at her. "Of course I would drive you home. There's no need to thank me for that."

Sabine glanced over her shoulder and found Jared out cold in his new car seat. "I think he likes it," she said. She glanced at her watch. It was a little after seven. It was earlier than Jared usually went to bed, and he'd probably beat the sun to rise, but that was okay. If she could get him upstairs, change his Pull-Up and take off his shoes without waking him up, she'd consider it a victory.

They got out of the car. Sabine walked around to the other side, but Gavin had already scooped up the sleepy toddler in his arms. Without waking, Jared put his head on Gavin's shoulder and clung to his neck. Gavin gently ran his palm over the child's head, brushing back the baby-soft strands of his dark hair and resting his hand on Jared's back to keep him steady.

Sabine watched with a touch of tears distorting her vision. It was sweet watching the two of them, like carbon copies of one another. It was only their second day together and already she could see Jared warming up to Gavin.

Gavin carried Jared through the building and into her apartment after she unlocked the door. Sabine led the way down the hall to the bedroom. Flipping on the lights, they were greeted with calming mint-green walls, cream wainscoting and a mural of Winnie the Pooh characters she'd painted above the crib. Her double bed was an afterthought on the opposite wall.

She slipped off Jared's shoes. His soft cotton pants and T-shirt would be fine to sleep in. She gestured for Gavin to lay him on the crib mattress and made quick work of changing him.

Jared immediately curled into a ball, reaching out for his stuffed dinosaur and pulling it to his chest. Sabine covered him with his blanket. They slipped out quietly, the night-light kicking on as the overhead light went out.

Sabine pulled the door closed gently and made her way back into the living room. She expected Gavin to make noises about leaving, but instead he loitered, his eyes focused on a painting on the wall over the dining room table.

"I remember this one," Gavin said, his fists in his pants pockets.

Sabine looked up at the canvas and smiled. "You should. I was painting that one while we were dating."

The background of the painting was intricately layered with a muted palette of white, cream, ivory, off-white and ecru. The design was extremely structured and orderly. The variations of the pattern were really quite remarkable if you could differentiate the subtle color differences.

It was Gavin on canvas. And across it, splatters of purple, black and green paint. Disorder. Chaos. Color. That was Sabine. It was a striking juxtaposition. One that when it was complete, was the perfect illustration of why as a couple they made good art, but not good sense.

"You weren't finished with it when I saw it last. Some of this is new, like the blue crosses. What did you end up calling it?"

The pale blue crosses were actually plus signs. The final addition to the work after seeing her own unexpected plus sign on a pregnancy test. "Conception," she said.

Gavin looked back at the painting and turned his head to look at it from a new angle. "It's very nice. I like the colors. It's a much-needed pop against the beige."

Sabine smiled. He didn't see the symbolism of their relationship in it at all and that was okay. Art was only half about what she created. The other half was how others perceived and experienced her work.

He turned back to her, his face serious. "You are a really talented artist, Sabine."

The compliment made her squirm a little. She was always uncomfortable with praise. Frankly, she wasn't used to it after growing up with parents who didn't understand why their daughter danced to a different drummer. "It's okay," she said with a dismissive wave of her hand. "Not my best work."

Gavin frowned and closed the gap between them. He clasped her hand in his and pulled it to the red silk of his tie. "No," he insisted. "It's not just okay. You're not just okay."

Sabine tried to pull away, but he wasn't having it. He bent his knees until he was at her eye level and she couldn't avoid his gaze.

"You are a gifted painter," he insisted. "You were then and you certainly are now. I was always amazed at how you could create such wonderful and imaginative things from just a blank canvas. You have a great deal of skill, Sabine, whether you think so or not. I hope our son has the same eye for the beautiful things in life."

The words were hard enough to hear when they were

about her, but knowing he wished the same for their son was too much for her to take. Her parents hadn't wanted her to be a painter. It was frivolous. They'd wanted her to stay home and work on the farm, grow up and marry a farmer, and then raise a brood of tiny farmers. She was absolutely nothing like they wanted. And the day she left for New York, they said as much.

Before she could change her mind, Sabine threw herself against the wall of Gavin's chest and hugged him tight. He seemed surprised at first, but then he wrapped his strong arms around her and pulled her close. "Thank you," she whispered into his lapel.

It felt good to be in his arms, surrounded in his warmth and spicy cologne. Good to be appreciated for her work even when she hadn't lifted a brush in two years. Good to have someone believe in her, even if it was the same man who let her walk away from him. She would be happy with his professional admiration if nothing else.

And yet, with her head pressed to his chest, she could hear his heart racing. His muscles were tense as he held her. He was either extremely uncomfortable hugging her or there was more than just admiration there.

Sabine lifted her head and looked up at him. Her breath caught in her throat as her eyes met his. They glittered with what could only be desire. His jaw was tight, but unlike last night, he wasn't angry. He swallowed hard, the muscles in his throat working hard down the column of his neck. She recognized the signs in Gavin. She knew them well but thought she'd never see him look at her like that again.

The intensity of his gaze flipped a switch in her own body. As it had in the restaurant, heat pooled in her cheeks and then rushed through her veins to warm every inch of her. She couldn't help it. There had been few things as exquisite in her life as being made love to by Gavin. It had come as a huge surprise considering how tightly buttoned-up he was, but there was no denying he knew just how to touch her. It was probably the worst thing she could do considering what was going on between them, but she wanted Gavin to touch her again.

He must have read it in her eyes because a moment later he dipped his head and brought his lips to hers. They were soft at first, molding to her mouth and drinking her in. Sabine gently pressed her hands against his chest, pushing up onto her toes to get closer to him.

His hands glided across her back, the heat of him penetrating through the fabric of her blouse and searing her skin. She wanted to feel those hands all over her body. It had been so long since someone had touched her that way. She didn't want it to stop. Not ever.

Sabine was about to lean in. She wanted to wrap her arms around his neck and press her body tight against his. As if he sensed the move, Gavin started to retreat. She could feel him pulling away, the cool air rushing between them and bringing with it reality. She pulled away, too, wrapping her arms across her chest to ward off the chill and its evidence on her aching body.

Gavin looked down at her and cleared his throat. "I'd better go."

Sabine nodded and moved slowly with him toward the door.

"Good night, Sabine," he said in a hoarse whisper. He took a step back, straightening his suit coat, and then gripped the brass knob in his hand.

"Good night," she whispered, bringing her fingers up to gently touch her lips. They were still tingling with his kiss as he vanished through her doorway. "Good night."

Four

"We have a date this afternoon. I mean a playdate. I mean, aw hell, I have no idea what's going on," Sabine lamented. She was folding a stack of shirts and paused with one clutched to her chest. "You know, a few days ago I was living my life like a criminal on the run, but I felt like I had a better grip on things."

Adrienne smiled at her and turned to change the outfit on the mannequin by the wall. "It's a big change," she said. "But so far, it's not a bad change, right?"

"That's true. I guess that's what worries me. I keep waiting for the other shoe to drop."

The boutique was open, but the foot traffic usually didn't pick up until closer to lunchtime on a Saturday. At the moment, Sabine and Adrienne were alone in the store and able to speak freely about the dramatic turn of events in her life. Normally, Sabine ran the shop alone until another employee, Jill, came in later in the day. Today, Adrienne came in as well to relieve Sabine so she could meet Gavin.

"I don't think he's going to steal Jared away from you, Sabine. It sounds like he's been pretty reasonable so far."

"I know," she said, folding the last shirt and adding it to the neat display. "But he doesn't have the DNA results back yet and won't until Monday. If he was going to make a move, it wouldn't be until he had the advantage. The Gavin I knew three years ago was…calculating and ruthless. He had absolutely no qualms about sitting back and waiting for the perfect moment to strike."

"This isn't a business deal and he's not a cobra. You two have a child together. It's different." Adrienne pulled out a pin and fitted the top of the dress to the form.

Sabine stopped and admired the outfit Adrienne had designed. The sexy sheath dress was fitted with a square neckline, but it had fun details like pockets and a bright print to make it pop. It was perfect for the summer with some strappy heels or colorful ballet flats. She'd been tempted to use her employee discount to buy it for herself, but there wasn't much point. That was the kind of dress a woman wanted to wear on a date or a night out with the girls. She hadn't had either in a very long time. And despite Gavin proposing one night and kissing her the next, she didn't think her Facebook relationship status would be changing anytime soon.

"Work and life are the same to Gavin. I mean, he didn't propose to me. Not really. It was more like an offer to buy out my company. A business merger. Just what a girl wants to hear, right?"

Adrienne turned and looked at Sabine with her hands planted on her hips. "And the kiss?"

The kiss. The one thing that didn't make sense. She knew he was her Achilles' heel so it didn't surprise her that she fell into his arms, but his motives were sketchy. "Strategy. He knows my weakness where he's concerned. He's just buttering up the competition to get his way."

"You really think that's all it was?" Her boss looked unconvinced.

Sabine flopped down onto an upholstered bench outside the changing rooms. "I don't know. It didn't feel like strategy. It felt…" Her mind drifted back to the way her body had responded to his touch. The way her lips tingled long after he'd left. She sighed and shook her head. "It doesn't matter what it felt like. The fact of the matter is that Gavin doesn't love me. He never has. His only interest in me back then was as a source of rebellion against his uptight family. Now, I'm nothing more than a vehicle to his son. And when he gets tired of the games, he'll remove the obstacle—*me*."

"You don't think he's interested in a relationship with you?" Adrienne sat down beside her.

"Why would he be? He wasn't interested the last time. At least not enough to so much as blink when it ended. I mean, I thought there was more between us than just sex, but he was always so closed off. I had no idea how he really felt, but when he let me walk out the door like I was nothing more than an amusement to occupy his time…I knew I was replaceable. Gavin never would've sought me out if it wasn't for Jared."

"You broke up with him," Adrienne reminded her. "Maybe his pride kept him from chasing after you. Listen, I'm married to one of those guys. They're all about running their little empires. They're the king of their own kingdoms. In the business world, showing weakness is like throwing chum in the ocean—the sharks start circling. They keep it all inside for so long that after a while, they lose touch with their own sense of vulnerability."

Her boss knew what she was talking about. Adrienne's husband was Will Taylor, owner of one of the oldest and most successful newspapers in New York. He came from a long line of CEOs, just as Gavin had. Even then, she'd seen Adrienne and Will together multiple times, and he was putty in her hands. And happily so. Will at work and Will at home were completely different people.

But somehow Sabine had a hard time picturing Gavin with a marshmallow center beneath his hard candy shell. They'd shared some intimate moments together while they'd dated, but there was always an element of control on his part. They were together only a short time, but it was an intense relationship. She gave so much and yet he held back from her. She had no way of knowing the parts he kept hidden, but more than likely, it was his apathy. "You're saying he let me walk away and cried himself to sleep that night?"

Adrienne chuckled. "Well, maybe that's taking it a little far. But he might have had regrets and didn't know what to do about it. Jared gives him a good reason to see you again without having to address any of those icky, uncomfortable feelings."

A pair of ladies came into the shop, so they put their conversation on hold for now. While the women looked around, Sabine moved over to the checkout counter and crouched down to inventory the stock of pink boutique bags with Adrienne's signature across the side. The passive activity helped her think.

Feelings were definitely not Gavin's forte. Or at least sharing them. She was certain he had them, he just bottled them up on the inside. But feelings for her? She doubted that.

Gavin might be attracted to her. The kiss they shared might've been him testing the waters of resuming a physical relationship. They'd always had an undeniable chemistry. She knew the minute she saw him the first time that she was in trouble. It was at a gallery showing for a local contemporary artist. Sabine had gotten lost in the lines and colors of one of the pieces and the rest of the world disappeared.

At least until she heard the low rumble of a man's voice in her ear. "It looks like an expensive mistake to me."

She'd turned in surprise and nearly choked on a sip of champagne when she saw him. He wasn't at all the kind of man she was used to. He wore an expensive suit and a watch that cost more money than she'd made in the past year. Men like Gavin typically turned their nose up at Sabine. But he'd looked at her with dark eyes that twinkled with amusement and desire.

Her pulse had shot up, her knees melted to butter beneath her, and she'd found herself without a witty response. Just that quickly, she was lost.

The weeks that followed were some of the greatest of her life. But not once in that time had he ever looked at her with anything more than lust. So as much as she'd like to think Adrienne was right, she knew better. He'd either been using their attraction to his advantage or using their situation to get laid.

One of the ladies tried on a blouse and then bought it, along with a scarf. Sabine rang her up and they left the store. The chime of the door signaled that her conversation with Adrienne could resume.

"So where are you guys going on your playdate today?" Adrienne called from the stockroom.

"We're going to the Central Park Zoo."

"That should be fun," Adrienne said, returning to the front with her arms full of one of her newest dress designs. "Was that his idea?"

"No," Sabine chuckled. She reached out to take several of the outfits from her. "He didn't have a clue of what to do with a two-year-old. I suggested the zoo because I wanted us to do something that didn't involve a lot of money."

Adrienne wrinkled her delicate nose. "What do you mean?"

They carried the dresses over to the empty rack and organized them by size. "I don't want Gavin buying Jared anything yet. At least not big, expensive things. He used to tell me that his father only ever took him shopping. I can't keep him from buying things forever, but that's not how I want to start off."

"Money isn't a bad thing, Sabine. I never had it until I married Will, and trust me, it takes some adjusting to get used to having a lot of it. But it can be used for good, too, not just for evil."

"It's also not a substitute for love or attention. I want Gavin to really try. Right now, Jared is still young, but before too long, he's going to be in the 'gimme' stage. I don't want Gavin buying affection with expensive gifts."

"Try to keep an open mind," Adrienne suggested. "Just because he buys Jared something doesn't mean he isn't trying. If getting him a balloon makes Jared smile, don't read too much into it. Just enjoy your afternoon." Adrienne stopped and crinkled her nose, making a funny face at Sabine.

"What's the matter?"

"I don't know. My stomach is a little upset all of a sudden. I think my smoothie is turning on me. Either that, or I'm nauseated by all your drama."

Sabine laughed. "I'm sorry my crazy life is making you ill. I've got some antacids in my purse if you need them."

"I'll be fine," Adrienne insisted. She looked down at her watch. "You'd better get going if you're going to meet him on time. Worry about having fun instead."

Sabine nodded. "Okay," she said. "We will have a good time, I promise."

She hoped she was right.

As Gavin stepped out of his apartment building onto Central Park South and crossed the street, he realized just how long it had been since he'd actually set foot in Central Park. He looked out at it every day but never paid any attention to the looming green hulk that sprawled out in front of him.

His first clue was that he was a little overdressed for a summer afternoon at the zoo. He'd left the tie at home, but he probably could've forgone the suit coat, too. A pair of jeans or khakis and a polo shirt would've suited just fine. He considered running his jacket back upstairs, but he didn't want to be late.

When he was younger, he'd enjoyed jogging along the paths or hanging out and playing Frisbee with friends in the Sheep Meadow. The more involved he got in the management of BXS, the less important trees and sunshine seemed in his agenda. He and Sabine had taken a horse-drawn carriage through the park one evening when they were dating, but the closest he had gotten to it since then was a gala at the Met last year.

By the time he reached the front entrance to the zoo, he could feel the sweat forming along his spine. He slipped out of the jacket and threw it over his arm after rolling up his sleeves. It helped, but not much. He was supposed to meet Sabine and Gavin just outside the brick archways that marked the entrance, but he didn't see them anywhere.

He unclipped his phone from his belt to look at the time. He was a few minutes early. He opted to flip through some emails. He'd hit a little bit of a snag with the Exclusivity Jetliners merger. The owner's son, Paul, had found out about his father's plans and was throwing a fit. Apparently he wasn't pleased about watching his inheritance getting sold off. Gavin was paying a pretty penny for the company, but Roger's son seemed to fancy playing CEO. Roger was starting to second-guess the sale.

He fired off a couple quick emails, but his attention was piqued by the sound of a child's laughter in the distance. It was one of those contagious giggles that made you smile just to hear it. He looked up in the direction of the sound and saw Sabine and Jared playing in the shade of a large tree.

Slipping his cell phone back in the holster, he made his way over to where they were. Sabine was crouched down beside Jared, dressed in capris and a tank top. Her dark hair was pulled back into a ponytail and a bright red backpack was slung over her shoulders.

Jared was playing with another one of his trucks. In the mud. Apparently, the kid had managed to find the only mud bog in the park. He was crouched barefoot in the brown muck, ramming his trucks through the sludge. He made loud truck noises with his mouth and then giggled hysterically when the mud splashed up onto his shirt. He was head-to-toe filthy and happy as a little piglet.

Gavin's instinct was to grab Jared and get him out of the dirt immediately. There had to be a restroom somewhere nearby where they could rinse him off. But then he saw the smile on Sabine's face. She wasn't even remotely concerned about what Jared was doing.

His mother would've had a fit if she had found him playing in the mud. His nanny would've had to hose him off outside and then thoroughly scrub him in the tub. When he was dry, he would've been given a lengthy lecture about how getting dirty was inappropriate and his nanny would've been fired for not keeping a better eye on him.

Jared dropped one of the trucks in the puddle and the water splashed up, splattering both him and Sabine. Gavin expected her to get upset since she'd gotten dirty now, but she just laughed and wiped the smear of muddy water off her arm. It was amazing. It made Gavin want to get dirty, too.

"Oh, hey," Sabine said, looking up to see him standing nearby. She glanced at her watch. "I'm sorry to keep you waiting. We got here a little early and Jared can't pass up some good mud." She stood up and whipped the backpack off her shoulders.

"Not a problem," he said as he watched her pull out

an assortment of things including wet wipes, a large, plastic zip bag and a clean shirt.

"All right, buddy," she said. "Time to go to the zoo with Gavin. Are you ready?"

"Yeah!" Jared said, immediately perking up at the suggestion of a new adventure.

"Give me your trucks first." She put all the muddy toys in the bag and then used his dirty shirt to wipe up a good bit of the muck off his hands and feet before shoving it in there, as well. The baby wipes made quick work of the rest, then the clean shirt and the little socks and sneakers she'd taken off went back on. "Good job!" she praised, giving him a tiny high five and zipping up the backpack.

Gavin was amazed by the process. Not only did she let Jared get dirty, she was fully prepared for the eventuality. He'd always just thought of Sabine as the artistic type. She was laid-back and went with the flow as he expected, but she also had a meticulous bit of planning underneath it all that he appreciated. She had the motherhood thing down. It was very impressive.

"We're ready," she said, bending down to pick Jared up.

Gavin had to smile when he noticed the speck of mud on Sabine's cheek. "Not quite yet," he said. Without thinking, he reached out to her, running the pad of his thumb across her cheekbone and wiping it away. The moment he touched her, he sensed a change in the energy between them. Her pale green eyes widened, the irises darkening in the center to the deep hunter green he remembered from their lovemaking. A soft gasp of surprise escaped her glossy pink lips.

His body reacted, as well. The touch brought on the

familiar tingle that settled between his shoulder blades and sent a shot of pure need down his spine. He wanted Sabine. There was no use in denying it. There was something about her that spoke to his most base instincts. Their time apart hadn't changed or dulled the attraction. In fact, it seemed to have amplified it.

That night at her apartment, he had to kiss her. There was no way he could walk out of there without tasting her again. Once he did, he could feel the floodgates giving way. He had to leave. And right then. If he had lingered a moment longer, he wouldn't have been able to stop himself.

Their relationship was complicated. There were a lot of proverbial balls still in the air. He wasn't dumb enough to get emotionally involved with Sabine again, but leaping back into a physical relationship with her, at least this soon, was a bad idea, too. For now, he needed to try and keep his distance on both fronts.

Why, then, was he standing in the middle of Central Park cradling Sabine's face with a throbbing erection? Because he was a masochist.

"A…uh…stray bit of Jared's handiwork," he said. He let his hand drop back to his side before he did something stupid in public. Instead, he turned to look at Jared. "Are you ready to see the monkeys?"

"Yeah!" he cheered, clapping his chubby hands together.

They bought their tickets and headed inside. Starting at the sea lion pool, they made their way around to visit the penguins and the snow leopards. He enjoyed watching his son's eyes light up when he saw the animals.

"Do you guys come here a lot?" he asked, leaning on

the railing outside the snow monkey exhibit. "He really seems to like it."

"We actually haven't been here before. I was waiting until he was a little older. This seemed like the perfect opportunity."

Gavin was surprised. Somehow he'd thought he had missed all his son's firsts, but there were more to be had than he expected. "I've never been here, either."

Sabine looked at him with disbelief lining her brow. "You've lived in New York your whole life and you've never been to the zoo?"

"Saying I lived here my whole life isn't entirely accurate. My family lived here, but I was gone off to school a lot of the time."

"So not even as a child? Your nannies never brought you here?"

"Nope. Sometimes we came to the park to play or walk, but never to the zoo. I'm not sure why. My boarding school took a field trip to Washington, D.C., once. We went to the Smithsonian and the National Zoo on that trip. I think I was fourteen or so. But I've never had the chance to come here."

"Have you ever been to a petting zoo?"

At that, Gavin had to laugh. "A petting zoo? Absolutely not. My mother would have a fit at the thought of me touching dirty animals. I never even had pets as a kid."

Sabine wrinkled her nose at him. "Well, then, today is your day. We'll head over to the children's zoo after this and you and Jared can both pet your first goat."

A goat? He wasn't so sure that he was interested in that. Sabine seemed to sense his hesitation. "Maybe we can start you off slow. You can hold a rabbit. They have places to wash your hands. I also have hand sanitizer in my bag. You'll be okay, I promise."

Gavin chuckled at Sabine. She was mothering him just the same as she did to coax Jared into trying something new. He wasn't used to that.

They were on their way to the children's zoo when he felt his cell phone buzzing at his hip. He looked down at the screen. It was Roger. He had to take this call.

"Excuse me one minute," he said.

Sabine frowned but nodded. "I'll take Jared to the restroom while we're waiting."

Gavin answered the phone and spent the next ten minutes soothing Roger's concerns. He didn't want this opportunity to slip through his fingers. Acquiring those private jets was as close to fulfilling his childhood dream as he might ever get. He had a plane of his own, but it was small and didn't have anywhere near the range of Roger's jets. He longed for the day when he could pilot one of those planes to some far-off destination. He was a falcon on a tether now. He wanted to fly free, and he wasn't going to let Paul Simpson's desire to play at CEO ruin it.

It was going well so far. He was able to address all of Roger's concerns. Things might be back on track if he could keep the owner focused on what was best for his family and his company. But it was taking some time. The conversation was still going when Sabine returned. She didn't seem pleased.

He covered the receiver with his hand. "I'm almost done. I can walk and talk," he said.

She turned and started walking away with Jared. He followed close behind them, but he was admittedly distracted. By the time he finally hung up, Gavin had already missed out on feeding the ducks. Jared was quacking and clumsily chasing one at the moment.

Sabine was watching him play with a twinkle in her eye. She loved their son so much. He could tell that Jared was everything to her. He appreciated that about her. His parents had never been abusive or cruel, but they had been distant. Busy. They weren't hands-on at all. Jared hadn't had all the privileges that Gavin grew up with, but he did have a loving, doting mother.

Who was frowning intently at Gavin.

"I'm sorry," he said. "It was important."

She shook her head and turned back to look at Jared. One of the zoo employees was holding a rabbit so he could pet it. "That's the most important thing, right there, Gavin."

Jared turned around and grinned at his mother with such joy it made Gavin's chest hurt. "A bunny," he exclaimed, hopping around on his little legs like a rabbit.

She was right. He needed to be in this 100 percent. Jared deserved it. And so did Sabine.

Five

There was a knock on the door early Sunday morning. Sabine was making pancakes while Jared played with blocks on the floor. Sunday was their easy day. There was no work or preschool. They were both still in their pajamas and not expecting company.

She was surprised to find Gavin on her doorstep. She was even more surprised to find he was wearing jeans and a T-shirt. It was a Gucci T-shirt, but at least it wasn't a suit. And it looked good on him. The black shirt fit his muscular frame like a second skin, reminding her of the body he hid beneath blazers and ties. And the jeans… they were snug in all the right places, making her mouth go dry in an instant.

He caught her so off guard, she didn't notice at first that he had a large canvas and a bag of painting supplies in his hands.

"Gavin," she said. "I wasn't expecting you this morning." After yesterday, she didn't figure she would see him until the test results came back. She could tell that he was trying yesterday, but his thoughts were being pulled in ten different directions. Even after he got off the phone, he was checking it constantly and replying to emails. He had a business to run.

And yet, here he was.

"I know. I wanted it to be a surprise."

Sabine wasn't big on surprises. With Gavin, it was more that he wanted to do something his way and to keep her from arguing, he wouldn't tell her until the last second. Surprise! But still, she was curious. "Come on in," she said.

Gavin stepped in, leaning the canvas against the bookcase. "Hey, big guy," he said to Jared. He got up from his blocks and came over to hug Gavin's leg. Gavin scooped the toddler up and held him over his head, and then they "soared" around the living room making airplane noises. Jared the Plane crash-landed onto the couch in a fit of giggles and tickling fingers poking at his tummy.

It had only been a few days, but she could tell that Jared was getting attached to Gavin. It was a good thing. She knew that. But still, she worried. He'd put in a decent effort so far, but could he keep it up for the next sixteen years? She wasn't sure. But she did know that he'd better not screw this up.

"I was making pancakes," she said, turning and heading back into the kitchen. "Have you had breakfast?"

"That depends," he said, pausing in the tickle fight. "What kind of pancakes are they?"

"Silver-dollar pancakes with blueberries."

"Nope." Gavin smiled. "I haven't had breakfast." He let Jared return to his blocks. "I'll be right back, big guy."

He followed her into the kitchen, leaning against the entryway. The kitchen was too small for both of them to be in there and get anything done. She tried to ignore his physical presence and how much of the room he took up without even entering, but she failed. The sight of him in those tight jeans was more than she could take. Her body instantly reacted to his nearness, her mouth going dry and her nipples pebbling against the thin fabric of her T-shirt.

She spun to face the stove before he could notice and decided to focus on pancakes, not the sexy man lurking nearby. Eyeing the batter, she decided she needed a larger batch to feed a man of his size. "So what brings you here this morning?"

Gavin watched her fold in another handful of dried blueberries. "I wanted to make up for yesterday."

Sabine tried not to react. She was happy that he was making the effort, but failing Jared and then making a grand gesture to appease his conscience was a dangerous cycle. She'd rather he just be present the first time. "How's that?"

"I saw in the paper that the Big Apple Circus is here. I got tickets for this afternoon."

Just as she'd thought. She had no problems with going to the circus, but he didn't ask her. He didn't call to see if that was something they might want to do. What if Jared was petrified of clowns? Or if they had other plans today? Gavin just bought the tickets and assumed that everything would go the way he'd planned.

But—he was trying, she reminded herself. "Jared

would probably enjoy that. What time do we need to leave for the show?"

"Well," Gavin said, "that's only part of the surprise. *We* aren't leaving. You're staying."

Sabine looked up from the griddle. "What do you mean?"

"I just got tickets for Jared and me. I thought you might enjoy an afternoon to yourself. I even brought you some painting supplies."

That explained the stuff he brought in with him. She'd been so thrown off by his unannounced arrival that she hadn't questioned it yet. She supposed that she should be excited and grateful, but instead, her stomach ached with worry. Gavin was taking her son someplace without her. She didn't really like the sound of that. He didn't know anything about children. What if Jared got sick? Or scared? Did Gavin even know that Jared wasn't fully potty trained yet? Just the idea of him changing dirty Pull-Ups started a rumble of nervous laughter in her chest that she fought down.

"I don't think that's a good idea," she managed to say.

Gavin's dark brow drew together in consternation. "Why not? You said you wanted me to be there. To be involved."

"It's been less than a week, Gavin. You've spent a couple hours with him, sure, but are you ready to take care of him on your own for a day?" Sabine turned back to the stove and flipped over the pancakes. She grabbed one of Jared's superhero plates and slid a couple tiny pancakes onto it beside the slices of banana she'd already cut up.

"You don't think I can handle it?"

She sighed heavily. Ignoring him, she poured some

blueberry syrup into the small bowl built into the dish and grabbed a sippy cup with milk from the refrigerator. She brushed past him to go into the living room. Jared had a tiny plastic table and chair where he could eat. She set down his breakfast and called him over. Once he was settled, she turned back to look at Gavin. He was still standing in the doorway to the kitchen looking handsome and irritated all at once.

"I don't know," she admitted. "I don't know if you can handle it or not. That's the problem. We don't really know one another that well."

Gavin crossed his arms over his chest and leaned against the door frame. His biceps bulged against the constraints of the shirt, drawing her eyes down to his strong forearms and rock-hard chest. It was easier to focus on that than the strangely cocky expression on his face.

"We know each other *very* well," he said with a wicked grin curling his lips.

Sabine approached him, stopping just short of touching him. "Your ability to give me an orgasm has no bearing on whether or not you can care for a toddler."

At the mention of the word *orgasm* his gaze narrowed at her. He swallowed hard but didn't reach for her. "I disagree. Both require an attention to detail. Anticipating what another person wants or needs. I don't think it matters if what they need is a drink, a toy or a mind-blowing physical release."

Mind-blowing. Sabine couldn't stop her tongue from gliding out over her lips. They'd gotten painfully dry. His gaze dropped to her mouth, then back to her eyes. There was a touch of amusement in his gaze. He knew he was getting to her.

"What if what they need is their poopy diaper changed? Or you gave them too much cotton candy and they spew blue muck all over the backseat of your Mercedes? Not quite as sexy."

The light of attraction in his eyes faded. It was hard to keep up the arousal with that kind of imagery. That's why she hadn't bothered dating in all this time. Maybe she should reconsider. She might not feel as vulnerable to Gavin's charms if she had an outlet that didn't involve him.

His expression hardened for a moment. He seemed irritated with her. "Stop trying to scare me away. I know taking care of a child isn't easy. It can be messy. But it's just a few hours to start. I can handle it. Will you let me do this for you? Please?"

"Do this for *me?* Shouldn't you be doing this for your son?"

"I am. Of course, I am. I want a relationship with Jared more than anything. But to do that, you have got to trust me. I will return him to you tonight, well fed, well cared for and, for the most part, clean. But you have to do your part. You have to let me try. Let me mess up. Enjoy your free afternoon. Paint something beautiful because you can. Go get a pedicure."

Sabine had to admit that sounded wonderful. She hadn't had an afternoon to herself since she went into labor. She didn't have any family here to watch Jared. She tried to only use Tina's services when she had to for classes. She hadn't had a day just to relax. And to paint…

She pushed past him into the kitchen to finish making pancakes. Gavin stayed in the doorway, allowing her the space to think, while also keeping an eye on Jared. She appreciated having someone to do that. She hadn't had another set of eyes to help before. Since Jared became mobile, she hadn't been able to shower, cook or do anything without constantly peeking out to check on him. Life was a little easier when he sat in his swing or bouncy chair while she did what needed to be done.

A whole afternoon?

She wanted to say yes, but she couldn't shake the worry. It was probably going to be fine. There was only so much trouble that could befall them in an afternoon at the circus. If Jared came home covered in blue vomit, the world wouldn't end. And it was a family-oriented event. She had no doubt that if another mother saw Gavin and Jared in a meltdown moment, she would step in to help.

Sabine finished the pancakes and turned off the burner. She slid a stack onto her plate and the other onto a plate for Gavin. Turning around, she offered one to him. When he reached for it, she pulled it back slightly.

"Okay," she said. "You can go. But I want you to text and check in with me. And if anything remotely worrisome happens—"

Gavin took the plate from her. "I will call you immediately. Okay?"

Sharing Jared with someone else was going to be hard, she could tell already. But it could be good, too. Two parents were double the hands, double the eyes, double the love. Right? "Okay, all right. You win. Just don't feed him too much sugar. You'll regret it."

Gavin couldn't remember being this tired, ever. Not when he was on the college rowing team. Not when he stayed up late studying for an exam. Not even after spending all night making love to a beautiful woman. How on earth did parents do this every day? How did

Sabine manage to care for Jared alone, work full-time, teach yoga…it was no wonder she'd stopped painting. He was bone-tired. Mentally exhausted.

And it was one of the best days of his life.

Seeing Jared's smile made everything worth it. That was what kept parents going. That moment his son's face lit up when he saw an elephant for the first time. Or the sound of his laughter when the clowns were up to their wacky antics.

The day hadn't been without its mishaps. Jared had dropped his ice cream and went into a full, five-alarm meltdown. Gavin knew Sabine didn't want him buying a bunch of things, but he gladly threw down the cash for the overpriced light-up sword to quiet him down. There was also a potty emergency that was timed just as they neared the front of the mile-long food line. Sabine had begun potty training recently and had told him that if Jared asked, they were to go, right then. So they did. And ended up at the end of the line, waiting another twenty minutes for hot dogs and popcorn.

But the world hadn't ended. There had been no tragedies, and he texted as much to Sabine every hour or so. The day had been filled with lights and sound and excitement. So much so that by the time they made it back to the apartment, Jared was out cold. Gavin knew exactly how he felt.

He carried the exhausted toddler inside, quietly tapping at the apartment door so as to not wake him up. When Sabine didn't answer, he tried the knob and found it unlocked. He expected to find Sabine frantically painting. This was her chance, after all, to indulge her suppressed creativity. Instead, she was curled up on the couch, asleep.

Gavin smiled. He had told her to spend the afternoon doing whatever she wanted. He should've guessed that a nap would be pretty high on the list. He tiptoed quietly through the living room and into the bedroom. Following the routine from Thursday night, he laid Jared in the crib and stripped him down into just his T-shirt and shorts. He covered him with the blanket and turned out the lights.

Sabine was still asleep when he came out. He knew he couldn't leave without waking her up, but he couldn't bear to disturb her. He eased down at the end of the couch and decided to just wait until she woke up.

He enjoyed watching Sabine sleep. She had always been one to work hard and play hard, so when she slept, it was a deep sleep and it came on quickly. There were many nights where he had lain in bed and just studied her face. Gavin had memorized every line and curve. He'd counted her eyelashes. There was just something about her that had fascinated him from the first moment he saw her.

The weeks they'd spent together were intense. He couldn't get enough of her. Sabine was a breath of fresh air to a man hanging from the gallows. She'd brought him back to life with her rebellious streak and quest for excitement. He'd loved everything about her, from her dazzling smile to her ever-changing rainbow-streaked hair. He'd loved how there was always a speck of paint somewhere on her body, even if he had to do a detailed search to find it. She was so different from every other woman he'd ever known.

For the first time, he'd allowed himself to start opening up to someone. He'd begun making plans for Sabine to be a permanent fixture in his life. He hadn't anticipated her bolting, and when she did, he shut down. Gavin hadn't allowed himself to realize just how much he'd missed her until this moment.

She didn't trust him. Not with her son and not with her heart. Gavin hadn't appreciated it when he had it— at least not outwardly. He never told her how he felt or shared his plans for their future. That was his own fault, and they missed their chance at love. But even with that lost, he wanted her back in his bed. He ached to run his fingers through her hair. Tonight, it was pulled up on top of her head, the silky black and bright purple strands jumbled together. He wanted to touch it and see it sprawled across the pillowcase.

His eyes traveled down her body to the thin shirt and shorts she was wearing. He didn't think it was possible, but she was more beautiful now than she had been back then. She wouldn't believe him if he told her that, but it was true. Motherhood had filled out some of the curves she'd lacked as a struggling artist. He remembered her getting so engrossed in her work that sometimes she would simply forget to eat. Gavin would come to the apartment with takeout and force her to take a break.

Now she had nicely rounded hips that called to him to reach out and glide his palms over them. He wanted to curl up behind her and press her soft body into his. He wanted to feel her lean, yoga-toned muscles flexing against him. The sight of her in that skimpy workout outfit had haunted him since that first night.

Her newly developed muscles didn't make up for the mental strain, however. Even in her sleep, a fine line ran between her eyebrows. She made a certain face when she was frustrated or confused, and that line was the result. There were faint circles under her eyes. She was worn out. He was determined to make things easier for her. No matter how their relationship ended or his feelings where she was concerned, she deserved the help he could provide.

She just had to let him.

"Gavin," Sabine whispered.

He looked up, expecting to see her eyes open, but she was talking in her sleep. Calling his name in her sleep. He held his breath, waiting to see if she spoke again.

"Please," she groaned, squirming slightly on the sofa. "Yes. I need you."

Gavin nearly choked on his own saliva. She wasn't just dreaming about him. She was having an erotic dream about him. The mere thought made his jeans uncomfortably tight.

"Touch me."

Gavin couldn't resist. He reached out and placed his hand on the firm curve of her calf. He loved the feel of her soft skin against him. It made his palm tingle and his blood hum in his veins. Just a simple touch. No other woman had had this effect on him. Whatever it was that drew them together was still here, and as strong as ever.

"Gavin?"

He looked up to see Sabine squinting at him in confusion. She was awake now. And probably wondering why the hell he was fondling her leg. He expected her to shy away from his touch, but she didn't. Instead, she sat up. She looked deep into his eyes for a moment, the fire of her passionate dream still lighting her gaze.

She reached up, cradling his face in her hands and tugging his mouth down to hers. He wasn't about to deny her. The moment their lips met, he felt the familiar surge of need wash over him. Before when they'd kissed, he had resisted the pull, but he couldn't do it any longer. He wanted her and she wanted him. They could deal with the consequences of it later.

Her mouth was hungry, demanding more of him, and he gave it. His tongue thrust inside her, matching her intensity and eliciting a groan deep in her throat. Her fingers drifted into his hair, desperately tugging him closer.

Gavin wrapped his arms around her waist and drew her up onto her knees. He explored every new curve of her body just as he'd fantasized, dipping low to cup the roundness of her backside. The firm press of her flesh against his fingertips was better than he ever could have imagined. He didn't think it was possible, but he grew even harder as he touched her.

Sabine's hands roamed as well, sliding down his chest, studying the ridges of his abs and then reaching around his back. She grasped the hem of his shirt and tugged until their lips parted and it came up and over his head. She did the same with her own shirt, throwing it to the floor and revealing full breasts with no bra to obscure them.

Before he could reach out to touch them, Sabine leaned back, cupping his neck with one hand and pulling him with her until she was lying on the couch and he was covering her body with his. Every soft inch of her molded to him. Her breasts crushed against his bare chest, the hard peaks of her nipples pressing insistently into his skin.

Gavin kissed her again and then let his lips roam along her jaw and down her throat. He teased at her sensitive skin, nipping gently with his teeth and soothing it with his tongue. He brought one palm to her breast, teasing the aching tip with slow circles and then massaging it with firm fingers. Sabine gasped aloud, her hips rising to meet his.

"I want you so badly," Gavin whispered against her collarbone.

Sabine didn't reply, but her hand eased between their bodies to unzip his jeans. She brought one finger up to her lips to gesture for him to be quiet, then her hand slipped under the waistband of his briefs. He fought for silence as her fingers wrapped around the length of him and stroked gently. He buried a moan against her breast, trying not to lose his grip of control. She knew just how to push him, just how to touch him to make him unravel.

He brushed her hand away and eased between her legs. He thrust his hips forward, creating a delicious friction as he rubbed against her through the thin cotton of her shorts.

"Ohh..." she whispered, her eyes closing.

She was so beautiful. He couldn't wait to watch her come undone. To bury himself deep inside her again after all this time.

"Please," he groaned, "tell me that you have something we can use." Gavin got up this morning thinking he was taking his son to the circus. He wasn't a teenager walking around with a condom in his pocket all the time. He hadn't come prepared for this.

Her eyes fluttered open, their green depths dark with desire. "I had an IUD put in after Jared was born," she said.

"Is that enough?" he asked.

At that, Sabine laughed. "It's supposed to be 99.8 percent effective, but with your super sperm, who knows? The condom didn't work so well for us the last time."

"Super sperm," Gavin snorted before dipping down

and kissing her again. "Do you want me to stop?" he asked. He would if she wanted him to, as much as that would kill him. But she needed to decide now.

"Don't you dare," she said, piercing him with her gaze.

With a growl, he buried his face in her neck. His hand grasped at the waist of her shorts, tugging them and her panties down over her hips. She arched up to help him and then kicked them off to the floor.

Sabine pushed at his jeans without success until Gavin finally eased back to take them off. She watched him with careful study as he kicked off his shoes and slipped out of the last of his clothes.

He looked down at her, nude and wanting, and his chest swelled with pride. She was sexy and free and waiting for him. As he watched, she reached up and untied her hair. The long strands fell down over her shoulders, the ends teasing at the tips of her breasts.

He couldn't wait any longer. Gavin returned to the couch, easing between her thighs. He sought her out first with his hand. Stroking gently, his fingertips slid easily over her sensitive flesh, causing her to whimper with need.

"Gavin," she pleaded, her voice little more than a breath.

His hand continued to move over her until she was panting and squirming beneath him. Then he slipped one finger inside. Sabine threw her head back, a cry strangling to silence in her throat. She was ready for him.

Gavin propped onto one elbow and gripped her hip with his other hand. Surging forward, he pressed into the slick heat of her welcoming body. He lost himself in the pleasure for a moment, absorbing every delicious sensation before flexing his hips and driving into her again.

Sabine clung to him, burying her face in his shoulder to muffle her gasps and cries. She met his every advance, whispering words of encouragement into his ear. The intensity built, moment by moment, until he knew she was close.

Her eyes squeezed shut, her mouth falling open in silent gasps. He put every ounce of energy he had left into pushing her over the edge. He was rewarded with the soft shudder of her body against him, the muscles deep inside clenching around him. The string of tension in his belly drew tighter and tighter until it snapped. He thrust hard, exploding into her with a low growl of satisfaction.

They both collapsed against the couch cushions in a panting, gasping heap. No sooner had they recovered than Gavin heard Jared crying in the other room.

Sabine pressed against his chest until he backed off. She quickly tugged on her clothes and disappeared into the bedroom.

Things were officially more complicated.

Six

Jared went back down fairly quickly. Sabine changed his Pull-Ups, put him in his pajamas and he fell asleep in minutes. Even then, she stayed in her bedroom longer than necessary. Going back into the living room meant facing what she'd just done. She wasn't quite ready for that yet.

Damn that stupid, erotic dream. When she fell asleep on the couch, she never expected to sleep that long. Or that she would have a sexual fantasy about Gavin while he was sitting there watching her. When she opened her eyes and he was touching her with the spark of passion in his eyes, she had to have him. She needed him.

And now it was done. She'd refused his proposal of marriage because he didn't love her, yet she'd just slept with him. She was throwing mixed signals left, right and center.

But she had to go back out there eventually. Steeling

her resolve, she exited the bedroom and pulled the door shut behind her. She made a quick stop in the restroom first, cleaning up and smoothing her hair back into a ponytail. When she returned to the living room, Gavin was fully dressed and sitting on the couch.

"Everything okay?" he asked.

"Yeah," she said. "He's back to sleep now. He probably won't wake up again until the morning." She nervously ran her hands over her shorts, not sure what to do with herself. "Did you guys have fun today?"

"We did. He's a very well-behaved kid. Gave me almost no trouble. Almost," he said with a smile.

Sabine was glad. She'd worried so much about them that she couldn't paint. At least at first. She'd tried, but it had been so long since she'd painted that she didn't know where to start. Instead, she'd taken a long, leisurely shower and indulged in extended grooming rituals she usually had to rush, like plucking her eyebrows and painting her toenails. One of her favorite chick flicks was on TV, so she sat down to watch it, and the next thing she knew, she was nodding off. She'd only expected to sleep for a half hour or so.

"I'm glad it went well." She eyed the spot on the couch where she'd just been and decided she wasn't quite ready to sit there yet. "Would you like some wine? I'm going to pour myself a glass."

"Sure," he said with a soft smile.

Sabine could tell this was awkward for him, too. And yet, he could've turned her down and left. But he didn't. She disappeared into the kitchen and returned a few minutes later with two glasses of merlot. "It came out of a box, but I like it," she said.

Gavin smiled in earnest, taking a large sip, then another. "It's pretty good," he admitted with surprise.

She sat down beside him and took her own sip. The wine seemed to flow directly into her veins, relaxing her immediately.

He pointed over at the blank canvas. "I'm surprised you didn't paint at all today."

Sabine looked at the white expanse that had been her nemesis for a good part of the afternoon. She couldn't count how many times she'd put her pencil to the canvas to sketch the bones of a scene and then stopped. "I think I've forgotten how to paint."

"That's not possible," Gavin argued. "You just need the right inspiration. I put you on the spot today. I bet if you relax and let the creative juices flow without the pressure of time, the ideas will come again."

"I hope so."

"You're too gifted to set your dream aside. Even for Jared. We can work together to get you back to what you love. I mean, after we get the results and I have visitation rights, you'll have more free time to yourself."

That was the wrong thing to say. She had been nervous enough about tomorrow and the lab results that were coming in. Knowing he was already planning to "exercise his rights" and take Jared for long stretches of time just made her chest tight with anxiety. It was a sharp reminder that even after they'd had sex, he was really here for Jared, not her. He hadn't mentioned anything about *all* of them spending time together. Or just the two of them. Any fantasies she had about there being any sort of family unit cobbled out of this mess were just that.

"And what about you?" she said, her tone a bit sharper than she'd planned. "You seem as wrapped up in the business as ever. We couldn't get you off your phone yesterday. I'm thinking you don't have much time to get in the cockpit anymore."

"It's been a while," he admitted. "But I'm working on it. All those calls I was taking at the zoo," he said, "were about a big deal I'm trying to pull together. Things were unraveling and I couldn't let it happen."

Sabine listened as he described his plans for BXS and Exclusivity Jetliners. It really did seem like a brilliant plan. There were plenty of wealthy and important people who would pay a premium for that kind of service. That didn't mean she appreciated it interloping on their day out together, but she could see it was important to him and not just day-to-day management crap.

"I'm hoping to fly one, too."

Her brows went up in surprise. "Did you get demoted from CEO to pilot?"

"I wish," he groaned. "But I've always wanted a Gulf-stream model jet. The ones we're acquiring could go over four thousand miles on one tank of gas. That could get me to Paris. I've always dreamed of flying across the Atlantic. But even if I can't manage that, I can take one out from time to time. Even if it's just to do a delivery. I don't care. I just want to get out from behind the desk and get up there. It's the only place I can ever find any peace."

She understood that. Yoga did a lot to help center her mind and spirit, but nothing came close to losing herself in her art.

"I want more time out of the office, and Jared finally gives me a real reason to do it. There's no point in work-life balance when you've got no life. But spending time with Jared needs to be a priority for me. I've already missed so much."

Sabine was impressed by his heartfelt words. Gavin had quickly become enamored with Jared, and she was glad. Part of her had always worried that he might reject his son. The other part worried that he'd claim him with such force that he'd rip her child from her arms. This seemed a healthy medium. Maybe this wouldn't be so bad. He was trying.

"I found a great apartment in Greenwich Village overlooking Washington Square Park," he said. "It has three bedrooms and it's close to the subway."

Sabine took a large sip of her wine. Here we go, she thought. "I thought you liked your apartment," she said, playing dumb. "Getting tired of living at the Ritz-Carlton?"

Gavin frowned. "What? No. Not for me. For you. I'd prefer you to be closer to me, but I know you'd rather live downtown. You work in SoHo, right? You could easily walk to work from this apartment."

Walking to work. She wouldn't even allow herself to fantasize about a life without a long train commute each day. Or three bedrooms where she didn't have to share with Jared. "I'm pretty sure it's out of my budget."

Gavin set his wine down on the coffee table. "I told you I wanted to help. Let me buy you an apartment."

"And I told you I wanted to take this slowly. I probably couldn't even afford the maintenance fee, much less the taxes or the mortgage itself. Homeowner's insurance. The utilities on a place that large would be through the roof."

He turned in his seat to face her, his serious businessman expression studying her. "How much is your rent here?"

"Gavin, I—"

He interrupted her with a number that was fewer than fifty dollars off the mark.

"Yes, pretty much," she admitted, reluctantly.

"Tack on a couple hundred for utilities and such. So what if I bought an apartment and rented it to you for the same amount you're paying now? That would be fair, right? You wouldn't have to worry about all the fees associated with owning the place."

She did have to admit that she preferred this idea. If she had to pay rent, she would continue working. She liked her job and wanted to keep doing it. But a three-bedroom apartment in the Village for the price of what she paid for a tiny place beyond the reach of the subway lines? That was insanity.

"That's a ridiculous suggestion. My rent is less than a tenth of what the mortgage on that kind of apartment would be."

Gavin shrugged. "I'm not concerned. You could live there rent-free for all I care. I just thought you would feel more comfortable if you contributed."

"There's a difference between helping us out and buying us a multimillion-dollar apartment."

"I want you close," he said. His dark eyes penetrated hers with an intensity that made her squirm slightly with a flush rising to her pale cheeks. Did he really mean *her*?

Sabine opened her mouth to argue, but he held up his hand to silence her protest. "I mean," he corrected, "living in Manhattan will make it easier to handle the custody arrangements and trade-offs. When he starts at his new school, he would be closer. It would be safer. More convenient for everyone."

Just as she thought. He wanted Jared close, not her. At least not for any reason more than the occasional booty call. "Especially for you," she snapped, irritably.

"And you!" he added. "If I got things my way, the two of you would just move in with me. That's certainly the cheapest option, since you seem so concerned about how much I spend, but I thought you would like having your own space better."

She must seem like the most ungrateful person on the planet, but she knew what this was. A slippery slope. He would push, push, push until he had things just the way he wanted them. If he wanted them—or Jared, she should say—living with him, eventually he would. This apartment in the Village would just be a pit stop to make it look as if he was being reasonable.

"I know it's a pain for you to drive all the way out here every time you want to see Jared. And I know that you and I just…" Her voice trailed off.

"Had sex?" he offered.

"Yes," she said with a heavy sigh. "But that doesn't change anything between us or about the things we've already discussed. We're not moving at all. Not in with you and not into that apartment. It sounds nice, but it's too soon. When we're ready, perhaps we could look together. I'd like some say in the decision, even if you're writing the checks. I'm pretty sure the place I pick will be significantly cheaper."

"I'm not concerned with the cost of keeping my child happy and safe."

A painful twinge nagged at Sabine right beneath her sternum. She should be happy the father of her child was willing to lay out millions for the health and welfare of their child. But a part of her was jealous. He was always so quick to point out that this was about their son. Each time he mentioned it, it was like he was poking the gaping wound of her heart with a sharp stick. She would benefit from the arrangement, but none of this was about her. The sex didn't change anything, just like it didn't change anything three years ago. He was attracted to her, but she was not his priority and never was.

"Thank you," she choked out. "I appreciate that you're so willing to create a stable, safe home for our son. Let's give it a week to sink in, all right? We've got a lot of hurdles to jump before we add real estate to the mix."

Gavin eyed her for a moment before silently nodding. Sabine knew this was anything but a victory. She was only pushing off the inevitable. He would get his way eventually.

He always did.

When Gavin arrived at Dr. Peterson's office at 10:00 a.m. Monday morning, Sabine was already there. She was lost in a fashion magazine and didn't notice him come in. "Morning," he said.

Sabine looked up and gave him a watery smile. "Hey." She looked a little out of sorts. Maybe she was nervous. Things would change after this and she probably knew it.

"Where's Jared?" he asked.

The smile faded. She slung the magazine she'd been reading onto the seat beside her. "At school, where he belongs. I'm sorry to disappoint, but you're stuck with me today."

He'd screwed up last night, he could tell. Not in seducing her—that would never be a bad idea—but in forcing the idea of the apartment on her. Anyone else would jump at the offer, but to her, it was him imposing on her. Demanding they be closer so he could see his son more easily. Not once mentioning that he'd like *her* closer as well because that opened the door to dangerous territory.

Sabine was skittish. She scared off easily last time. He wasn't about to tell her that he wanted to see her more because he was still fighting himself over the idea of it. He was usually pretty good at keeping his distance from people, but he'd already let Sabine in once. Keeping her out the second time was harder than he expected. Especially when he didn't want to. He wanted her in his bed. Across from him at a nice restaurant. Certainly he could have that and not completely lose himself to her.

"That's scarcely a hardship," he said, seating himself in the empty chair beside her. "I find your company to be incredibly…*stimulating*."

Sabine crossed her arms over her chest and smothered a snort of disbelief. "Well, you'll be stimulating yourself from now on. Last night was—"

"Awesome?" he interjected. Their physical connection could never be anything less.

"A mistake."

"Sometimes a mistake can be a happy accident. Like Jared, a happy accident."

Her moss-green eyes narrowed at him. "And sometimes it's just a mistake. Like sleeping with your ex when you're in the middle of a custody negotiation."

Gavin nodded and leaned into her, crossing his own arms. She really thought last night was a mistake? He hadn't picked up on it at the time. She was probably just worried it would give him the upper hand somehow. Knowing just how to touch a woman was always an advantage, but he didn't intend to use that knowledge against her. At least outside the bedroom.

"So I suppose you've got no business going to dinner with me tonight, either."

Her gaze ran over his face, trying to read into his motives. "Listen, Gavin," she started with a shake of her head. "I know I told you that I wanted you to put in quality time with Jared, but that doesn't mean you have to come see him *every* day. I know you've got a company to run and a life in progress before all this came out. I only meant that you had to keep your promises and make an effort."

She thought this was about Jared. Apparently he had not made it abundantly clear how badly he wanted her last night. Their tryst on the couch was nice, but it was just an appetizer to take the edge off three years apart. He wouldn't allow himself to fall for Sabine, but he wasn't going to deny himself the pleasure of making love to her. "Who said anything about Jared? I was thinking about you and me. Someplace dark and quiet with no kid's menu."

"That sounds lovely," she said, "but Jared isn't a puppy. We can't just crate him while we go out."

"I can arrange for someone to watch him."

A flicker of conflict danced across her face. She wanted to go. He could tell. She was just very protective and worried about leaving their son with a stranger. Hell, she hadn't even wanted to leave Jared with *him*.

"Someone? You don't even know who?"

"Of course I do. I was actually considering my secretary, Marie. She's got a new grandson of her own that she fawns over, but he lives in Vermont, so she doesn't see him nearly as much as she wants to. I asked her this morning if she was willing to watch Jared tonight. She'll even come out to your apartment so you don't have to pack up any of his things and he can sleep in his own bed when the time comes."

Sabine pursed her lips in thought and flipped her ponytail over her shoulder. "So you were so confident that I would go to dinner with you that you arranged a babysitter before you even bothered to ask if I wanted to go."

Her dream last night had tipped her hand. "Your subconscious doesn't lie."

Her cheeks flushed red against her pale complexion. She turned away from him and focused her attention on the television mounted on the opposite wall of the waiting room. "What if I have plans?"

"Do you have plans?" he asked.

"No," she admitted without facing him. "But that's not the point. You assume too much. You assume that just because we have a child together and we went too far last night that I want—"

"Brooks!" The nurse opened the side door and called out their name to come back.

Sabine's concerned expression faded, the lines disappearing between her brows. She seemed relieved to avoid this conversation. He wasn't going to let her off that easily.

"To be continued," Gavin said, looking her square in the eye. She met his gaze and nodded softly.

He climbed to his feet and offered his hand to help Sabine up. They made their way back to Dr. Peterson's personal office and sat in the two guest chairs across from his desk. It didn't take long before his physician strolled in with a file in his hands.

Dr. Peterson eased into his seat and flipped open the

paperwork. His gaze ran over it for a moment before he nodded. In that brief flash of time, Gavin had his first flicker of doubt. Jared looked just like him. There was no real reason to believe he wasn't his son, but Sabine had seemed nervous in the lobby. He didn't know anything for certain until the doctor told him the results. He hadn't even wanted a son a week ago, and now he would be devastated to know Jared wasn't his.

"Well," the doctor began, "I've got good news for you, Mr. Brooks. It appears as though you're a father. Congratulations," he said, reaching across the desk to shake his hand.

"Thank you," Gavin replied with relief washing over him.

Dr. Peterson pulled out two manila envelopes and handed one to each of them. "Here's a copy of the DNA report for each of you to give your lawyers."

This apparently was not the doctor's first paternity test rodeo. "Thank you," he said, slipping the envelope into his lapel pocket.

"Let me know if you have any questions. Good luck to you both." Dr. Peterson stood, ushering them out the door.

They were back in the lobby of the building before they spoke again. Gavin turned to her as she was putting the envelope into her purse. "Now about that dinner. You never answered me."

Sabine looked up at him. She didn't have the relieved expression he was expecting. She seemed even more concerned than she had going in. "Not tonight, Gavin. I'm not much in the mood for that."

"What's the matter?" he asked. Some women would be leaping with joy to have scientific evidence that their child was the heir to a multibillion-dollar empire. Sabine was a notable exception. "This was your idea," he reminded her.

She sighed. "I know. And I knew what the results would be, but I wasn't prepared for the finality of it. It's done. Now the wheels start turning and the child that has been one hundred percent mine for the past two years will start slipping from my arms. It's selfish of me, I know, and I apologize, but that doesn't make me leap for joy."

Gavin turned to face her, placing his hands reassuringly on her shoulders. It gave her no real choice but to look at him. "Sabine, what can I possibly say to convince you that this isn't a bad thing?"

Her pale green eyes grew glassy with tears she was too stubborn to shed in front of him. "There's nothing you can say, Gavin. Actions speak louder than words."

Fair enough. "How about this," he offered. "I'll get Edmund to start the paperwork and put together a custody proposal for you to look over. When you're happy with it, we'll share a nice dinner, just the two of us, to celebrate that the sky didn't fall and things will be fine."

Her gaze dropped to his collar and she nodded so slightly, he could barely tell she'd agreed. "Okay," she whispered.

"Clear your schedule for Friday night," he said with confidence. "I have a feeling we're going to be sharing a lovely candlelit dinner together before the weekend arrives."

Sabine curled up on the couch and watched Gavin and Jared play on the living room floor. They were stacking Duplo blocks. Gavin was trying to build a plane, but

Jared was determined to make a truck and kept stealing pieces off the clunky blue-and-red jet. It was amazing to see them together, the father and his tiny toddler clone.

It made her smile, even when she wasn't sure she should be smiling.

Gavin had done his best to reassure her that things would be fine. His lawyer had presented a very reasonable custody agreement. Her relief at reading the briefing was palpable. They were both giving a little and taking a little, which surprised her. Gavin got Jared on alternate weekends, rotating holidays and two weeks in the summer, but he would continue to reside primarily with Sabine. Her concession was to agree to move to Manhattan to make the arrangement easier on everyone.

They'd built in flexibility in the agreement to accommodate special requests, like birthdays. Unless Gavin pushed her, she intended to let him see Jared as often as he liked. How could she turn away a scene like the one playing out on her floor?

Tonight, they were telling Jared that Gavin was his father. It was a big moment for them. The DNA test had made it certain, but telling Jared made it real.

"Hey, big guy?" Gavin said.

Jared dropped a block and looked up. "Yep?"

"Do you know what a daddy is?"

Sabine leaned forward in her seat, resting her elbows on her knees. She agreed to let Gavin be the one to tell him, but she wasn't certain how much Jared would understand. He was still so young.

"Yeah," he said cheerfully, before launching into another of his long-winded and unintelligible speeches. Jared was a quiet child, slow to speak, although it seemed more that he didn't have a lot he wanted to say.

Only in the past few months had he started rattling on in his own toddler-speak. From what pieces she could pick out, he was talking about his friend at school whose daddy picked him up every day. Then he pointed at Sabine. "Mommy."

"Right." Gavin smiled. "And I am *your* daddy."

Jared cocked his head to the side and wrinkled his nose. He turned to Sabine for confirmation. "Daddy?"

She let out the breath she'd been holding to nod. "Yeah, buddy. He's your daddy."

A peculiar grin crossed Jared's face. It was the same expression he made when she "stole" his nose and he wasn't quite sure he believed her. "Daddy?" He pointed at Gavin.

Gavin nodded, having only a moment to brace himself before his son launched into his arms.

"Daddy!" he proclaimed.

Sabine watched Gavin hold his son as fiercely as if someone were going to snatch him away. She understood how he felt. And then she saw the glassy tears in the eyes of her powerful CEO, and her chest tightened with the rush of confusing emotions. It hadn't taken long, but Gavin was completely in love with his son.

She couldn't help but feel a pang of jealousy.

Seven

"**D**amn you for always being right."

Gavin stood on Sabine's doorstep holding a bouquet of purple dahlias. She had opened the door and greeted him that way, stealing his "hello" from his lips. Fortunately she was smiling, so he did the same.

He held out the bundle of flowers with the nearly black centers that faded to bright purple tips. "These are for you. They reminded me of your hair."

Sabine brought the flowers up to her nose and delicately inhaled their scent. "They're beautiful, thank you."

"So are you," he added. And he meant it. She looked lovely tonight. She was wearing a fitted white dress with brightly colored flowers that looked like one of her watercolor paintings. It was sleeveless and clung to every curve of her body.

She smiled, wrinkling her nose with a touch of embarrassment. The movement caught the light on the tiny pink rhinestone in her nose. It was the same bright color as her lipstick and the chunky bracelet on her wrist. "Let me put these in some water and we can go."

Gavin nodded and stepped across the threshold into the apartment. It was Friday night and as predicted, they were having dinner. Everything had gone smoothly. The paperwork had been filed in family court to add Gavin's name to the birth certificate. Along with the addition, Jared's last name would be updated to Brooks. He'd suggested making Jared's middle name Hayes, but she said the name Thomas was more important to her. He'd thought Sabine would pitch a fit on the subject of Jared's name, but it hadn't concerned her.

The custody proposal Edmund put together was approved by both of them on the first draft. He hoped that he would see Jared more than required, but this established a minimum they were both comfortable with.

He noticed Marie's coat hanging by the door when he came in, so he knew she was already there to watch Jared. Gavin looked around the apartment, but he didn't see Marie or Jared anywhere. "Where is everyone?"

Then he heard giggles and splashing from the bathroom. He smiled, knowing Marie was probably soaked. After they'd told Jared that Gavin was his daddy, he'd insisted *Daddy* give him his bath that night. Gavin had gotten more water on him than the toddler in the tub, he was pretty certain.

Aside from that, the night had gone pretty smoothly. Apparently toddlers didn't angst about things the way grown-ups did. Gavin was his daddy—*great*. Let's go play.

"Marie is giving Jared a bath, although I think they're

probably having more fun with the bathtub paints than actually washing."

Gavin wanted to peek in and say hello before they left, but he resisted. He'd gotten Sabine to agree to this dinner and the babysitter he provided. Right now, Jared was happy. If they went in to say goodbye, the giggles might disintegrate into tears. "Are you ready?"

She nodded, the luxurious black waves of her hair gracefully swaying along her jawline. "I already told Marie goodbye a few minutes ago so we could slip out. She seems to have everything under control."

Since it was just the two of them tonight, he'd opted for the Aston Martin. He held the door for her, noting the elegant curve of her ankles in tall pink pumps as she slipped inside. Gavin had no clue how women walked in shoes like that, but he was extremely thankful they did.

They had seven-thirty reservations at one of the most sought-out, high-end restaurants in Manhattan. He'd made the reservation on Monday, feeling confident they would come to an agreement in time, but even then, it had taken some persuading to get a table. Most people booked a table several months in advance, but they knew better than to tell a Brooks no. He tended to get in wherever he wanted to, and he made it worth the maître d's efforts.

They checked in and were immediately taken to an intimate booth for two. The restaurant was the brainchild of a young, up-and-coming chef who snagged a James Beard award at the unheard-of age of twenty-two. The decor was decidedly modern with lots of glass, concrete and colored lights that glowed behind geometric wall panels.

Their table was like a cocoon wrapping around them

and shielding them from the world. A green glass container on the table had a flickering candle inside, giving a moody light to their space. It was just enough to read their menus, but not enough to draw attention to who was inside the booth. It made the restaurant popular with the young celebrity set who wanted to go out but maintain their privacy.

"Have you ever been here?" Gavin asked.

Sabine took in all the sights with wide eyes. "No, but I've heard of it. My boss said her husband took her here for her birthday."

"Did she like it?"

"She said the food was good. The decor was a little modern for her taste, which is funny considering her clothing design has a contemporary edge to it that would fit right in."

"I've been here once," Gavin said. "It's fine cuisine, but it's not stuffy. I thought you'd like that."

Sabine smiled and looked down. "Yes, there aren't fifteen pieces of silverware, so that's a relief."

Gavin smiled and looked over the menu. He'd learned his lesson the first time they dated. His attempts to impress her with nice restaurants had only intimidated her and pointed out the wide gap of their social standings. She wasn't like other women he'd dated. A lot of women in Manhattan expected to be wined and dined in the finest restaurants in town. Sabine was just as happy with Thai takeout eaten on the terrace of his apartment, if not more so.

This place was his attempt at a compromise and so far, it seemed to be a good choice. There wasn't a fixed tasting menu like so many other restaurants. Foie gras and caviar wasn't her style, and she wouldn't let him pay two hundred dollars a head for a meal she wouldn't eat.

Here, diners got to mix and match their choice of Asian fusion dishes for the six courses.

The waiter brought their drinks, presenting him with a premium sake and Sabine with a light green pear martini that was nearly the color of her eyes. They ordered and the server disappeared to bring their first course selection.

"I'm glad we got everything worked out with Edmund. I've been looking forward to this night all week." He met her eyes across the table and let a knowing smile curl his lips. Gavin expected tonight to go well and for Sabine to end up back in his bed. He'd fantasized about her naked body lying across his sheets as he lay in bed each night.

Holding up his drink for a toast, he waited for Sabine to do the same. "To surviving the terrible twos," he said with a grin, "and everything else the future may hold."

Sabine tipped her glass against his and took a healthy sip. "Thank you for handling all of this so gingerly. You don't know how much I've worried."

"What are we drinking to?" A nasal voice cut into their conversation.

They both turned to find a blonde woman standing beside their table. *Ugh.* It was Viola Collins. The Manhattan society busybody was one of the last people he wanted to see tonight. She had a big mouth, an overabundance of opinions and a blatant desire for Gavin that he'd dodged for years.

"Viola," he said, ignoring her question and wishing he could ignore her, as well. "How are you?"

She smiled and showed off her perfect set of straightened, whitened teeth that looked a touch odd against her too-tan skin. "I'm just great." Her laser focus shifted toward Sabine, taking in and categorizing every detail with visible distaste. "And who do we have here?"

Gavin watched his date with concern. He wasn't certain how Sabine would react to someone like Viola. Some people might shrink away under Viola's obvious appraisal, but she didn't. Sabine sat up straighter in her seat and met Viola's gaze with her own confident one.

"Viola Collins, this is my date, Sabine Hayes."

The women briefly shook hands, but he could tell there was no friendliness behind it. Women were funny that way, sizing one another up under the cool guise of politeness.

"Would I have met you before?" Viola asked.

"I sincerely doubt it," Sabine replied.

Gavin couldn't remember if they had or not. "You may have. Sabine and I dated a few years back."

"Hmm…" Viola said. Her nose turned up slightly, although Gavin thought that might be more the result of her latest round of plastic surgery. "I think I would've remembered *this*. That's interesting that you two are dating again. I would've thought the novelty would've worn off the first time."

"Oh, no," Sabine said, a sharp edge to her voice. "I'm very bendy."

Viola's eyes widened, her tight mouth twisting at Sabine's bold words. "Are you?" She turned to Gavin. "Well, I'll have to tell Rosemary Goodwin that you're off the market. *For now*," she added. "I think she's still waiting for you to call her again after your last hot date. I'll just tell her to be patient."

"You'll have to excuse me." Sabine reached for her purse and slipped out of the booth, deliberately sweeping the green martini off the table. The concoction splattered across Viola's cream silk dress. "How clumsy of me!"

she said. Ignoring the sputtering woman, Sabine bent down to pick up the glass and set it back on the table. "That's better." At that, she turned and bolted from the restaurant.

Viola gawked at Sabine as she disappeared, sputtering in outrage. The silk dress was ruined. No question of it.

Gavin didn't care. Viola could use a fist to the face, but no one wanted to pick up her plastic surgery tab to repair the damage. He got up, throwing cash onto the table for the bill and pressing more into Viola's hand for a new dress. "That wasn't your color anyway."

He jogged through the restaurant, pushing through the crowd waiting to be seated, and bursting out onto the street. He spied Sabine about a block away, charging furiously down the pavement despite the handicap of her heels.

"Sabine!" he yelled. "Wait."

She didn't even turn around. He had to run to catch up with her, pulling alongside and matching her stride.

"I should've known," she said, without acknowledging him. "You know there was a reason I ended this the last time. One of the reasons was that everyone in your world is a snob."

"Not everyone," he insisted. He wrapped his fingers around her delicate wrist to keep her from running off again and pulled her to a stop. "Just ignore Viola. She doesn't matter to anyone but herself."

She shook her head, the waves of her hair falling into her face as she looked down at the sidewalk. "It's the same as last time, Gavin. People in your world are never going to see me as anything other than an interloper. Like you're slumming for your own amusement. I don't fit in and I never will."

"I know," he said. "That's one of the many things that make you great."

Her light green eyes met his for a moment, a glimmer of something—hope, maybe—quickly fading away. "Stop fooling yourself, Gavin. You belong with someone like Viola or this Rosemary woman that's waiting on you to call again. We're all wrong for each other. You're only here with me now because of Jared."

"Let me assure you that if I wanted a woman like Viola I could have one. I could have *her,* if I wanted to. She's made that very clear over the years, but I'm not interested. I don't want her." He took a step closer, pulling Sabine against him. "I want you. Just as you are."

"You say that now, but you wouldn't answer her question," she said, resisting his pull on her.

"Answer what question?"

"She asked what we were drinking to. You don't want anyone to know about Jared, do you? Are you ashamed of him? Or of both of us?"

"Absolutely not!" he said as emphatically as he could. "I will gladly shout the news about my son from the rooftops. But I haven't told my family yet. If Viola found out, it would be all over town. I don't want them to hear it from her."

Gavin slipped his arms around her waist, enjoying the feel of her against him, even under these circumstances. "I'd like to tell them tomorrow afternoon. Would you be able to bring Jared to meet them? Maybe around dinnertime? That would give them some time to adjust to the idea before you show up."

"Why don't you just come get him?" she said. Her bravado from her interaction with Viola had crumbled. Now she just looked worn down.

"Because I want them to spend time with you, too,"

Gavin added. "I know you've met them before, but that was years ago. This is different."

"And say what, Gavin? 'Hey, everyone, you remember Sabine? Since you saw her last, she's had my son and lied to all of us for over two years. We've got that worked out now. Don't mind the nose ring.'"

"Pretty much," he said with a smile. "How did you guess?"

Sabine's gaze shot up to his. Red flushed her cheeks and she punched him in the shoulder. She hit him as furiously as she could and he barely felt it. He laughed at her assault, which only made it worse. She was like an angry kitten, hissing and clawing, but not dangerous enough to even break the skin. "I'm serious, Gavin!"

"I'm serious, too." He meant every word of it. Gavin had gone into this thinking that he could indulge in Sabine's body and keep his heart thoroughly out of the equation. She had no idea how badly she'd hurt him when she left, and he didn't want her to know. But he'd opened the door to her once. No matter how hard he fought, it was too easy to open up to her again. It wasn't love, but it was something more than his usual indifference.

Perhaps this time would be different. Even if they weren't together, they would always be connected through Jared. They would be constants in an ever-changing life and he welcomed it, even if he didn't know what they would do with it.

He slipped his finger under her chin and tipped her face up to him. "Serious about this."

Gavin's lips met hers before she could start arguing with him again. The moment he kissed her, she was lost. She melted into him, channeling her emotions into the kiss. Sabine let all of her anger, her frustration, her fear flow through her mouth and her fingertips. She buried her fingers through his dark hair, tugging his neck closer.

He responded in kind, his mouth punishing her with his kiss. His hands molded to her body, his fingers pressed hard into her flesh. The rough touch was a pleasure with a razor's edge. She craved his intensity. The physical connection made everything else fade away. At least for tonight. Tomorrow was…tomorrow.

"Take me to your place," she said.

Gavin reluctantly pulled away. "I'll have the valet bring the car."

Within a few minutes, they were strolling into the Ritz-Carlton Tower. They took the elevator up to Gavin's apartment. It had been a long time since she'd been here. She'd walked alone down this very hallway after she broke up with him. Pregnant and unaware of that fact. It felt strange to traverse the same carpeting after all these years.

Inside the apartment, little had changed. The same elegant, expensive and uncomfortable furniture that was better suited for a decorating magazine than to actually being used. The same stunning view of Central Park sprawled out of the arched floor-to-ceiling windows. There was a newer, larger, flatter television mounted to one wall, but that was about it.

"You've done a lot with the place since I saw it last," she said drily.

"There's new additions," he insisted. He pointed to a corner in the dining room where there was a stack of children's toys, new in the packages, and the car seat from the Mercedes. "I'm also doing some renovations to one of the bedrooms."

Gavin led her down the hallway to the rooms that had once functioned as a guest room and his office. Inside the old guest room, a tarp was draped over the hardwood floors. Several cans of paint were sitting in the middle of the floor, unopened. Construction was under way for some wainscoting and a window seat that would cover and vent the radiators. Jared was too young to enjoy it now, but she could just imagine him curling up there, looking out over Central Park and reading a book.

"You said his favorite color was red, so I was going to paint the walls red." He gestured over to the side. "I'm having them build a loft with a ladder into this niche here, so he'll have his own tree house–like space to play when he's older. They're delivering a toddler bed in a few days with a Spider-Man bedding set and curtains."

"It's wonderful," Sabine said. And it was. A million times better than anything she could afford to get him. "He will love it, especially when he gets a little older. What little boy wouldn't?"

Sabine took a last look and moved back out into the hallway and past the closed door to his home office. She didn't begrudge her son anything his father gave him, but it was hard for her to face that Gavin could provide Jared with things she couldn't. "What's this?" she asked, pointing toward a touch panel on the table near the phone.

Gavin caught up with her in the living room. "It's the new Ritz-Carlton concierge system. We didn't have dinner. Would you like me to order something?"

"Maybe later. It's still early." Sabine kicked off her heels and continued through the apartment to the master suite. She reached behind her and began unzipping her dress as she disappeared around the corner.

She'd barely made it three feet inside before she felt Gavin's heat against her back. He brushed her hands away, tugging her zipper down the curve of her spine. His fingertips brushed at the soft skin there, just briefly, before he moved to her shoulders and pushed her dress off.

Sabine stepped out of her clothing, continuing across the room in nothing but the white satin bra and panties she'd worn with it. There were no lights on in that room, so she was free to walk to the window and look outside without being seen.

She heard Gavin close the door behind them, ensuring they were blanketed in darkness. The moonlight from outside was enough to illuminate the pieces of furniture she remembered from before.

She felt Gavin's breath on her neck before he touched her. His bare chest pushed into her back, his skin hot and firm. He swept her hair over her left shoulder, leaning down to press searing kisses along the line of her neck. One bra strap was pushed aside, then the other, before he unhooked the clasp and let the satin fall to the floor.

Sabine relaxed against him, letting her head roll back to rest on his shoulder and expose her throat. She closed her eyes to block out the distraction of the view and focus on the feeling of his lips, teeth and tongue moving over her sensitive flesh. His palms covered her exposed breasts, molding them with his hands and gently pinching the tips until she whimpered aloud with pleasure.

"Sabine," he whispered, biting at her earlobe. "You don't know how long I've waited to have you back in my bed." He slid his hands down to her hips, holding her steady as he pressed his arousal into her backside with a growl.

The vibration of the sound rumbled through her whole body like a shock wave. Her nipples tightened and her core pulsed with need. Knowing she could turn him on like this was such a high. She never felt as sexy as she did when she was with Gavin. Somehow, knowing she could bring such a powerful man to his knees with desire and pleasure was the greatest turn-on.

Sabine turned in his arms, looking up at the dark shadows across his face before she smiled and slipped out of his grasp. Her eyes had adjusted to the light. It made it easy for her to find her way to the massive bed in the center of his room. She crawled up onto it, throwing a glance over her shoulder to make sure he was watching the swell of her backside peeking out from the satin panties. Of course he was.

"This bed?" she asked sweetly, although she felt anything but sweet.

Gavin had his hands balled into fists at his side. "What are you trying to do to me?"

He was fighting for control, but she didn't want him to win. She wanted him to break, to lose himself in her. It would only require her to push a little bit harder. She climbed up to her knees and hooked her thumbs beneath her panties. Looking him in the eye, she bit her lips and glided the slick fabric over her hips.

His breath was ragged in his chest, but he held his place. Gavin's burning gaze danced between the bite of her teeth into her plump pink lips to her full, pert breasts, to the ever-lowering panties. When the cropped dark curls of her sex peeked out from the top, he swallowed hard. His hands went to his belt. His eyes never left her body as he removed the last of his clothes.

Now they were both naked with no more barriers between them. She was ready for him to unleash his passion on her.

With a wicked smile, Sabine flicked her dark hair over her shoulder and curled her finger to beckon Gavin to come to her. He didn't hesitate, surging forward onto the bed until she fell backward onto the soft comforter.

Every inch of her was suddenly covered by the massive expanse of his body. The weight of him pressed her into the mattress, molding her against him. He entered her quickly as well, causing Sabine to cry out before she could stop herself.

"Yes," Gavin hissed in encouragement. "Be loud. You can scream the walls down tonight." He thrust hard into her again. "I want hotel security knocking on the door."

Sabine laughed and drew her knees up to cradle him. When he surged forward again, he drove deeper. She groaned loud, the sound echoing off the walls of the room. He wanted her loud and she would be happy to oblige.

Eight

Sabine rang the doorbell with her elbow, fighting to keep ahold of her son. Jared squirmed furiously in her arms, and she didn't blame him. For their trip to see Gavin's parents she'd dressed him in his best outfit—a pair of khakis, a short-sleeved plaid shirt and a little bow tie. Adrienne had bought the outfit for him and he looked adorable in it. When he stopped squirming. His two-year-old heart much preferred hoodies and T-shirts with cartoon characters on them.

Putting him on the ground, she crouched down to his level and straightened his clothes. "Hey, buddy," she said. "I know you don't like this, but I need you to be a good boy today. You're going to see Daddy and meet some nice people who are very excited to see you."

"Don't wanna." He pouted, with one lip sticking out so far, she was tempted to kiss it away. "Want truck."

"I've got your truck in my bag, and you can have it later. If you're a good boy today, we'll get ice cream on the way home, okay?"

The dark, mischievous eyes of her son looked up at her, considering the offer. Before he could answer, the door opened and Sabine looked up into the same eyes. Gavin was in the doorway.

"Hi, Jared," Gavin said, his whole face lighting up at the sight of his son. He knelt down and put out his arms, and Jared immediately stopped pouting and ran to him. Gavin scooped him up and swung him in the air while Jared giggled hysterically.

Sabine stood and smiled, nervously readjusting her purse on her shoulder and smoothing a hand over her hair. She'd pulled the black-and-purple strands back into a bun at the nape of her neck. The violet highlights were still visible, but not so "in their face." Adrienne had insisted she wear one of her newly designed tops today, a silky, scoop-neck red top that gathered at the waist. She'd paired it with some black pants and a patent leather belt. It looked good on her, but it was hardly the armor she'd wanted going into this.

She sucked a deep breath into her lungs, trying to even out her frantic heartbeat, but it did little good. She was about to see Gavin's parents again, and this time, as the mother of their grandchild. They had been polite but distant the last time. Obviously, they hadn't felt the need to get invested in Gavin's latest dating novelty.

She didn't anticipate this going well. They might hate her for keeping Jared a secret. They might turn their noses up at her like Viola had. Only today, she couldn't dump a drink on the bitch and run out.

"How'd it go?" she asked.

Gavin settled Jared in his arms and turned to her. "Well, I think. They were surprised. Okay, *more* than surprised. But we talked a lot, and they've had some time to process it. Now I think they're excited at the prospect of their first grandchild."

It was too early for Sabine to feel optimistic. She was about to reply when she heard a woman's voice from inside the apartment. "Are they here? Ohmigosh, look at him!"

Sabine was expecting his mother, but instead, the face of a younger woman appeared over Gavin's shoulder. She had long, dark brown hair like his, but her eyes were a steely gray color. It had to be his sister, Diana.

Gavin turned toward her, showcasing his son. "This is Jared. Jared, this is your auntie Diana."

Jared played shy, turning his face into Gavin's shirt when Diana tried to coax him to say hello. More voices sounded inside with footsteps pounding across the floor. How many people were in there? A crowd of four or five people gathered, all fussing at Jared and Gavin at once.

"He looks just like you did at that age!"

"What a handsome boy!"

Sabine was happy to stay safely in the hallway and play spectator for the moment. It was easier. She always knew they would accept Jared. He was their blessed heir. The vessel that brought him into existence was another matter.

She could feel the moment the first set of eyes fell on her. It was Diana. She slipped around Gavin into the hallway, rushing Sabine with a hug she wasn't anticipating.

"It's so nice to finally meet you," Diana said.

Sabine patted weakly at the young woman's back and pulled away as soon as she could. "Finally?"

Diana smiled and threw a conspiratorial look over her shoulder. "Gavin had mentioned you to me when you were first dating. He just went on and on about you. I'd never heard him do that about another woman before. And then it ended and I was so disappointed. When he called and asked me to come over today to meet his son, I was so happy to hear that you were the mother." She grinned wide and nudged Sabine with her elbow. "I think it's fate."

Sabine tried not to laugh at the young woman's enthusiasm. She couldn't be more than twenty-two or twenty-three. She still believed in all that. And since Diana was the beautiful only daughter of a billion-dollar empire, Sabine was pretty certain no man had the nerve to break her heart. At least, not yet.

Diana snatched up Sabine's hand in hers and tugged her over the threshold of the entryway. The polished parquet floors were too slick for her to resist the movement and before she knew it, the door was closed and she was standing in the apartment of Byron and Celia Brooks.

Okay, apartment was a misnomer. This was a mansion slapped on the top of an apartment building. In front of her was a grand marble staircase with a gold-and-crystal chandelier twinkling overhead from the twenty-foot ceilings. On each side of the doorway were large urns filled with bouquets of fresh flowers that were nicer than the arrangements at some people's weddings.

That was all she could see with the press of people, but it was enough to let her know she wasn't in Nebraska anymore.

"Everyone, you remember Sabine Hayes. She's Jared's mother."

Sabine's chest tightened instantly, her breath going

still in her lungs of stone. Every eye in the room flew from Jared to her. His father's. His mother's. His brother Alan's. She tried to smile wide and pretend she wasn't having a panic attack, but she wasn't certain how convincing she was.

His mother stepped forward first. She looked just as she had the last time. Sabine and Gavin had run into them at a restaurant as they were going in and his parents were leaving. It had been an accidental meeting really, given their relationship hadn't called for the meeting of the parents yet. Sabine had been struck by how refined and effortlessly elegant his mother was. Today was no exception.

Celia's light brown hair was pulled back in a bun like Sabine's. She was wearing a gray silk dress with a strand of dark gray pearls around her neck and teardrops with diamonds from her ears. The dress perfectly matched her eyes, so much like Diana's. Her gaze swept quickly over Sabine from head to toe but stopped at her eyes with a smile of her own. "It's lovely to see you again, Sabine."

"Likewise," she said, politely shaking the woman's hand. Every description Gavin ever gave her of his mother had built an image of a cold, disinterested woman in Sabine's mind. Their meeting before hadn't been very revealing, but today, she instantly knew that was not the case. There was a light in her eyes that was very warm and friendly. Celia Brooks had just been raised well and taught early the rules of etiquette and civility that a woman of her class needed. Yes, she could've been a more hands-on mother and let her children get dirty every now and then, but that wasn't how she was brought up.

"Please, come in and meet everyone. You remember my husband, Byron, and this is my other son, Alan."

Sabine shook each of their hands and was amazed at how much alike the Brooks men looked. Thick brown hair, eyes like melted dark chocolate, strong builds. Just one glance and Sabine could tell exactly how Jared would look when he was twenty-five and when he was fifty-five.

"Nora has refreshments set up for us in the parlor," Celia said, ushering everyone out of the hallway.

The farther they went into the apartment, the more nervous Sabine became. Not because of his family, but because of their stuff. Every item her eyes lit upon looked fragile and priceless. "Do not put him down," Sabine whispered to Gavin.

At that, Gavin chuckled. "Do you have any idea how many things my siblings and I have broken over the years? I assure you, if it's important, it's not sitting out."

"Oh, yes," Celia insisted. "Don't worry about a thing. It has been quite a while since we had a youngster here, but we'd better get used to it, right?" She got a wistful look in her eye and glanced over at Jared. "A grandchild. What an unexpected and wonderful surprise."

Sabine wasn't quite sure what to say. She expected the other shoe to drop at any moment. But time went on, and it didn't. They chatted and nibbled on treats their housekeeper, Nora, made. His family asked questions about her with genuine interest. Jared was turned loose and managed not to break anything. To her shock, Byron, the former CEO of BXS, got on the floor and played with him and his dump truck.

She had made herself sick worrying about today. Thinking they would hate her. That they'd never accept her or her son. But as time went by, she found herself to be incredibly at ease with his family. They were polished and polite, but not cold and certainly not blatantly rude like Viola. It was nothing like she'd expected.

It seemed Sabine was as guilty of prejudice as she worried they would be. Just as she feared they would look at her and make snap judgments, so had she. She had this idea of what rich people were like. Gavin's stories of his distant, workaholic family had only reinforced the image in her mind.

But she was wrong. And it made her angry. People like Viola had made her believe that she could never have Gavin. That she would never fit in. She was angry at herself, really. She was the one who was too afraid to find out if their wicked whispers were true. She pushed away the only man she'd ever loved, deprived him of his son for two years, because she was certain they could never last.

She was wrong. At least in part. They might never truly be together as a couple again, but they could be a family and make it work.

Sabine had wasted so much time being afraid. She wasn't about to make the same mistake twice.

"You don't have to keep trying to take me out to dinner, Gavin."

"If at first you don't succeed, try, try again." Gavin smiled and helped her out of the car and onto the curb outside a restaurant.

"You didn't fail the last time." Sabine slowly approached him, pressed herself against the length of his body and wrapped her arms around his neck. "I seem to recall that evening ending in quite a…spectacular fashion."

"Spectacular, eh?" Gavin growled near her ear. "I'm

glad you seemed to think so. But—" he planted a kiss on her neck and whispered to her "—we never actually ate."

"That was okay with me." She looked up at him with her wide green eyes and a wicked smile curling her lips. "We could have the same thing tonight, if you'd like."

He smiled and let his hands roam across the silky fabric of her dress. She was trying to lure him back to bed, but he wouldn't let her. Couldn't let her. At least not tonight. "Well, as tempting as that is, I'll have to pass. You see, I brought in reinforcements to make sure this meal was a success. We can't stand up our guests."

Sabine frowned at him, her nose wrinkling. "Guests?"

"Sabine!"

She pulled away from Gavin and turned to find Adrienne and Will behind her. "Adrienne? Will? What are you two doing here?"

Adrienne leaned in to give her a hug with an amused smirk on her face. "Gavin invited us to have dinner with you tonight. Did he not tell you?"

"Uh, no, he didn't." Sabine looked over her shoulder at Gavin, who appeared appropriately admonished, at least for the moment. "How did you even know how to get in touch with either of them?"

"Gavin and I have been acquaintances for several years," Will said. "We play the occasional game of racquetball together."

Sabine just shook her head. "So…what? Do all young, rich guys know each other? Is there some kind of club or something where you all hang out and be rich together?"

"Yes, we have a support group—Rich and Sexy Anonymous," Gavin offered with a smile. "Let's get inside or we'll be late for our reservation."

They were seated at a table for four near the window.

He'd known Will for several years but hadn't connected that the Adrienne that Sabine worked for was the same Adrienne that married Will the year before. When the pieces finally clicked, he thought having dinner together would be nice. Not even Viola would have the nerve to come up to a table like this and make a fuss. They were guaranteed a fun night out with people that he already knew would make Sabine comfortable.

He had also been curious to meet Adrienne in person. He'd read about her in the newspaper a few years ago after her plane crash and the scandal that followed. She had lost her memory for weeks, and everyone thought she was Will's fiancée, who actually died in the wreck. It was the stuff of dramatic movies, but she had made herself into quite the success story. Her clothing line had soared in the past year, and her boutique was one of the most popular destinations for the young and hip in Manhattan. He just never thought to look for his runaway girlfriend behind the counter of the store.

The waiter came to take their drink orders. "Is anyone interested in some wine?"

"None for me," Adrienne said.

"We can order something sweeter," Sabine offered. "I know you like a Riesling or a Moscato, right?"

"I do normally—" she smiled "—but I'm not drinking at all for the next eight months or so."

The sharp squealing noise that followed was nearly enough to pierce Gavin's eardrums. Sabine leaped up from her chair and ran around to embrace Adrienne. That kicked off a rapid-fire female discussion about things that Gavin would rather not be privy to. Instead, he ordered sparkling water for Adrienne and wine for everyone else.

"Congrats, Daddy," he said to Will.

Will chuckled. "Congrats to you, as well. It seems to be going around."

"It has. I can assure you that mine was more of a surprise, since my child was walking and talking by the time I found out about it."

"Yeah, but you lucked out. You missed the morning sickness, the wild hormonal swings, the Lamaze classes, the birthing room where she threatens to castrate you. After the child is born there's the midnight feedings, the colic…"

Gavin listened to Will talk for a moment and shook his head to interrupt. "I'd gladly take all that and more in exchange for the rest of what I missed. I also didn't get to be there when she heard his heartbeat or saw his image on the sonogram for the first time. I missed his birth, his first steps, his first words…. Enjoy every moment of this experience with Adrienne. Things that don't seem very important now will be the very stuff that will keep you up at night when you're older. One day, you'll look up from your BlackBerry and your kid will be in high school."

Gavin couldn't stop the words from flying out of his mouth. Every single one of them was true, although he'd barely allowed himself the time to think about what he'd missed. He tried to focus on what was ahead. Jared wasn't going to drift in and out of his life like so many others, so he had no excuse. If he missed moments going forward, it was his own fault. He didn't want any more regrets.

The waiter brought their wine, and Gavin took a large sip. "Sorry about that," he said.

"No, don't be," Will answered. "You're right. Time goes by so quickly, especially to guys like us. The priorities start to change when you fall in love and even more so when kids come into the picture. I'll try to keep it in perspective when she's sending me out in the night on strange cravings runs."

"Gavin is taking us to look at apartments on my day off," he heard Sabine say.

"There's an apartment down the street from us that's for sale," Adrienne said. "A really nice brownstone. It's on the second floor, so there's some stairs, but not many."

"I think I'd prefer her to be in a building with a doorman and some security. It would make me feel better."

"It's not like my current apartment has surveillance cameras and security," Sabine said.

"It doesn't matter. If you continue to refuse living with me, I want you in someplace secure. I don't want just anyone strolling up to your door. This can be a dangerous town sometimes, and I want you and Jared protected when I can't be there."

"Yes, that viciously dangerous Upper West Side," Sabine said with a smile. "I actually read that the Village has one of the higher crime rates, but you seemed okay with that."

"Hence the doorman."

"Okay, fine, no brownstones." The two women exchanged knowing looks and shrugged.

They placed their orders and continued chatting easily during the meal. Given they actually got as far as having food on the table, this was their most successful dinner yet. At this point, Gavin was thinking of opening a door to a line of conversation he was extremely interested in. He hadn't brought it up to Sabine—she would likely shoot him down—but with Will and Adrienne as backup, he might be successful.

"So, are you guys planning to take any romantic pre-baby vacations sometime soon?"

The couple looked at each other. "That's not a bad idea," Will said. "We honestly haven't given it much thought. It really will be a challenge to travel with little ones. Honey," he said, turning to Adrienne, "we should definitely do something. Let's go somewhere glamorous and decidedly un-kid-friendly to celebrate. We're going to be making pilgrimages to the Mouse from now on, so we need to enjoy an adult vacation while we can."

"You really should," Sabine echoed. "That escape to your place in the Hamptons this summer was the only vacation I've taken since Jared was born. You should take the time to pamper yourself now. The spring lines are almost finished for Fashion Week. You should definitely go somewhere after the show."

Gavin perked up at her words. That was exactly what he was hoping to hear. "You've only had one vacation in two years?"

"More than that, really," she admitted. "Since I had Jared, I haven't had the time. Before I had Jared, I didn't have the money. Adrienne twisted my arm into going this summer. Prior to that, the last real vacation I took was my senior trip to Disney World in high school."

"That hardly counts," Will pointed out.

"Yes," Adrienne agreed. "You need a vacation as badly as I do. Maybe more. Thank goodness I got you to come to the beach house. I had no idea you were so vacation-deprived."

"I save all my hours in case Jared gets sick. And I don't have anyone to watch him while I'm gone. Tina had him over the Fourth of July trip, but I think that was too much for her. I couldn't ask her to do it again."

"You wouldn't have to," Gavin said.

"Are you offering to watch him while I go on vacation?" she challenged with a smile.

"Not exactly."

Nine

"This one is nice."

Sabine was gripping the handles of Jared's stroller as she shot him a glance that told him he was incorrect. She wasn't impolite enough to say that in front of the Realtor, though.

They were in the seventh apartment of the day. They had crisscrossed Manhattan, looking at places uptown, downtown, east and west. This last apartment, in midtown, had three spacious bedrooms, a large kitchen, a balcony and a spa tub in the master bath. And of course, it did not impress her nearly as much as some of the others. Unfortunately, it was the closest of all the apartments to his own place.

She favored the West Village, and there was no convincing her otherwise.

"This is probably a no," he said. "And I think we're

done for the day. The kid is getting tired." That was an understatement. He'd been conked out in his stroller since they arrived at this building.

"I really do like the one in the Village. I just want to know what all my options are before we spend that much. It's more than we need, really."

The woman sighed and closed her leather portfolio. "I'll keep looking and contact you next week with a list of other options. I worry you might lose out on that place if you don't put an offer in soon."

The Realtor was eyeing him from the other room. She was far too eager to push him into an expensive sale, and he wouldn't be rushed. Sabine would have what she wanted, and for the price he was willing to pay, this lady needed to find it for them.

"There are two million apartments in Manhattan," Gavin said. "We'll find another one if we have to."

They were escorted out of the apartment and downstairs. After they parted ways with the Realtor, they started strolling down the block. The street sounds roused Jared from his nap just as they neared Bryant Park.

"Could we take Jared over to the carousel? He loves that."

"Absolutely."

They took Jared for a spin on the carousel and then settled onto a bench to enjoy the nice afternoon. Gavin went to buy them both a drink, and when he returned, Jared was playing with another child who'd brought bubbles to the park.

"I've got a surprise for you."

Gavin had to smile at the mix of concern and intrigue on Sabine's face. He was excited about the prospect of what he had planned, but he also enjoyed watching her twist herself into knots trying to figure out what he was doing. She hated not knowing what was going on, which made him all the more determined to surprise her.

"Really?" Sabine turned away, feigning disinterest and watching Jared play with the bubbles.

It had been a couple days since she'd met his family. Things seemed to be going well on all fronts. Edmund said the custody and other legal paperwork should be finalized any day now. Gavin and his legal team were signing off on the merger agreement with Exclusivity Jetliners next week. Roger Simpson's son had finally stopped his loud protests about the acquisition, and things were moving forward.

Everything was going to plan, and Gavin wanted to celebrate the best way he knew how—an exhilarating flight and a luxurious weekend on the beach. For the first time in his life, he wanted to share that experience with someone else. He wanted Sabine beside him as he soared through the clouds and buried his toes in the sand. He just had to talk her into going along with it, which would be harder than securing an Exclusivity Jetliners jet and reserving a private beachfront bungalow in Bermuda on short notice.

"When you go home tonight, I want you to pack for a long weekend away."

Her head snapped back to look at him, a frown pulling down the corners of her pink lips. "I have to work this weekend, Gavin. I've already taken off too much time from the store. I can't go anywhere."

"Yes, you can," he said with a wide smile. Did she really think he would make a suggestion like this without having every detail handled? He ran an international shipping empire; he could manage taking her away for the weekend. "The lovely Adrienne and I spoke about my plans at dinner while you were in the ladies' room. She seemed very enthusiastic about it. You have the next three days off. She told me to tell you to have a good time and not to worry about anything."

Red rushed to Sabine's pale cheeks as her brow furrowed and she started to sputter. "What? You—y-you just went to my boss and made arrangements without asking me? Seriously? Gavin, you can't just make decisions like this and leave me out of them."

"Relax," he said, running a soothing hand over her bare shoulder. She was wearing a sleeveless blouse in a bright kelly green that made her eyes darken to the color of the oak leaves overhead. It was almost the same shade as when she looked at him with desire blazing in her eyes. "I'm not trying to take over your life. I'm just trying to take you on a little surprise getaway. You wouldn't do it if I didn't twist your arm."

His fingertips tingled as they grazed over her skin, rousing a need inside him that was inappropriate for the park. He hadn't made love to Sabine since they went to his apartment. She might have her concerns, but he was determined to take her to a tropical location where he could make love to her for hours, uninterrupted.

He wasn't sure whether it was his words or his touch, but the lines between her brows eased up. With a heavy sigh, she turned her attention back to the playground. "What will we do about Jared? You haven't mentioned him coming with us."

It was all handled. "My parents have volunteered to keep him for the weekend. They're quite excited about the prospect, actually."

Sabine's lips twisted as she tried, and failed, to hold in her concerns. "Your parents? The ones who left you with nannies, refused to let you get dirty or be loud or do anything remotely childlike? I don't see that going very well, to be perfectly honest."

Gavin shrugged. What was the worst that could happen? His parents had all the resources in the world at their fingertips. They could manage any contingency, even if it meant breaking down and hiring in someone to help them for the weekend. "I think it will be fine. This is completely different. From what I hear, being a grandparent has a different set of rules. They were distracted by work and responsibilities when I was a kid. Now, they've got nothing but time, cash and two years of indulging to catch up on. Worst-case scenario, we come home to a spoiled-rotten brat."

A soft chuckle escaped Sabine's lips as she turned back to the playground again. He followed her line of sight to the patch of grass where Jared and another little boy were chasing bubbles and giggling hysterically.

She was a great mother. She worried about their son and his welfare every second of the day and had done so for two straight years all on her own. A mother's protective nature never really went away, but Sabine needed a break. A weekend trip wouldn't hurt anything. In fact, she might come home refreshed and be a better parent for it.

"If it helps," Gavin added, "Nora, the housekeeper, used to work as a nanny. She's great with kids. If my parents need reinforcements, she'll be there to help. Nothing will go wrong. You deserve some time to relax."

"I don't know, Gavin. When you took him to the circus, I was nearly panicked the whole time. That was the first time he'd gone somewhere without me aside from day care. And now you want to take me on a trip? How far are we going?"

"Only a short plane ride away."

"Plane?" she cried, turning on the bench to face him full-on. "I really don't want to be that far from him, Gavin."

"It's only about a two-hour flight. If we drove to the Hamptons it would take just as long to get back home with summer traffic." He reached out and took her hand, relishing the cool glide of her skin against his. She had such delicate, feminine hands, more so than he remembered. He was used to them being rough with calluses from her wooden brushes, with paint embedded under her nails and along her cuticles. He hadn't managed to get her back to painting yet, but this trip was a sure start.

"Please let me do this for you. Not only will you have a great time, but it's my chance to share my passion with you the way you once shared your painting with me."

Her green eyes met his, and he felt some of her resistance fading away. She knew how important this was to him. "You're flying us there?"

Gavin smiled and nodded. It hadn't been an original part of his plan, but when he asked Roger about chartering one of his jets, he'd laughed and told him they were practically his already. If he wanted to take one, he was welcome to it, and he could fly it himself.

"Roger is loaning me one of his jets for the trip. I've been dying to fly one, and I really want you to be up there with me when I do. That would make the experience that much more special."

He loved to fly. Soaring through the air was the greatest high he'd ever experienced. It wasn't the same when you weren't sitting at the controls. The only thing that could make it better would be sharing it with her. Somehow, the idea of having Sabine beside him in the cockpit made his chest tight. He wanted to share this with her. He wanted to spoil her. She just had to let him.

She finally let the slightest smile curl her lips. He'd won, he could tell. The tiny smirk made him want to lean in and kiss her until she was blushing again, but this time with passion instead of irritation. But he'd have time soon enough. He wanted her in a swimsuit, her skin glistening with suntan oil. He couldn't wait to feel the press of her bikini bottom against him as he held her in the ocean. They both needed this trip away for a million different reasons.

"I suppose you're not going to tell me where we're flying to."

"Nope." He grinned.

"Then how do I know what to pack?"

"Dress for sizzling-hot days lounging on the beach and cool nights overlooking the ocean. Throw a couple things in a bag and leave the rest up to me."

Sabine wasn't a big fan of flying, but she wasn't about to tell Gavin that. It was his big love, like painting was for her, so she took her Dramamine, packed her bag and hoped for the best.

"You look nervous," Gavin said after locking the door and sliding into the cockpit beside her.

"Me?" she asked with a nervous twitter of laughter. "Never." She was thankful she'd worn large sunglasses today. Maybe he wouldn't notice her eyes were closed the whole time.

The taxi down the runway wasn't so bad. Gavin

seemed very at ease with his headset on and vast display of controls in front of him. He had given her a headset of her own to wear so she could hear the air traffic controllers talking. She heard the tower give them clearance to take off.

"Here we go," Gavin said with an impish smile that reminded her of Jared when he thought he was getting away with something naughty.

Gavin eased the accelerator forward and the jet started down the runway. At that point, Sabine closed her eyes and took a deep breath. She felt the lift as the plane surged into the sky, but she didn't open her eyes.

"Isn't it beautiful?" Gavin asked after a few minutes.

"Oh, yeah," she said, seeing nothing but the dark inside of her eyelids.

"Sabine, open your eyes. Are you afraid to fly?"

She turned to him with a sheepish smile. "No, I'm afraid to crash. You know my boss survived a plane crash a few years ago, right? When you know someone it happened to, it makes it more real in your mind." It was then that she looked through the glass and noticed nothing but ocean around them. He hadn't mentioned flying over the ocean. She swallowed hard. She could do this. She didn't really have a choice.

"We're not going to crash."

"No one plans to."

"Just breathe and enjoy the freedom of zooming through the sky like a bird. Soaring above everyone and everything."

She pried her gaze away from the vast stretch of ocean that surrounded them and decided to focus on Gavin instead. His eyes were alight with excitement. Her serious businessman was grinning from ear to ear like a child with his first bicycle. He adjusted the controls like a pro, setting the cruising altitude and putting them on a course to...*somewhere.*

It was an amazing transformation. Sabine had seen Gavin happy. Angry. Sad. She'd watched his face contort in the pinnacle of passion and go blank with deep thought. But not once had she ever seen him truly joyful. It suited him. He should've joined the Air Force. He might not have a thirty-million-dollar apartment on Central Park South, but he would've been happier. Sometimes you have to make the hard choices to chase your dream. She'd left her entire family behind to follow hers and had rarely regretted the decision.

Two hours later, Gavin started talking into the headset again, and they were granted permission to land although she didn't see anything but miles of blue sea. The plane slowly dropped in altitude. The ocean lightened to a bright turquoise blue, and mossy-green islands appeared through the clouds. She closed her eyes when they landed, but Gavin did a great job at that.

They taxied around the small island airport, finally passing a sign to help her figure out where she was. Welcome to Bermuda.

Bermuda!

At the hangar, they were directed to a location to leave the jet. Gavin shut all the equipment down and they opened the door, extending steps to the ground. Sabine was excited about the trip but grateful to finally have her sandals touching the earth again.

Gavin directed a couple men to unload luggage from the cargo hold and move it to a black town car waiting outside. The driver then whisked them through the narrow, winding streets. After a while, they turned off the main road to a sand-and-gravel drive that disappeared through the thick cover of trees. The world seemed to slip farther away with every turn until at last they came upon a secluded two-story home right on the beach. The house was bright yellow with a white roof and white shutters around each window.

The driver carried their bags inside, leaving them on the tile floor of the master bedroom suite. Sabine followed behind him, taking in every detail of their home away from home. It was decorated in a casual beach style with bright colors and lots of light. There were large French doors off the living room that opened onto a deck. She walked outside, stepping onto it and realizing that it actually extended out over the water.

Sabine leaned against the railing and looked all around her. She didn't see another house or boat anywhere. There was nothing but palm trees, black volcanic rock, clear blue water and pink sand. It was unexpected, but peachy-pink sand stretched out on either side of them.

"The sand is pink," she said, when she heard Gavin step out onto the patio behind her.

"I thought you'd like that." He pressed against her back and wrapped his arms around her waist.

Sabine sighed and eased against him. She could feel the tension start to drift away just being here in his arms. He was right. As much as she'd protested, she needed this vacation.

"I didn't even know such a thing existed. It's beautiful." Her gaze fell on some multicolored glittering stones in the sand. "What is that?" She pointed to the beach. "Shells?"

"Sea glass. They have some beaches here that are just covered in it."

Sabine had the urge to walk along the beach and collect some glass to take home. Maybe she could work it into her art. She hadn't done any painting yet, but she had begun allowing herself to think about it again. The ideas were forming, waiting for her to execute when she was ready. Sea glass might very well feature prominently in the first piece.

"This place is amazing. I want to paint it."

Gavin nuzzled his nose along the shell of her ear. "Good. I want you to paint. I even brought supplies with me."

Sabine turned in his arms with a small frown. "I didn't notice any canvases."

He grinned and planted his hands on the railing to trap her there. "That's because they're body paints. I'm your canvas."

"Oohhh…" Sabine cooed, the possibilities flowing into her mind. This could certainly be fun. "When can we start my next masterpiece?"

Gavin captured her lips with his own, coaxing her blood to move faster and her skin to flush with the heat of desire. One hand moved to her waist and slid beneath her shirt to caress her bare skin. "Right now," he whispered against her lips.

He took her hand and led her back inside. In the bedroom, his luggage was open, and sitting on the dresser was a box of body paints. Gavin must've unpacked it after their driver left. She picked up the pink box and eyed it with curiosity. "You didn't mention it was edible."

"I thought it might bother you to destroy your own creation."

Sabine pulled a jar of strawberry-flavored red paint

from the box with a wicked grin. "Given I'd be destroying it with my tongue, I don't mind so much."

She advanced toward the bed, Gavin stepping backward until his calves met with the mattress. Sabine set down the paints long enough to help him slip out of his clothes and lie out on the king-size bed.

There wasn't anything quite as inspirational as seeing his powerful, naked body sprawled in front of her. His arms were crossed behind his head, his rock-hard chest and chiseled abs just waiting for her artistic improvements. This was an exciting new canvas, and unlike the one he brought to her apartment, there was no blank, white surface to mock her.

Easing onto the bed beside him, she arranged her jars and pulled out the brush that came with it. It wasn't exactly the highest-quality equipment, but this wasn't going to hang in the Louvre one day.

Thinking for a moment, she dipped the brush into the blueberry paint and started swirling it around his navel. He hissed for a moment at the cold paint and then smiled. Next, she added some strawberry paint. Then green watermelon and purple grape. She lost herself in the art, mixing the colors around his skin until he looked like her own twisted, edible version of an abstract Kandinsky painting.

After nearly an hour, she sat back on her heels and admired her canvas. She liked it. It really was a shame it wouldn't last through his next shower.

"I like watching you work."

Sabine turned to look at him, his face one of the only parts of his body that didn't look like a unicorn had thrown up a rainbow on him. "Thanks."

"You get this intensity in your eyes that's amazingly

sexy." He sat up to admire his body. "I can say with certainty that this is probably the greatest abstract art piece ever created with edible body paints. And," he added with a grin, "the only one that smells like a bowl of Froot Loops."

She reached out with her brush and dabbed a dot of purple paint on his lips, then leaned in to lick it away. Her tongue glided slowly along his bottom lip, her gaze never leaving his. "Tasty."

He buried his fingers in her hair and tugged her mouth back to his. His tongue dipped inside and glided along her own. "Indeed. The grape is very tasty."

Sabine smiled and pushed him back against the bed. "That was fun, but now it's time to clean up."

She started with his chest, licking a path across his pecs and flicking her tongue across his nipples. She made her way down the flavorful canvas, teasing at his rib cage and the sensitive plane of his stomach. When she glanced up, she noticed Gavin watching just as eagerly as when she was painting.

"I told you I liked watching you work," he said with a grin.

Sabine dipped lower to the firm heat of his erection and wiped away his smile with her tongue. Taking it deep into her mouth, she worked hard to remove every drop of paint, leaving Gavin groaning and clutching at the blankets with his fists.

"Sabine," he whispered, reaching for her wrist. He found her and tugged until her body was sprawled across his. "You're wearing too much clothing," he complained.

Sitting astride him, Sabine slipped out of her top and bra and then stood to push down her capris and panties. She tossed everything onto the floor and crouched back down. With little effort, she was able to take him into her body and thrust him deep inside.

His hands moved quickly to her hips, guiding her movements. Sabine closed her eyes and tried to absorb the sensations, but found that without the distraction of painting, her emotions were starting to creep in.

From the moment he first kissed her, Sabine had worried that she was fighting a losing battle. Not for custody of Jared, but for custody of her heart. No matter how many times she told herself that none of this was about them, that it was about his son, she couldn't help but think it was more.

Sure, everything he offered would make her a happier mother for their child. But he didn't need to bring her here, to make love to her like this. He didn't have to be so supportive of her art when no one else was. It made it seem like more. And she wanted it to be more. She was just afraid.

Sabine loved him. She always had. There were plenty of reasons why they wouldn't make a good couple, but in the end, only one reason mattered. She left because she loved him enough to change for him—the one thing she swore she'd never do. She'd been disowned by her family for her unwillingness to bend, and yet she would be whatever Gavin wanted her to be. And it scared the hell out of her. So she made her excuses and ran before she did something she might hate herself for.

There was no running from Gavin now. He would forever be a part of her life. And she didn't have the strength to keep fighting this. He might never love her the way she loved him. But she couldn't pretend that this meant nothing to her.

Gavin groaned loudly, pulling her from her thoughts. He moved his hand up to cup her breast, the intensity of their movements increasing with each moment that went by. She wouldn't be able to hold out much longer.

Opening her eyes, she looked down at Gavin. His eyes were closed, his teeth biting down on his lip. He was completely wrapped up in his desire for her. For *her*. Just the way she was. He'd told her that the night she fought with Viola, but she wasn't ready to listen. Perhaps he really meant it. Perhaps he wouldn't ask her to change and she wouldn't betray how weak she was by giving in to his demands.

Perhaps one day he might love her for being herself.

That thought made her heart soar with hope and her body followed. The pleasure surged through her, her cries echoing in the large, tile-floored room. Gavin quickly followed, digging his fingers into the flesh of her hips and growling with satisfaction.

When their heartbeats slowed and they snuggled comfortably into each other's arms, Sabine spoke. Not the words she wanted to say, but the ones she needed to say. "Thank you."

"For what?"

"For the paint. And all of this, really. But mostly the paint."

"I assure you, the pleasure was all mine."

Sabine laughed and nestled tighter against his still somewhat rainbow-colored chest. "That's not what I meant. You've always been such a big supporter of my work. I haven't…" Her voice trailed off as tears crept into her words. She cleared her throat. "I haven't always had that in my life.

"After I had Jared and stopped painting, I began to worry that I might lose my touch. When you brought that canvas the other day and the ideas didn't come, I was really worried my art career was done. Today showed me that I still have the creativity inside me. I just need to not put so much pressure on myself and have fun with it again. It doesn't seem like much, but those body paints were a big deal. For me."

"I'm glad," Gavin said, holding her tight. "I have to say it's the best fifteen bucks I've ever spent at the adult novelty store."

Ten

"We should really call and check in on Jared."

Gavin tugged her tight against him and shook his head. They had made love, showered off her artwork, eaten—as body paints are not a replacement for real food—made love again and taken a nap. He wasn't anywhere near ready to let go of her. Not even just so she could grab her phone from the other room.

"I told my parents to call if there was a problem. I want you one hundred percent focused on enjoying yourself and relaxing. They've got it under control. We've only been gone for eight hours."

He could feel her start to squirm, but he wasn't budging. "How about we call in the morning?"

"Okay. I'm sure everything's fine, but I'm just a nervous mama. I worry."

"I know. But remember, our parents raised us, at least

yours did. Mine hired very qualified people to do it. They know what they're doing."

"I'd rather you not use my parents as an example of good parenting."

Gavin had never heard Sabine speak at length about her family or where she grew up. He knew it was somewhere in the Midwest, but she always seemed hesitant to talk about it. Since she opened the door, he'd take the opportunity. "Do your parents know about Jared?"

He felt Sabine stiffen in his arms. "No," she finally said.

"Why not?"

She wiggled until he allowed her to roll onto her back and look at him. "They are very religious, very hard-working Midwestern farmers. They worship God, the Cornhuskers and John Deere, in that order. I grew up in a small town that was nothing but cornfields and the occasional church for miles. From the time I was a teenager, I started to divert from the path they all followed. My parents tried their hardest to guide me back, but it didn't work. They decided they didn't want anything to do with me and this crazy life I wanted to lead. I refuse to expose Jared to grandparents that would just look at him as my shameful illegitimate son that my wild city life earned me."

"What happened between you and your family?" Gavin asked.

Sabine sighed, her kiss-swollen lips pursing in thought. She didn't really want to talk about it, but she needed to and they both knew it.

"Like I said, I wasn't the child they wanted. I wasn't willing to change who I was or what I dreamed of for them. They wanted me to be a quiet, mousy girl that would get up at dawn to cook for my husband and the other farmhands, take care of a brood of children and be content to sit on the porch and snap green beans. My two sisters didn't see anything wrong with that, but it wasn't what I wanted for my life. They couldn't understand why I wanted a nose ring instead of a wedding ring. The first time I dyed my bangs pink, my mother nearly had a heart attack. My art, my dreams of New York and being a famous painter…that was all childish nonsense to them. They wanted me to 'grow up' and do something respectable."

Gavin knew what it was like not to have his family support his choices. But he hadn't been brave like Sabine. He'd caved to the pressure. He envied her strength, especially knowing the high price she'd paid for her dreams. She had no contact with her family at all?

"You don't even speak to your sisters, then?"

"Very rarely. They're both older than I am, but the younger of the two talks to me on Facebook now and then. When we do talk, it's like chatting superficially with an old friend from junior high you barely remember. We don't share much. I don't post anything about Jared online, so none of them know about him. It seems that when I refused the life they chose I was insulting them, too. In trying to make myself happy, I made everyone else mad."

"So how did you end up in New York?"

"After graduation, I was toying with the idea of leaving Nebraska. I was working as a checkout girl at the grocery store and hoarding every penny I made. My parents had started this ridiculous parade of eligible farmers through the house each week at Sunday dinner just like they had with my older sisters. I could feel my opportunity to leave slipping away. If I wasn't careful, eventually one of the men would catch my eye. Then I'd end up pregnant or married, and I'd never get to New York.

"One night, after I walked the latest guy out, I returned to the living room and announced to my parents that I was moving out. I'd finally saved up enough to get there and a little money to live on. I told them I had a bus ticket to Manhattan and I would be leaving in the morning. It scared the daylights out of me, but I had to do it."

Gavin noticed the faint shimmer of tears in her eyes. The room was dark, but there was enough moonlight to catch it. Her parents hurt her and he hated them for it. "What did they say when you told them?"

She didn't reply right away. When she finally spoke, the tears had reached her voice, her words wavering with emotions. "They said to go on and go, then. Why wait for the morning? My dad grabbed the bag I had packed and threw it in the back of his truck."

Sabine sniffed delicately and wiped her eyes. "They were done with me. If I wasn't going to be the daughter they wanted me to be, then I just wouldn't be their daughter. My mama didn't say a word. She just shook her head and went to do the dishes. That's all she ever did was clean that damned kitchen. So I climbed into the truck and left. I wasn't even finished packing, but I couldn't make myself go upstairs to get the last of my things. I ended up sleeping in the bus station that night because I couldn't change my ticket."

"Just like that?"

"Just like that." She sighed, pulling her emotions back into check. "They disowned me. I don't know if they secretly thought I would fail and come running home, or if they were just tired of dealing with my eccentricities.

I wasn't the town tramp. I wasn't pregnant or on drugs. I was smart, I graduated high school with good grades. I worked and did my share around the farm. But I didn't fit this mold they tried to force me into.

"That was the last time I saw or spoke to my parents. The saddest part is that despite the fact that I wanted to go, I wanted them to ask me to stay. But they didn't. They just let me walk out like I meant nothing to them."

Gavin felt a sick knot start to form in his stomach. He'd done the exact same thing to her. All this time, he'd only focused on the fact that Sabine had left like everyone else in his life. He'd never considered that she might stay if he'd asked. And he'd wanted to. Every nerve in his body was screaming for him to say something—do *something*—to keep Sabine from leaving him, but he'd sat quietly and let her walk away.

"You know, people make mistakes. I'm willing to bet that they love you and miss you. Maybe they thought they were giving you one of those hard life lessons thinking you would come back and be more grateful for what you had. And when you didn't…they didn't know what to do. Or how to find you."

"I'm not that hard to find. Like I said, I'm on Facebook. For a while, I even had a website for my art."

Gavin shook his head. "It's not always as easy as that, especially when you know you're in the wrong. I mean, I did the same thing, didn't I? I was stupid and stubborn and let you walk away. I had a million idiotic reasons for it at the time, but none of them held up the moment that door slammed. Whenever I think back on that day, I wonder what would've happened if I'd run after you. If I'd pulled you into my arms and told you that I needed you to stay."

"You wanted me to stay?"

There was such astonishment in her voice that made him feel even worse. She thought he didn't care. All this time. A part of her probably still did. He hadn't asked for more than her body. Perhaps that's all she thought he wanted. It was all he thought he wanted, until this moment.

"Of course I wanted you to stay. I was just so caught off guard. I had let myself believe that you were different, that you wouldn't leave because you cared about me. When you broke it off, my world started to crumble. I just didn't know how to ask you to stay. You know that I'm not good with that kind of thing. Feelings…" His voice drifted off as he shook his head. He sucked at the emotional stuff.

"It's easier than you think."

Gavin planted a kiss against the crown of her head. "It is?"

"Yes." She propped up onto one elbow and looked him in the eyes. "All you had to say is 'stay.' Just that one word is enough."

"If I had said it the day you left…" He hated to ask, but he had to know.

"I would have stayed."

Gavin swallowed hard and nodded. So many people had come and gone from his life. How many of them might still be around if he'd had the nerve to ask them to stay? Some things were out of his control, but at least he could've salvaged the past few years with Sabine.

It was hard to face the fact that one little word could've changed their entire lives. But sometimes that was all it took. He looked down at the beautiful woman in his arms, the mother of his child, and he vowed he would never let something that insignificant get in the way again.

* * *

Sabine stretched out on the lounge chair and sighed. Gavin was snoozing in the chair beside her as they both soaked in the warm sunshine and light breeze. She was really enjoying this little vacation. They had eaten too much, drank too much, slept late and made love more times than she could count. Gavin had even taken her to the Bermuda Botanical Gardens and the art museum there. She'd lost herself in room after room of paintings and sculptures, lighting the fires of her long-cold creative flames.

It was all too perfect.

She couldn't believe how wrong she'd been. About everything. From the day she took that first pregnancy test, she worried that Gavin would take over her life, steal her son and leave her powerless to stop him. So far, he'd wanted to help, wanted to have his time with his son, but had respected her boundaries. Things would change, but they would compromise on the decisions. There would be no boarding schools, no nannies taking the place of loving parents…

She'd thought Gavin didn't want her, only to find out he'd been devastated when she left. He hadn't told her that he loved her, but she could tell he had feelings for her. They might not be as strong as what she felt for him, but it was more than she ever expected to have.

She thought that she would never fit into Gavin's world or be the woman he wanted her to be. Now, she realized he didn't want her to fit in. He wanted her to be herself. There would always be people with something rude to say, but if his family welcomed her with open arms, she didn't really care what anyone else thought.

Things were going amazingly well.

A soft chirp distracted Sabine from her thoughts. It was Gavin's cell phone. It had been remarkably quiet since they'd arrived. He'd done well in focusing on their vacation, too. She watched him reach for it and frown at the screen before answering.

"Hi, Dad," he said. "Is everything okay?"

Immediately, Sabine's stomach sank. They had called yesterday to check in and everything was fine. He'd told her that his parents would only call if there was a problem. She tried to will herself to relax as she listened to half of the conversation.

"What?" Gavin's tone was sharp and alarmed. He shot up on the lounge chair, his worried gaze searching the ocean for answers he wouldn't find there. "Are you sure? Did you look in all the closets and under the beds? He likes to play hide-and-seek."

Sabine sat up in her chair, swinging her legs over the side to turn toward him. "What is it? Is Jared okay?"

Gavin wouldn't look at her. He was totally focused on the call. "How did they get in the apartment?"

They? Her heart was racing.

"Did you call the police?"

"Gavin!" Sabine cried, unable to stand not knowing what was going on any longer. If Jared fell and skinned his knee, the police wouldn't be involved. This was something far worse than she could imagine.

"No, that was the right thing to do. We'll be home in three hours." Gavin turned off his phone and finally looked at her. He had the shimmer of glassy tears in his eyes as he spoke. "Jared is gone."

A strangled cry escaped her throat. "Gone? He's missing? How?"

Gavin shook his head softly. "Not missing. Kidnapped. A ransom note was left."

Sabine's brain started to swim in panic. She could barely follow his words. She couldn't possibly have heard him right. No one would take Jared. Why would anyone take Jared? "What?" she said, but she couldn't understand his answer. Nothing made sense.

Gavin stood up and offered his hand to her, but she didn't know why. "Sabine, please," he said at last. "We have to get back to New York."

She took his hand, standing slowly until she was looking into his eyes. His eyes. Just like her son's. That's when the fog in her brain cleared, and all that was left behind was red fury.

Her baby had been taken. Her sweet little boy, who had been nothing but safe under her care. Until now. Until he became the son of one of the wealthiest men in Manhattan. Then he was just a pawn in the games of the rich.

"Sabine?"

Her gaze locked on his, her lips tightening with anger. Gavin reached out to touch her face, but she swatted his hand away. "Don't you touch me," she warned through gritted teeth. "This is all your fault."

It was as though she'd slapped him across the face. He flinched and stepped back. "What?"

"I never should've listened to you. You said he would be safe with your parents."

"Of course. Why would I think someone would kidnap our son?"

"Because that's the world you live in, Gavin. You might be appalled by the way we lived with our tiny apartment and our old, worn furniture, but you know what? Jared was safe! He was a safe, happy little boy who didn't know what he was missing. And now he's a rich little boy, scared and alone because being *your son* made him a target."

"You think I'm the reason he was kidnapped?"

There was hurt in Gavin's eyes, but she ignored it. She was too deep in her rage to care. "You are *absolutely* the reason he was kidnapped. What did the ransom note say? Did they want millions of dollars? They wouldn't have gotten that from me, no matter what. I have nothing to offer, nothing anyone could possibly want, unlike you."

"I don't know what the ransom note said aside from the fact that they would call with instructions at 5:00 p.m. If we leave now, we can get back in plenty of time. Can you stop yelling long enough to pack and get on the plane?"

"You bet I can. I don't want to be on the island with you for another minute anyway." Sabine spun on her heel and ran from him, kicking pink sand as she headed for the stairs. She leaped up them two at a time until she reached the deck and raced for the master bedroom.

"What is that supposed to mean?" he said, charging in behind her.

"It means I wish I'd never run into Clay on the street. That the last two weeks had never happened. I should've gone home to Nebraska so you could never find me. If you weren't a part of Jared's life, I would have my son with me right now. This is exactly why I didn't tell you that you were a father."

The hurt expression on Gavin's face quickly morphed into anger. His dark eyes narrowed dangerously at her. "That is a load of crap and you know it. You didn't tell me about Jared because you're a control freak who couldn't stand someone else being involved in decisions for *your* son. You didn't tell me because you're selfish and you wanted him all to yourself, no matter what the cost to him."

"You bastard! I was protecting him from the life you hated."

"Yes, because it was so much better to suffer for your child and get sympathy than to give up your child dictatorship. Martyrdom doesn't look good on you, Sabine."

Her cheeks flushed red with anger. She didn't know what to say to him. There wasn't anything else to say. She turned her back on him and focused on packing and getting home to her son. She threw open her bag and chucked everything within reach into it. Whatever was too far away wasn't important enough to worry about. By the time she had her things together, so did he. He was standing at the front door, a car waiting for them in the driveway.

She couldn't speak. If she opened her mouth, she would say more horrible things. Some she meant, some she didn't. It was probably the same for him. Yelling made her feel better when she felt so helpless. Instead, she brushed past him to the car, giving her bags over to the driver and climbing inside.

The ride to the airport was just as silent. Her anger had begun to dissipate; this wasn't the time to start blaming and arguing. That time would come later, when Jared was home safely and she could think of something, anything, but her son's welfare.

The plane was well on its way back to New York before she so much as looked in Gavin's direction. There was only a foot between them, but it could've been miles. "Listen, fighting isn't going to get us anywhere, so let's call a truce until this whole mess is over."

Gavin's fingers flexed around the controls with anger

and anxiety, but the plane didn't so much as waver under his steady command. "Agreed."

"What else did your parents say when they called?"

"They had taken him to the park and then brought him home to take a nap before lunch. My mother said she fell asleep herself on the chaise in the living room. When she got up to check on him, he was gone and the ransom note was left on the bed."

"No one else was home?"

"My father was in his office. Nora had gone out to pick up groceries."

Sabine shook her head and focused her gaze on the miles of ocean between her and her baby. "How can someone just walk into a multimillion-dollar apartment building and walk out with our son? Did no one see him? Not even the doorman? Surely there are cameras everywhere."

"Whoever it was didn't go through the front door. They probably went in through the parking garage. There are cameras all over, but it requires a police request for them to pull the surveillance tapes."

"And?"

"And," Gavin said with a heavy sigh, "we haven't called the cops yet. The note threatened Jared's safety if we involved the police. I want to wait and take the kidnapper's call tonight. Then we might have a better idea of who we're working with here. At that point, we might get the NYPD to come in."

Sabine wasn't sure if she liked this plan or not. This was her first involvement with a kidnapping outside episodes of *Law & Order,* but calling the cops always seemed to be step number one in those situations. But perhaps Gavin had more insight into this than he was sharing. "You said 'a better idea of who we're working with.' Do you know who might be involved in this?"

Gavin shrugged, the dismissive gesture making her angrier than she already was. "It might not be anyone I know. With this kind of thing, it could just be some random creep out to make a quick buck in ransom money. You were right to say that claiming my son made him a target. It did. I hadn't really considered that until now.

"But I can't help but think this is someone I know. Jared isn't common knowledge yet. I can't be certain, but I've got a pretty short suspect list. Despite what you might think, I don't go around ruining my competitors and giving them reason to hate me."

"Who, out of those people, would despise you enough to kidnap your son?"

"Three, tops. And that's a stretch."

"And how many," Sabine asked with a tremble in her voice, "would be willing to *kill* your son for revenge?"

Gavin turned and looked at her, the blood draining from behind his newly tanned skin. "No one," he said, although not with enough confidence to make her feel better. "No one."

Eleven

Truthfully, Gavin only had one suspect on his list. As the time drew close for the call from the kidnappers, he was fairly certain who would be on the other end.

They had arrived safely at the airport and made their way to his parents' apartment as quickly as they could. His parents looked nearly ill when they walked in. His father's larger-than-life confidence had crumbled. His mother looked paper-thin and fragile. This had shaken them and it was no wonder. Their home, the one they'd shared for over thirty years, had been tainted by someone bold enough to stroll inside and walk out with the most precious treasure in their possession.

Sabine and his mother hugged fiercely and then went to sit together on the couch. His father paced in the corner, staring out the window at the city that had somehow betrayed him. Nora brought a tray with hot tea and nibbles that no one could stomach touching. Gavin just sat and waited for the call.

When the phone finally rang, Gavin's heart leaped into his throat. He answered on the second ring, gesturing for silence in the room. They had not called the police, but if the four nervous adults swarming him weren't quiet, the kidnapper might think the mansion was overrun with investigators and hostage negotiation teams.

"Hello?" he choked out.

"Gavin Brooks," the man said with an air of confidence that bordered on arrogance. Gavin didn't recognize the voice, but he hadn't spoken to his primary suspect. "So glad you could come home from your luxury vacation for our little chat."

"I want to talk to Jared," Gavin demanded as forcefully as he could.

Sabine leaped up and sat beside him on the couch. They hadn't really spoken much since their fight, and things might be irrevocably broken between them, but in this moment, they were united in finding their son and making sure Jared returned home safe and sound. He reached out and took her trembling hand in his. He was just as nervous, just as scared as she was, but he was better at not showing it. Holding her hand and keeping her calm was like an anchor on his own nerves. It kept the butterflies in his stomach from carrying him off into the sky.

"I bet you do. But you're not in charge here. I am. And you've got a couple hoops to jump through before that's even on the table."

"How do I know that you really have him?"

"If I don't...who does? You haven't misplaced your son, have you?"

"Is he okay?"

"For now. I haven't harmed a hair on his handsome little head. If you want to keep it that way, you'll do exactly as I ask and not involve the police. If you call the cops, we're done negotiating and you'll never see your little boy again."

Gavin nervously squeezed Sabine's hand. She smiled weakly at him, confusing his gesture as one of reassurance. He felt anything but sure. "I'm not calling the police. I want to keep this between you and me. But I have to know. What, exactly, do you want, Paul?"

The man on the other end of the line chuckled bitterly. "Aww, shoot. I was hoping it would take longer for you to figure out who was behind this. How did you guess it was me? I thought you'd be ruining the lives of half a dozen people right now, but you narrowed the field pretty quickly."

Paul Simpson. He had been right on the money with his original guess. Roger's irresponsible only son was the heir to Exclusivity Jetliners. At least until his father signed over the company to Gavin on Tuesday. The looming deadline must have pushed Paul too far. He had no choice but to act. That left little question of what his ransom demand would be.

"Only a handful of people knew I was going out of town. Even fewer knew that I had a son. That's not common knowledge yet."

Gavin had mentioned the trip to Roger when they spoke on the phone Thursday. He'd mentioned taking Sabine to Bermuda and that his parents would be watching Jared. That's when Roger had graciously offered the jet. If Paul was listening in on their conversation, all he had to do was wait for the right moment to slip in and steal away their son. He had handed his enemy the ammunition to attack him and didn't even realize it.

The only plus to this scenario was that Paul was spineless. Or so he seemed. Roger didn't have much faith in his son. When he snapped, Paul jumped to attention. That said, Gavin wouldn't have given him the credit to plan a scheme like this, so maybe he was wrong. He wouldn't push Paul to find out.

"Ahh. Well, mistakes are bound to be made in a scenario like this. Fortunately, we don't have to worry about any of that because this is going to go smoothly and without issue."

Somehow, Gavin doubted it. "What do you *want,* Paul? You still haven't told me what you're after with all this, although I have a pretty good guess."

"It's simple, really. First, you're going to call my father. You tell him that you have to back out of the merger deal. Give him whatever excuse you want to. Aside from blackmail, of course. But end it, and now."

The sinking feeling in his gut ached even more miserably than it had before. His dream of having his own jet fleet was slipping through his fingers. Everything he'd worked for, everything he'd built toward in the past few years would be traded away for his son. Gavin hadn't been a father for long, but he would do anything to keep Jared safe. If that meant losing Exclusivity Jetliners, that was the price he would pay. But that didn't mean it wouldn't hurt.

He should've seen this coming. Paul had silenced his complaints about the sale recently. Roger had thought that he had finally convinced his son to see reason, but

the truth was that Paul was quietly looking into alterna-
tives to get his way. Going around his father was the best
plan. But it wouldn't solve all of his problems.

"If I don't buy the company, your father will just sell
it to someone else."

"No!" Paul shouted into the line. "He won't. If this
falls through, he'll give me the chance to try running
the company on my own. Then I can prove to him that
I can do it and he won't sell."

Gavin wanted to tell Paul he was delusional, but he
couldn't. The moment Jared was safely in his arms, he'd
have the NYPD swarming this guy and hauling his ass
to Rikers Island for the foreseeable future. He wouldn't
be running a company anytime soon.

"After I call Roger and cancel the deal, we get our
son back?"

"Not exactly," Paul chuckled. "First, I have to confirm with my father that the merger is out for good. After
that, I need a little financial insurance. I expect to see
you at the bank bright and early in the morning—and
yes, I am watching you. You'll withdraw a million in
small bills and put it into a backpack. I'll call again in
the morning with the rendezvous point."

"And then we get Jared back."

"And then," Paul sighed in dismay, "yes, you get your
precious little boy back. But first, phone my father and
call off the deal. I'll be calling him in half an hour, and I
expect him to share the disappointing news when I speak
to him. You'll hear from me at 10:00 a.m. tomorrow."

The line went dead.

Gavin dropped the phone onto the table and flopped
back into the cushions of his couch. He was fighting

to keep it together, but inside, it felt as if his world was crumbling. His son was in danger. The one person he believed was in his life for good could be permanently snatched away on the whim of a ruthless man. His dreams of owning private jets were about to be crushed. The woman he cared for blamed him for all of it and might never forgive him if something went wrong. She was already one foot out of his life, he could tell.

But nothing he could say or do would guarantee that Jared would be handed over, unharmed. Or that Sabine would ever look at him with love in her eyes again.

She was watching him silently from the seat beside him. He was still clutching her hand, worried if he let go, he'd lose her forever. "Well," she said at last. "What did you find out?"

"Is Jared okay?" his mother asked.

"Yes, I think so. I know who has orchestrated this and why. I don't have any reason to believe that he won't return Jared to us safe and sound as long as I meet his demands."

She breathed a visible sigh of relief. "Who has him?"

"Paul Simpson. No one you know."

"What did he ask for?" His father finally entered the conversation.

"A million-dollar ransom, delivered tomorrow in exchange for Jared."

"Our accountant can make that happen," Byron confirmed.

"And today," Gavin continued, "the cancellation of my latest business deal."

Sabine gasped and squeezed his hand even tighter. "The one you were working with the private jet company?"

Gavin nodded, his gaze dropping down to his lap.

"Yes. I hope you enjoyed riding in that plane to Bermuda. That will probably be the last time."

"Oh, Gavin, I'm so sorry." Her pale eyes, lined with worry, were at once glassy with tears. For a moment he was jealous that she could cry for what he was losing and he couldn't. "I know how important that was to you. Maybe you can still—"

Gavin pulled his hand away and held it up to silence her. He wasn't in the mood to deal with the maybes and other consolations she could offer. It wouldn't matter. "Even if this all works out, I think my dealings with the Simpson family are over."

"We can acquire more planes, son."

He shook his head at his father. "Finding another company with a quality fleet I can afford is nearly impossible. The shareholders won't back a more expensive merger. The whole concierge plan is dead."

He turned away from his family and picked up his phone. He needed to call Roger, but that would wait a few more minutes. More important was calling his accountant. He didn't exactly leave thousands of dollars just lying around, much less a million. Some things would need to be shifted around so he had liquid assets for the ransom. His accountant would get everything together for him with little fuss.

The awkward call to his accountant took only a few minutes. The man seemed confused by the sudden and out-of-ordinary request, but he didn't question it. The money would be ready for pickup in the morning. That done, he couldn't put off the inevitable any longer.

Gavin slowly dialed the familiar number of Roger Simpson. With every fiber of his being, he didn't want to back out of this deal. It was everything he'd desired, and it was mere days from being his at last. He wasn't even sure how he would say the words out loud. His tongue might not cooperate. He'd rather shout at Roger about how his son was volatile, if not plain disturbed. But he wouldn't. Not while Jared's life was in another person's hands.

"Gavin?" Roger answered. "I didn't expect to hear from you today. You're back early from Bermuda. Did something happen? Was something wrong with the jet I loaned you?"

"The jet was fine. Don't worry about any of that. Something came up and we had to come back ahead of schedule." He just couldn't tell him that the something involved blackmail and kidnapping. "I—I'm sorry to have to make this call, Roger. I'm afraid I have to withdraw my offer to buy Exclusivity Jetliners."

"What?" Roger's voice cracked over the line. "You were thrilled about the offer when we last spoke just a few days ago. What's wrong? What happened to change your mind so suddenly? Did you find a better company to meet your needs? Our arrangement is completely negotiable."

"No, please, Roger. I'm sorry, but I can't really elaborate on the subject. I hate that I have to do this, but I must. I'm sorry for the trouble I'm causing you, but I have to go."

Gavin hung up the phone before Roger could grill him for more information. He did what he had to do for Jared's sake, but he didn't have to like it. Dropping his phone onto the coffee table, he got up, brushing off the questions and sympathetic looks of Sabine and his family, and walked out of the room. He needed some space to mourn his dreams, privately.

* * *

It was 10:00 a.m. and Gavin had returned from the bank with the million-dollar ransom a few minutes ago. The whole family was gathered around the phone waiting for Paul's call and the instructions for today's trade-off.

Sabine hadn't slept. They had all stayed at the Brooks mansion, but even an expensive mattress with luxury linens couldn't lure her to sleep. And from the looks of it, Gavin hadn't slept, either. Never in her life had she seen him look like he did right now. His eyes were lined with exhaustion and sadness. Gray smudges circled beneath them. He wasn't frowning, but he wasn't smiling, either. He had shut everything off. She recognized that in him. There was too much to deal with, too much that could go wrong, so he had chosen to numb himself to the possibilities.

She knew it was hard on him. Not only because of his concern for Jared but what it cost him to ensure his son's safety. That jet acquisition had meant everything to him. Seeing him in the cockpit of that plane had been an eye-opening experience. She had experienced what she thought was the pinnacle of passion when she made love to Gavin. But for him, there was a higher joy, a greater pleasure.

He'd been so close to merging his work and his dreams. And he'd been forced to throw it away.

Sabine placed a reassuring hand on his knee, and he covered it with his own. The warmth of his skin against hers chased away the fears that threatened from the corners of her mind. She wouldn't allow herself to indulge those thoughts. She'd be no good to her son if she was a hysterical mess.

As much as she'd yelled at Gavin, and blamed him for this whole mess, she was glad to have him here with her during this. No one should have to deal with this sort of thing alone. He had handled everything, and well. There were benefits to having a take-charge man in her life, even when it was sometimes frustrating.

Gavin would do whatever it took to see that their son came home safely. Jared was their number one priority.

The phone rang. The loud sound was amplified in the silent room, sending Sabine straight up out of her seat. Gavin calmly reached out and hit the button for the speakerphone. Sabine hated listening to only half the conversation and had asked him to let her listen this time, as well.

"Yes?"

"I'm surprised, Gavin." Paul's voice boomed through the speaker. "You've done everything I've asked so far without a whisper to the police. My father was quite disappointed that your deal fell through. It was hard not to laugh in his face. You've been so cooperative you must really care about this brat. Funny, considering you've only known about him for two weeks."

Sabine fought back her urge to scream profanities into the phone. They were too close to getting Jared home safely. She could say or do whatever she wanted after that.

"I've got the money," Gavin said, ignoring his taunts. "What now?"

"Meet me in an hour in Washington Square Park. I'll be waiting by the arch with junior. You hand over the backpack, I hand over the kid."

"I'll be there."

"If I so much as smell a cop, we're done. And so is the kid."

Paul hung up, leaving them all in a stunned silence. After a moment, Celia started crying. Byron put his arm around her.

"Don't worry, dear. He doesn't have the nerve to actually hurt Jared, no matter what he says."

Gavin stood up and nodded. "He's right. Roger told me once that Paul didn't have enough ambition to get out of bed before noon most days. This is just the quickest, easiest way to make some money and get his father to do what he wants." He slung the backpack with the money onto his shoulder. "I'd better go."

Sabine leaped up, as well. "I'm going with you."

Gavin's jaw tightened. He looked as though he wanted to argue with her, but he didn't. Gavin might be able to get his way when it came to unimportant things, but that was because most times, Sabine didn't care. She cared about this, and she wouldn't take no for an answer.

"Okay. Let's go."

Sabine grabbed her own red backpack. It had a change of clothes, Pull-Ups, dry cereal, Jared's favorite stuffed dinosaur and one of his trucks. She wanted to have everything she needed to clean him up and comfort him the minute she could finally get herself to let go.

Gavin had a car drive them downtown. It let them off about a block from the park and would circle until he called to be picked up. If all went well, this shouldn't take long.

Sabine's heart was pounding wildly in her chest as they walked through the park and headed toward the arch. She could barely hear the sounds of the traffic and people surrounding them. Gavin clutched her hand in his, steadying and guiding her to the rendezvous point.

They were about five minutes early. She didn't know what Paul Simpson looked like, but Jared was nowhere in sight.

The minutes ticked by. Anxiously waiting. Then she heard it.

"Mommy!"

Like an arrow through her brain, Sabine immediately recognized the voice of her child amid the chaos of downtown. Her head turned sharply to the left. There, an older man was walking toward them carrying Jared in his arms.

She broke into a sprint, closing the gap between them. It wasn't part of the plan, but Sabine didn't care. She could hear Gavin running behind her. She stopped herself short of the man, who looked nothing like she expected him to. He was in his late fifties easily, in a nice suit. He also immediately lifted Jared from his hip and handed him into her arms.

Something about this didn't seem right, but it didn't matter. All that mattered was the warm, snuggling body of her baby back in her arms. Jared clung to her neck, his breathing a little labored as she nearly squeezed the life out of him. When she could finally ease up, she inspected her son for signs of his abduction. He was clean. Rosy-cheeked. Smiling. He actually didn't appear to think anything was awry.

What the hell was really going on?

"Roger?"

Sabine pried her attention away to listen to Gavin's conversation. Roger? That was Paul's father. Was he involved in this, too?

"Gavin, I am so sorry. You have no idea how disturbed I was to find out what was really going on. My son..." His voice trailed off. "It's inexcusable. There are no words to express how horrified I am. This must have been a day of pure hell for you both."

"What happened, Roger? We were supposed to be meeting Paul here." Gavin's dark eyes flickered over Sabine and Jared, but he didn't dare try to hold his son. He'd have to pry him from Sabine's dead arms.

"After your call last night, I got concerned. When I went into the office this morning, I heard Paul talking to someone in the day care center of our offices. He doesn't have children, so there was no reason for him to be there. Later, I overheard him talking on the phone to you. After he hung up, I confronted him and he confessed everything to me. My wife and I have been concerned about him for a while, but you never believe your children could ever do something as horrible as this."

"Where is he now?"

"He's in one of my jets on his way to a very expensive long-term rehab facility in Vermont. It was that or I disinherited him. If you want to press charges, I completely understand. I can give you the facility address for the police to pick him up. I just wanted to start getting him help right away. It seems he had more problems than even I knew, including an expensive drug habit. He owed his dealer quite a bit and had worked out a deal where he would let them use our planes to import and export drugs. That was the only reason he wanted the company. Can you imagine?"

"I'm sorry to hear that, Roger."

The old man shook his head sadly and looked over at Jared. It must be hard to know your child did something terrible when all you can see is them when they were little.

"I want you to know your little boy was in the best possible care the entire time he was gone. Paul put him in the Exclusivity Jetliners day care center. We run a twenty-four-hour facility for our employees who might have to go on long flights or overnight trips. Jared spent the last day playing with the other children. I personally guarantee there's not a scratch on him."

Sabine felt a wave of relief wash over her. No wonder Jared seemed perfectly contented. He thought he had spent the day at school with new friends and had no clue he was a kidnapping victim. Thank goodness for that. She ran her palm over his head, messing up the soft, dark hairs and standing them on end.

Jared rubbed his hair back down with both hands. "Dinosaur?" he asked.

Sabine crouched down, settling him on his feet and pulling her bag off her shoulder. "He's right here." She pulled out the plush triceratops from their trip to the American Museum of Natural History.

Jared happily hugged the dinosaur and leaned against her leg. He wasn't traumatized by the whole ordeal, but Mommy was gone a little too long for his taste. She wasn't going to be out of his sight for a while, and she knew exactly how he felt.

"I want to make this up to you," Roger said. He was shuffling awkwardly in his loafers. "At least I want to try. I doubt anything can make it better."

"Don't beat yourself up over this, Roger. You can't control what your kids do when they're adults."

"No, Gavin. I'm taking responsibility for this whole mess. I kept waiting for him to grow up, and I let things go too far. Now I want to change what I can. If you're still interested, I want to make sure you get these planes you're after. There's no way in hell I want my son to ever have his hands in the company—rehab or no. Because of everything that happened, I'd like to sell it to you for twenty percent less than we previously negotiated. How's that sound?"

Sabine watched Gavin's eyes widen in surprise. Twenty percent of the money they were talking about was apparently a huge amount. She couldn't even imagine it.

"Roger, I—"

"And I'll throw in *Beth*."

"No." Gavin shook his head. "Absolutely not. That's your private jet. You named it after your wife!"

Roger smiled and patted Gavin on the shoulder. "My first wife," he clarified. "She's not a part of the Exclusivity Jetliners fleet, I know. But I want to give her to you. Not to BXS, but to *you*. Even if the merger is off the table. I know you've always wanted your own jet, and it doesn't get much better than my *Beth,* I assure you."

"What about you?" Gavin asked.

"I'll take some of the money I make off the sale and maybe I'll buy a smaller plane. I don't need such a big one anymore. Anyway, I don't want to give Paul too many options. Maybe I'll just get a nice yacht instead and take the missus to Monaco."

"Are you sure?"

"Absolutely. I'll have my lawyers redraft the agreement and we'll be back on for Tuesday." Roger smiled and looked down at Jared with a touch of sadness in his eyes. "Again, I'm sorry about all of this. Please, take your son home and enjoy your afternoon with him."

Then he leaned in closer to Gavin. "And for the love of God, stop by the bank and get that cash put back someplace safe. You can't just walk around with a million dollars in a backpack."

Twelve

"Well," Gavin said, breaking the long silence. "Tomorrow I'm going to call the Realtor and let her know that the apartment overlooking Washington Square Park is out."

"Out? Why?" Sabine asked from the seat beside him. The town car had picked them up after Roger left and was taking them back uptown to his apartment.

"I'm not paying five million dollars for a place that will do nothing but remind you of all of this every time you look out the window. This location is tainted."

Sabine sighed. "We looked at over half a dozen apartments last week, and that was the only one I really liked. I understand your concerns, but I hate to start over."

Thankfully, Gavin had no intention of putting her through all that again. There was only one apartment she needed to tour. It had taken him a long time to come to this conclusion, but now his mind was made up. "We're not. A place has come available that no one knows about yet. I think you're really going to love it."

Her brows arched in question, but she didn't press him. At least not now. She was too busy holding a squirming Jared in her lap. After the past twenty-four hours of hell, she probably didn't think apartment hunting was high on their agenda. She would question him later.

Besides, they hadn't spoken—really spoken—since their fight on the beach. They were angry with one another and then they set that aside while they focused on getting Jared back. Now, with all of that behind them, they had nothing to do but deal with each other and the fallout of their heated and regretful words.

Gavin wasn't ready to start that awkward conversation yet. He was much happier to watch Sabine and Jared interact as they drove home. Occasionally she leaned down and inhaled the scent of his baby shampoo and smiled, very nearly on the verge of tears. How could she ever have thought he could split the two of them up? It was an impossible task.

And as time went by, splitting Gavin from Sabine and Jared was an even more impossible task.

He'd signed off on the custody agreements because they were fair and reasonable, but he didn't like them. He wouldn't see Jared nearly enough. And aside from the occasional custody trade-off, nowhere in the pile of paperwork did it say how often he would get to see Sabine. There was no such thing as visitation with the mother.

At this point, she might not want anything else to do with him. They had both said terrible things to each other. He hadn't meant a word of it. He'd been hurt by her blame and flung the most convenient insults he could find. He could tell her that. But he knew Sabine. She wouldn't pay any attention to his apologies. They were just words, and she had told him more than once that actions spoke louder.

Now was the time for action.

The car finally pulled up outside of the Ritz-Carlton. He ushered them both inside through the crowd of tourists and over to the residential elevator. He swiped the card that had special access to his floor of the hotel. In his apartment with the door locked, Gavin finally felt secure again. His family was safe and intact and he was never going to let them out of his sight again.

Once they settled in, he called his parents to let them know Jared was okay. He should've called from the car, but he needed time to mentally unwind and process everything that happened.

Jared was playing with his dinosaur on the floor when he got off the phone. Sabine was staring out the window at Central Park, her arms crossed protectively over her chest.

"Sabine?" She turned to look at him, an expression of sadness on her face. "Are you okay?"

She nodded softly. "Yes. I wanted to tell you that I'm sorry about everything I said to you. I was upset and scared when I found out something had happened to Jared. Blaming you was the easiest thing to do. It was wrong of me. Your son was in danger, too."

"I said things I didn't mean, too."

"Yes, but you were right. I was being selfish. I was so afraid of not having Jared all to myself that I kept him from you. I shouldn't have done that. I'm glad that Clay saw me and told you about him. It was a step I couldn't make on my own. I'm really glad you're going to be a part of his life."

"What about your life?"

Sabine's eyes narrowed. "Of course Jared is already a huge part of my life. Any more, he is my life."

Gavin took a few steps closer to her. "I wasn't talking about Jared. I was talking about me. Will I get to be a part of your life, too?"

She sighed and let her gaze drop to the floor. "I don't know, Gavin. The last few weeks have been nice, but it has been a lot, and fast. We have a lifetime of sharing our son. I don't want anything to mess that up. I know how important he is to you."

"*You're* important to me," he emphasized. "Both of you. Not just Jared. All this time, all that we've shared together these weeks… It wasn't just about our son or wooing you into giving me what I wanted. You know that, right?"

Sabine looked up at him, her pale green eyes still sad and now, a touch wearier than before. "I want to believe that, Gavin. Truly, I do. But how can I know anything about our relationship when you won't tell me how you feel? You'd rather let me walk away than tell me you want me to stay. I can't spend all our time together guessing. I need you to talk to me."

"You know that's hard for me. I've never been good at voicing my feelings. I've spent my whole life watching people walk away and never come back. My parents were always busy, foisting me and my siblings off on one nanny after the next until I was old enough for boarding school. They were so worried about keeping up appearances that I changed schools every few years to move on to a more prestigious program. It didn't take long for me to learn to keep my distance from everyone."

"Not everyone is going to leave you, Gavin."

"You did. You said that you would've stayed if I had asked, but how do I know that for certain? What if I told them how I felt and they left anyway? I'm not good with words. Can't I just show you how I feel?"

"More kisses? More gifts and fancy dinners? That doesn't mean anything to me. I need more, Gavin. I need to hear the words coming from your lips."

He reached out for her hand. "I'm offering more. But first, please, I want to show you something." He tugged gently until she followed him down the hallway toward Jared's newly renovated bedroom.

"You already showed me Jared's room."

"I know. This time I want to show you the other room."

Gavin turned the knob and pushed open the door to what used to be his office. When he flipped on the light switch, he heard Sabine gasp beside him.

"Remember in the car when I said that I knew of an available property that you would love? This is it. I had the old office done up for you. An art studio just for you to work. You don't have to share it with a toddler or storage boxes or cleaning supplies. It's all yours for you to do whatever you like."

Sabine stepped ahead of him into the large, open room. He'd had the hardwood floors refinished. The walls were painted a soft, matte green very close to the color of her eyes. "The consultant I worked with told me that this shade of green was a good choice for an art studio because it wouldn't influence the color of your work and would provide enough light with the off-white ceilings."

There was one large window that let in plenty of natural light and several nonfluorescent fixtures that he was told were good for art. A leather love seat sat along one wall. Several cabinets lined the other, each filled with every painting supply he could order. Several easels were already set up with blank canvases perched on them, and a few framed paintings were hanging on the walls.

"That shade of green also looked wonderful with the paintings I had of yours."

"It's beautiful. Perfect." Sabine approached one of the three canvases hanging on the wall and let her finger run along the large wooden frame. "I didn't know you had bought any of my work. Why didn't you tell me?"

"Because I bought the pieces after you left me. It was my way of keeping you in my life, I guess."

She spun on her heel to face him, her brow knit together with excitement tampered by confusion. "When did you decide to do all this?"

"Three years ago."

"What?" she gasped.

"The room was nearly finished when you broke it off. I was planning on asking you to move in with me and giving you the room as a housewarming gift. I decided to go ahead and complete it, and then I didn't have the heart to do anything else with it. I've just kept the door shut."

"You wanted me to move in with you?" Sabine's hands dropped helplessly at her sides. "I wish to God you would've said something. I didn't think I mattered to you. I loved you, but I thought I was a fool."

"I was the fool for letting you walk away. I wanted you here with me then, and I was too afraid to admit to myself that I still wanted you here with me now. I would've bought you any apartment you chose, but I knew you were meant to be here with me."

"Why didn't you tell me about it when you showed me Jared's new room?"

Gavin took a deep breath. "I thought it was too soon to show it to you. We were slowly rebuilding our relationship. I didn't know where we would end up. I thought that I might scare you away if you saw it. Too much, too soon."

"Why would you think that?"

"You'd already laughed off my proposal and shot down any suggestion of moving in with me."

"To be fair, it wasn't much of a proposal."

"True. Which is why I worried you would think the studio was my way of trying to bribe you into moving in with me after you told me no already. It's not a bribe. It's a homecoming gift. I started working on this place years ago because I wanted it to be a home for us. Now, a home for *all* of us. Not a part-time, alternate weekends and holidays home. For every day. All three of us together."

He watched tears start welling in her eyes and didn't know if it was a good or bad sign. He decided to go with it. The moment felt right even though he wasn't as prepared as he would like to be.

"Sabine, I know I'm no good at talking about my feelings. I built this space for you because I...I love you. I loved you then and I love you now. This was the only way I could think of to show you how I felt."

"You love me?" Sabine asked with a sly smile curling her lips.

"I do. Very much."

"Then say it again," she challenged.

"I love you," he repeated, this time without hesitation. A grin of his own spread wide across his face. It was getting easier every time he said it. "Now it's your turn."

Sabine leaned into him, her green gaze focused intently on him. "I love you, Gavin," she said without a moment's indecision. Then she placed her hands on his face and leaned in to kiss him.

Gavin wrapped his arms around her, thankful to have this again after two days without her touch or her kisses to help him get through it. He'd worried that he'd ruined it again.

"I'm glad you do," he said. Gavin pulled her hands from his face and held them in his. "That will make this next part less embarrassing. I want to ask again if you'll marry me, but this time, even if the answer is no, please don't laugh. A man's ego can't take that twice."

"Okay," Sabine said, her face now perfectly solemn in preparation for his query.

Gavin dropped down to one knee, her hands still grasped in his own. "Sabine Hayes, I love you. And I love our son. I want us to be a family. There is nothing on this earth—not a jet, not money—that I want more than for you to be my wife. Will you marry me?"

Sabine could barely withstand the rush of emotions surging through her. She really was on an emotional roller coaster. She'd experienced the highest of highs and the lowest of lows all in a few hours' time. If Gavin wasn't looking up at her with dark, love-filled eyes, she might start nervously twittering with laughter again simply from the stress of it all.

But she couldn't laugh. Not this time. Gavin wanted to marry her and there was nothing funny about that.

"Yes. I will marry you."

Gavin stood back up and swept her into his arms. His mouth eagerly captured hers, sealing their agreement with a kiss that made her blood sizzle through her veins. She wanted to make love to him on the leather couch of her new studio. The sooner she could start creating memories in her new home, the better.

Of course, that would have to wait for nap time.

Instead, she looked up into the dark eyes of her fiancé. The man she loved. The father of her child. There, in his arms, everything felt right. This is what she'd missed, the thing that made all those other apartments seem cold and unappealing.

"Gavin, do you know why I didn't like any of the apartments we looked at?"

He gave her a lopsided smile in response to her unexpected question. "You wanted crown molding and granite countertops?"

"No. Guess again."

He shrugged. "I'm out of guesses. Why didn't you like them?"

"Because they were all missing something—*you*."

Gavin laughed. "Of course. There's only one apartment in Manhattan that comes equipped with Gavin Brooks. It's a very exclusive address. The only way to get into the place is through marriage."

"Well, wouldn't you know that THE Gavin Brooks just asked me to be his wife?"

He picked up her left hand and eyed the bare ring finger. "This won't do. The first thing everyone will do when you tell them we're engaged is look at your hand. We need to get you an engagement ring."

"Right now?"

"We're two blocks away from Tiffany's. Why not right now?"

Sabine sighed. It had been an exciting couple of

days. Too exciting if you asked her. She was happy to spread out some of the big moments to later in the week. "There's no rush. I know you're good for it. There's a million dollars in cash lying around on the living room floor in a JanSport."

"Okay, you win. What about tomorrow?"

"I have to work tomorrow morning."

Gavin eyed her with dismay. "No, you don't."

"Yes, I do. I'm not going to abandon my wonderful, pregnant boss when she needs me. You're the one that suggested a vacation. I at least have to stay at the store long enough for her to take one."

"What about if we go early, before the boutique opens?"

"Okay," Sabine relented. If he wanted so badly to put a dangerously expensive rock on her hand, she would let him. "But make sure you don—"

"Spider-Man!"

Sabine and Gavin turned to find Jared standing in the doorway of his new bedroom. He flung the door the rest of the way open and charged in the space that was custom-made for a little boy with dreams of being a superhero.

The workers had done an excellent job on the room. It was just as Gavin had described. Red walls, a loft with a rope swing for an adventurous young boy, and a comic-book motif sure to please. All it needed was his favorite toys from their place in Brooklyn and it would be perfect.

Jared crawled up on the new bed, bouncing ever so slightly on the new Spider-Man comforter. "Big bed!"

"Yep, it's a big boy bed."

"Mine?"

"It is," Gavin replied. "Do you like it?"

Jared flipped two thumbs up. "Love Spider-Man!"

Sabine was nearly overwhelmed by the joy and excitement on their small son's face. Gavin turned to look at her and frowned when he noted the tears pooling in her eyes.

"And I love you," she said.

"More than Spider-Man?" Gavin asked.

"Oh, yeah," she replied, leaning in to kiss him and prove her point.

Epilogue

Sabine was exhausted. There wasn't really another word to describe the state a woman was in immediately following childbirth. The messy business was over. The doctors and nurses had cleared out and the family went home. Now it was just Sabine and Gavin in a quiet hospital suite.

Well, make that just Sabine, Gavin *and* the brand-new Miss Elizabeth Anne Brooks in a quiet hospital suite.

Beth made her arrival at 4:53 p.m., weighing seven pounds, two ounces and shrieking with the finest set of lungs to ever debut at St. Luke's Hospital. They named her after Gavin's private plane—*Beth*—and Sabine's mother, with whom she'd recently reconciled.

Gavin's parents, siblings and the housekeeper had left a few hours ago with Jared in tow. Their son had been very excited to see his new sister, but the novelty wore off pretty quickly when she didn't do anything but sleep.

He insisted that Grandpa and Grandma take him for ice cream and when visiting hours ended, they relented.

It had been a long day filled with excitement, nerves, joy and pain. And now, she was enjoying a private moment she would remember for her whole life.

Gavin was beside her in the reclining chair. Beth was bundled up in a white blanket with pastel stripes. She was perfect, tiny and pink with Sabine's nose. The nurses had put a hat on to keep her head warm. It hid away the wild mohawk of dark hair she'd been born with. Gavin said her crazy hair was from Sabine, too. Beth had fallen asleep with her small hand clutching his pinky finger, content, warm and safe in her daddy's arms.

But the best part was watching Gavin.

The past nine months had been an adventure for her husband. Since he'd missed out on her first pregnancy, Gavin wanted to be a part of every moment from sonograms to Lamaze classes. Sometimes she wondered if he regretted getting so immersed in the details of the process.

He could handle running shipping empires and flying jets, but preparing for the arrival of a new baby—and a girl at that—nearly did him in. During labor, he was wide-eyed and panicked. Occasionally even a little green around the gills. It was pretty adorable.

Then she was born, shouting her displeasure to everyone in the maternity ward. Of course, Sabine looked at her baby first, cataloging fingers and toes and noting how beautiful and perfect she was. But the moment Beth was laid on her chest, Sabine's eyes went to Gavin. The expression on his face was priceless. It was quite literally love at first sight.

And now, while he held her, a marching band could parade through the room and Gavin probably wouldn't notice. He couldn't tear his gaze away from his daughter. It was as though the answers to all the questions in the universe were wrapped up in that blanket. It was the most precious thing Sabine had ever seen.

"You're my hero."

Sabine didn't realize Gavin was looking at her until he spoke. "Your hero?"

"Absolutely. You were amazing today." Gavin stood slowly so he didn't wake their daughter and carried Beth over to her.

Sabine accepted the bundle and smiled up at him. "Eh, piece of cake. I think I only threatened your life once."

"Twice, but who's counting?" Gavin eased down to sit on the edge of the bed and put his arm around her shoulders. "Seriously, though, I don't know how you did it. *Before*. With Jared. I mean, I knew that *I* had missed a lot, but one thing I never really considered was how it was for you. To do this all alone…"

It certainly was different this time. Before, one of her gallery friends came by the next day. That was it. This time, she had an entire cheering squad waiting in the next room, a crew in Nebraska staying up to date on Facebook and a husband holding her hand. What a difference a few years could make.

"That was the choice I made." She shrugged. "The wrong one, obviously. It was definitely better with you here."

Gavin leaned in to place a kiss on her lips and another on Beth's forehead. "I have to say I agree."

They both spent a moment looking down at their daughter. "She looks like you," Gavin said.

"That's fair since Jared looks like you. Besides, it would be unfortunate for a girl to have your chin."

"I can tell she's going to give me trouble. If she's half as beautiful and smart and talented as her mother, the boys will be lined up the block."

"She's four hours old. I don't think you need to start polishing the shotgun just yet. You've got years of ballet recitals and princess parties before we need to start worrying about that."

Gavin smiled and leaned his head against hers. "I'm looking forward to every pink, glittery second."

* * * * *

BABY FOR KEEPS

BY
JANICE MAYNARD

I dedicate this book to children everywhere who think
they are not smart. Don't ever believe it! It's a great big
world out there. Follow your dreams. . .always!

One

Saturday nights were always busy at the Silver Dollar Saloon. Dylan Kavanagh surveyed the crowd with a gaze that catalogued every detail. The newlyweds at table six. The habitual drunk who would soon have to be booted out. The kid who looked nervous enough to be contemplating the use of a fake ID.

Around the bar—a winding expanse of wood that dated back to the 1800s and had been rescued from a building in Colorado—the usual suspects ordered drinks and munched on peanuts. The tourists were easy to spot, not only because Dylan knew most of the locals, but because the out-of-towners scanned the room eagerly, hoping to spot celebrities.

Western North Carolina's natural beauty drew people for many reasons. Families on vacation, for sure. But the state was also a hot spot for location scouts. Dylan's home, the elegant town of Silver Glen, was no stranger to famous faces. Just last week one of Hollywood's iconic directors had wrapped production on a civil-war picture.

Dylan shrugged inwardly. He had no interest at all in the famous or the infamous when it came to the world of filmmaking, no matter how many A-listers dropped by for a drink or a meal. Once burned, twice shy.

Suddenly, he realized that he had unconsciously been watching something that sent up a red flag. The woman at the other end of the bar was knocking back drinks at an alarming rate. He frowned, surprised that his head bartender, Rick, hadn't already cut her off.

Working his way behind the bar, Dylan inched closer to Rick. Two other servers were helping out because things were so hectic. And that wasn't counting the three waitresses handling food orders out on the floor.

When Dylan was in earshot of his employee, he tapped him on the shoulder and muttered, "You need to pull the plug on the lady in pink. She's had enough, I think." The woman exhibited an air of desperation that didn't mix well with alcohol.

Rick grinned, his big hands busy filling drink orders. "Not to worry, Boss. She's drinking virgin strawberry daiquiris."

"Ah." It was blisteringly hot outside, an airless summer evening that justified anyone having a cold one…or two or three. The AC was working very well in here right now, yet the woman swallowed her icy drinks with reckless precision. With a nod, Dylan moved away, aware that he was creating a traffic jam in the narrow space.

Rick, who was two decades his senior, cocked his head toward the door. "Go home, Boss. We got this." The big, burly man with the country accent was perfectly suited to his job. And he was a pro. He and the rest of the staff didn't need Dylan hovering and giving the impression he didn't trust them.

But the truth was, Dylan loved the Silver Dollar. He'd bought it as a twenty-year-old kid, and after renovating the old building from the ground up, he'd opened what was to become one of Silver Glen's most thriving businesses.

Dylan had been a wealthy man when he bought the bar. And if the place ever went belly-up, he'd be a rich man still. As one of the Kavanaghs, the family that put Silver Glen on the map back in the mid-twentieth century, Dylan could easily afford to spend his days and his dollars on idle living. But his mother, Maeve, had brought up all seven of her boys to respect the value of a hard day's work.

That wasn't why Dylan was hanging around the Silver Dollar on a Saturday night. He had put in plenty of hours this week. The reason was far more complex. This bar was proof—hard-core evidence—that he wasn't a total failure in life. Despite his youthful stumbles, he had made something of himself.

He didn't like thinking about his adolescence. Parts of it had been a nightmare. And the ugly reality that he was never going to match his older brother in academic achievement had tormented him right up until the day he admitted defeat and dropped out of college.

The truth was, he felt more like himself here at the saloon than most any other place. The Silver Dollar was laid-back, sometimes rowdy, and always interesting. It felt comfortable. Nobody here knew about his failings. No one, even the locals, seemed to remember that Dylan had been metaphorically voted "student most likely to be a bum."

He'd absolutely hated not being able to master the required subjects in school, but he had masked his anger and frustration by building a reputation for insolence, irresponsibility and wild partying.

Only when he had found this old building disintegrating and in disrepair had he finally settled down and found his passion. Like the building, there was more to Dylan than met the eye. But he'd had to prove himself. So the Silver Dollar was more than a project. It was his personal declaration of independence.

Besides, Dylan was *between relationships* at the moment, and he'd rather be here mingling than sitting at home watching summer reruns. He was a people person, plain and simple. That brought him back to the puzzle of the woman in pink.

Ignore her. Rick was right. Dylan *should* go home. As much as he enjoyed spending time at the Silver Dollar, there was more to life than business. Before he departed, though, he knew he had to check on his unusual and intriguing customer. When the stool beside her became available, Dylan took it as a sign. He had Irish blood running in his veins. Sometimes the universe pointed toward a clear and obvious path.

It wasn't strange to have a single lady drinking at the bar. But the ones who did were usually trolling for a pickup. This slight, harried-looking woman seemed to be encased in a bubble of solitude, her eyes focused on her drink. Quietly, he sat down to her left and only then saw what he hadn't been able to see from his previous vantage point.

She was holding a baby.

An infant, to be exact. Cradled in the woman's right arm, resting in her lap, was a tiny, sleeping child. A girl, if the little pink ribbon stuck to her one curl of dark hair was any indication.

Already regretting his impulse, Dylan assessed the situation instantly, realizing that more was at work here than a woman needing a drink. If he were smart, he would back away. His impulse to wade in and help people often went unappreciated, or even worse, blew up in his face.

When the woman didn't so much as acknowledge his presence, even though they were sitting practically hip to hip, his gut told him to stand up and walk away. He would have. He should have. But just then the slender female plopped her glass on the bar, hiccuped and gave one of those little multiple-hitching sighs that said louder than words she had been crying, was about to cry or was trying *not* to cry.

Female tears scared the crap out of Dylan. He was no different than any other member of his sex in that regard.

He had grown up without sisters, and the last time he saw his mother cry was at his dad's funeral years ago. So the urge to run made complete sense.

But something held him in his seat. Some gut-deep, chivalrous desire to help. That, and the faint female scent that made him think of summer roses blooming in the gardens up at the Silver Beeches, his brother's ritzy hotel on top of the mountain.

Still debating what he should say or do, he paused for another careful, sideways glance. His mystery lady was sitting down, so it was hard to gauge her height, but *average* was his best guess. She wore khaki pants and a pale pink, button-down shirt. Dark brown hair pulled back in a ragged ponytail revealed her delicate profile and a pointed chin with a bit of a stubborn tilt.

Something about her was very familiar, perhaps because she reminded him of the actress Zooey Deschanel, only without the smile or the joie de vivre. The woman at Dylan's side was the picture of exhaustion. Her left hand no longer held a drink, but even at rest, it fisted on the bar. No wedding ring. That, however, could mean anything.

Stand up. Walk away.

His subconscious tried to help him, it really did. But sometimes a man had to do what a man had to do. Grimacing inwardly, he leaned a bit closer to be heard over the music and the high-decibel conversations surrounding them. "Excuse me, ma'am. I'm Dylan Kavanagh, the owner here. Are you okay? Is there anything I can do to help?"

If Mia hadn't been holding her daughter, Cora, so tightly, she might have dropped the sleeping baby. The shock of hearing Dylan's voice after so many years burned through her stupor of despair and fatigue and ripped at her nerve endings. She had walked into the Silver Dollar because she heard he was the owner and because she was curious about how things had turned out for him. She hadn't really expected him to be here.

Looking up, she bit her lip. "Hello, Dylan. It's me. Mia. Mia Larin."

The poleaxed look that crossed his face wasn't flattering. Only a blind woman could have missed the mix of emotions that was a long way from "Great to see you." He recovered quickly, though. "Good Lord. Mia Larin. What brings you back to Silver Glen?"

It was a reasonable question. She hadn't lived here since the year she and Dylan graduated from high school. He had been eighteen and full of piss and vinegar. She had been sixteen and scared of what lay ahead. She'd also been a social misfit with an IQ near 170 and little else to commend her. While she was in graduate school, her parents had sold the family home and retired to the Gulf Coast, thus severing her last connection to Silver Glen.

She shrugged, feeling her throat close up at the memories. "I don't really know. Nostalgia, I guess. How are you doing?"

It was a stupid question. She could *see* how he was doing. The boy with the skinny, rangy frame had filled out, matured, taken a second helping of tall, dark and gorgeous. His warm, whiskey-brown eyes locked on hers and made her stomach do a free fall, even though she was sitting down.

Broad shoulders and a headful of thick, golden-chestnut hair, along with a hard, muscled body added up to a man who oozed masculinity. She wondered if he was still as much of a badass as he had been as a teenager. Back then his aim in life seemed to be seeking out trouble.

He was the first boy she'd ever had as a friend, the only boy who had ever kissed her, until she got out of college.

And here he was, looking too damned appealing for his own good.

Dylan grinned, the flash of his smile a blow to her already damaged heart. In an instant, she was back in school, heartsick with a desperate crush that was laced with the knowledge she had as much chance of ever becoming Dylan Kavanagh's girlfriend as she did of being voted Homecoming Queen.

He raised a hand, and at some unseen signal, the bartender brought him a club soda with lime. Dylan took a drink, set down his glass and flicked the end of her ponytail. "You've grown up."

The three laconic words held equal measures of surprise and male interest. Her stupid heart responded with adolescent pleasure despite the fact that she was now past thirty, held two doctoral degrees and, as of twelve weeks ago, had become a mother.

"So have you." Though it galled her to admit it, she couldn't hold his gaze. She was no longer the painfully shy girl she had been when he knew her before, but even the most confident of women would have to admit that Dylan Kavanagh was a bit overwhelming at close range.

He toyed with the straw in his glass, not bothering to disguise his curiosity as he looked down at Cora. The baby, bless her heart, was sleeping blissfully. It was only at two in the morning that she usually showed any aversion to slumber.

"So you have a child," he said.

"What tipped you off, smart guy?"

He winced.

Appalled, she realized that her careless comment must have sounded like a reference to the past. She'd tutored him because he had dyslexia. As a senior, Dylan had hated being forced to take help from a classmate, especially one who had skipped two grades and was only fifteen. The pride of a cocky teenage boy had taken a beating at having Mia witness his inability to read and master English textbooks and novels.

"That's not what I meant," she said quickly. "I'm sorry. I'm a little self-conscious about having a baby and not being married. My parents are adjusting, but they don't like it."

"So where's the kid's dad?" Dylan seemed to have forgiven Mia for her awkward comment. His eyes registered more than a passing interest in the answer to his question as he waited.

"I'm not really prepared to go into that."

The man on her right reared back in raucous laughter and jostled her roughly. Mia cuddled Cora more tightly, realizing that a bar was the last place in the world she should have brought her infant daughter.

Dylan must have come to the same conclusion, because he put a hand on her arm and smiled persuasively. "We can't talk here. Let's go upstairs and get comfortable. It used to be my bookkeeper's apartment, but she moved out last Tuesday."

Mia allowed him to help her to her feet. Grabbing the diaper bag she'd propped on the foot rail, she slung it over her shoulder. "That would be nice." For a woman with a genius IQ, she probably should have been able to come up with a better adjective. But this encounter seemed surreal. Her social skills were rusty at best. Given the fact that she hadn't slept a full night since Cora had been born, it was no wonder *nice* was the best she could do..

"Follow me." Dylan led her across the restaurant floor to a hallway at the back of the building. The steep, narrow staircase at the end was dimly lit.

He insisted on taking the diaper bag and would have taken Cora as well, but Mia clutched her tightly. "I can carry her." She trailed in his wake as they ascended, trying not to ogle his tight butt packaged nicely in well-washed jeans.

She knew the man in front of her was a millionaire several times over. Yet somehow, he had the knack of appearing to be just one of the guys. It was a talent she had envied in high school. Mia hadn't fit in with any crowd or clique. Shy and serious, she had been all but ostracized by her classmates who were two years or more ahead of her in adolescence.

On the landing, Dylan paused, giving her a chance to catch up. "The area to our left is storage. As I said, this apartment up here was my bookkeeper's. But she got engaged and moved across the country. You can imagine what a mess I've made of things. I need to hire somebody soon or I'll have the IRS on my back for not paying my quarterly taxes."

He opened the nearest door and ushered her inside. Mia looked around with interest. They stood in a good-size living area furnished with a sofa, loveseat and two chairs upholstered in a navy-and-taupe print. The neutral rug was clean but unexceptional. Faded patches on the walls indicated where pictures had hung. "How long was she with you?"

Dylan dropped the diaper bag on a chair. "Nearly since the beginning. Her first husband died and left her with almost nothing. So this job was a godsend both for her and for me. But a couple of months ago, she met a trucker downstairs, and the rest is history."

Mia sank onto the sofa with a sigh and laid Cora beside her. The baby didn't stir. "Life is full of surprises."

He sprawled in a chair at her elbow. "It sure as hell is. You remember my brother Liam?"

"Of course I do. He always scared me a little bit. So serious and intimidating."

"He's loosened up a lot since he met Zoe. She's his new

wife. You should meet her. The two of you would probably get along."

"Really? Why?"

Obviously his throwaway statement was meant to be
rhetorical, because he hesitated. "Oh, you know. Girl
stuff…"

Her face flushed. This was always her problem. She
had never mastered the art of careless chitchat. Fussing
with Cora's blanket for a moment gave her a chance to
look away. She should probably go. But she'd made such a
complete and total mess of her life, she was deeply grateful
to have an excuse to focus on someone other than herself
for a moment. Gathering her composure, she leaned back
and gave Dylan a pleasant smile. "Well, other than your
brother's marriage, what's been going on in Silver Glen
since I've been gone?"

Dylan propped an ankle on the other knee and tucked
his hands behind his head. "Have you had dinner?" It
wasn't an answer to Mia's question, but he was starving.

"No. Not really. But you don't have to feed me."

"It's on the house. For old time's sake." He pulled out
his cell phone and sent a text to the kitchen. "They'll bring
something up as soon as they can."

"Sounds good." Mia's smile was shy. He remembered
the slight duck of her head and the curve of soft pink lips
when something pleased her. Not that pleasing Mia had
been Dylan's forte. He'd resented like hell the fact that he
had to take help from a fifteen-year-old kid. And truth
be told, he had probably made Mia's life a misery more
often than not.

"Why did you do it?" he asked. The question tumbled
out. He hadn't even known he was going to ask it.

A slight frown creased her forehead. "Do what?"

"Tutor me." His face was somber.

"Wow, Dylan. It's taken you this long to ask that question?"

He shrugged, making her more aware than ever of the breadth of his shoulders. "I was busy before."

"You were, at that," she agreed. "Football, basketball, dating hot girls."

"You noticed?"

"I noticed everything," she said flatly. "I had the worst crush on you."

He blanched, remembering all his careless cruelties to her. Even though in private he'd been pathetically grateful when she helped him make sense of a Shakespeare play, in public he had shunned her...or made jokes about her. Even at the time, with all the cluelessness of an adolescent boy, he'd known he was hurting her.

But maintaining his image as a badass had been his one and only goal. While some of his classmates were getting scholarship offers from Duke or the University of North Carolina, Dylan had struggled to pretend he didn't care. College was stupid and unnecessary. He'd said it enough times that he almost believed it. But when he slunk off to community college and couldn't even make passing grades there, his humiliation was complete.

"I owe you about a million apologies," he said, his mouth twisting in a grimace of regret. "You tried so hard to help me."

"I might point out that you did pass senior English."

"True. And without cheating, if you remember."

"You wrote an essay about why Romeo and Juliet was such an unbelievable story."

"Well, it was," he protested. "What kind of idiot takes poison when he could have kidnapped the girl and run away to Vegas?"

Mia chuckled, the laughter erasing her air of exhaustion and making her look more like the girl he'd known in high school. "It wasn't your fault, Dylan. The problems you had. Someone should have diagnosed you in elementary school, and your educational career would have been entirely different."

"You can't blame them too much. I did a damned good job of pretending that I was lazy and unmotivated."

"You may have fooled a lot of people, but you never fooled me."

Two

Dylan's wry smile and self-deprecating assessment made Mia's heart hurt. Dyslexia was no minor roadblock. Mia knew that Dylan had scored above average on intelligence tests. When it came to creating ideas and working with people, he far outstripped her in ability. Dylan was smart and gifted. Unfortunately, his talents didn't align with the way traditional education evaluated achievement.

She circled back to his earlier question. "You asked me why I tutored you."

"Well, why did you?"

"I suppose it was for lots of reasons. For one thing, the teacher asked me to. And for another, I was no different than any other girl at Silver Glen High. I wanted to spend time with you."

He rubbed his jaw. "Is that all?"

"No." Time for brutal honesty. "I wanted you to succeed. And I thought I could help. No matter how hard you tried to pretend differently, I knew you hated feeling—"

"Stupid," he interjected with some heat. "The word you're looking for is *stupid*."

She stared at him, taken aback that his intelligence still seemed to be a sore spot for him. "Good grief, Dylan. You're a successful, respected businessman. You work for a living even though you don't have to. You've made the Silver Dollar Saloon into something special. Why does it matter *now* that you struggled in school? We're not kids anymore. You've more than proven your capabilities."

His jaw clenched, his eyes stormy, though somehow she knew his agitation was not directed at her. "And what about you, Mia? What do you do?"

"I'm a medical researcher. Over in the Raleigh/Durham area. My team has been working to prove that the standard series of childhood vaccines is safe for everyone."

"And I sell beer for a living."

"Don't be flip," she said, her temper starting to rise. "It's not a competition."

"Of course not. I was never competition for you. How many languages do you speak?"

His sarcasm nicked her in ways she couldn't explain. She hadn't asked to be smart. In fact, there had been many days in her life when she would have given almost anything to be the epitome of a dumb blonde joke. She glanced at Cora, who was still sleeping peacefully.

"I should go," she said quietly. "I didn't mean to stir up the past. It was nice seeing you again." A chill of disappointment clenched her heart and brought back unpleasant memories of being out of step with the world.

She and Dylan stood at the same moment.

His face registered consternation and shame. "Don't leave. I'm being an ass. It's not your fault you're a genius."

"I'm a woman," she said flatly. "And will it make you feel better to know that I've made an absolute mess of my life?" Her voice broke on the last word. Tears she had worked so hard to keep at bay for the past several hours burst forth in an unattractive sobbing mess.

Inside her chest, a great gaping hole filled with uncertainty and fear made it hard to breathe. She didn't feel smart at all. What she really felt was panicked and desperate.

She put her hands over her face, mortified that Dylan was here to witness her inevitable meltdown.

Without warning, she felt his warm hands on her shoulders. "Sit down, Mia. Everything's going to be all right."

"You don't know that," she said, sniffling and, as usual, without a tissue.

"Here. Take this." The pristine square of white cotton he pulled from his back pocket was still warm from his body. She blew her nose and wiped her eyes, feeling hollow and shaky.

Dylan tugged her down beside him on the sofa, both of them glancing at Cora automatically to make sure she was in no danger. The baby was oblivious. "Don't worry," she said, trying to laugh. "I'm not going to have a nervous breakdown."

He grinned, revealing the slightest hint of a dimple. "Why don't you tell me what's going on?"

"It's a long story."

"I've got all night."

The genuine concern in his eyes disarmed her, despite her embarrassment. It couldn't hurt to have an impartial opinion. She was at a crossroads, and perhaps she was too close to the situation and too sleep-deprived to make a rational decision.

"Okay," she said. "You asked for it."

"Start at the beginning." He stretched a muscular arm along the back of the sofa, making her uncomfortably aware of his masculine scent and closeness. His khaki slacks and navy knit polo shirt with the bar's name embroidered on the chest fit him in a way that emphasized everything about him that was male.

Her hands shook, so she clasped them in her lap. "After I turned twenty-nine, I realized that I wanted a baby. A cliché, I know, but my biological clock was ticking so loudly, I couldn't ignore it."

"Did the man in your life agree?"

"There was no man at that moment. Well, there was one. For about fifteen minutes. But we were a terrible match, and thankfully we both recognized it before we did anything irrevocable."

"So who did you have in mind for a daddy?"

"Nobody," she said simply. "I was well educated and financially secure. I decided that I could raise a child on my own." She couldn't fault the skepticism she saw on his face. In retrospect, she had been both naive and overly confident in her abilities.

"There's still the matter of sperm."

His droll comment made her cheeks heat again. "Well, of course, but I had that all figured out. As part of the scientific community in Raleigh, I possessed a working knowledge of what was going on in most of our experimental labs. And of course, fertility research was and still is a majorly funded arm of study."

"Still no sperm."

"I'm getting there. Once I found a doctor and a facility that I trusted, I had all the initial tests to see if I was healthy and ovulating well."

"And were you?"

"Definitely. So I knew the timing was right. Then all I had to do was visit a sperm bank and select the proper donor."

"Who, I'm assuming, would be a doctoral student with intellectual capabilities matching your own."

He was entirely serious.

She shook her head vehemently. "No. Not even close. I would never do that to a child of mine. I wanted a normal baby."

"Good Lord, Mia. You mean to tell me you deliberately tried to make little Cora less smart than her mother?" The baffled shock on his face gave her a moment's pause.

"I wouldn't say that." She heard the defensiveness in her words and winced inwardly. "But I selected a candidate who was a blue-collar worker with average intelligence."

"Why?"

"I wanted her to have a happy life."

Dylan honestly didn't know what to say. *I wanted her to have a happy life.* Those eight words, quietly spoken, told him more about Mia than if he'd had her résumé in front of him. For the first time, he understood that even if his school career had been painful and difficult, Mia's had also, but in an entirely different way.

The knock on the door saved him from having to respond to that last, heart-wrenching statement. Soon he and Mia were enjoying appetizers and burgers. Based on the drinks she had ordered downstairs, he avoided anything alcoholic and instead opted for Cokes to accompany their meal.

Mia ate like she hadn't eaten in a week. "This food is amazing," she said. "Thank you so much. I've been living off frozen dinners and frozen pizza for days. My mom helped out for the first week and a half, but the baby exhausted her, so I finally encouraged her to go home."

He lifted an eyebrow, helping himself to another handful of French fries. "You've left me hanging," he said. "Finish your story, please."

"I was hoping you'd lost interest. The whole sorry tale doesn't put me in a very good light."

When she wiped a dab of ketchup from her lower lip, to his surprise, he felt a little zing that was a lot like sexual interest. Squashing that thought, he leaned back in his chair. "I'm all ears."

Mia was slender and graceful. Though she wore neither makeup nor jewelry, she carried herself with an inherent femininity. Back in high school, he had kissed her once upon a time, more out of curiosity than anything else. The heat had surprised and alarmed him. He needed Mia's help with schoolwork. He couldn't afford to alienate her, just because his teenage libido was revving on all cylinders.

Now, thinking back to how he had perceived the fifteen-year-old Mia, he wondered what had attracted him. She'd been quiet and timid, although she *had* managed to stand up to him on more than one occasion when he tried to blow off a project or an assignment.

Her looks and figure had been nothing spectacular in the eyes of a teenage boy. Mia had been on the cusp of womanhood, with no breasts to speak of, and a body that was still girlish despite her maturity in other ways. Yet something about her had appealed to him. In all of their interactions, she had never once made fun of his ineptitude, nor had she patronized him.

Now, from the vantage point of adulthood, he marveled that she had put up with his arrogance and antagonism. Though eventually they had become friends, for weeks at the beginning of their relationship he had acted like a total jerk. And an ungrateful jerk at that.

He kept silent, counting on the fact that she would eventually talk to him if he didn't push.

Mia finished the last swallow of her drink, stacked her dishes neatly and curled her legs beneath her. "The thing is," she said, wrinkling her nose as if about to confess to a crime, "artificial insemination is expensive. I assumed, quite erroneously, that since I was young and healthy I would get pregnant the first time."

"But you didn't."

"No. And every month when I got my period, I cried."

"Why was it so important to you?"

She blinked, her expression one of shock, as though no one had ever dared ask her that question. "I wanted someone of my own to love. You may not remember, but my folks were older parents. They had me when my mom was forty-three. So though I love them very much, I understood why they wanted to retire and move south. Even when we lived in the same state, we didn't see that much of each other."

"Why not?"

She hesitated. "They were proud because I was smart, but they had no idea what to do with me. Once I was out on my own, the gulf widened. I'm sure part of it was my fault. I never quite understood how to talk to them about my work. And besides…"

"Go on."

"I found out when I was a teenager that my parents had never really wanted children. It was a Pandora's box kind of thing. I read one of my mom's journals. Turns out that when I was conceived, my mother was going through menopause and thought she couldn't get pregnant. So I was an unwelcome surprise in more ways than one. They did the best they could. I'm grateful for that."

Dylan thought of his big, close-knit, sometimes rowdy family. And of the way his mother cherished and coddled each of her sons though they were now grown men. They all had their moments of discord, of course. What family didn't? But he couldn't imagine a life where his brothers and his mom weren't an integral part of who he was. "I'm sorry," he said quietly. "That must have hurt."

Mia shrugged. "Anyway, you asked why the baby was so important. The truth is, I wanted someone to love who would love me back. I wanted a family of my own." She laid a hand gently on the baby's blanket. "It took eight tries, but when the doctor told me I was pregnant, it was the most wonderful day of my life."

Since Dylan had witnessed her tears not so long ago, he surmised that the euphoria hadn't lasted. "Was the pregnancy difficult?"

"Oh, no. Not at all."

"And did people ask questions?"

"My staff was actually fairly small. And we each worked on a particular aspect of the project. So we were more like professional acquaintances than the kind of deeper connections you sometimes make in an office environment. My friend Janette knew the truth. Frankly, she thought it was a bad idea all along…tried to talk me out of it more than once. But she was supportive once I actually became pregnant. She even went with me to childbirth classes and stayed with me at the hospital when Cora was born."

"So what went wrong? Why did you come back to Silver Glen and walk into my bar?"

She leaned her head against the back of the sofa, her gaze bleak. "A dreadful domino of events. My job paid well, and I had a healthy savings portfolio. But I drained all of it trying to get pregnant. Even that didn't seem *so* irresponsible, because I knew that I could live on a strict budget and build up my savings again. Only I hadn't counted on the fickle finger of fate."

"Meaning?"

"While I was on maternity leave, the funding for my research and my lab was eliminated. Big-time budget cuts. So now I had a brand-new baby and no job. And, as a wonderful dollop of icing on the cake, my roommate with whom I rented a condo decided to move in with her boyfriend."

He leaned forward and rested his hands on his knees, smiling at her with an abundance of sympathy. "That sucks."

She managed a somewhat teary chuckle. "I probably wouldn't be such a basket case if little Cora here slept at night. But no matter how many books I read and how many theories I try, all she wants to do is snooze during the day and play all night."

"I don't blame her. That's my M.O. sometimes."

His droll humor made her smile, when the last thing she felt like doing was smiling. She remembered that about him. Dylan was always the life of the party. He could rally a crowd around a cause, and best of all, he wasn't moody. Some guys like him, i.e. rich and handsome, were egotists. But Dylan was the opposite.

He'd spent his high school years trying to prove that he was one of the gang. No one special.

She felt embarrassed suddenly. He must think she was a total nutcase. It was time to go. But just as she was gathering herself to depart, little Cora stirred and cried out.

Dylan's face softened as he focused on the tiny hands that flailed above the edge of the blanket. "Somebody is about to get mad."

"I need to feed her."

"Do you have baby food with you? I can send one of the staff to the store to get some."

"Um…no…thanks. *I* need to feed her. You know… nurse her."

His neck turned red. She could swear his gaze brushed across her breasts before landing somewhere on the far wall. "Of course. No problem. There's a comfy chair in the bedroom. Will that work?"

"That would be perfect." She rummaged in the bag for a clean diaper and a pack of baby wipes, conscious that he noted her every move. "I won't be too long. But don't feel like you have to entertain me. It's been fun catching up. I'll leave when I'm done."

He stood when she did, watching intently as she scooped Cora into her arms and bounced her so the baby's displeasure didn't escalate into a full-blown crying fit. Fortunately, Cora settled down and even smiled.

"Don't be ridiculous," Dylan said. "I don't want you to rush off. In fact, I'd love to hold Cora for a little while when you're done. Would you mind?"

She gaped at him. Big, brawny Dylan Kavanagh wanted to hold a baby? The thought sent a warm curl of *something* humming in the pit of her stomach. What was it about men and babies that made women go all gooey inside? "Of course I don't mind. But don't you have things to do?"

He tucked his hands in his back pockets and shook his head, his face alight with mischief. "Are you kidding? Mia Larin has come back to town all grown up. This is the most interesting encounter I've had in a month. Go feed the little one. I'll be here when you get back."

Three

Dylan watched Mia walk into the bedroom and push the door closed, though the latch didn't click shut. His brain whirled with a dozen thoughts and emotions as he wondered what would have happened if he hadn't sat down beside her at the bar. Would Mia have taken the baby back out to the car and driven away?

The thought made him uneasy. Had she sought him out on purpose, or was their meeting an accident?

He paced the room, wondering how long it took a woman to nurse a baby. Thinking about Mia baring her breasts and feeding her child was not wise. He had the weirdest urge to go in there and watch. Such a normal, *human* activity shouldn't affect him so strongly. Maybe it was because in his memories Mia was little more than a young girl herself.

Women were always at a disadvantage when it came to child rearing. It was all well and good to say a mother could have everything—career and family life. But it required a hell of a lot of juggling and tag-team parenting to make it work. Dylan's mother, when widowed long ago with seven boys, had leaned on her eldest son, Liam, to help carry the load.

Mia had no one.

Dylan could have gone back downstairs for a few minutes. He could have turned on the television. He could have sat down and relaxed after a long day. But instead, he paced. Things he didn't even know he remembered came rushing back from his subconscious. The way young Mia had chewed on the ends of her erasers. The little huffing sound of exasperation she made when she thought Dylan wasn't trying hard enough. The small frown that appeared between her eyebrows when she concentrated.

Oddly enough, he had found the eraser thing endearing. It made her seem human. Most of the time Mia's grasp of the kind of books that befuddled Dylan either baffled him or angered him or embarrassed him. As an adult, he understood that his academic difficulties were the result of a very specific problem. But he still reacted to the memories with an inward wince that told him he had a chip on his shoulder, even now.

Without thinking about what he was doing, he worked his way toward the bedroom door. Because the door didn't latch and because it was old and not level, the crack between the door and the frame had gradually widened. Dylan stood mesmerized, seeing only a slice of the room beyond. But it was enough to witness the quiet radiance on Mia's face. The way she looked at her baby made his chest tighten.

He rested a hand on the doorframe, swallowing hard as he realized that one of Mia's breasts was bare. He couldn't really see all that much from his vantage point. Spying on her was unforgiveable. But he couldn't look away from the picture of mother and child. The entire world was made up of moments like these, day after day.

For Dylan, however, it was brand-new. Witnessing it wrenched something inside his chest. Seeing Liam with Zoe these past few months had made Dylan vulnerable somehow...as if he couldn't help but wonder whether he would ever want that kind of tie...that kind of bond.

As Mia buttoned her blouse, he retreated hurriedly. By

the time she walked into the living room, he was leafing through a magazine that had been left behind. He looked up and smiled. "Is her tummy full?"

"It is indeed. She's very happy at the moment if you were serious about holding her."

"Of course I was." As he took the baby from Mia, his hand brushed her chest inadvertently. He was a grown man. It shouldn't have embarrassed him. But all he could think about was the curve of Mia's breast as she offered it to this infant. He turned away so he could hide the fact that he was flustered. "She's beautiful."

"I think so, but I suppose I'm prejudiced."

In his peripheral vision he saw Mia sit down on the sofa again. He circled the room slowly, singing nonsense songs, crooning bits of nursery rhymes he remembered from his childhood. He could swear that Cora's big, dark eyes, so like her mother's, focused on his face.

Half turning, he spoke softly. "She's going to be a charmer. I think she's flirting with me." When there was no response from Mia, he looked over his shoulder. She was curled up on the sofa, her cheek pillowed on one hand. Apparently she had plopped down and simply gone to sleep. Instantly.

He shook his head at Cora. "You're going to have to give Mommy a break, little one. She's worn out."

Debating his options, he decided to sneak downstairs and let Mia rest. The town had declared all public buildings no-smoking zones last year, so there would be nothing to harm the baby. And besides, Mia had been the one to bring her child into the bar. Surely she wouldn't mind.

Mia awoke slowly, completely disoriented. Had Cora cried out? She listened for a moment, and then in a blinding rush of recollection she realized where she was. But as she sat up and glanced around, she noted that her daughter and Dylan were nowhere to be found.

Telling herself there was no need to panic, she scrubbed her hands over her face and tried to shake off the feeling of being drugged. The nap had helped, but it wasn't the same as a full night's sleep. She stood up and stretched.

Grabbing her things, she smoothed her shirt and her hair and walked downstairs. The bar was still noisy and busy. When she actually looked at her watch, she groaned. It was after midnight. She found Dylan seated in a booth playing patty-cake with her baby. Standing two deep at his elbow was a group of fawning women. Now *this* was the Dylan she remembered. She wasn't sure, however, that she appreciated his using her baby as entertainment for his admirers.

Behind the bar, the big man who had poured her drinks earlier sketched a wave as he continued serving customers. Good heavens, what must Dylan's employees think of Mia's presence? Of Cora's?

Screwing up her courage, she edged toward the booth. Though she was no longer a social disaster, approaching a cluster of strangers still wasn't easy for her. She cleared her throat to attract Dylan's attention. "I need to go," she said.

Dylan had the good sense to look abashed. "Sorry. I didn't see you standing there. Did you sleep well?"

The expression of every woman in earshot was the same. Shock. Dismay. Vested calculation.

Mia wanted to tell them not to worry, but it didn't seem the time. She held out her arms for Cora. "I'll take her. Thanks for dinner."

As Dylan wiggled his way out of the booth, his entourage melted away. He moved closer to Mia, forcing the two of them into an intimate circle. "Don't be in such a damned hurry."

She put her hands over Cora's ears, scowling. "Watch

your mouth. I'm surprised to see you looking so comfortable and domesticated with Cora. Or was that nothing but an act for your groupies?"

His eyebrows rose to his hairline, but still he didn't surrender the baby. "The little Mia I knew was never sarcastic."

"The little Mia you knew wouldn't say *boo* to a goose. I'm not a child anymore."

He stared at her. Hard. The way a man stares at a woman. "No, you definitely are not."

It appeared that the man flirted indiscriminately, because she knew for a fact that he had no interest in her. "Give me my child."

Holding Cora even more tightly, he nodded his head toward the back. "I've got a closet-size office back there. Give me fifteen minutes. Then if you want to go, I won't stop you."

She was confused and tired and more than a little depressed. But short of wrestling him to the ground and making a scene, it appeared she had no choice. "Fine. Fifteen minutes."

Dylan's office was a wreck. He must have been telling the truth about his bookkeeper, because there was easily a week's worth of receipts and purchase orders stacked haphazardly across the surface of the scarred oak table he used as a desk. Still holding Cora, he motioned Mia into one of two chairs in the small space. "I have a proposition for you."

"You must be hard up if you're propositioning a nursing mom with a bad haircut and legs that haven't been shaved in two weeks."

This time she definitely saw him wince. "You used to be a lot sweeter, Mia Larin."

"I'm a mom now. I can't be a pushover. Are you ever going to give her back to me?"

He kissed the top of Cora's downy head. "You forget that I have five brothers younger than me. I've changed more than my share of diapers over the years."

"But not recently."

"No. Not recently."

If he had an agenda for this awkward meeting, he was taking his good easy time getting to the point. "What do you want from me, Dylan?"

His smile could have charmed the bloomers off an old-maid schoolteacher. "I want to offer you a job."

"Doing what?"

He waved a hand at the mess. "Being my new book-keeper."

"That's absurd. I'm not an accountant."

He propped a hip against the table, forcing her to look at all the places his jeans were soft and worn. "You're a genius," he said, the words oddly inflected. "Keeping the books for the Silver Dollar Saloon isn't exactly rocket science."

"I don't need you to bail me out, Dylan. But thanks for the offer." Watching him absently stroke her daughter's hair undermined her hurry to leave. Dylan was big and strong and unabashedly masculine. But his hands held Cora gently.

"We'd be helping each other," he insisted. "The job comes with room and board. Or at least until you get tired of the food downstairs. I live five miles away, so you don't have to worry about me getting underfoot. There's an alarm system. You would be perfectly safe alone here when we're closed. I know the bar gets pretty noisy at times, but a fan or a sound machine would probably do the trick. The insulation between the floors is actually pretty good."

"Why are you doing this?"

"You need some time to regroup. I need a bookkeeper.

You won't have to worry about day care. Cora is welcome here always. And with a salary coming in—though I'm sure it's not even in the ballpark of what you were making in your field— you'll be comfortable and settled while you look for a new position."

It was a testament to her desperation that she considered it. Her résumé would have to be updated before she could job hunt. And the thought of spending more time with Cora was irresistible. Doing Dylan's books could be handled while Cora napped. But still she wasn't satisfied.

Shaking her head, she studied his face. "You can't tell me that you offer jobs to every hard-luck case who walks through the door. Why me? Why now?"

"I think you know why," he said quietly, meeting her gaze squarely. "I owe you more than I can ever repay. I'm sorry that I was a stupid teenage boy too proud to acknowledge what you were doing for me. But I'm saying it now. Thank you, Mia. For everything. The job is real. Please let me do this for you. It would mean a lot to me."

"You're serious? It was a long time ago, Dylan. And I liked tutoring you. You don't owe me anything."

"Then do it for Cora. Before you lost your job, you would have had to go back to work soon. Now you have a chance to spend several more weeks with her. Isn't that enough to make you say yes?"

Forty-five minutes later, Mia found herself checking into a hot, musty, generic motel room out at the interstate. Dylan had tried hard to get her to spend the night upstairs above the bar. But she needed some space and distance to weigh the pros and cons of his unexpected offer. He had the uncanny ability to make people see things his way. She wanted to be sure she was considering all the aspects of his proposal before she gave him an answer.

The pluses were obvious. Time with her daughter. An

immediate paycheck. No need to look for a new place to live when her lease ran out in a week. And it wasn't as if she had a lot of other appealing choices. She would get a job in the Raleigh/Durham area eventually, once she found another lab looking for her set of skills. If she were lucky, the employer might even offer on-site, discounted day care. She knew of several companies that did so. But tracking down such a position would take time—time when she wasn't bringing in money and didn't have a place to live.

Or if she agreed to work for Dylan, she would have a roof over her head, food to eat and more time with Cora while she looked for employment in her field. Only a fool would say no—right?

Then why was she hesitating?

It all came down to Dylan. It was one thing for a young girl to have a crush on a popular senior jock. That was practically a rite of passage. But as Dylan had pointed out, Mia was all grown up. And her reactions to the equally grown-up Dylan were alarming.

The times she had tried dating in her adult life had been either disastrous or disappointing. Until she walked through the doors of the Silver Dollar Saloon, she had honestly thought she didn't have much of an interest in sex or men. But coming face-to-face with Dylan exposed the lie she had told herself for years.

Dylan wasn't a high school crush. He was the boy, now the man, who had made her aware of her sexual self. His masculine strength and power made her feel intensely *female*. In every other area of her life, people looked at her as a *brain* first and foremost.

She did valuable work. She knew that. Her intelligence had led her to projects and challenges that were exciting and fulfilling. But sometimes it felt that she could have just as easily been a robot. No one cared that she had emotions or, heaven forbid, *needs*.

That wasn't *entirely* fair. Janette was a dear friend. And Janette was the one who'd introduced Mia to Howard, the botany professor who dated Mia for six months, courted her circumspectly and eventually shared her bed. Their relationship had been comfortable and undemanding, laden with pleasant conversation as well as shared interests and backgrounds.

But in the end, the absence of sparks between them meant a sad, inevitable breakup due to lack of sizzle.

With Dylan, there was plenty of sizzle—an entire forest fire of sizzle. Not necessarily on his part, but definitely on Mia's. All she had to do was look at him and she remembered exactly how she had felt as a girl of fifteen. Perhaps the tutoring had erased some boundaries between them. Or maybe because they had kept their relationship secret, it had felt safe to her. But whatever the reason, Dylan was the only male to make her feel this way.

Discovering that truth was disheartening. If she had let a teenage crush spoil her for other men, she was doomed to a single, celibate life. On the other hand, maybe she could make her obsession work *for* her, not against her. A hefty dose of exposure to the mature Dylan could prove to her that the boy she had idolized was just a guy like any other. She could flirt with him, maybe even sleep with him, and then go on her way.

She tucked Cora into the portable crib and sighed with relief when the baby actually curled into a ball and went still. Cora had fallen asleep on the ride over, but Mia had anticipated another long night of being up and down with her. Maybe Dylan had worn her daughter out.

Showering and changing as quietly as she could, Mia crawled into bed and yawned. She had promised Dylan an answer tomorrow. He had given her both the bar's number and his cell-phone number. But now she had more to think about. Her limbs felt restless and her body heavy. If she stayed in Silver Glen for six weeks, or maybe eight, however long it took to find another position suited to her skills and experience, would that be long enough to get Dylan out of her system?

Merely the thought of it made her breath catch and her thighs clench.

Janette hailed from Silver Glen as well. Though she was older than Mia, their hometown connection was what led them to become friends in Raleigh. Janette kept up with several family members in Silver Glen, and it had been a source of hot gossip when Dylan's engagement to a young starlet ended abruptly a few years ago.

As far as Mia knew, Dylan had played the field since. If there was no one special in his life, she wouldn't have to feel guilty about using him for her own personal entertainment.

Maybe if she could work up the courage to let him know what she wanted, they could have a mutually satisfying sexual relationship, and then as soon as Mia got a job, she and Cora would move back to Raleigh.

Cora was sleeping, but Mia was not. Her pulse jumped and skittered. Her breath came in short bursts. The exhilaration she experienced was couched in incredulity and terror. What on God's green earth led her to think she could seduce any man, much less the gorgeous Dylan Kavanagh?

Before she could lose her nerve, she reached for her cell phone on the bedside table. Hands trembling, she sent a text. I'll do it. But only until I get a job in my field. Working for you will be strictly temporary. As she hit Send, she wondered whom she was trying to convince.

Ninety seconds passed before he responded. Had he been sleeping? Imagining him naked and warm beneath a thin sheet made her hot enough to toss back the covers.

A quiet ding signaled his answer.

Good. Need help moving?

No. Friends will help me pack or keep the baby. When should I come?

A week? Ten days? The sooner the better. I'm drowning in ledgers.

If you find somebody else in the meantime, let me know.

I don't want anybody else. I want you.

Four

As soon as Dylan hit Send, he groaned. That last text could be misconstrued. But surely the prim and proper Mia wouldn't read it that way. All he had in mind was repaying Mia for what she had done for him so long ago. Any man worth his salt knew that an honorable guy settled his debts.

He'd thought about Mia over the years, usually with guilt for the way he had treated her. Sure, they had ended up being friends before it was all over, but it had been a clandestine bond. He'd been too macho and too ashamed of his academic weaknesses to let anyone see that he actually liked and respected a mousy little fifteen-year-old.

Even if his bookkeeper hadn't quit, he would have found some way to help Mia. He had lots of friends in town. But serendipity meant that not only did he really need Mia's help, but he was able to provide a place for her and Cora to stay rent-free. This arrangement was going to go a long way toward easing his conscience.

He turned over in the bed and sprawled on his stomach, feeling sleep struggle to claim him. At times like this, he envied his brother Liam. What would it be like to have the woman you loved tucked up in bed beside you every night? Zoe's effervescence was the perfect foil for Liam's serious side.

Dylan had heard his brother laugh more in the past few months than he had since they were kids. Liam was happier, less stressed, infinitely mellower. Even when it came to Liam, Dylan had guilt. When their father disappeared two decades ago, Liam, a mere lad of sixteen, had manned up to help their mother run the Silver Beeches Lodge, the extremely high-end hotel that had built their family finances.

While the rest of them were exploring options and making mistakes and generally learning what life was all about, Liam had stepped forward in a course already mapped out. He claimed not to resent his lot. He'd told Dylan more than once that running the hotel with Maeve Kavanagh was something he enjoyed.

Even so, Dylan hoped that Zoe would help Liam take care of a few items on his bucket list. His older brother was a hell of a guy, and he deserved the best.

Dylan sighed deeply, his body boneless as it succumbed to sleep. He'd have to paint the apartment before Mia came, and rearrange furniture to make space for the baby bed... and maybe even...

Fortunately for Mia, she wasn't a pack rat. Most of her belongings consisted of books and bookcases, kitchen items and clothes. With Janette's help, she spent one weekend boxing up most of the contents of her condo and ferrying it a bit at a time to a storage unit. She paid for three months in advance, knowing that surely by that time she would be back on her feet.

She still had her suspicions that Dylan was inventing work for her. His need to say thank-you, or do penance, was not something she took seriously. Anything she had done for him in the past had been freely offered. But she wasn't going to turn down the chance to have a safety net while she looked for a new job and to spend time with Cora. Eight weeks...twelve at the most. That seemed reasonable.

Having a shot at becoming one of Dylan's *flings* was merely a bonus. He was a man. She was a woman. All she had to do was get him to concentrate less on her IQ and more on her curves.

Cora, bless her, had been in a sunny mood most of the time, snoozing in her crib until it had to be dismantled. Janette's boyfriend offered to pick up the small U-Haul trailer Mia had rented. He insisted on hooking it to her SUV and helping her load everything that was going to Silver Glen.

By the time Mia pulled away from her building, waving at Janette in the rearview mirror, she was exhausted, but the sense of turning a new page in her life was infinitely preferable to the miasma of panic and failure that had dogged her the last month. All of her misgivings had dissipated. Returning to Silver Glen was going to be wonderful.

Five hours later, she turned onto the street where the Silver Dollar was located and hit her brakes to avoid crashing into a fire engine. In front of her, two white-and-orange barricades made it clear that she had reached the end of the road.

She rolled down her window and leaned out to speak to a uniformed cop. "What's going on?" She couldn't see far enough ahead to tell what had caused the commotion.

The cop shrugged. "Fire at the Silver Dollar, but they've got it under control now."

All the breath left her lungs. "Dylan?"

Her pale-faced distress must have registered, because he backpedalled rapidly. "No one hurt, ma'am. It happened early this morning. The building was empty."

She leaned back in her seat and tried to catch her breath. "I'm supposed to meet someone there."

The officer glanced in the backseat where Cora was

sucking enthusiastically on a pacifier. "At the bar?" His skepticism made her feel unaccountably guilty.

"Mr. Kavanagh has hired me to be his new bookkeeper. I'm moving into the upstairs apartment."

The man shook his head, sympathy on his weathered face. "Not today, you're not. I hope you have a plan B. The second floor is a total loss."

Dylan leaned against a lamppost, grimly studying what was left of his saloon. Thankfully, the main floor had sustained mostly smoke and water damage. But it would be quite a while before the Silver Dollar could reopen for business. He would pay his staff full wages, of course. But that still left the problem of his newest employee. And her child.

As he pondered his next steps, someone tapped him on the arm. When he turned, Mia stood looking at him, Cora clutched to her chest. "What happened, Dylan?" Her eyes were round.

"My own damn fault, apparently. It's been hot as Hades this last week, so I left the window AC units in the apartment running on high all night. I didn't want you or the baby to be uncomfortable today while you were getting settled. From what the fire marshal tells me, it looks like one of them shorted out and started the fire."

Mia turned to stare at the building, her expression hard to read. The scene still crawled with firefighters and investigators. No one wanted to take a chance that nearby structures might get involved.

Her shoulders lifted and fell. "Well, I guess that's that."

"What do you mean?"

"It means Cora and I will be driving back to Raleigh."

He heard the resignation in her voice. "Don't be ridiculous. Nothing has changed except where you and Cora will be sleeping. My house is huge, with more than enough room for guests."

Her chin lifted. "I'm not a charity case. It's out of the question."

For a moment he saw a spark of the temper he hadn't known existed. Perhaps Mia wasn't so meek after all. "I hired you in good faith. I'll sue for breach of contract if you leave."

Her eyes narrowed. "Don't be absurd."

"The building may be a mess at the moment, but I still have a business to run on paper."

"I'll have to find a place to rent until the repairs are finished."

"First of all, rental property in Silver Glen is slim pickings. And even if you found something, they'd want you to sign a twelve-month lease. You and Cora won't be here that long."

"You have an answer for everything, don't you?"

He had ruffled her feathers for sure. "It won't be so bad, I swear. My place is plenty big. I won't bother you at all."

"And what if the baby bothers you? What if she cries in the middle of the night?"

He grinned, feeling his mood lift despite the day's events. "I think I can handle it. C'mon, Mia. Think outside the box. We were friends once upon a time."

"I've changed. I don't let people push me around anymore."

"From what I remember, that was never the case with us." He shrugged. "If anything, you were the one ordering me to do this and that."

"I wouldn't have had to get tough if you hadn't been so stubborn."

"I've changed," he said, echoing her assertion and giving her his most angelic smile.

"I'll have to see it to believe it."

"Then that settles it. Let me get my car and you can follow me home."

"I never agreed to this nonsensical plan."

"But you know you're going to in the end. From what I can tell, you're stuck with me for a few weeks. Chin up, Mia. It won't be so bad."

Mia knew Dylan Kavanagh was rich. Everybody knew it. But when you spent time with him, that knowledge tended to get shoved into the background. He had spent his life proving that he was just an ordinary guy. No flashy clothes. No Rolex watch on his wrist. No silver spoon.

The truth, however, was somewhat different. Mia had plenty of opportunity to chew on that fact as she followed Dylan's big, black pickup truck all the way outside of town and along a winding country road. When they turned off the main highway onto a narrow lane, weeping willows met overhead, creating a cool, green, foliage-lined tunnel that filtered sunlight in gentle rays.

Occasionally a pothole left over from the winter gave one of Mia's tires a jerk, but all in all, the road was in good repair. Cora slept through the trip, though soon she would be demanding to be fed. Thankfully, they rounded a bend in the road and Dylan's home came into view.

To call it a house would be like calling the Mona Lisa a finger painting. Dylan and his architect had created a magical fairy tale of a place. The structure, built of mountain stone, dark timbers and copper, nestled amidst the grove of hardwood trees as if it had been there forever. A small brook meandered across the front of the property. Someone had built a whimsical bridge over one section and a gazebo near another.

Flowers bloomed everywhere, not in any neat garden, but wild and free, as if they had claimed the space for their own. Mia rolled to a halt behind Dylan and turned off the car. She wanted to take in every wonderful detail, but Cora awoke as soon as the engine stopped.

Even now, Mia marveled that someone so small and perfect was hers to love. Except for getting her nights and days turned around, Cora was a very easy baby. She had already learned to smile and coo, and her pudgy arms and legs were the picture of health.

Try as she might, Mia couldn't see any evidence of traits from the anonymous man who had donated his sperm. Sometimes she felt guilty for robbing Cora of the chance to have a father, but other times she was simply happy to have a healthy child.

Dylan came back to help her with the diaper bag and the small suitcase that held immediate necessities. "You can have your pick of rooms," he said, ascending the wide stone staircase in step with her. "There are four bedrooms on the second story, but I'm sure you don't want to lug Cora up and down the stairs all the time. I think you'll like the guest suite on the main level. It has a small sitting room where you can put the baby bed, so you won't have to sleep in the same room with her."

As he opened the massive front door and ushered Mia inside, she almost gasped. The interior was straight out of an architectural magazine. Vaulted ceilings soared over the living area. Above them, a corridor with a fancy carved railing circled three sides. Doors opened off of it at regular intervals, presumably the bedrooms Dylan had mentioned.

On this level, however, the central open floor plan was flanked by wings to the left and right. "Kitchen, etcetera over there." Dylan pointed. "And in the opposite direction, two large suites."

Her cheeks heated. He was telling her that she and Cora would be staying in the wing that housed his quarters. She could ask for one of the rooms upstairs, but he was right.

Who wanted to carry a baby up and down the stairs for every nap and diaper change?

Cora began to whimper. Mia realized that feeding time couldn't be delayed much longer. Thankfully, Dylan was perceptive. He motioned toward the right side of the house. "If you go through the kitchen, you'll find a sunroom that has comfy chairs. It looks like she's getting hungry." He touched her head gently, stroking her silky hair. "She's been an angel, hasn't she?"

Mia nodded, feeling her breathing get jerky because he was so close. "It's actually easier to travel with her now than it will be in a few months. Once she's mobile, all bets are off."

His big body loomed over hers, his clothes smelling faintly of smoke, but not masking the aroma of shaving soap and warm male. Smiling, he cocked his head toward the opposite side of the house. "If you trust me to unload the trailer and set up the crib, I can get started on that while you're feeding her."

"I can't let you do all that," she protested weakly.

"Exactly how did you expect to hold an infant and unpack at the same time?" he asked.

"Quit being so damned logical." It had been a very stressful day, and it wasn't even dinnertime yet.

Dylan put an arm around her shoulders and steered her toward the kitchen. "It takes a village to raise a child—don't you know?" he said, grinning. "It wouldn't kill you to say 'Thank you, Dylan.'"

She sighed inwardly, feeling as if she were being railroaded, but not really having a choice at the moment. "Thank you, Dylan."

"That's better. Much better. Now go feed the kid before she gets any redder in the face. I'll handle all the rest."

Mia fell in love with the sunroom. It didn't really look like a Dylan room at all. At least not the Dylan she knew.

Cozy furniture covered in expensive chintz fabric beckoned a visitor to sit and fritter away a few hours. The windows were screened, so clearly when the temperatures allowed, they could be raised easily.

Bookcases lined the wall that bordered the hallway. Their presence gave her pause. Dylan had a long-standing battle with the written word, but maybe he had learned to enjoy some of volumes he had collected. In one corner of the room, a hammock suspended from a metal frame rocked slightly, as if propelled by an unseen hand. *Thou shalt not covet.* Mia remembered her mom's gentle admonition when she had wanted a shiny red bicycle like the one the girl next door owned.

Bicycles were one thing, but this room—oh, the temptation. Mia could see herself studying here, playing with Cora when she learned to crawl, perhaps knitting a sweater for someone she loved. In that instant, she realized that she had walked into danger.

Seeing Dylan every day in a business setting, even if it was a bar, would have been far less personal than staying in his house tucked away in the woods. Despite her silly fantasy of seducing him, she knew in her heart that the best course of action would be to keep her distance for however long she chose to stay in Silver Glen.

It was easy to imagine using him for a sexual fling, but she wasn't really that kind of woman. No matter how much she told herself she had come out of her shell, she wasn't in the category of females who took relationships in stride…who used sex as a game.

Case in point, her love life was so sterile, she'd chosen to conceive a baby with the help of an anonymous donor. That said louder than words she wasn't good at connecting with the opposite sex.

Sitting down and propping her feet on an ottoman, she settled Cora at her breast and gazed out over Dylan's backyard. It was a veritable Garden of Eden, filled with trees perfect for climbing. Why had he built such a house for himself? Did he plan to get married one day? Or had his aborted engagement soured him on the idea of wedded bliss?

It didn't really matter. The only thing Mia needed to know was that he was willing to play host to her and her baby until his building was repaired. At the rate of most home improvement projects, that could be well after Mia was gone.

Cora ate hungrily, her quiet slurping sounds making Mia smile. Even in the darkest moments when she had lost her job and her roommate had moved out and Cora had been wide-awake at three o'clock in the morning, Mia had not regretted getting pregnant, not at all. Being a mom was hard. But she had done a lot of difficult things in her life. Starting school at age four. Skipping two grades. Entering college at sixteen. Tutoring a moody boy with enough anger and testosterone to make a girl feel faint.

He had tried so hard to pretend that he didn't care. But Mia had known. Dylan hated feeling stupid. He resented needing her help as much as he'd been relieved to have it.

Maybe this arrangement would give him some kind of closure. Seeing Mia's predicament should reassure him that intelligence was no buffer against the difficulties of life. No matter his challenges as a youth, he had far surpassed what many people had thought him capable of accomplishing. Even without the backing of his wealthy family, Mia was convinced that Dylan would have been just as successful. It might have taken him longer, but he would have gotten there eventually.

He had drive and determination and the kind of creativity that saw ideas and possibilities. Mia envied his fearlessness. It had taken her years to escape the prison of feeling socially inept and painfully shy.

Cora pulled away and looked up at her with bright eyes. Carefully balancing the baby on her knees, Mia buttoned her shirt and wondered whether to stay put or to seek out her host. "We're in uncharted waters, my little beauty."

Cora gurgled what might have been agreement. Mia put the baby on her shoulder and patted her back until a definite burp emanated from the tiny body. "Let's go find Dylan."

Five

Dylan gave the bed a shake to make sure it was steady. No squeaks. No wobbles. He plopped the mattress into place and stepped back to admire his handiwork. Printed instructions were often useless to him. Fortunately, he had a knack for three-dimensional reasoning that allowed him to construct almost anything that required wood and screws and nails.

"Wow, that was fast."

He turned and saw Mia and Cora staring at him with identical wide-eyed expressions. "It's not too complicated. But I didn't know where you'd packed the crib sheet. I put your three suitcases in the next room. I'm assuming the boxes can wait until morning?" He glanced at his watch. "I hate to be a poor host, but the fire marshal called to say I can come downtown now and go inside to assess the damage. And I promised some friends of mine we'd play pool at a buddy's house tonight. I can cancel, though...."

Mia straightened her spine, her arms wrapped protectively around Cora. "We don't need you to look after us. We'll be fine. Go. Do whatever you have to do."

As he drove away from the house a few minutes later, he told himself that the weird feeling in the pit of his stomach wasn't disappointment. Of course Mia didn't need him. This whole setup was for *his* benefit...so he could assuage some lingering guilt from high school. He was giving her a place to stay, sure. But she would more than earn her keep when she combed through the mess that was his bookkeeping system.

Dylan had tried to make sense of the various computer files. But in the end, he'd been nothing but frustrated. He suspected that he'd done more harm than good when he'd tried to enter recent debits and credits. Though he had learned to read for pleasure, it was a slow process. Numbers were a nightmare.

When he pulled up in front of the bar, the fire marshal waved him forward. "The upstairs is not safe to access, but you're welcome to take anything you need from the main level."

Dylan wrinkled his nose at the acrid odor of burnt wood. "My insurance company is in Asheville. They're sending someone out tomorrow."

"The numbers will add up. You'd be amazed at how much it costs to recover from water damage alone, much less the smoke."

"Yeah. But I'm more worried about the time. I'd like to reopen in a month. You think that's possible?"

The other man shook his head. "I don't know, Mr. Kavanagh. Money can grease a lot of wheels. But it's still a cumbersome process. Be careful in there. The floors are slick."

Dylan walked through the door of the Silver Dollar and groaned inwardly. The place over which he had labored so hard and so long was a wreck. He didn't have to worry about vandals. There was nothing much left worth stealing at this point.

His main objective was to recover anything Mia might need from his office. The small space smelled as bad as the rest of the building, but it wasn't as wet. Fortunately, he had a remote server at home that served as a backup for all his work files. His computer now stood in a puddle of water, so he didn't have much faith that it would reboot.

He found a cardboard carton that was mostly intact and scooped all the papers off the top of his desk. They could be dried out, and if worst came to worst, he'd ask vendors to resend their invoices.

This wasn't how he had anticipated getting reacquainted with Mia. He wanted to give her the impression that he was a solid businessman with an enthusiastic clientele. Instead, he was left with a smelly, sodden mess.

All in all, it could have been worse. At least the outer structure was intact. Since there was no rain in the forecast, he loaded everything into the back of his truck. He definitely didn't want that smell in the cab.

Over beer and burgers, his friends grilled him about the fire. They were equal parts sympathetic to his predicament and bummed out that their favorite watering hole was closed down indefinitely. Dylan managed to change the subject eventually, uncomfortably aware that several of these men barely managed to make ends meet from paycheck to paycheck. He didn't want anyone feeling sorry for him when all he had to do was throw money at his problem, and eventually it would resolve itself.

If the men sitting around the table ever resented the fact that his bank account ran to seven figures, they never showed it. But he had to wonder if his connection to the Kavanagh fortune at times made them uncomfortable.

Shaking off the odd sense that he didn't belong, he finished off his drink and stood. "Who's gonna be first in line for an ass-kicking at eight ball?"

When Cora went down for an early-evening nap, Mia snooped unashamedly. She'd put the baby monitor beside Cora's bed and carried the receiver in her pocket. That left her free to roam Dylan's gorgeous house at will. She started with the upstairs bedrooms. They were immaculately decorated and looked ready to welcome guests at any moment.

Despite that, they had an air of emptiness about them. Exactly how often did Dylan actually have overnight company?

His kitchen was a dream, especially the fancy appliances. Mia knew how to nuke anything, but the largesse in Dylan's refrigerator made her stomach growl. He'd told her his housekeeper kept him well stocked with food, but that was somewhat of an understatement. Mia found a freezer full of packages labeled with names like chicken parmesan, vegetable soup, whole-wheat bread. Added to what was in the fridge itself, she surmised that Dylan could easily hole up here and not go hungry for a month or more.

Since he had enjoined her to make herself at home and help herself to anything she wanted for dinner, she wasted no time in picking out what looked to be an individual serving of chicken potpie. While it thawed in the microwave, she glanced at the monitor, making sure Cora was still asleep. The little girl was in her favorite position, with her butt lifted in the air and her knees pulled beneath her.

Shadows fell as Mia ended her meal. She would have to wake the baby up soon or Cora would never sleep tonight. Although Mia was not particularly anxious about staying alone, the house did seem bigger and emptier with dark on the way. She wondered how long Dylan would stay out.

None of her business, she reminded herself. If the original plan had worked out, she and Cora would be alone in the apartment over the bar. But at least the people and the noise would have kept her company until closing time.

Cora was in her usual sunny mood when Mia got her up. Somewhere in the car there was a plastic storage box with the baby's bathtub and other important items, but Mia decided to do without them tonight. She put Cora in the sink and managed to bathe her quickly before the odd circumstances could unsettle the infant.

Smelling like lotion and clean baby, Cora wriggled as her mother tucked her into pajamas. For an hour, they played on the king-size bed that was to be Mia's for the next several weeks. If Mia listened occasionally for the sound of a vehicle coming up the road, it was only because she was a little nervous about being so far out in the woods all alone.

It certainly wasn't because she was hoping to see Dylan again before she went to sleep.

Cora, for once, was cooperative when it came to bedtime. Her little eyelids drooped as Mia stood rocking her back and forth and singing one of the songs that was part of their bedtime ritual. When Mia laid Cora carefully in the bed, the baby wiggled for a moment and then curled her arms on either side of her head.

Turning out the light, Mia tiptoed backward out of the room and eased the door shut. Her heart jumped in her chest when she bumped into something big and warm. A hand came over her mouth, muffling her shriek.

"Easy, Mia. It's just me."

She struggled until he freed her. "You scared the heck out of me," she cried, glaring at Dylan as she tried to breathe normally.

"Sorry." He didn't seem overly penitent. "I thought you would hear me come in the front door, but you must have been busy with the baby. You want some ice cream?"

His prosaic question was at odds with the way his gaze roved over her body. She had changed into thin knit sleep pants and a spaghetti strap tank top. It was a perfectly respectable outfit for a hot summer night, even if it did reveal her nipples a tad too much.

"Ice cream would be nice," she said, crossing her arms over her chest. "Let me put a robe on."

His half smile made her knees quake. "Not on my account," he said. "I like you just the way you are. Follow me."

The house didn't seem nearly as big and threatening with the owner in residence. Mia sat down at the small table in the breakfast nook and watched as Dylan dished up enormous servings of praline pecan for each of them. Judging from the condition of his body, he clearly expended calories somehow, because there wasn't an ounce of fat on him anywhere.

He was lean and muscular. Physical power was on display, but restrained. Dylan was the kind of man a woman would want at her side if she were lost in the wilderness.

Joining her at the table, he offered her a bowl. "Dig in."

After four bites, she put down her spoon. "You're staring at me."

"Sorry." He leaned forward and wiped a smudge of caramel off her chin. "I'm still trying to match the grown-up Mia to my memories of a young girl."

His touch rattled her. "I'm surprised you remember anything at all about me. You were a senior, an exalted star, and I wasn't even in the same orbit."

"You were a senior, too," he pointed out, studying her as he licked his dessert off the back of his spoon.

She had never before seen anything sexy about eating ice cream, but Dylan was in a class by himself.

"I wasn't a *real* senior," she said, remembering the taunts and ostracism. The pecking order in high school was rigid and unbending. The fact that she was only fifteen years old and about to get her diploma was a sore spot for many of her classmates struggling to pass required courses.

"You had a hard time, didn't you?" In his eyes she saw dawning adult comprehension of what her life must have been like. "I'm sorry, Mia."

She shrugged. "I was used to it. And besides, I was neither the first nor the last high-school kid to be bullied. It could have been a lot worse. I always wondered if you had something to do with the fact that after Christmas, a lot of the kids suddenly changed toward me. They weren't exactly nice, but they weren't outright hostile anymore. Did you say something?"

"I might have. A bunch of us went on a ski trip over New Year's weekend. A couple of the jocks were talking about getting you in bed to prove that they could. I shut them down. That's all."

She paused, her spoon halfway to her mouth. "Why, Dylan Kavanagh…you were looking out for me." The knowledge gave her a warm fuzzy feeling.

His quick grin made him look more like the kid from high school. "Don't make me out to be a hero. I'm well aware that I gave you plenty of grief."

"And yet you kissed me once."

The words tumbled out of her mouth uncensored. She froze, aghast that she had dropped a conversational bomb.

Dylan was shocked that she had brought it up. And vaguely uncomfortable. He'd wondered if she even remembered the spring night right before they graduated.

"I never should have done that," he muttered, taking another bite of ice cream and hoping she didn't notice that his face had flushed. Even now, he could remember the taste of her lips.

But she had been fifteen, her sixteenth birthday still two months away, and he had been a man of eighteen by that time. His awkward embrace and quick, furtive kiss had felt both deliciously sweet and at the same time terribly wrong.

Mia set her spoon in her empty bowl and propped her

chin on her hand. "I always wondered why you kissed me. Was it a dare?"

"No. Hell, no." The idea was insulting. That would have made it even worse. "I had the urge, that's all. We'd been together all year, more hours than I cared to admit, and we were getting ready to graduate. Probably never going to see each other again, since you were headed off to school at some brainiac university."

"You can't tell me the Dylan Kavanagh I knew back then was sentimental. Try again."

"You were pretty in the moonlight," he said flatly. "I went to get something from the concession stand and there you were." They'd both, separately, been at Silver Glen's one and only drive-in theater. The place was in business even today. The owners were careful to keep it in good shape and to hire off-duty police officers for the premises so parents would still let their kids go there.

"You were with a date, weren't you?"

How could big dark eyes make him feel like such a heel? "Yes."

"So again…I have to ask. Why?"

"Damn it, Mia, I don't know." He stood and took his bowl to the sink, dropping it with a clatter. "You fascinated me. And intimidated me."

Her jaw dropped. "That's the most outrageous thing I've ever heard you say. You hated me for a long time. And after that you barely tolerated me."

"Not true." He leaned against the counter, his hands propped behind him on the sink. "I never hated you. It may have seemed that way in the beginning, but it was really myself I hated. You just caught the fallout. I may have acted like the biggest horse's ass ever, but I thought you were sweet and impossibly complicated."

She looked at him as if he had grown horns and a tail.

"Why won't you tell me the real reason you kissed me, Dylan?"

Fed up with her stubbornness and her utter lack of faith in her appeal, he strode to the table and grabbed her wrist, pulling her to her feet. "I kissed you because you made me hard and I dreamed about you most nights." Without thinking about the ramifications or the consequences, he lowered his head, muttering softly as he brought his lips close to hers. "You were an angel to me, the one and only person who could rescue me from the mess that was my life."

He came so close to kissing her, he could taste it. But Mia was rigid in his embrace. For about thirty seconds. Then something unexpected struck him in the chest and spread throughout his body. It was a feeling like being caught in a summer rain, drenched to the skin and laughing because it felt so good.

She hugged him. Her technique was awkward and tentative. The very lack of confidence in the way she responded stole beneath his defenses and swamped him with tenderness. She was not a young girl anymore. She was a grown woman with a soft body and full breasts and curvy hips that begged for a man's touch.

Much longer, and he'd be tempted to take her standing up. *Bad idea, Dylan.* He backed away reluctantly, breaking the physical connection though he couldn't deny a less tangible link that bound them together.

Mia stared up at him with an expression that was impossible to define. "You almost kissed me," she said.

He shrugged. "I thought better of it. You didn't believe me about that night at the drive-in, but it's true. I had a little bit of a forbidden crush on you back then."

"Forbidden?"

"You were too young, even if we *were* in the same grade. I may have been a hormonal teenage boy, but I knew you were off-limits."

"I was headed to college, same as you."

"Didn't matter. You were a kid, a very pretty, not-old-enough-to-be-legal kid."

"Am I supposed to be grateful that you kept your hands to yourself?"

He might not be the smartest man in the world, but he knew a pissed-off woman when he heard one. "What do you want from me, Mia?"

She was silent for so long, he began to sweat. And when she spoke she didn't really answer his question. "If we're being honest here, I suppose I should tell you that I didn't happen upon the Silver Dollar by chance."

His eyebrows went up. "You didn't?"

"No. I wanted to see you, and it wasn't hard to find out that you owned the saloon."

"You couldn't have known about the job, so why did you come?"

Mia sat back down, resting her elbows on the table and putting her face in her hands before she looked up at him with a crooked smile. "I've screwed up just about every aspect of my life. At the moment, I'm a homeless single mom with a helpless baby and limited funds. I thought it might make me feel better if I could be sure that *you* were doing well…that the tutoring I did in high school meant something. So I came back to Silver Glen for a visit."

"How did you know I would sit down at the bar and speak to you?"

"I didn't. But it wouldn't have mattered if we never came face-to-face. I could see right in front of me what you had created. A thriving business. People eating, drinking, having fun. Camaraderie. You're a success, Dylan. And that makes me feel good."

Six

Mia almost regretted her honesty. Dylan's visible discomfort was not the reaction she had expected. But he responded gruffly, "I'm glad."

"Don't get me wrong," she said quickly. "I'm not taking credit for your success. That's all you. But in high school you were at a critical juncture, and I like to think I helped…at least a little."

"Of course you did." He glanced at the clock on the wall. "If you have everything you need, I think I'll turn in. Whenever the baby naps tomorrow, you and I can go over the books, and hopefully you can get started when time permits."

The switch from personal to business gave her mental whiplash. Had Dylan been offended by what she said? Perhaps he thought she was presumptuous to pat herself on the back. Maybe the feeling she was trying to express had come out all wrong. "Dylan, I didn't mean that you couldn't have done it without me. That's not what I was saying."

He shoved his hands in his pockets, the line and angles of his face set in stone. "But it's true, isn't it? Without your help, I would have flunked out of high school. And when I dropped out of college, if my family hadn't had money I would have ended up flipping burgers at a fast-food place."

"That's crazy, I—"

He strode out of the room so quickly she was caught off guard. Running to catch up, she followed him across the huge, open living area. Just before he reached the wing where their bedrooms were located, she grabbed his sleeve. "Listen to me, Dylan. Your money isn't what made the saloon a success. It's you. The way you draw people together. Everybody loves hanging out at the Silver Dollar because you've made it comfortable and fun. Do you know how much I wish I had your gift for reaching people?"

He stopped. Not much choice, really, with her hanging on to his arm. But his face softened. "Still trying to save me from myself, Mia?"

"You don't need saving," she insisted. "But that chip on your shoulder must be getting hard to carry."

He ignored her deliberate provocation. "I'm meeting with the insurance adjustor at ten tomorrow. I should be back sometime after lunch. We can work on the bookkeeping stuff then. My housekeeper will be here in the morning. Please make yourself at home."

Before she could respond, he disappeared into his suite of rooms and closed the door firmly behind him.

Mia stood, nonplussed, and felt a rush of mortification. She shouldn't have brought up the past. Clearly it was still a sore spot. But it baffled her that no one else saw this side of Dylan. At the saloon, the customers related to him like he was a rock star, the women giggly and starry-eyed and the men standing a little straighter and pulling in their beer guts in an attempt to emulate the man whom everyone admired.

Dylan, by every definition, was a success in life, both professionally and personally. Despite his aborted engagement, he had surrounded himself with a wide circle of family and friends. Someday there might be a woman lucky enough and smart enough to snag him for a husband.

Turning and tiptoeing into her suite so as not to wake

the baby, Mia crawled into bed and turned out the light. In the dark, and in a strange place, she heard all sorts of pops and creaks as the house settled for the night. To take her mind off the unfamiliar noises, she imagined what Dylan might be doing. Perhaps he had showered and walked nude back into his bedroom. It was safe to imagine that a man like him slept in the buff. Just thinking about it made Mia shiver.

Sex with the professor had been unexceptional. Unlike Indiana Jones, Mia's short-lived lover had a body almost as soft as a woman's. The most physical thing he ever did was lift his arm as he wrote on the dry-erase board. Surely she wasn't so shallow that she had to have rock-hard abs and spectacularly defined muscles to get turned on.

A more likely and more palatable explanation was the fact that Dylan had stolen a piece of her heart when she was fifteen, and she had never gotten it back. She was an adult woman now. With needs. Needs that went beyond the necessity of finding a job or a place to live.

Sometimes at night, she lay in bed imagining what it would be like if she had a husband tucked in beside her, a soul mate to share the ups and downs of being a parent. It wasn't that she was afraid to work hard. She would do anything to ensure Cora's happiness and well-being. But even so, single parenting was lonely.

She didn't regret getting pregnant. Cora was a gift unlike any she had ever received in her life. Perhaps she was overthinking her decision. In the end, it didn't really matter if she had chosen a less-than-perfect route to motherhood. The deed was done. She had a baby. And the two of them were a family.

Moments later, hovering on the edge of sleep, deliciously drowsy and comfortable in Dylan's luxurious guest bed, Mia groaned when she heard the unmistakable sound of her daughter's cry.

Dragging herself upright on the side of the bed, she scraped her hands through her hair and rubbed her temples. Judging by the experience of past nights, she had about sixty seconds to pacify her baby before Cora launched into full-scale squalling. With a deep breath and a prayer for patience, she headed for the adjoining room, wondering if she would ever again get a full night's sleep.

Dylan heard Cora cry out. His first instinct was to get up and go see if he could help. But that seemed uncomfortably intimate in light of the fact that he and Mia had barely reconnected after not seeing each other for a dozen years. He had certainly never anticipated having her live in his house.

The truth was, he could more than afford to put her up at a hotel. Hell, his family owned the swank, exclusive Silver Beeches Lodge on top of the mountain. The hotel was no place for a baby, though. Not only might the other guests complain, but Mia and Cora needed privacy and space to be comfortable. He had more than enough room. One slip of a woman and her tiny infant were hardly likely to cramp his style, and besides, part of him wanted them close by.

He turned over in bed and lay on his stomach, his face buried in one arm. The air-conditioning was set at the usual temp, but he felt hot and restless. It had been too long since he'd slept with a woman. Seeing his brother's happiness made him jealous.

There…he'd admitted it. Which made him a pathetic lowlife. Knowing that his own engagement had crashed and burned when the woman he'd loved decided Hollywood had more to offer than Dylan Kavanagh had been a blow to his heart and his ego. He didn't begrudge Liam his happiness. Not at all. His older brother deserved every ounce of joy he'd found in the exuberant Zoe.

But Dylan's failure in the relationship department made him wonder if his judgment about women was as screwed up as his perception of numbers and letters.

Self-pity was a disgusting emotion. Normally, he spent little time bemoaning the defection of his fiancée, or even the fact that his reading comprehension sucked even now. But getting to know Mia again, on top of seeing the business he'd worked so hard to establish going up in smoke, had rattled him.

Tomorrow morning he'd get his head on straight. Tomorrow morning he'd make a fresh start in more ways than one.

In the meantime, surely it wasn't hurting anyone if he imagined what Mia Larin looked like all grown up. And naked.

When light filtered into Mia's room, she wanted to pull the covers over her head and pretend that it was still the dead of night. Cora had played on Mia's bed, cooing and clutching a rattle, until almost one in the morning when she finally wore herself out and fell asleep. Mia had laid her daughter gently in her crib, returned to her own room and been comatose almost instantly. The baby awakened at five for her usual feeding, but thankfully, had gone right back to sleep.

Mia felt sluggish and hungover, which really wasn't fair since she hadn't consumed so much as half a glass of wine since the first day she decided to get pregnant. Before launching on her solo adventure, she had read book after book about nutrition, ovulation, maternal health and mental preparation. Given the repeated disappointments she had weathered as the months passed, there had been more than one occasion when a good, stiff drink might have helped.

Rolling onto her side, she glanced at the clock. The

thought of another hour's sleep sounded like heaven, but her stomach rumbled, and she knew that once Cora was up, Mia's morning meal would consist of little more than a banana eaten standing up and a cup of coffee.

Ever so quietly, she dressed in jeans and a yellow cotton shirt that buttoned up the front. Maybe the cheery color would help cut through the fog of sleep deprivation.

Though she had never exactly been a fashion icon, her wardrobe lately tended more toward practical than stylish. Though she would have liked to appear trendy and put together for Dylan's benefit, it probably wasn't going to happen. Lately, more often than not, she noticed halfway through the day that Cora had spit up on her shoulder. Not exactly the way to entice a man.

With the baby monitor tucked in her pocket, Mia crossed the living room in her bare feet, making a beeline for the kitchen and the smell of coffee. Though Dylan had warned her his housekeeper would be in residence this morning, it was still somewhat of a shock to come face-to-face with an angular woman whose short-cropped gray hair—along with a black uniform—gave her a stern look. Mia judged her age to be between sixty-five and seventy.

"Oh," Mia said, pulling up short. "I'm Mia Larin. And you must be Dylan's housekeeper."

When the woman smiled, her entire demeanor transformed. "That's me," she said. "My name's Gertie. What can I get you for breakfast, dear?" Without asking, she poured a cup of coffee and pressed it into Mia's hand, pointing out the sugar and creamer on the table.

Mia shook her head. "Please don't think you have to wait on me. I'm here to work for Dylan. In fact, I was supposed to be living above the bar, but, well…you know what happened."

Gertie grimaced. "A damn shame. But Dylan will put it to rights. That boy never loses sight of a goal. And by the way, my job is to take care of Mr. Kavanagh and his guests. He specifically asked me this morning to make sure you and the baby were settled in. So no back talk from you, young lady." Her smile indicated that she was joking, but Mia had a feeling that crossing Gertie wouldn't be a good idea.

"Well, in that case, I'd love some toast and one of those grapefruits over there."

Gertie hunched her shoulders and scowled. "You nursing?"

It was a rather personal question from someone she had just met, but Mia answered anyway. "Yes, ma'am." She'd been brought up to respect her elders. Despite Gertie's position as housekeeper, Mia felt deference was in order.

"Then you need more food than that. You like your eggs scrambled?" At Mia's nod, Gertie turned toward the refrigerator. "Newspaper's on the counter. I know you young people get the headlines on your fancy phones or whatever, but in my opinion, nothing gets the day off to a good start like reading the comics and the obituaries over a decent cup of coffee."

Mia, somewhat chastened, picked up the copy of the *Asheville Citizen-Times*. "Dylan subscribes to this?"

Gertie snorted. "No. I bring my copy from home. But I've caught him checking his stocks a time or two."

"Have you worked for him very long?"

"Ever since he built this house. So, I suppose we're closing in on three years or so."

That answered the question of whether or not Dylan had put down roots when he fell in love. The engagement had been longer ago than that, so he must have broken ground for this amazing house simply because he wanted a place of his own.

Mia pretended an interest in the paper, but she was more enthralled in watching Gertie. The older woman moved about the kitchen with an economy Mia admired. Mia rarely cooked, and when she did, the results were never the same. She knew how to read a formula and how to follow rules. But somehow, her culinary efforts always fell short. Perhaps she could pick up a few tips while she was here.

In no time, Gertie set a plate of eggs, sausage and biscuits in front of Mia, flanked by a small bowl holding a perfectly sliced and sectioned grapefruit half. "Thank you," Mia said. "This looks delicious."

"It is." Gertie's grin was smug. "Mr. Dylan likes a clean house, but he didn't hire me 'cause I know how to vacuum. That boy loves his food."

"You'd never know it to look at him." Mia's face flamed, realizing that it probably wasn't good form to exhibit such oblique though obvious appreciation of her landlord's physical attributes.

Gertie merely chuckled. "He burns it off. Never sits still that I can tell. How do you two know each other?"

"We were in school together."

"Ah." Gertie washed the iron skillet she'd used to fix Mia's eggs and dried it with a paper towel. "Mr. Dylan told me you're going to be doing the books for him. I want you to know that I'd consider it an honor to take care of the baby whenever you ask."

Mia gaped. "Well, uh…"

"Oh, you can trust me, honey. I've got five kids of my own and twelve grandchildren. Don't get to see them as much as I'd like. They're spread all over the country. But I'm good with babies."

"That's a lovely offer," Mia said faintly, feeling a bit overwhelmed. "I'm sure it will take me a few days to get into the swing of things, but I'll keep that in mind."

"I'd do anything for Mr. Dylan."

There was a certain level of fervor in the terse statement that begged for a question. "Because he pays well?"

"No." Gertie paused. "Well, yes, he does. But that's not what I meant. Mr. Dylan helped me out of a tight spot once, and I owe him."

Mia wasn't nosy as a rule. And she certainly wasn't assertive in situations like this. But Gertie seemed primed to share information. "How so?"

The housekeeper poured herself a cup of coffee, leaned against the counter and took a sip. Black. No sugar. "One of my grandsons came to live with me three summers ago. He'd been raisin' hell back home and his momma and daddy thought a change of scenery would do him good. But the little weasel brought drugs with him here to Silver Glen and tried to sell them. Sheriff caught him and tossed him in jail. I had to bail him out."

"So Dylan loaned you the money?"

"I had the money. It wasn't that. But I'm an old woman. A fifteen-year-old boy with an attitude won't take advice, even from me. Dylan hauled his butt out of jail and gave him a tongue-lashing for upsetting his grandmother. The boy had a choice between doing jail time, going home to his momma and daddy or working for Dylan all summer."

"I'm assuming he chose Dylan?"

"Sure did. In ten weeks, Mr. Dylan talked more sense into that hardheaded rascal than the rest of us put together. The kid looked up to him, and the lectures came easier from his mentor than from me or his parents. My grandson is in college now. Making straight As. And he hasn't touched drugs since he left Silver Glen. Mr. Dylan did that."

Mia ate her breakfast in silence, her respect for Dylan growing. Perhaps because he'd been such a hell-raiser himself, he understood the mind-set of a rebellious teenage boy. Not that Dylan had ever dabbled in drugs. He'd been a sports fiend, determined to keep his body in top physical shape. But he had definitely taken pride in flouting authority.

It didn't take a psychologist to see that Dylan had been compensating for his struggles in the classroom. It was no help that his older brother, Liam, had breezed through high school and gone on past college to get an advanced degree.

Sibling rivalry at that age was tough. Dylan must have felt the sting of not measuring up. So to prove he didn't care, he'd pulled stunts like kidnapping Mr. Everson's prize bull and tying it to the flagpole in the center of town. Dumping a case of red food coloring and a gallon of detergent into the fountain in front of the bank. Snitching the principal's ugly burgundy blazer and literally running it up the flagpole.

No one was ever harmed by Dylan's pranks. And he was usually the one who had to pay the price for cleaning up his messes. But his antics had worked. In Silver Glen High School, by the time Dylan reached his senior year, he was the most popular guy around, hands down. Mia had been an invisible nobody.

She finished the last bite of her lighter-than-air biscuit and pushed back from the table. "That was wonderful, Gertie. Thank you so much."

"Glad you enjoyed it. Lunch will be ready at twelve-thirty, as long as Mr. Dylan makes it back from town. Anytime you need washing done for you or the baby, just drop it on the floor in the laundry room."

"Oh, but I—"

Gertie held up a hand. "It's my job. *Your* job is to look after the baby and the books. Don't be tryin' to wash dishes or mess around in my kitchen. This is my turf. And I'm going to make your life easier, because that's what Mr. Dylan wants."

Seven

Dylan had a good news/bad news kind of morning. On the upside, he had very good insurance. The financial hit wasn't going to be too bad at all. But in the negative column was the fact that the contractor he wanted to do the renovation couldn't start for three weeks. In other words, hurry up and wait.

He swallowed his impatience as best he could. Sooner or later the bar would reopen, and he was confident that his regulars would return. Nothing could be done about the lost business in the meantime.

When he was satisfied that he had taken care of the essential details to get the ball rolling with the adjustor and the repair work, he jumped in his truck and headed for home. Knowing that Mia and Cora would be there when he arrived was another item for the plus column.

He found his houseguests in the sunroom. Pausing in the doorway, he absorbed the picture they made. Mia was down on the carpet, stretched out on her side. Where her yellow top buttoned near her waist, one side of the fabric gaped, giving him a tantalizing glimpse of pale white skin. Cora lay on a fuzzy pink blanket, kicking her legs and rolling from side to side as Mia laughed softly. "It won't be long, sweet pea."

"Won't be long until what?" Dylan strolled into the

room and sprawled into his favorite recliner that just happened to be at Mia's elbow.

She sat up and straightened her clothing, her cheeks flushed, either from playing with her daughter or because seeing Dylan flustered her. "Until she rolls over completely. The doctor says Cora's at the top of the charts physically."

"You may have an athlete on your hands."

Mia shook her head. "Not if she has my genes. I was lucky that my high-school gym classes were pass/fail, or my grade point average would have suffered. I've been known to trip over my own feet."

"That's only because your super impressive brain is tied up with loftier matters."

She gazed at him askance. "Are you making fun of me, Kavanagh?"

He reached down and tugged her ponytail. "Maybe. What are you going to do about it? I'm bigger and faster than you."

She scooped Cora into her lap and nuzzled her head. "I like the grown-up Dylan."

Her non sequitur caught him off guard. "What does that mean?" It sounded like a compliment, which made him suspicious. The Mia he had once known would never have been confident enough to flirt with a guy, even one she felt comfortable around.

"It means that I'm impressed with the man you've become. You're not angry anymore. And not out to prove anything, at least I don't think so. Some people would have been apoplectic after the fire yesterday, but you've handled it all so calmly."

The praise made him oddly uncomfortable. "Believe me, Mia, I'm nothing special. I have the luxury of a safety net. Not everyone is so lucky. It's not like I'm going to be destitute and on the street if the Silver Dollar goes belly-up."

She frowned. "Do you think it will?"

"I hope not. The guy I trust to do the restoration can't get to me until three weeks from now. Which means a long wait until I can reopen. But I'm pretty sure my regulars will come back."

"I can't imagine that they wouldn't." She glanced at her watch. "We'd better head for the kitchen. I don't want to get my knuckles rapped with a ruler if we're late for lunch. I think I'm scared of Gertie."

"Her bark is worse than her bite." He extended a hand and helped Mia to her feet. Cora yawned hugely, making him laugh. "Maybe I'm prejudiced, but she's really cute. Did she sleep okay last night?" He had heard her only that one time, but he didn't know how long the baby had stayed awake.

"So-so."

"Do you mind if I carry her?"

Mia surrendered the baby without comment, walking ahead of him as they followed their noses to the appetizing aromas of Gertie's handiwork. Dylan enjoyed the feel of the infant in his arms. The smell of baby shampoo brought back good memories from his childhood. Cora was still young enough that having a stranger hold her wasn't alarming.

That first evening at the Silver Dollar, she had gone to him without protest, her big brown eyes and pink dimpled cheeks the epitome of a happy baby. Dylan wondered which, if any, of her anonymous male parent's traits she had inherited. Dylan wasn't sure where he stood on the whole nature/nurture thing. But his gut told him that what mattered most was the love a child received *after* birth.

In the kitchen, Gertie bustled about, shooing them to

seats at the table and pouring iced tea and lemonade to go along with the home cooked vegetables.

Mia's face lit up. "Food, real food. I've about had my fill of microwave dinners."

Dylan sat down with Cora in his lap, scooting his silverware out of the way when the baby predictably reached for a fork. "You won't go hungry while you're under this roof. Gertie is so good she could be on one of those reality cooking shows."

Gertie turned bright red. "Oh, hush, Dylan. You're exaggerating."

At that very moment, Mia realized that the housekeeper loved her boss like a son. It was cute actually. The woman obviously doted on Dylan, and he treated her with a mixture of respect and affection that was very sweet to watch. He would probably hate knowing Mia thought anything about him was sweet. He might not *need* to prove he was a bad boy anymore, but there was nothing overtly soft about him.

He exuded masculinity effortlessly. It was in the way he walked and in the breadth of his shoulders and in the low rumble of his laughter. This Dylan might be older and more sophisticated than the boy she had known in school, but beneath the skin he was still a rough-and-tumble guy.

With Dylan behind the bar at the Silver Dollar, there would be no need for a bouncer. He could probably corral a rowdy drunk with one sharp frown and a quick trip through the front door. Dylan had never initiated fights as a teenager, at least not that Mia remembered. But there was no doubt in her mind that he possessed the physical strength and agility to handle himself in any situation.

Back in high school, he had been on the wrestling squad for a little while. But though he was very good at the sport, he hadn't seemed to enjoy it the way he did football and baseball. Dylan liked being part of a team and thrived on the camaraderie of the locker room. His leadership skills were apparent even then.

As Gertie refilled Mia's glass, Mia wondered if the other two had noticed her silence. She had "checked out" for a few minutes thinking about Dylan. Somehow, he managed to clear his plate and have second helpings while still holding Cora in the crook of his left arm. The baby had actually fallen asleep.

Gertie cleared away the dishes and stopped at Dylan's elbow. "I know you two have business to discuss. Miss Mia, what if I take the baby for a walk in the backyard? I promise I'll keep her in the shade."

Dylan looked at Mia inquiringly. "It's up to you."

Mia nodded. "Of course. If you don't mind. And please call me Mia."

Gertie seemed pleased. Dylan handed Cora over to her so carefully that the baby never stirred. Mia realized ruefully that being spoiled was dangerously addictive. Suddenly, she had a beautiful, albeit temporary, home, and on top of that no need to cook or clean. She even had a built-in babysitter when needed. The change from desperate exhaustion to a return of her usual energy told her how much she had been struggling.

Once it was just the two of them in the kitchen, Mia cocked her head and smiled at Dylan. "You're a natural with kids. Do you think you'll want a big family someday? Another limb on the Kavanagh family tree?"

His face darkened and he got up from the table, turning his back on her as he poured himself a cup of coffee. "I don't plan to have children."

The words were curt. His tone of voice said *not up for discussion.* Mia, however, was so shocked she didn't pause to consider dropping the subject. "Why not?"

The glance he shot her over his shoulder was stormy.

"Because I might have a kid just like me. And I wouldn't wish that on anybody. No kid deserves to feel stupid."

The vehemence in his voice stunned her. "Is that why your engagement broke up? She wanted kids and you didn't?"

He faced her now, nursing the mug in his big hands. His face was wiped clean of expression, but there was turmoil in his gaze. "Having kids never even came up. We didn't get that far."

"Sorry," she muttered. Seeing the way he interacted with Cora told her that he would be a wonderful father.

He shrugged. "Anyone in town could fill you in on every titillating detail of my engagement and its ignominious end."

"Forget it. I shouldn't have asked. Why don't we get started looking at the saloon books?"

"Not yet. Obviously you're interested. And I've got nothing to hide. I fell for a cute blonde with a bubbly personality that nicely disguised a streak of ambition a mile wide."

"There's nothing wrong with having ambition."

"True. But it's not like I was planning to keep her barefoot and pregnant. The thing is, I was embarrassingly infatuated with her. Bought her a flashy engagement ring. Showered her with gifts. Maybe dating a movie star fed my ego, who knows?"

"I'm sure it was more than that."

"I never have been able to decide if it was my heart or my pride that took a hit. Doesn't really matter, though. She was here for three months filming a movie. When it was over, she had convinced herself that she loved the pace of life in Silver Glen, the sense of community and me."

"But she didn't."

"Let's just say that when her favorite director called

with an offer for the role of a lifetime, she hit the road so fast I never saw it coming."

"Surely you could have worked something out."

"She didn't want to. And in the end, that was probably for the best, because I belong in Silver Glen and she doesn't. She gave the ring back, kissed me with a tearful apology and left."

"I'm sorry, Dylan. That must have been a wretched time for you."

"It's worse in a small town. No place to hide."

His crooked smile tugged at her heartstrings. Mia couldn't imagine walking away from Dylan Kavanagh if he were in love with her. Clearly, the actress wanted success more than she wanted love. Or maybe she realized that whatever she and Dylan shared wasn't love at all.

"I hope I didn't bring back bad memories," she said.

It surprised Mia a little bit that she still felt so comfortable around him. Much like catching up with a cousin you hadn't seen in years, she and Dylan seemed to have picked up where they left off. But that analogy went only so far. There was nothing familial about her reaction to him.

"We all learn from our mistakes. Mine was a big one, but I've moved on." He took a cautious sip of coffee. "What about you? Is there a romantic debacle in your past?"

She sat back in her chair, enjoying the picture he made. Despite the fact that he leaned against the counter by the kitchen sink, there was nothing domesticated about him. He was a natural with children, but he didn't want any of his own. The knowledge made Mia sad.

The Kavanaghs had always seemed like a fairy-tale family to her. Despite the tragedy of losing Reggie Kavanagh, their close-knit relationships as they pulled together after his death fascinated an only child. As adults, the siblings probably had busy lives and didn't see each other as often as they liked. Maybe there were even sibling rivalries that carried over into adulthood. But despite any possible tensions, Mia envied them.

"I wouldn't call it a debacle," she said. "I dated a professor for a while. We had a lot in common, but not much sizzle."

One corner of Dylan's mouth lifted in a sexy grin. "Why, Mia. I didn't even realize you knew what sizzle was."

"I'm neither a prude nor an innocent. Though I will concede that my sexual experience compared to yours is probably the equivalent of comparing miniature golf to a professional game."

"Balls? Really? That's the metaphor you're going with?"

His wicked teasing shouldn't have rattled her. But he'd always had the ability to throw her off-kilter. "Behave," she muttered. "If you know how." She stood and faced him. "Shouldn't we get down to business?"

Dylan was somewhat perturbed that everything Mia said sounded sexual to him. She wasn't doing it on purpose. At least he didn't think so. Maybe having a woman sleeping in his house was not such a good idea. Too intimate. Too accessible. Too everything.

"The office is this way," he said gruffly.

Fortunately she followed him down the hall without comment. Dylan's home office opened off the corridor opposite the sunroom. He didn't spend much time there. It was mostly a repository for business paperwork, because at the saloon his walled "cubicle," as he liked to call it, was much too small to house file cabinets. This room had windows that let in the summer sun, and thick navy carpet that made a man want to go barefoot.

Today, however, he was the boss showing a new employee the ropes. As he glanced around the room, he felt his neck flush. The place was a wreck. He hadn't realized how bad it looked. Picking up a stack of *Sports Illustrated* magazines, he shoved several bunches of mail on top of them, attempting to clear a spot where Mia could work.

"Sorry," he said. He hadn't realized what a mess the room had become. "It's usually just me in here, so I don't bother much with cleaning."

Mia looked around with interest. "Don't worry about it. I'm sure you're always busy down at the bar. But I'd be happy to take a shot at organizing things a bit…if you trust me."

"Of course I trust you." He picked up a flat package that he had already opened with a knife and handed it to her. "I bought this to get you started."

Mia opened the carton and stared. "You got me a laptop?"

"It's top-of-the-line. And I had the guy at the computer store move all the files from the desktop at the Silver Dollar onto this baby. Fortunately, I had already dealt with that last week, because I think the old computer sustained some water damage."

Mia looked at the slim piece of technology with appreciation. "I've always wanted one so thin and light. Not that this one is mine, but it will be fun to use."

He pulled out the leather desk chair. "Sit down. Fire it up."

While he plugged in the power cord in case the unit wasn't fully charged, Mia opened the new toy and turned it on. When he stood from his crouched position on the floor beside her chair, her fingers were flying over the keys. "It's so fast," she said, her voice laden with excitement.

Rolling his eyes, he wondered if she had forgotten his presence. Testing a theory, he leaned forward and rested his forearms on the back of the chair. Now his head was close to hers, close enough that he could have kissed her cheek if he had been so inclined. He hadn't really *stopped* thinking about kissing her since last night.

She smelled good. The temptation was almost irresistible. But she was a guest in his home. His gut-deep need to nibble the curve of her ear was inappropriate. He did touch her hair, but so softly that he was sure she wouldn't notice.

Mia never flinched. "Where are the bookkeeping files?" she asked.

"Everything you need is right here." He reached around her and pointed to a tab. The faint, pleasing scent of her perfume teased his nose. Her hair, tucked up in a ponytail again, was silky and thick—the color of rich chocolate. The urge to press his lips to the nape of her neck almost shredded his resolve.

When her hands went perfectly still on the keyboard, he knew she had finally realized that he was practically embracing her. "Dylan?"

She turned her head and looked up at him. Without analyzing it, he brushed the pad of his thumb across her soft cheek. "What?"

Mia's small white teeth worried her lower lip. "I wondered when I accepted this job if we might become lovers."

He jerked upright so fast he practically cracked his spine. It was one thing for him to try and rattle the sweetly serious girl he had known in high school. Apparently this new Mia was bolder. And apparently he wasn't as slick an operator as he thought, because the light of interest in her eyes threatened to knock him on his ass.

How had he lost control of the situation so quickly?

"That's not funny," he said. "Open one of those files and let me show you how things work."

She swiveled her chair until she faced him. Her lips twitched. "I'd like that. A lot."

"Stop it," he demanded.

"Stop what?"

"Acting like you want me to seduce you."

"I don't," she said simply, her hands now tucked primly in her lap. "I'm more interested in seducing *you*."

Maybe he had stepped through some kind of time warp into a parallel universe. It was the only explanation for this surreal conversation. He ran a hand across the back of his neck. "Are you trying to get back at me for being such a jerk in high school? Is that the reason for this charade?" She couldn't be serious.

Mia smiled sweetly. "You seem upset."

"I'm not upset, I'm just..." He trailed off, not quite able to articulate his feelings. It certainly wasn't unusual for a woman to come on to him. But Mia? Even in the midst of his consternation, his libido was at work, urging him to stop rationalizing and take advantage of the situation. "Maybe you're suffering from stress," he said desperately, reaching for any feasible explanation for her attitude. "Perhaps you should go lie down."

"Is that an invitation, Dylan?"

Eight

Mia wanted to laugh out loud at Dylan's hunted expression. He was the one who had touched her, not vice versa, but clearly he hadn't expected her reaction. Truthfully she was surprised at herself. When had she decided to reach for what she wanted? Both literally and metaphorically?

Perhaps trying so hard to get pregnant and finally succeeding had given her the confidence to face her fears. She had never had any trouble with academic challenges, but steering her personal life in a positive direction? That was a bigger hurdle to jump.

"Oh, forget it, Dylan," she said, keeping her tone light and teasing. "You're looking at me like I sprouted two heads. Your virtue is safe. Go away and let me get started on this."

The naked relief on his face was comical. "That's a good idea," he said heartily. "Having me here will be an interruption. That's my old bookkeeper's cell number there on the bulletin board. She said for you to call her anytime if you have questions."

The next thing Mia knew, she was alone in Dylan's office. His defection disappointed her. But she knew he was interested. The signs were all there. That *almost* kiss when they'd shared ice cream. His soft touch on her hair when he thought she didn't notice. He kept reaching out to her. She would give him time to get used to the idea.

Glancing at her watch, she realized that Cora would be ready to eat soon. Still, there was enough time to comb through the Silver Dollar's accounts-payable and accounts-receivable files. As she delved into her task, she saw that the computer program was straightforward. Her math skills were almost as strong as her language skills, so she soon felt confident that she could help Dylan.

That he would be helping her as well was a given.

By the time she shut everything down and went in search of her baby, Dylan was nowhere to be found. Gertie was sitting in the living room bouncing Cora on her knee. The baby was happy, but when she saw her mother, Cora wanted her.

Gertie handed Cora over with a smile. "Cute kid. Looks like you."

"Thank you for looking after her."

"Glad to do it."

"Is Dylan still around?"

"Nope. He lit out of here like a crazy man, mumbling something about a meeting in town. But it was the first I heard of it."

Mia grimaced inwardly. "I'm sure the fire has created a host of problems for him. Once I get the baby down for her afternoon nap, I plan to spend a couple of hours in the office seeing what things are urgent and which ones can wait. You don't have to cook for me if Dylan will be out. I'll be fine with a sandwich."

Gertie bristled. "Nonsense. You and the baby are my responsibility. That's what Dylan wants."

Dylan drove around town aimlessly. He couldn't go to work and he couldn't go home. That was a hell of a thing for a man to admit. Now that Pandora's box had been opened, all he could think about was what it would be like to have Mia Larin in his bed.

His fingers gripped the steering wheel as he broke out in a cold sweat. No good deed went unpunished. All he had wanted to do was give her—temporarily— a job and a place to live. To express his appreciation for what she had done for him in high school.

That was a noble goal. Right? So why was he hiding out? He was a man, damn it. Mia was a little mouse of a woman.

Except that she wasn't. Even as he said the words out loud, he knew they weren't true. Maybe Mia had been bashful and socially backward at fifteen, but definitely not now. She was a grown woman with goals and dreams. She'd wanted a baby, and she'd made it happen.

Was she serious about wanting Dylan?

Even as his body tightened at the thought, he acknowledged that it was a bad idea all the way around. Not on a physical level. Hell, he'd been on board with that since the moment he realized the grown-up Mia was a sensual, alluring woman.

But Mia didn't belong in Silver Glen, and he didn't want a woman getting close enough to him again to make him do something stupid. It didn't help that Mia had a beautiful little baby. The two of them together were a temptation he didn't need.

The idea of family and hearth and home had become more appealing to him in recent months. After his broken engagement, he had closed himself off emotionally. Aside from work, he was interested only in fun and games… having a good time. But after Liam and Zoe's wedding, some of the ice around Dylan's heart began to thaw.

Now he had brought two females into his home. Females who brightened up the place and gave it new life. So the temptation returned.

When his relationship with Tara ended, it had been tough. But there were no children involved. That experience had taught him a bitter truth. Either he picked the wrong women, or he himself wasn't very good in the relationship department.

Regardless, he was skittish about getting serious again. Especially with a woman who was already a parent. Dylan liked kids. No question there. But he doubted his ability to be the kind of parent who could nurture and care for a child of his own.

The only example he'd had growing up was Reggie, his feckless father. Dylan's dad was a Peter Pan at heart, always chasing the next crazy idea, leaving it to Maeve to do the lion's share of guiding seven boys. Dylan suspected he had inherited some of his dad's lack of focus. He'd be damned if he would ruin some kid's life.

Dylan had to keep reminding himself that Mia was passing through. Like his ex-fiancée, Mia would not be sticking around when the right job offer came along. Even if she *was* attracted to him, it was up to Dylan to be strong for both of them. Mia's defenses were down. She'd been through a grueling few weeks. An honorable man would not take advantage of that weakness. No matter how very badly he wanted to.

By the time he returned home in the late afternoon, he was certain he had a handle on the Mia situation. What he hadn't counted on was finding his mother, Maeve, sitting on his sofa conversing with his new houseguest. It wasn't entirely unheard of for his mom to drop by, but she usually called first. Maybe the gossipy grapevine had alerted her to Mia's presence. Maeve had been doing her best to play matchmaker for Dylan since the Tara incident.

Every one of his bachelor survival skills kicked into gear. "Hello, Mom. What brings you here?"

Maeve Kavanagh was an attractive woman in her early sixties. Her auburn hair with touches of gray, habitually kept in a bun, gave her an air of authority, but there was nothing matronly about her. Along with Liam, Maeve ran the Silver Beeches Lodge.

Dylan tossed his keys in a disk on the credenza by the front door and took a seat across from the two women. His mother cuddled Cora, a look of absolute joy on her face as she played with the baby.

Mia shot him a look that could have meant anything. "Your mother was worried about you. Because of the fire."

"I'm fine, Mom. But I appreciate your stopping by. Mia is staying with me for a bit. I guess you've already introduced yourselves by now. Do you remember her at all?"

Maeve tore her attention away from the infant long enough to frown at her son. "Of course I do. I thanked God for her every minute of your senior year. You were so busy being a rebellious adolescent that I couldn't get through to you, so I looked on Mia's assistance as a miracle."

Mia frowned. "It hadn't been that long since Dylan lost his dad. I think his behavior was understandable."

Dylan squirmed when his mother raised an eyebrow. He didn't need Mia defending him. Especially not to the parent who remembered all too well the many ways that he'd once tried to ruin his life. He stood, not caring if he was being rude. "I'll walk you out to the car, Mom."

Maeve grinned at Mia. "I believe that's 'Here's your hat, what's your hurry.' But since I do have a million things waiting to be accomplished, I'll go. It was lovely to see you again, Mia. I hope you'll join me for dinner at the Lodge one evening soon."

"Thank you, Ms. Kavanagh. I'd like that."

"As long as you bring the baby and call me Maeve."

Dylan escorted his mother out of the house, well aware he was about to get the third degree. What he hadn't expected was the way his parent looked at him with calculation in her eyes.

Opening her car door, but not getting in, she rested her arm on the frame. "Tell me the truth, Dylan. Is that baby yours?"

Startled shock tensed every one of his muscles. "Good God, Mother, no. I haven't seen the woman since high school."

"And yet she's tucked up nice and cozy in your house."

If anyone else, including his brothers, had subjected him to this line of questioning, he'd have told them to mind their own damn business. Unfortunately, that wasn't an option with his mother.

"Mia lost her job. I needed a bookkeeper. It's temporary. The plan was for her to live in the apartment over the saloon. Obviously, that's not an option right now."

Maeve's expression didn't change. "I don't want to see you get hurt. I don't want anyone taking advantage of your kind heart. You have this wonderful capacity for helping people, but it doesn't always serve you well in the end."

He stared down at the driveway, kicking a pebble with enough force to express his frustration. "You're talking about my ex-fiancée."

"Tara, the tramp, we call her. She used you, Dylan. It fed her ego to have a handsome hulk of a young man—a wealthy one at that—squiring her around town. I know the shape you were in when she left. You care, Dylan. Sometimes too much. Because people are not always what they seem."

"Mia's not like that. And the situations are totally different."

"I saw the way she looked at you when you walked into the room a moment ago."

He would have liked to argue the point, but given the surprising turn of events in his office earlier, he couldn't. "You have nothing to worry about. Mia's time here is very short. A woman with her qualifications and capabilities will have another job in no time."

"Bring her to dinner at the hotel. Zoe has been dying to cook for us in their suite."

Dylan's brother and his new wife lived on the top floor of the Silver Beeches Lodge, but they already had plans underway to build an incredible house. "I think being included in a family dinner would make Mia uncomfortable."

"Nonsense. I already invited her."

"She's nursing. I doubt she'd want to leave the baby for that long."

"Bring the baby with you. Maybe little Cora will give Liam and Zoe ideas. I'd like to be a nana before I have one foot in the grave."

"You never give up, do you?" He smiled, acknowledging the love and affection he felt for his mother. She had been widowed very young and yet managed to raise seven rambunctious boys and keep the family fortunes afloat. "I love you, Mom."

He kissed her cheek and tucked her into the car.

She stuck her arm out the window and waved a finger at him. "I'll check with Liam and Zoe and see what night works for them. No excuses."

Without answering, he watched her drive away. Hearing someone who cared so much about him put into words some of what he had been thinking sobered him. Was he susceptible to Mia simply because of auld lang syne and propinquity?

When he went back inside the house, he stopped to speak to the woman who had occupied his thoughts for most of the day. "Mia."

She looked up at him and smiled. "Your mother is sweet."

Dylan thought about that for a minute. Maeve had been

called headstrong and caring, but sweet? He squelched the instinct to plop down beside Mia and play with the baby, reminding himself of his recent resolve to keep them at a distance.

"I have several calls to make this evening, so I'm going to have dinner in my suite. You and Cora are welcome to make yourself at home anywhere in the house. I'll talk to you tomorrow."

I'll talk to you tomorrow.
But he didn't.

Mia was first surprised, then angry, then sad when she realized Dylan was making a concerted effort to be invisible. For five straight days, she never saw him nor heard from him. Gertie said he was hard at work tearing out the insides of the bar so that when the contractor was ready, the work could begin at once. None of which explained why a man with Dylan's fortune hadn't hired a crew to take over the dirty, smelly work. At night she caught sounds that might be him moving around in his room, but he came and went like a ghost.

It didn't take a genius to understand that Dylan was not going to follow up on her blatant invitation. Something inside Mia shriveled and died with the knowledge that for once in her life she had made the first move with a man, and now he was avoiding her as if afraid she might somehow jump him in his sleep. *Embarrassed* didn't begin to describe how she felt.

When she had been in residence almost a week, it became clear that she needed to be proactive about finding a *real* job. Living in Dylan's house was an untenable situation. The man was literally skulking around like a phantom because she had told him she wanted him.

Besides that, she needed to get back to work. As much as she adored Cora—and as lovely as it was to be waited on hand and foot—her brain needed the challenges it was accustomed to handling. The work she did was important. Her skills were a rare gift, one she could not in all good conscience fritter away.

One morning when Cora napped and after the records for the bar were in good shape, Mia used the laptop to write a new résumé. She'd been in her last job a very long time, so it wasn't hard to piece together her employment history.

Dylan had dangled the prospect of spending more time with Cora as an incentive for Mia to take the flexible bookkeeping job. But no matter how much she cherished being with her child all day, it was equally necessary to set a good example for her daughter. Mia's career was important. It changed lives. The work she was trained to do, the work she enjoyed, was more than a means of income. It was what she was good at…what she contributed to the world at large.

Once the résumé was polished, she compiled a list of all the influential contacts she knew in her field and emailed them her portfolio. After she clicked the send button, she felt her heart sink. She wished she had time to follow up on her attraction to Dylan. But if he was not interested, then the sooner she left, the better. Besides, getting involved with him would only lead to heartbreak. Dylan belonged in Silver Glen. Sadly, there was nothing here for Mia.

That night, Cora did not sleep well at all. She was restless and cranky, perhaps picking up on her mother's unsettled feelings. At two in the morning, Mia wandered to the other side of the house to get a glass of milk. Cora whimpered and squirmed in her arms, her little face red and blotchy from crying.

Mia knew how she felt. For two cents, she would plop down on the floor and bawl herself.

Instead of reaching for the light switch—because she definitely wanted Cora to know it was not morning—she tiptoed carefully across the kitchen, hoping to avoid a stubbed toe. But when she did run into something, it was big and warm and solid. Her muffled shriek came seconds before the realization that Dylan held her by the arms.

Her pulse racing like a train bound for the station, she wriggled free. "You've got to stop doing that. My heart can't take it." The complaint didn't hold much heat, since she was whispering.

He ran a hand over Cora's downy head. "You think she's getting a tooth?"

Mia yawned, not even protesting when Dylan reached for Cora. "It's a little too soon for that. Maybe I'm being punished for something."

"You want some company while she's awake?" His question was quiet, but it seemed significant somehow.

"I haven't seen you for days."

"Did you miss me?" Even in the gloom she could see the flash of white teeth.

"Barely noticed you were gone," she lied. "And yes…if you have insomnia, I'd love to have an adult to converse with. My repertoire of baby talk is all panned out."

Dylan brushed past her. "Follow me."

In the living room, he flipped on the gas logs, even though it was the height of summer. The dancing flames cast a rosy glow of illumination that was gentle enough not to stimulate Cora.

Mia collapsed onto the sofa, so tired she could barely sit up straight. "I can hold her," she said.

"Relax, Mia. I've got this."

As she watched through heavy-lidded eyes, Dylan walked Cora around the room, singing to her in a voice that was pleasant but definitely off-key. His husky serenade seeped into Mia's bones and muscles, relaxing them until she slid further down into the cushions.

Only then did it dawn on her that he was naked from the waist up. In the illumination from the fire, she could see the beautiful delineation of his muscles. He looked powerfully masculine, and—in spite of the baby cradled in his arms—untamed, pagan. His drawstring pajama pants, navy with a yellow stripe, were most likely a concession to his houseguests.

Cora quieted finally, lashes settling on rounded cheeks. Mia knew she should get up and take the baby, but she couldn't seem to move....

Dylan cuddled Cora. Sweet, snuggly, pudgy Cora. She rested against his chest trustingly, a little streak of drool wetting his skin. He loved babies, always had. They smelled like home and happiness and love. An infant's smile was the greatest promise that the world would go on, no matter how much the grown-ups mucked around with it. When he was sure she was out for the count, he laid her in the crib, crossing his fingers that she would stay asleep.

When she didn't stir after a full minute, he was fairly certain she was down for the night. Returning to the living room, he found Mia fast asleep, as well. She had tugged an afghan from the back of the sofa. All he could see of her was the top of her head. Smiling wryly, he bent and scooped her into his arms.

If Cora reminded him of peace and security, Mia's warm body had just the opposite effect. The weight of her in his arms gave him a jolt of excitement and possessive hunger. Holding her, he wanted to believe that it was possible to keep her here. Silver Glen was his home. If he tried hard enough, he could envision Mia returning to her roots as well.

Although he had worked hard to create himself in the

image of a carefree, never-serious party guy, he knew in his heart that the fabric of life was more than that. It was woven of simple pleasures like holding a quiet, complicated, soft-skinned woman in your arms and wondering what it would be like to kiss her.

From happier days of his childhood, he remembered his family sitting around the table playing board games and laughing, always laughing. After Reggie's death, much of the laughter had stopped. Perhaps that was why Dylan had tried so hard to be the life of the party. He remembered those good times and yearned to recreate them.

Mia reminded him anew of what he was missing. She spoke to him at a visceral level, underscoring the value of things like hard work and loyalty and selfless giving. Seeing her with Cora made him want to be a better man.

Mia's room was semidark. She had left a light on in the bathroom with the door cracked, so Dylan was able to carry her easily without crashing into furniture. With one hand he straightened the tousled sheets and spread. The state of her bed told him more than words about her interrupted night.

When he folded back the covers and laid her gently on the mattress, she stirred, her eyes opening slowly. "Cora?" She sat up on her elbows.

Dylan smoothed the hair from her face. "She's asleep. In her bed."

"Oh. I'm sorry."

"Nothing to be sorry about. There's no reason not to ask for help, Mia. As long as you're here."

"I'm making you uncomfortable. Your family has questions. And you want to draw a line in the sand between business and personal. I'll go as soon as I can find somewhere else to live."

Nothing she said was untrue. But it wasn't the whole truth. "What makes me uncomfortable," he said slowly, "is that I want you and I'm not sure if I should."

Nine

He hadn't meant to be quite so honest.

Mia's nose wrinkled. "Ouch. Am I that much of a liability?" Though she said it jokingly, he fancied that in her eyes he saw vulnerability and hurt. But that might have been a trick of light and shadow.

He sat down beside her on the bed. "You don't belong in Silver Glen, Mia." The truth might hurt, but it was better that they each acknowledge the reality of their situation. "Your intellectual gifts can make a difference in the world. For now, you've had a hiccup. You need time to regroup. That's understandable. And I'm happy I can help. I owe you that. But we can't forget that your stay here is temporary. I've already had one relationship with a woman who was just passing through. It was a messy, public breakup. No one gets privacy in a small town. I'd rather not repeat the experience."

"That's quite a speech. Would you care to cut to the bottom line and tell me what the heck you're saying?"

"I'm saying that I want you."

He stroked her arm as he said the words, completely aware that Mia was unlike anyone he had cared about before. Beneath the very real sexual hunger he felt for her was a vein of something he couldn't pin down...tenderness maybe, but more than that. She was a part of his past, a very significant part. She had helped shape him into the man he had become.

After his blunt statement, she sat straight up, crossing her legs pretzel style and staring at him. "You may be disappointed. I'm not very good at it. Sex, I mean."

Humor slipped in unannounced, lightening the mood. "In this particular situation, I think it's safe to assume that I won't have any complaints. Not that I'm bragging, but you probably were with the wrong men before."

"Man. Only one."

"Ah, yes. The professor. I may not have his brains, but I've researched the hell out of this particular topic." Perhaps he shouldn't have alluded to other women, even obliquely. Mia was acquainted with his past exploits, but she flinched when he mentioned them.

"Are you sure, Dylan?"

Again that heartbreaking vulnerability. "We were friends once. I hope we still are. But the connection I feel to you, to the grown-up Mia, is brand-new. I'd like to see where it goes."

Only a prospective lover with Mia's IQ could induce Dylan to use such an academic approach to sex. Ordinarily, a couple of drinks, soft lighting and a willing woman took care of any negotiations in that arena. But for whatever reason, it seemed important to him that she knew he had thought about this. That he wasn't being ruled by his baser instincts.

On the other hand, his carefully worded analysis of the spark between them didn't seem to be making her very happy. Hell, why was he second-guessing everything?

Carefully, giving her one last moment to change her mind, he slid both hands beneath her sleep-ruffled hair and cupped her neck. His head lowered. Women normally closed their eyes at this point. Mia didn't. She watched him with fascination in her dark-eyed gaze.

He hesitated. "You make me a little nuts," he confessed.

"Why?" This close he could see how thick her lashes were.

"I sometimes feel like you're studying me."

"Why on earth would I do that?" Sexual anticipation was replaced by frustration on her face and in her voice.

"You're the only genius I've ever met. I don't know what goes on inside your head." Why he was baring his soul like this, he hadn't a clue. But it obviously was the wrong tack to take with Mia.

Her chin wobbled. "I'm no different than any other woman, Dylan. Same body parts, same emotions, same wants and needs. I hate it when you say things like that."

"I'm sorry." And he was.

"Forget all that other stuff. Pretend you picked me up at a bar. Not the Silver Dollar. Someplace else. We met and flirted and all we could think about was jumping each other's bones."

In that moment, he understood what she wanted. Mia needed to feel like an ordinary woman. She wasn't ordinary. Far from it. But he was hurting her by hiding the depth of his hunger, when all he had ever wanted to do was protect her.

Deliberately, he reached for the hem of her tank top and peeled it upward, forcing her to raise her arms as he lifted it over her head. His sharp, audible intake of breath was loud in the hushed silence of her room. "God, you're beautiful," he muttered. White-skinned and pleasingly curved, she was a sculptor's dream. But unlike marble, she was real and soft and warm. Locking his gaze with hers, he cupped her breasts with his hands, testing their weight and fullness.

This time Mia closed her eyes.

He took that as a positive sign. Suddenly, he felt like a kid in a candy shop, not sure what he wanted first. A linear approach seemed feasible. He started with her delicate eyelids, drifted down her perfect nose, and settled his lips over hers. The contact rocked him on his ass. Nuclear fission couldn't have been any hotter.

Even as his hands kneaded her flesh and teased her nipples, his mouth ravaged hers. Tongues tangling. Breath laboring. She was as eager as he was, her slim arms going around his neck and tightening as he deepened the kiss. It wasn't what he expected at all.

He had thought Mia might be tentative or clumsy or awkward. Instead, he—Dylan—felt completely out of his depth. She was intensely female despite the fact that she did little to enhance her looks with the usual feminine paints and potions. He had barely touched her, and already he was hard enough to make his position on the bed uncomfortable.

"Mia?" he asked hoarsely, not really sure what he wanted her to say or do.

"Take off your clothes, Dylan. Come to bed with me."

Mia couldn't believe it was really happening. All the fantasies about Dylan she had entertained over the years were pale imitations of the real thing. His skin was hot beneath her touch, though the room was plenty cool. The muscles that rippled in his arms and torso were strong and defined. She stroked him with giddy delight. He was hers. Maybe only for tonight. But he was hers.

Her confidence wavered when she saw him fully nude. Standing beside the bed, arms crossed, shoulders squared, he projected determination and an unmistakable intent to have his way. His erection bobbed high and strong against his flat, corded abdomen.

She swallowed against the sudden lump in her throat. "You're a very striking man," she said quietly.

He tugged her toward the edge of the bed and dragged

her sleep pants down her legs, along with her undies. She was a grown woman. Not without experience. But allowing Dylan to look his fill of her naked body required a surprising amount of courage. Her belly was no longer as flat as it once was, and she had a couple of stretch marks.

In her imagination, this was the moment when he joined her beneath the covers. The reassuringly *covering* covers. But he took her off guard again. Gently, he took both of her hands in his, gripped them, and pulled her to her feet. She was not a noticeably short woman. But toe-to-toe with Dylan she felt small and defenseless.

His devilish grin warmed the cold places in her body. "Touch me, Mia. Please."

It reassured her to realize that his need was every bit as great as hers. She went up on tiptoe and kissed his mouth, lingering to slide her tongue between his teeth, relishing the response that quaked through his frame. Against her belly, his eager flesh twitched. She clasped him in one hand, squeezing gently. His clenched jaw and damp forehead revealed the extent of her power. Power she had never claimed before.

Tilting back her head, she searched his gaze. "Is that what you meant?"

"Damn, woman. I thought you said you weren't good at this."

She rested her cheek against his chest, feeling the steady thump of his heart. When her arms clasped his waist and his circled hers, she felt as if something precious had been born. "These are just the preliminaries," she whispered. "Don't get too excited, Dylan. I may not measure up in the main event."

She'd spent most of her life being judged on her abilities. Here, now, on the verge of having sex with the man of her dreams, it had never mattered more that she did and said the right things. It would be crushing if Dylan found her naiveté boring or, even worse, amusing.

But he totally disarmed her by laughing. "Good Lord, Mia. It isn't an exam. And besides, I'm supposed to be the one pleasing *you* tonight, not the other way around. You'll get your turn. Relax, sweetheart."

He scooped her into his arms and sprawled on the bed with her, his big, hairy legs tangling with her smaller, paler ones. Though he kept most of his weight on his hands, she shivered at the delicious feel of his tough, honed body pressing hers into the mattress. Such a primitive response. But entirely inescapable.

Scraping her thumbnail along his chin, she smiled. "I like you all rough and scraggly."

Nuzzling her neck, he chuckled. "You may sing another tune when you wake up in the morning wearing my marks. If I'd known this was a possibility, I'd have shaved for you."

She cocked her head, staring up at him. "Do things usually start off this slowly? Not that I'm complaining."

"Well, Miss Impatient, do you have condoms?"

"Um, no…" She flushed from her throat to her hairline. Just when she thought she was giving a great performance as a woman of the world having casual sex with a hot, hungry guy, she betrayed her true colors.

Though a pained look crossed his face, he spoke gently. "I'll go get some." Climbing off the bed, he towered over her. "You won't change your mind?"

She pulled the sheet over her nudity, not quite as nonchalant as she hoped to be in this situation. "I won't change my mind."

Dylan must have dabbled in time travel, because he made it to his bedroom and back to hers in a nanosecond.

After dropping a handful of packets on the bedside table, he held one out to her. "You want to do the honors?"

"No. Thank you." To be honest, she wasn't at all sure that little piece of latex was going to fit over and around Dylan's aroused shaft.

Nevertheless, he rolled it on with an economy of motion she admired and then climbed back in bed. "Move over, woman."

"Your feet are freezing," she exclaimed.

"Then warm me up."

After that, any conversation gave way to sheer physical sensation. Despite his chilled feet, the rest of Dylan's body radiated heat. He settled between her thighs with a groan that sounded as if he had waited a hundred years to find that exact spot. She wrapped her legs around his waist, lifting her hips to urge him on.

And yet still, he didn't join their bodies. His erection, hot and firm, rubbed lazily against the cleft between her legs. Zings of sensation flooded her pelvis with restless pleasure. She had known that sex with Dylan would be incredible. Sheer physical delight. What she hadn't expected was the rush of emotion. Tears stung her eyes, though she wouldn't let them fall for fear he would misunderstand.

He was so dear, so special, so deserving of a woman's love. It was incomprehensible to her that his fiancée had walked away from him. Perhaps one day the woman would realize what she had lost. Or perhaps she and Dylan were never really right for each other at all.

The girl Mia had been in high school still lived somewhere deep inside the adult Mia. That shy, backward teenager who had adored the angry, sullen Dylan now wanted the stronger, happier Dylan with equal measure. He'd thrown up barriers between them already. Telling her she didn't belong. Making his learning challenges and her intellectual capabilities some kind of überforbidden matchup.

They weren't the Montagues and Capulets.

When he braced himself on one hand and stroked his fingers over her lower lip, she tasted him involuntarily, her tongue wetting the pad of his thumb. He shuddered. She bit the same spot with a sharp nip.

Clearly Dylan had himself on a tight leash. She was well aware that he was holding back. But she didn't want his gentleness, at least not right now. Hunger rose like an irrepressible tide, making her reckless.

"I won't break," she muttered. "I want you in me, over me, on me."

His pupils expanded as hot color flushed his cheekbones. He dropped his forehead to hers. "You've got it, Mia." The words were guttural, a hoarse accompaniment to the forceful thrust of his hips that buried him deep inside her.

She was fairly certain they both gasped in unison, but with the sound of her heartbeat loud in her ears, she couldn't be sure.

Mia had the ability to convert complicated numerical equations into their metric equivalents without using a calculator. Her papers had been published in academic journals and had even been presented at international conferences. Abstract ideas and three-dimensional thinking were her bread and butter.

But what she couldn't fathom was how one man, *this* one man, could reduce her from a practical, down-to-earth scientist and mom to a shivering mass of nerves and need. She swallowed hard and tried to force words from a dry throat. "That's more like it."

Dylan nibbled her collarbone, his lower body momentarily still. His pause gave her a chance to absorb the effects of his possession. Pleasantly stretched and undeniably filled, her sex welcomed him enthusiastically, little muscle flutters massaging his length.

The hair on his chest tickled her breasts. She liked the sensation. Their coupling had an earthy, elemental rightness to it that she and the professor had never quite attained. This breathless moment seemed preordained, as if long ago, Dylan and Mia's teenage friendship prepared the ground for what was to come.

He moved his hips without warning, gaining another half inch of penetration. "You're tight," he groaned. "I don't want this to end."

"You've barely started yet," she pointed out, a little miffed that her charms weren't sufficient enough to drive him insane with lust.

Dylan didn't answer with words. Instead, he began moving slowly, drawing a tremulous cry from her parched throat. Beneath her, his expensive sheets were cool and smooth against her heated flesh. Above her, his big, hard body enveloped her in a stimulating mélange of sight and sound and touch. The room smelled of warm skin and hot sex.

"Open your mouth, baby."

When she obeyed, the thrust of his tongue mimicked the movements of his hips. The dual possession melted her, incinerated her. Feverish and desperate, she raked his shoulders with her fingernails, barely conscious that she did so. "Please," she whispered. "Please."

Impossible pleasure beckoned, her orgasm building with the heat of a thousand suns, barely contained. Dylan took her again and again, his movements bold, giving no quarter. She would be sore tomorrow. That fleeting thought escaped from some last coherent corner of her brain.

"Come for me, Mia," he rasped, the words barely audible.

And she did....

Dylan held her as she writhed and cried out. He ground the base of his erection against her mound, sending her up yet again. Feeling her climax, watching the sharp jolt of completion paint her face with rosy color, sent exultation fizzing in his veins, despite the fact that he had thus far denied himself release.

Holding back was next to impossible, but he wanted to enjoy her pleasure. When she was sated and still, her eyes closed, he withdrew and leaned down to whisper in her ear. "You screamed my name," he said smugly.

Mia opened one eyelid. "Did not."

"Did, too."

Playing with her was fun. But fun was not even on the scale of what he needed now. "I'll let you sleep soon," he promised, not at all sure he wasn't lying. He rolled to his back, taking her limp body with him. Arranging her like a sleepy rag doll with her legs straddling his hips, he lifted her gently, positioned the head of his erection at her entrance and pushed.

Mia's lips parted, an arrested expression on her face. "Oh," she breathed, her hands settling on his shoulders.

Oh, indeed. The new angle put increasing pressure on his hypersensitive sex. Straining to give her as much as she could take, he flexed his hips and drove upward, shaking the bed with the force of his rhythmic movements. Mia's hair fell around her face. Her breasts swung enticingly above him.

Rearing up, he captured one nipple with his teeth and sucked it into his mouth. Mia moaned. He felt the clasp of her inner flesh tighten around him. The visual stimulation and the feel of her in his arms snapped the last of his control. He rolled the two of them again, needing the mattress to brace against as he lunged wildly toward the finish.

Holy hell. Sharp yellow lights obscured his vision. Uncontrollable trembling sapped his muscles of their strength. Lightning struck his groin with paralyzing heat, and he slammed into the end with a shout.

Ten

Dylan lay stunned on top of Mia, barely able to breathe. What in the hell had happened to him? Instinctively, he gathered his defenses, unwilling to let her see that their lovemaking was anything out of the ordinary. Already, Mia knew far too much about his psyche for him to feel completely at ease with her. A man liked to hide his weaknesses.

It remained to be seen, however, if the last hour was a weakness or a catastrophic shift in the continental plates.

When he thought he could force his muscles to move, he lifted away from her, stumbled to his feet and went into the bathroom to take care of the condom and splash water on his face. In the mirror his eyes were overbright, feverish. He ran both hands through his hair, raking his fingers across his scalp.

When he returned to the bedroom, braced for the inevitable postcoital conversation, Mia was sound asleep. She lay on her back where he had abandoned her, arms outflung, hair mussed, her body bare as the day she was born. He couldn't decide if relief or disappointment held the upper hand. Looking at her made his chest hurt and his head throb.

What had he done?

The clock ticked away the minutes before dawn. Mia needed her sleep. Even if he was already partially erect and wanted her again with an alarming desperation, it would be cruel to wake her. Cora was a lively handful. A rested Mia would be better able to handle her daughter's demands.

Quietly picking up his scattered pieces of clothing, he bundled them into his arms and lingered by the bed. Mia and his ex-fiancée, Tara, were as different as two women could be—in looks, in temperament, in every way. What did it say about him that he had so quickly recovered from a broken heart? Had Tara's defection been more a blow to his pride?

In all honesty, the sex with Tara had been fun. And she had been fun. Always urging him on to the next wild adventure. In retrospect, it was kind of ironic. Tara was a female version of himself, or at least the self he had been in high school and later as a young adult.

Maybe that had been the attraction. He understood her.

Mia, on the other hand, was a complete mystery. Even given her history of crippling shyness, it was hard to imagine that no man had managed to put a ring on her finger. She was warm and funny and loyal and brave. That she had resorted to a sperm donor to become pregnant baffled him.

Such an action pointed to the fact that she didn't want any messy involvement with a man who might make demands. Had she never been in love? Ever?

Now that he thought about it, he surely hadn't. The relationship with Tara had been two parts lust and one part male hubris. Dating a beautiful actress made him feel like a million bucks. He could be excused for believing their short-lived engagement was the real thing, because he'd been thinking with his male anatomy and not his brain.

He liked to imagine that in the intervening years he had matured. At least he'd been smart enough not to get entwined in any further unsuitable relationships. His dating nowadays was light and fun. No commitment, no complications.

Up until tonight.

He backed away from the bed a step at a time, his feet silent on the plush carpet. When he reached the door, he opened it quietly. Mia slept so deeply, she never even stirred.

The bed and the woman were inviting. All he had to do was lift the covers and take her in his arms. His hands tingled as he imagined the feel of her skin. Warm. Incredibly soft.

Damn. He had a sick feeling that he had let the genie out of the bottle. What was he going to do about Mia and Cora now?

Mia rolled over and glanced at her phone to see what time it was. Weak, early-morning sunlight filtered into the room through a crack in the heavy brocade drapes that matched the moss-green color palette of the room. Her breasts ached, heavy with milk. Cora would be awake any moment now. On the monitor, the grainy picture of Mia's daughter showed a reassuring image of the infant sleeping peacefully.

Concentrating on the baby wasn't working. Movielike flashes spun through Mia's head. Arousing, incredible memories. She needed to believe that the stimulating pictures were nothing more than a surreal dream. But the fragrance of a man's skin lingered on her sheets.

Even as her legs moved restlessly, her heart and soul ached with the breath-stealing certainty that she and Dylan had been lovers last night. In the wee hours when rational thought was easily subverted by yearning and need. During the drowsy moments when phantoms seemed real and the concrete world faded into shadows.

The emptiness of the bed mocked her. If the dreams were real, where was Dylan? Why wasn't he curled up with her beneath the sumptuous covers, his body warm and hard and ready for a morning tête-à-tête?

Shaking all over, she fled to the bathroom, taking the baby monitor with her. If she were lucky, she would have time for a quick shower before Cora demanded her breakfast. Beneath the hot, pelting spray, Mia soaped herself furiously, trying to erase the feel of Dylan's touch.

His absence spoke volumes. Even in the beginning, he had expressed his doubts. Perhaps he had been looking to her to put a stop to the madness that had caught them up in the middle of the night.

Mia hadn't been interested in making rational, grown-up decisions. Dylan had stood before her, wanting her. So she took without asking, without considering Cora, without deciding if her selfish behavior had consequences. What did Dylan think of her? Why wasn't he here?

Closing her heart to the pain she didn't want to face, she returned to the bedroom to dress. By the time she had finished, Cora was stirring. As she went to scoop up her daughter and change her diaper, Mia reminded herself how lucky she was. Cora was the sunshine in her life. The one true lodestar that kept her focused and reminded her that a mother's job was to be selfless…to put her child's well-being ahead of her own.

Mia was in Silver Glen so Cora would have a roof overhead while her mother found a job. Touching base with Dylan had accomplished that. He needed Mia's help, and she heeded his. But their bargain had a definite timeline. A beginning and an end.

As she sat in the rocking chair nursing her daughter, the familiarity of the routine brought some peace to her heart. Dylan wasn't hers. She'd known that at fifteen and she knew it now. Her only mistake had been thinking sex with him would end the wondering and the wanting.

Well, now she knew. Sex with Dylan was deserving of

all the superlatives she could summon. But she wouldn't embarrass him by letting him think she was expecting more. Neither more intimacy nor more attention. She was living in his house because of a fluke. It would be wrong to put him in an awkward position by burdening him with her feelings.

When Cora was finished, Mia dressed her in a teal-and-yellow sundress. Mia's stomach was growling so loudly she knew it was impractical to put off breakfast any longer. As she suspected, when she and Cora entered the kitchen, there was no sign of Dylan. Only Gertie…frying bacon.

The older woman turned and smiled. "There you two are. I had a feeling someone kept you up during the night, Mia."

Mia felt her cheeks redden and hoped the housekeeper didn't notice. "Yes, as usual. I came in here for a glass of milk, but thankfully Cora finally settled down and slept until morning."

Without asking, Gertie waved Mia to a seat and put a bowl of fresh strawberries and blueberries in front of her. "I've got some cinnamon muffins coming out of the oven in about a minute. Eat up."

"Did Dylan have an early appointment?"

"Not to my knowledge. He left about thirty minutes ago to head down to the Silver Dollar. Why? Did you need to speak to him?"

"I did have a few questions about the books. But it can wait."

Mia had barely finished her meal when the landline phone rang. Gertie answered it and then held out the cordless receiver to Mia. "It's for you. Ms. Kavanagh."

Gertie swooped in and scooped Cora from Mia's lap. Mia answered reluctantly. "Hello?"

"Good morning, Mia. This is Maeve. Zoe and I have put our heads together, and we would like for you and Dylan to come to dinner tonight up at the lodge. Zoe wants to cook for us. We have several portable cribs here for the hotel guests. We can set one up in Zoe and Liam's bedroom, so you can put Cora to sleep and not have to rush off."

"But, Ms. Kavanagh, I have no idea if Dylan is available."

"Call me Maeve. Please. I've already talked to him this morning. He said it was up to you."

Mia was stuck. Social convention dictated that she accept the invitation, but she could think of nothing more awkward than sitting across the dinner table from the mother of the man with whom she'd been naked the night before. Since she didn't have a valid reason to decline, however, she was forced to agree. "Well, yes, then. That would be lovely. And thank you for making arrangements for Cora. Since I'm nursing, I don't want to be away from her for too long."

"I understand completely. We'll look forward to seeing the three of you around six-thirty. Oh, and Mia?"

"Yes?"

"Would it be a problem to dress for dinner? Zoe has worked hard on this meal, and I thought it would be fun to celebrate."

"Not a problem at all. See you soon."

Mia hung up the phone wondering ruefully when she had become such a good liar. Dress for dinner? Good grief. She had brought all of her clothes with her to Silver Glen except for winter things that were in storage, but she had no idea if she could find anything suitable, since most of the cartons were still out in the garage.

When she asked Gertie to help with the baby so Mia could rummage in her boxes, Gertie offered a solution. "After the baby's next feeding, why don't you put her down for a nap and let me keep an eye on her? You could go into town and visit that cute little shop called Silver Linings.

They have beautiful things for women your age. I'm sure you can find what you want."

"I hate to take up your time, Gertie."

The woman, still holding Cora, waved a hand dismissively. "If I have to choose between babysitting or doing the laundry, it's no competition. Go. Have a few hours to yourself. All new moms need that. I swear I'll take good care of her."

"I know you will."

Mia's other problem wasn't so easily solved. It seemed self-indulgent in the extreme to buy a new dress for herself when her finances were so tight. On the other hand, wearing the appropriate feminine armor for the night to come would go a long way toward helping her face Dylan.

She needed something that would make it clear, without words, that she knew the score and was confident in her own skin. A sexy frock that would knock his socks off and at the same time convince him she had no designs on his bachelorhood.

By the time Cora fell asleep right after lunch, Mia was itching to get out of the house. She hadn't realized how much she had been *chained* to Cora's side until she had the opportunity to be out and about without a diaper bag or a stroller. Not that she was unhappy with her new role. She loved being Cora's mom. Every minute of it.

Still, the prospect of stealing away for a couple of carefree hours held definite appeal.

Gertie's directions were spot on. Silver Linings had not been around when Mia was a girl. The trendy shop occupied the ground floor of a historic building adjacent to the bank. When Mia parked and got out to glance in the storefront windows, a little flutter of excitement skittered down her spine. There, on a mannequin, was the exact dress she'd imagined.

Nursing moms were often limited in their choice of

clothing due to necessity, but this dress opened down the front. Without wasting further time, she went inside to try it on.

The salesclerk was a young woman several years younger than Mia. "I'm Dottie. May I help you find something?" she asked politely. Her nose was pierced and she had a tattoo down her left forearm. In high school, this was the sort of person who'd looked down at Mia and made fun of her. But Mia was an adult now and no longer cowed by the idea of someone judging her. It had been a long road, but she was happy with who she was.

"The red dress in the window? May I try it on? I became a mom not that long ago, and my wardrobe is in need of help." Fortunately, the store had her size. Otherwise she would have had to swallow her disappointment and choose something else. Though she took three additional dresses into the changing room, she had her heart set on the sexy one from the window display.

Stripping down to her bra and panties, she stepped into the sleeveless, cocktail-length dress. It was not at all conventional. The fabric was a heavy watered silk. The design featured a nipped-in waist and a skirt that flared slightly in a bell shape. The back was scooped out, but the front dipped into a low V topped with a single pea-size clear crystal that served as the zipper pull.

Even before she zipped up the dress, Mia knew her bra would have to go. Unfastening the undergarment and dropping it onto a stool, she stared at her bare breasts in the mirror, reminded of the hungry way Dylan had gazed at her. And then touched her....

Her nipples ached as they furled tightly. She would have liked to blame the telling response on the air-conditioning, but the small space was actually quite warm.

As Mia struggled to close the bodice, the saleslady

spoke from just outside the door. "How are you doing in there?"

Mia grimaced at her reflection. "This is the same size I always wear, but…"

The clerk's voice was sympathetic. "Don't worry if you still have a few pounds of baby weight to lose. It will come off in no time. Do you need me to bring you another size?"

"It's not that. Look at me." She opened the door. "Tell me what you think."

The young woman's eyes widened and she grinned. "Ah. Now I get it. You've got nursing boobs. I say enjoy them while they last. Same thing happened to me when my son was born. My husband loved it."

Mia's cheeks warmed. The woman in the mirror had Mia's face and hair, but beyond that she seemed like a stranger. The bombshell image made her uncomfortable. She'd spent most of her life trying to blend into the woodwork. This dress made a statement, even more so because of her breasts. "You don't think there's too much…"

"Cleavage?"

"Yes."

"Not at all. You're probably not used to showing off your body. I see it all the time. Just because you've got a kid doesn't mean you have to wear a shroud. You've got a kickin' figure. And if I'm not mistaken, you're hoping to catch someone's eye with this—right?"

"It's a small dinner party."

"You didn't answer my question. Which is as good as a yes. Buy the dress. You know you want to." She glanced at the three hanging on a hook at Mia's shoulder. Turning up her nose, she shook her head. "Those other ones are fine if you're presenting an award to the parent-teacher association or visiting your grandma's church. But if you want to say, 'I'm available,' then the red is your best bet."

Mia swallowed her misgivings. "I'll take it."

Three hours later she had a mild panic attack. If it had been feasible, she would have ripped open every one of her moving boxes until she found a nice, safe, boring outfit to wear tonight. But it was about a thousand degrees out in the hot, muggy garage, and besides, Dylan was going to be ready to leave in less than half an hour.

She still hadn't seen or heard from him today. Not so much as a peep, other than a terse text indicating their time of departure. Clearly, he had chatted with his mother and knew the plan.

Once more, Mia looked in the ornate, full-length mirror. Her strappy black sandals were not new, but they were comfy and flattering. She had left her hair loose and wavy on her shoulders. For once, the style was cooperating, though all bets were off when she had to step outside into the heat and humidity.

But between her head and her toes, there was a revolution going on. Somehow, the new dress looked even more outrageous than it had in the store dressing room. The fit was perfect at the waist. The hemline was elegant, flattering her legs. But the top? Holy cow. She looked like a Victoria's Secret model. Breasts that had never been more than a B cup now thrust up and out in all their rounded glory.

How had she not noticed before? On maternity leave, her clothing of choice had been T-shirts, nursing bras and sweatpants. Her biggest goal during the first six weeks had been not to burst into tears more than once a day. With her hormones all over the map, she had felt frumpy, overwhelmed and inexperienced.

Noticing that her breasts had morphed from barely there to bountiful hadn't been on her radar.

Tucking her hair behind her ear, she made one last pirouette and put a hand to her fluttery stomach. For better or for worse, it was showtime.

Eleven

Dylan ran a finger inside his collar, trying to loosen his tie without removing it and starting all over again. What had his mother and Zoe been thinking? He hated wearing a tux. The more formal dress reminded him that he was a Kavanagh and thus on display to the community all the time. Dylan didn't want to be *anyone's* role model.

He much preferred the comfort of his jeans and cowboy boots. In his role at the Silver Dollar, he could pretend he was like all the rest of the working stiffs. But tonight, dressed in an expensive European-made jacket and trousers that he wore as seldom as possible, he felt as if he were playing a part. Liam wore dress clothes effortlessly. In fact, Dylan sometimes wondered if his older brother had his boxers starched and pressed.

It was no picnic following along in school behind the sibling who excelled at everything. Liam's academic awards and accolades had taken over his bedroom bookshelves by the time he was sixteen, along with an equal number of sporting trophies.

Dylan had his own ribbons and medals and letterman jackets, but he would have traded it all for just one visible, pen-on-paper acknowledgement that he had a decent brain.

Shaking off the stupid childhood trauma of never measuring up, he pulled the car around front, turned on the AC and moved Cora's infant seat from Mia's vehicle to his. Since they were both going to be dressed to the nines, he wanted to pamper his date in something other than his utilitarian, though expensive, pickup truck. The late model Mercedes had been a gift from his mother, a reminder that he was one of the family no matter how hard he tried to pretend otherwise.

The Kavanagh wealth made him uncomfortable. Especially since he was the only one in the family with no discernible talent or passion. He didn't *excel* at anything.

As he walked back through the front door into the house, he stopped dead in his tracks. Mia had just stepped into the living room. When she saw him, she halted as well. "Hello, Dylan." Her voice was polite…cool…no inflection at all.

Despite her somewhat chilly greeting, his temperature shot through the roof and his mouth dried like a snowflake in Death Valley. The woman standing in front of him was no longer merely an attractive female with whom he'd had sex. She was a goddess…or an angel. He couldn't decide which. Dark, shiny hair tumbled artfully onto white shoulders. Deft, completely natural-looking makeup accentuated her eyes, making them bittersweet chocolate instead of the lighter, milkier variety.

Dangling earrings fabricated of some clear, faceted material caught the light, drawing attention to her swanlike neck. Her lips were red. Sin-red. A shade to match her dress and make a man shudder with desire.

But it was the single glittery bead at the top of her bodice that caught his attention. The small piece of glass was attached to a zipper that ran the entire length of the dress. All a man would have to do is tug gently, but inexorably, and in seconds the woman would be naked.

He cleared his throat. "You look very nice."

A small frown creased the space between her eyebrows. "So do you."

Gertie, toting the baby on her hip, came in from the kitchen at that moment, rescuing Dylan and Mia from their awkward conversation. She whistled. "Lord, have mercy. You two clean up real nice. See, Cora. Look how pretty your mama is. And my boy, Dylan. Why, if I was forty years younger, I'd take a run at him myself."

Dylan kissed Gertie's cheek and the top of Cora's head. "You're good for my ego, but don't go overboard. You know you'll always be my favorite." He took the baby, who immediately tried to grab for his bow tie. "You ready, Mia?"

She nodded. "Yes."

Her stilted response pretty much set the tone for their drive up the mountain. The Silver Beeches Lodge, constructed after the Second World War, was an elegant and outrageously expensive hotel that catered to high-end clients who demanded privacy and discretion. From the silver screen to politics, the majority of guests had money and wielded power.

As they drove up onto a sweeping flagstone apron, Dylan shot a sideways glance at his passenger. She sat primly, knees pressed together, hands clasped on the small black clutch purse in her lap. Cora had babbled happily during the short trip, diverted by the sights and sounds outside the car.

As the valet approached, Dylan drummed his fingers on the steering wheel. "Shouldn't we get our stories straight?" he asked.

For the first time, Mia looked straight at him, her gaze stormy. "I don't think we have a story. So no problem."

"You're mad because I wasn't there when you woke up." He still felt bad about that. But he'd had to get out of the house, had needed physical distance to clear his head and analyze what had happened to him when he made love to Mia. If he'd had his way, he would have avoided her even longer, but tonight's dinner was in the nature of a command performance.

Mia's eyes narrowed. "I'm not mad. Not at all. Sleep is far sweeter than anything else I could be doing these days."

Wow. Direct hit. She'd just relegated mind-blowing sex to a spot somewhere below snoozing. Fair enough. If that's how she wanted to play it… Opening his car door with a jerk that nearly twisted it off the hinges, he went to the back and talked to Cora while he released her from her seat. The baby's smile took the sharp edges off his anger.

In his peripheral vision, he saw Mia get out of the car and smooth her skirt. Five men stood on the steps of the hotel, some guests, some employees. Five sets of eyes locked on Mia and stared. He couldn't blame them. She radiated sexuality. Her lush breasts were evidence of the elemental, primitive truth that mankind needed a fertile woman for the continuation of the species.

Except for the occasional moment of temptation, Dylan had little interest in fathering children. But Neanderthal or not, he understood the urge to mate. Only in his case, the urge was surprisingly more than physical. He was proud of Mia, not for her breasts or her killer legs, but for her incredible brain that had so much to offer society. And for other equally important things like her care with Cora, and her gentle acceptance of a high-school boy who had done his best to alienate her.

Even if she *was* pissed at him, he was glad they were friends. Although after last night, the *friend* word could be called into question. She certainly deserved to be angry. Walking out on her after sex had been unconscionable, despite the fact he *had* needed to retreat and figure out what was going on inside his head.

In spite of all his reservations, he liked the family tableau they made. Mia insisted on taking the baby as they ascended the shallow steps. "I'll carry her."

He surrendered without protest, guessing that the baby acted as a sort of shield. It had to be intimidating for Mia to walk into the Silver Beeches knowing that she was going to be sharing dinner with Maeve Kavanagh. His mother came by her reputation honestly. She was kind and fair, but he'd seen big strong men quake in their boots when she was displeased about something.

"Liam and Zoe have an apartment on the top floor," he said. The elevator ride was silent, save for Cora's little baby sounds. She enjoyed playing with her reflection in the mirror. Fortunately, she was too young to comprehend that the adults momentarily caged in the small space were not speaking. Or to notice that their body language was hostile.

When they exited the elevator, Dylan took Mia's elbow and steered her to the right. Liam answered the doorbell on the first ring. The eldest Kavanagh son greeted them warmly. "Zoe's been on pins and needles. It's about time you got here."

Dylan curled an arm around Mia's waist, surprising her. "This is Mia. Mia, Liam."

Liam shook Mia's hand, but his attention was on Cora. "May I?" he asked. At Mia's bemused nod, he reached for the baby and called out over his shoulder. "Zoe. Come see what I found, my love."

Zoe Kavanagh was bright and beautiful and artlessly charming. The gold lace camisole and flirty skirt she wore along with gold, high-heeled pumps suited her airy personality. Even without the bright clothing, she would have lit up the room. Mia envied her easy social skills. The slender blonde rarely sat still, scooting back and forth from the kitchen to grab something or the other. "It's almost ready," she said.

Liam's smile as he watched his wife was telling. He

was deeply in love and not afraid to show it. "My Zoe insists on cooking for me even though we have a five-star chef presiding over the restaurant downstairs. But I have to admit she's a natural. I'm sure I've gained five pounds or more since we got married."

Given that Liam was as lean and toned and muscular as his brother, Mia wondered if he were joking. She had refused a glass of wine and was sipping tonic water when the door of the apartment burst open after a brief knock and Maeve Kavanagh sailed into the room followed by a handsome man who bore a striking resemblance to the two male Kavanaghs already present.

"Look who I brought with me," Maeve beamed. "I convinced Aidan to fly down for the evening." Maeve's plum Jackie-O sheath was accessorized with a matching short-sleeved jacket.

After a flurry of introductions all around, and lots of hugging, Mia found herself shaking hands with Aidan, who was as tall as his brothers, but even more suave and polished than Liam. "I feel like I'm intruding," she said, shooting a sharp, disapproving glance at Dylan.

Aidan kissed the back of her hand with a gesture that seemed completely natural. "Not at all. I'm the party crasher. I live in New York, but you'll find me here in Silver Glen frequently. Despite being a city dweller now, I can't resist the lure of home. I was hoping the whole gang would show up here tonight."

Zoe wrinkled her nose. "Conor, Patrick, Gavin and James all *claimed* to be otherwise occupied."

Liam put an arm around his wife's waist. "It's hard to corral everyone on short notice. But we'll try again soon."

Maeve threw up her hands and made a beeline for Mia. "There's that precious baby."

Dylan and Liam snickered. "You know that's the only reason she came," Dylan said in a stage whisper.

As Maeve took Cora from Mia's arms, Zoe paused long enough to put her hands on her hips and pout. "Hey, I think I've been insulted."

Liam gave his wife a long, enthusiastic kiss that soothed her ruffled feathers. When they came up for air, his throat was flushed and his eyes glittered. "I'm sure she'll be just as excited, my love, when and if you give her a grandchild."

Mia was the only one standing close enough to hear his muttered comment. And she was sure it wasn't for public consumption. Zoe's cheeks turned a delightful shade of pink and her smile softened before she escaped to the kitchen.

Amidst conversation and laughter, the finishing touches were added to the table. Mia helped, since her child had been kidnapped by the force of Maeve's personality and seemed quite happy. Just before they sat down, a second knock sounded at the door.

"I'll get it," Maeve said, the baby comfortably settled on her hip. "I asked one of our summer employees to come up and entertain Cora in Liam and Zoe's den. Paula is a senior at the University of North Carolina, majoring in child development. I hope you don't mind, Mia."

What could she say? "Of course not. It will be nice to enjoy an uninterrupted meal." Honestly, she was being spoiled. After all the help from Gertie and Dylan's family, it might be a challenge to manage on her own.

Dylan came close enough to whisper in her ear. "I'll apologize in advance for anything my mother says or does to upset you."

Mia shook her head briefly. "It's fine." She was still trying to get accustomed to Dylan's magnificence in formal attire. The snowy white shirt brought out his tan, and the traditional black tux fit his body as if it had been made for him. It probably had.

She liked the casual Dylan very much. But this sophisticated Dylan made her shiver.

As the adults seated themselves at the table, Zoe brought out the last dish and joined them. "We won't stand on ceremony," she said. "Pass the food and help yourself."

Amidst the clatter of silverware and china and crystal, Mia absorbed the atmosphere and studied the Kavanagh family. Zoe seemed a natural part of the bunch, even though she and Liam hadn't been married all that long. She laughed and shared anecdotes and teased her husband. Liam and Dylan and Aidan bickered amiably, as siblings did, covering every subject from sports to movies to politics. Maeve had strong opinions and wasn't afraid to express them.

Only Mia was silent. She wasn't *afraid* to speak. But the conversational dynamic was such that she found it difficult to get a word in edgewise. During a momentary lull in the rapid-fire back-and-forth chatter, Maeve launched her first volley, taking Mia completely off guard.

The older woman took a sip of wine, set down her glass and pinned Mia with a deceptively gentle stare. "So tell me, Mia," she said. "Is the baby's father in the picture?"

Mia choked on a piece of walnut in her salad and Dylan had to pat her on the back. Hard.

He glared at his mother. "I thought you were the woman who hated gossip."

Maeve didn't look the least bit repentant. "I do. Which is why I'm going directly to the source. But Mia can tell me to mind my own business if she wants to." She smiled at Mia. "You can, my dear, honestly."

Mia felt her face and neck turning red as the eyes of her dinner companions fixed on her with varying degrees of sympathy. "It's no secret," she said. "I was ready to have a baby, and since there was no man in my life, I chose to use a sperm donor."

Silence fell.

"I see." Maeve's perplexed expression held a hint of disapproval.

Mia was used to that by now. If she had decided as a single person to adopt an infant, no one would have batted an eye, but somehow, the path she had chosen was far less acceptable. Perhaps it was the clinical nature of the process. Or the lack of loving conception.

Zoe broke the uncomfortable impasse. "So, Mia. How did you and Dylan meet?"

Again, Mia was taken aback. She had assumed someone would have filled Zoe in before Mia and Dylan arrived, but maybe this was supposed to be a secret. Liam had been away at college when Dylan was a senior, so he and Mia had never met. But surely the family had realized Dylan was getting tutoring help. Aidan had been a sophomore or junior at the time.

Mia opened her mouth to speak, but before she could explain, Maeve rushed into the breach, addressing her daughter-in-law. "Dylan and Mia knew each other back in high school. They reconnected recently."

Zoe nodded, satisfied with that explanation. "And what do you do for a living, Mia?" she asked.

"I'm a medical researcher. But the funding for my lab and my program was cut off recently. I came back to Silver Glen for a visit and ran into Dylan at the Silver Dollar."

Dylan picked up the tale. "My bookkeeper quit, so Mia is helping me out temporarily since she's between jobs."

Zoe's eyebrows went up. "You must be very smart," she said, studying Mia's face as if she could see IQ points written there.

"Off-the-charts smart," Dylan said, his smile rueful. "I'm lucky she was available to help me out."

Mia was desperate to change the subject. As Zoe stood and began to clear the dessert plates, Mia leaped to her feet as well. "Let me help," she said. "Please. The dinner was amazing."

In the kitchen Zoe began rinsing china. "Liam tells me to let the housekeeper take care of this in the morning, but I can't stand a messy kitchen." She handed Mia a plate to put in the dishwasher. "What about you? Do you like to cook?"

"I don't really have much opportunity. I worked all the time before Cora was born, and now I'm still learning how to care for an infant. There don't seem to be enough hours in the day."

Zoe nodded, her expression thoughtful. "The Kavanaghs can be a bit overwhelming, especially when the whole clan gets together. You and I should stick together."

"I think you have the wrong idea. I work for Dylan."

"Maeve told me you're living with him."

"Only because the building burned. I was supposed to be staying in the apartment upstairs above the Silver Dollar."

Zoe rolled her eyes. "Men don't take women into their homes without some kind of ulterior motive."

He feels like he owes me something for the past.

But Mia couldn't say that. Not when Dylan's brother and sister-in-law apparently did not know how severely Dylan had struggled in high school. "Dylan is a kind man. He told me that rental property is hard to find in Silver Glen. If it had been just me, I'm sure he would have let me fend for myself. But he has a soft spot for Cora. That's probably why he suggested that she and I move in."

Zoe dried her hands on a towel and turned on the dishwasher. "Is the baby his?"

Because the other woman's back was turned, Mia couldn't see her face. "No. Of course not."

Mia's hostess faced her with a look in her eyes that told Mia she was not easily duped. "You might have concocted that story to give yourself time to figure out what to do. Not that I would blame you. The Kavanaghs would go nuts if they thought Cora was the first of the next generation. I should know. The hints have been flying thick and fast for me to get pregnant."

"Well, she's not," Mia said, the words flat. "Maybe I was naive to do what I did, but I adore Cora and I wouldn't change a thing. I know the father was healthy and normal in every way. That's enough for me."

"I didn't mean to make you angry." Zoe's big blue eyes shimmered with emotion.

Mia swallowed her pique. "I'm not angry. More defensive, I guess. I never expected people to react so strongly, my parents included."

"Do they live close by?"

"No. They're in Florida. My mom came up for the first ten days to help. She loves the baby, of course, but I could tell from the first moment I told them I was pregnant that they thought I needed a flesh-and-blood man and not an anonymous donor."

"Dylan's a man." Zoe's sly smile was not at all hard to decipher.

"Dylan and I are *not* an item."

"I watched the way he watches you. He's possessive. Though I suppose he might not even realize he feels that way. Men can be clueless about these things."

"You're way off base, Zoe. His broken engagement burned him. He's not interested in marriage or fatherhood or any commitment at all, for that matter. If you're planning on matchmaking, you should know that he and I are not a couple. Period."

Twelve

He and I are not a couple. Period.

Dylan winced, pausing just outside the kitchen door. He'd caught only the tail end of Mia's statement, but it was enough to understand the gist of her conversation with Zoe. Apparently, Dylan's sister-in-law had been understandably curious about Mia's relationship with Dylan, and Mia had set her straight.

Dylan should be elated that Mia knew the score. No need for an embarrassing face-to-face where he had to explain that he had no plans to settle down, much less with a ready-made family.

In that case, why did he feel like he'd been punched in the stomach? Striding into the kitchen, he faced the two women whose faces held identical guilty looks. "Paula says Cora is getting fussy. They're waiting for you in Zoe and Liam's bedroom. Isn't it time to feed her and put her down?" He addressed his comments to Mia impassively.

Mia, clad in the ruby dress that made her look more like a Russian princess than a new mom, glanced at the clock on the wall. "Oh, gosh, yes. Zoe and I were having so much fun getting to know each other I lost track of time."

"I'll bet you were." He wanted Mia to squirm a little, wondering whether or not he had heard what she said.

Zoe piped up, her expression beseeching. "Would you

like me to sit with you while you feed her? I assume you're nursing?"

Dylan kissed his sister-in-law's cheek. It wasn't her fault that things were weird. "I'll sit with her, Zoe. But thanks for offering. Go snuggle up with your husband on the sofa. He's looking neglected."

They exited the kitchen as a trio. Zoe headed for the living room, and Dylan and Mia searched out the master suite. As promised, the crib was set up and ready. Two comfy armchairs by the window, each with matching ottomans, offered an ideal spot for Zoe to feed Cora.

The young college student handed Cora over with a smile. "Your baby is adorable, and so even-tempered. Thank you for giving me the opportunity to play with her. The diaper bag is there on the bed. If you need babysitting help any other time this summer, please feel free to call me. Mrs. Kavanagh has my contact info."

Mia smiled. "Thank you, Paula. I'll keep that in mind."

When the door closed, Dylan rummaged in Cora's tote for pajamas, diapers, wipes and a changing pad to protect the bedspread. "There you go," he said, determined not to give Mia a chance to kick him out. "All set."

Mia clutched the baby. "Why are you in here? This is pretty much a solo operation."

He shrugged. "Give me the kid. Go sit in the chair and I'll bring her to you." It was a matter of minutes to change the diaper and tuck Cora into soft pajamas that snapped up the front. In his peripheral vision, he was aware that Mia had cooperated with his instructions. He was under no illusions. If she told him to leave, he would have to obey her wishes. But he was counting on the fact that she would let him stay.

When he turned and walked toward the window and the woman who stared at him with big, dark eyes, he felt something shift inside him. The setting lent a certain note of intimacy, but it was more than that.

Mia took Cora from him, her gaze unreadable. "Will you turn your back, please?"

He crouched beside her. "I'd rather not. I've seen all there is of you to see, Mia. Remember? Last night?" Slowly, giving her time to protest, he caught the crystal at the center of her bodice and began to pull.

She slapped at his hand, her cheeks hot with what appeared to be mortification. "Don't be ridiculous, Dylan. There's nothing remotely sexy about what I'm getting ready to do."

Surprisingly, a lump in his throat made it hard to speak. "That's where you're wrong." Locking her gaze with his, never looking down, he opened the zipper, hearing the soft rasp as the sides of the dress parted. In Mia's eyes he saw confusion and vulnerability and something else. Desire.

The desire was a welcome sight, because he had been wondering if it was wrong to be turned on by the prospect of Mia offering her breast to a hungry child. At last, the zipper reached the end of its track. Unable to resist any longer, he stared at the bountiful sight that was Mia's bosom. A single drop of pale milk clung to one nipple. He caught it on his finger and tasted it. "Lucky baby," he said. The words were hoarse.

Mia's lower lip trembled. What was she thinking as she stared at him so intently? As he watched, she tucked the infant in her arm and let Cora nuzzle until she found her goal and latched on. As the child sucked at her mother's breast, Dylan felt an answering pull in his groin. He shifted the second chair closer and sat down, wrapped in some mystical moment that shut out the world and enclosed Mia, Cora and him in perfect intimacy.

Mia kept her eyes downcast, her free hand coming up now and again to stroke Cora's small, perfect head. When it was time, she switched the baby to the opposite breast. Without asking, Dylan reached in his back pocket and extracted a handkerchief. Leaning forward, he carefully dried Mia's skin where the baby had eaten so enthusiastically.

He didn't linger, nor did he do anything else that might be construed as sexual. The quiet tableau was almost sacred to him. This ancient, elemental, perfectly *right* moment where life, *literally* life, was offered to the helpless in an act of love.

When Cora's long eyelashes settled on rounded cheeks, Mia pulled her away from the breast and handed her to Dylan. "Hold her please."

As he watched in silence, Mia removed the last of the sticky milk and refastened her gown. When she was fully clothed once more, she held out her arms. "I'll put her in the bed."

"Let me." He deposited Cora in the crib, smiling when she never even moved. Poor babe was tired out from an evening of fun and attention. He turned to face Mia. "Thank you."

She was still seated, her fingers moving restlessly on the arms of the chair. "For what?"

"For letting me be here. For sharing Cora. For trusting me." He pulled her to her feet. "I'm sorry I didn't stay last night."

Mia had kicked off her shoes before she fed the baby, and now, standing in front of him, she seemed fragile and helpless. Even though Dylan liked the role of protector, he knew Mia didn't need him. Not really. She was strong and smart and well able to care for herself and her offspring.

She pulled away from his grasp, her expression guarded. "Why didn't you stay?"

"Lots of reasons." *I was getting in too deep. You'll be*

gone soon. "I knew you needed your rest to take care of Cora."

"A weak excuse at best. I'd have thought a man with your experience would have come up with a better line than that."

Ouch. Not helpless at all. "It's the truth."

She crossed her arms, perhaps unaware that the action threatened to topple her breasts from their crimson cage. "Let's get something straight, Dylan. I appreciate your helping me out in a bad situation. But I'm not going to get any crazy ideas. You've told me I don't belong in Silver Glen, and you're right. I'm not stupid enough to think that you and I are in some kind of relationship. So relax."

"Impossible," he muttered. "When I'm in the same room with you, relaxing is the last thing on my mind." He toyed with the seemingly innocuous crystal zipper pull. There was something intrinsically sexual about the damn thing. Gently, he lowered it two inches. Mia's sharply indrawn breath told him volumes. The curves of her pale breasts beckoned a man to touch, to worship.

When she didn't protest, he tugged again, this time uncovering her to the navel. "Lord, Mia," he said as his hand trembled. "You have the most incredible body. I can't stop thinking about last night."

Her head dropped backward. Her eyes closed as he traced the faint, silvery lines that marked places where her body had readied itself to give life. Slowly, he pushed the dress down her arms until it hung from her hips. Now she was naked from the waist up, a lush, erotic invitation. He gathered her close and held her, stroking her bare back.

They were standing in his brother's bedroom. Behind them a baby lay sleeping. Close by, a dinner party awaited their return. He shook with the urge to lift her against the wall and fill her. His erection was full and ready. Desire was a writhing, clawing beast inside him. He could lock the door. Pretend that Mia was still nursing Cora.

It was a measure of his desperation that he seriously considered it.

Instead, he released her and did the only thing left to him. Fisting one hand in her hair at the back of her head and using the other to tip up her chin, he kissed her roughly, forcefully. "Tonight, Mia. I want you again. And this time I won't leave." He wouldn't be able to, not again. He didn't have the will to walk away from something so perfect, even if the outcome would never fall in his favor.

Her arms twined around his neck. "Yes." The single word was a barely audible whisper.

He knew on some hazy, faraway level that they were crushing her dress. Imagining what she would look like if he helped her step out of it only made the ache in his gut worse.

Her lips were soft beneath his, unbearably sweet. For a split second he flashed back to that stolen kiss in high school, the one that had confused him and made him ashamed. Even then, there had been something about Mia that drew him. Some essential goodness that he sensed he lacked. As a seventeen-year-old, he'd known it, and he knew it now.

He didn't deserve a woman like this. He was selfish and focused on the here and now. Mia had a child to consider. She contributed to the greater good with her work. Frivolity wasn't in her repertoire. But perhaps in the short time she was with him he could teach her the benefits of being naughty once in a while.

When her small hands tugged at his shirttails and slipped beneath to settle on the bare skin at his waist, he flinched. He'd kept a tight rein on his libido this far, but feeling her fingers on him made his vision go fuzzy. "We have to stop," he said gruffly, cursing the situation and the lousy timing that ensured, at a minimum, a miserable hour ahead.

Mia moved her hands, now pushing against his chest. When she was free, she tugged at her dress, pink-cheeked.

At that very moment, a quiet knock sounded at the door and Liam's voice came softly. "Dessert and coffee on the table. You guys ready?"

Dylan brushed the hair from Mia's flushed cheeks. "On our way," he said. Carefully, he raised the zipper of her dress all the way to the top and smoothed her skirt with two hands. "You okay?" he asked, gazing at her intently. He couldn't read the secrets hidden in her eyes.

She nodded. "Let's go. They're waiting."

He allowed her to pass him, but at the last moment snagged her wrist and reeled her in for one last quick kiss. Thank God she was wearing smudge-proof lipstick. "I'm glad you came back to Silver Glen," he said, resting his forehead against hers.

"Me, too." She touched his cheek with a fleeting caress that made him shiver. "Me, too."

Mia had never been in such a situation. Dylan ushered her to the dining room, his hand at the small of her back. She felt exposed and embarrassed, but at the heart of it, disappointed that she and Dylan were not alone.

Zoe had made an angel food cake from scratch and topped it with a fresh strawberry compote. "Is Cora asleep?" she asked.

The question was innocent, but Mia blushed anyway, as if the three adults at the table knew exactly what she and Dylan had been up to. "She went down without a peep," Mia said, sitting down as Dylan took the chair to her right. "*Getting* her to sleep is never a problem. It's the two a.m. playtime that's killing me."

Maeve sat at the head of the table, Aidan at the foot.

The two couples occupied either side. Mia liked Maeve, though the woman's personality was one part steamroller and one part matriarch.

The older woman waved a hand. "Hang in there, my dear. I went through that with at least three of my boys. It will pass. In my experience, parenthood is an endurance test, a marathon where the stubborn win out in the end."

Mia laughed. "I hope you're right. But at this point, my chances of *winning* are no more than fifty-fifty at best."

Dylan interrupted. "Don't let Mia fool you. She's doing a wonderful job as a mother." He poured himself a cup of black coffee from a fancy silver pot. "Cora clearly is thriving."

Maeve focused her gaze on Mia. "So what will you do with Cora when you get a new job?"

There was no mistaking the note of disapproval. Mia felt her defenses go up, but tried to answer calmly. "I'll find a reputable day care, of course. There are quite a few good ones in the Raleigh/Durham area."

"Have you considered taking a leave? I know how hard it is to deal with an infant and be productive during the day."

It was Zoe's turn to jump into the conversation. Apparently she wasn't scared of her mother-in-law. "That's not always feasible, Maeve. Most women have to work outside the home. Particularly single moms. Not everyone has a fortune like the Kavanaghs. And besides, from what Liam has told me, Mia's work has far-reaching applications."

Mia gave Zoe a grateful smile. "I hope to find a balance that works for Cora and me. As much as I love my baby, my career is also important. I find it challenging and fulfilling. Ultimately, I think Cora will benefit from having a mother who uses her abilities and contributes to society. But I know that life is never perfect."

She saw the three brothers glance at each other. The

Kavanaghs had certainly known their share of heartache over the years. Losing a parent was never easy, and Reggie Kavanagh's body had never been recovered. Maeve had stepped into the breach, giving her boys all the love and support they needed to become successful adults. Perhaps she thought Mia was selfish to get pregnant as a single woman, because Maeve knew exactly how difficult it had been to be both mother *and* father. Mia wondered how the other brothers had fared in the absence of a male parent.

Dylan put an end to the awkward conversation. "I think Mia and I will call it a night. Zoe, the meal was fantastic. Feel free to try your culinary skills on me anytime."

Liam gave him a mock glare. "Quit flirting with my wife."

Dylan raised an innocent eyebrow. "Who, me?" As the group stood, he kissed Zoe on the cheek. "My brother is a Neanderthal. It's perfectly acceptable for men and women to be friends."

Zoe pinched his cheek. "You are such a rascal. Behave yourself and take Mia and little Cora home. I promise to feed you another day."

When Mia excused herself to put the baby in the infant carrier, she could hear the five Kavanaghs talking animatedly. Clearly they enjoyed spending time together. It made her realize that she wanted more children, at least one more. Cora would need a sibling, someone to have her back when life was hard. But in some corner of her heart, Mia knew that Cora needed a daddy as well. In all the struggle of trying to get pregnant, it had honestly not seemed like that big a deal.

Now, however, the truth stared her in the face. Seeing Dylan with Cora was an inescapable revelation. As she grew, Cora would want a father. And at some point, she would ask questions.

On a more practical note, having so much help with

Cora in recent days showed Mia that she was missing out on many things by trying to do it all herself. For a woman who was supposedly a genius, she had been woefully unprepared for the consequences of her actions.

As she gathered up her purse and the baby's accoutrements, Dylan came to help her carry Cora. They said their goodbyes and finally escaped into the hallway. Mia wondered if Maeve and Aidan were lingering with Liam and Zoe to discuss what was going on in Dylan's life and whether or not Mia was taking advantage of him.

In the elevator, Dylan was suspiciously quiet. Cora had stayed asleep through all the noisy goodbyes. Mia stared down at her skirt, trying not to remember how the fabric had pooled around her hips when Dylan half undressed her. She couldn't figure him out. At times he seemed intent on seducing her into his bed, and at others he kept his distance…almost as if Mia was a threat to him.

She wanted to talk to him during the ride home, but maybe there was nothing to say. He was a Kavanagh and she was a new mom with a baby and no real job at the moment. They had a tenuous connection at best, even though they had added a sexual component to their relationship.

Men liked sex. Men, as a rule, took sex when it was offered. What they did not do was give up their bachelor status without a fight.

Fortunately for Dylan, Mia had no intention of fighting. If she ever did get married, she wanted a man who wanted her. Completely. Brains and all. Dylan still wasn't comfortable with Mia knowing about his past struggles. If Mia's hunch was correct, no one in his family knew except for Maeve.

She wanted to whack him over the head and get him to admit that he was a smart man in all the ways that counted. But she had a feeling he wouldn't listen. Dylan was stubborn.

Her brain ran in circles searching for solutions. She couldn't turn her back on a lifetime of study and work that was significant and valuable. That would be selfish and irresponsible. But every day the prospect of staying in Silver Glen with Dylan held more and more allure.

As they neared the turn to his property, she took a deep breath, mentally gearing up for the evening ahead. In Liam and Zoe's bedroom, she and Dylan had seemed in perfect accord. But what would happen now?

Gertie had left lights on to welcome them home. For Mia, the sight of Dylan's beautiful house elicited much more than gratitude for the roof over her head. She loved the way he had made his place seem like part of the countryside. Privacy and seclusion created peace and a feeling of home in the deepest sense of the word.

For one fleeting second, she allowed herself to acknowledge the truth. She had feelings for Dylan Kavanagh. Messy, wonderful emotions that couldn't be organized in spreadsheets or analyzed by computer programs. Exhilaration and panic duked it out in her stomach.

Dylan had made Mia comfortable and welcome in his home. He had been charming and gentle with Cora. He had even tried to protect Mia from his desire for her, though that hadn't lasted long.

But what if she admitted she was equally hungry? Would it make a difference if she told him what she wanted? Was there a chance Dylan might want something more, as well?

She was in trouble either way. If his answer was no, she faced humiliation and hurt. But if his answer was yes, she faced another set of problems. Could she give up her career and be content as a wife and mother? No matter how wonderful living in Silver Glen might be, it would mean relinquishing an entire part of the life that had defined her since she'd become an adult.

All of her life she had dealt with difficult challenges. But this situation she *now* faced would require hard choices. If she took the wrong path, the consequences for her and for Cora could be devastating.

Thirteen

Dylan scooped the infant seat out of the car and followed Mia up the stairs. Unlocking the front door while juggling a baby was a skill he hadn't known he possessed, but something about it was satisfying. Cora was so innocent, so perfect. It made him feel good to know that in some small way, he was helping protect her.

In deference to the sleeping child, they made their way across the living room without turning on additional lights. Mia had been remarkably quiet on the way home. He wondered if his mother's veiled criticisms had pissed her off. She'd be justified.

After they put Cora down and closed the door, he took Mia's hand. "Let's have some coffee and sit in front of the fire."

"It's late."

He lifted her fingers to his lips and kissed them. "Are you going to turn into a pumpkin?" She had already kicked off her shoes. The disparity in their heights emphasized the contrast of male to female.

Mia shrugged, her expression difficult to decipher. "I'll change and meet you in the kitchen."

"Don't," he said gruffly. "Don't change. Please. I have a few fantasies about this dress."

That brought a smile to her face. "It *is* a nice dress," she said, the words demure.

"Very user-friendly." He cupped a hand behind her neck and massaged the spot beneath her ear. "Maybe we don't need coffee." He'd never brought a lover to this house. Perhaps his social skills were rusty. Or maybe he was simply losing control.

Mia strained on her tiptoes to kiss him, her lips warm and eager against his. "I'm not at all thirsty," she said. "Maybe we should go to bed and get some rest."

"Rest?" He was befuddled by her scent and by the feel of silk beneath his fingertips. Silk fabric. Silky-skinned woman.

She drew him toward her bedroom. "We *will* rest. Afterward."

It boded well for him that Mia made no pretense of resistance. He liked not having to guess whether or not she wanted him. No mixed messages. No hidden agendas. Just a man and a woman sharing pleasure.

For a moment, he wanted to take her to *his* suite…to play sexy games on his turf. But there was Cora to consider, and besides, perhaps he would regret making erotic memories in his bed when Mia was gone.

Thinking about her departure gave him an uneasy feeling. So he shut down that particular train of thought and focused on the temptress in the red dress.

Once the bedroom door closed, Mia stepped away from him and seemed to lose her courage. She fidgeted.

He put his arm around her waist and walked her to the bed. Sitting on the edge of the mattress, he positioned her in front of him, still standing. "You are a beautiful woman, Mia Larin, but in this dress… Lord, have mercy. It's a good thing my heart's in good shape."

Her tense posture relaxed. "You're really good at that."

"At what?"

"Making a woman feel special."

"You *are* special," he insisted. There was doubt in her

eyes, so he set out to make a believer out of her. Tracing the edge of her bodice with a fingertip, he grinned when gooseflesh erupted on her bare arms. "Do I make you nervous, Mia?"

"A little." Her arms hung at her sides, but her fingers curled, indicating that she was not completely at ease.

"I'm the most amiable guy on the planet. No one is scared of me."

At last she moved. Running her thumb across his bottom lip, she knocked the breath out of him with her tender caress. "I don't have a great deal of experience with men, but you're different."

He didn't know whether to be pleased or annoyed. "That doesn't sound entirely like a compliment."

Her skin was pale in the dimly lit room, her dark-eyed gaze impossible to decipher. "I don't want to fall for a guy who has *carefree bachelor* tattooed across his libido." She ruffled his hair. "You make a woman want things you're not willing to give."

He felt a twinge of guilt. Mia wasn't wrong. "We never had any idea that this was anything more than fun."

"I know."

"And besides," he said, feeling defensive, "there's nothing for you here in Silver Glen. You know that."

"There's you." The absolute conviction in those two words rocked him on his heels.

His heart twisted…hard. She was making herself completely vulnerable to him, but he couldn't reciprocate. "I'm not anyone's prize. Trust me. If you want fun and games, I'm your man. But don't expect more from me than I can give, Mia. I thought you'd learned that lesson a long time ago."

Nothing on her face indicated that his blunt refusal of her unspoken request had hurt her. But she took a ragged little breath that could have meant anything. "You're honest. I'll give you that. I won't embarrass you anymore. Make love to me, Dylan."

He felt a lick of relief that she had dropped the subject, but at the same time a raw feeling he was closing a door that might never reopen. "I can do that." The words were forced from a tight throat.

That damned crystal beckoned him irresistibly. He toyed with it, the backs of his fingers stroking her cleavage. "I feel like it's Christmas morning and Santa brought me a special package wrapped in red."

The anticipation was almost more than he could take. But he wanted to draw out the pleasure until they were both drunk with it.

When he tugged at the faux jewel, the zipper gave easily. Too easily. He forced himself to stop at two inches.

Mia's eyes closed, her chest rising and falling with rapid breaths. "I swear I would have pegged you as one of those guys who rips off the paper to see what's inside."

He spanned her hips with his hands trying to decide if she was wearing panties. Surely so. His Mia was shy… though present evidence didn't support such a hypothesis.

"I am," he admitted. "But sometimes patience is a virtue."

"Not at the moment," she muttered.

He played with the clear stone again. Such a simple thing to torment a man—but oh-so-effective. Any other day, if he and Mia had shared more than a single encounter prior to tonight, he might have submitted to his caveman instincts and yanked the sparkly pull as far down as it would go in one rash movement. Even thinking about it gave him chills.

But he needed to work up to that. By her own admission, Mia was not widely experienced in the erotic arts. He didn't want to scare her by coming on too strong.

The zipper conceded another four inches. Now the dress

was in danger of falling. It clung to Mia's breasts tantalizingly, held there by nothing more than a whisper.

When he teased her tummy with a fingertip, he evoked a surprisingly strong reaction. Mia grabbed the top of her dress and held it close, her hand batting his away. "Stop that," she hissed. "I'm ticklish."

"I'll keep it in mind." Allowing her the pretense of holding him at bay, he took the zipper to its final destination. "Move your hands, Mia."

When she shook her head, a lock of dark, wavy hair fell over her almost bare shoulder. "You're still dressed," she protested.

"My turn will come." He grasped both of her wrists in one of his hands and held them away from her body. Gently, awkwardly—since he had only one hand to work with—he peeled the dress down her arms. Clearly, he hadn't thought this through, because Mia's bound wrists halted his progress. "Well, damn."

She had the audacity to laugh. "Now what? Maybe you're not as smooth an operator as I thought."

"You have a sassy mouth for someone who's supposed to be shy."

"I've changed, Dylan."

"I noticed."

The act of trapping her delicate wrists with one of his big hands had aroused him even more if that were possible. But his ultimate goal meant he had to release her in the short-term. Before she could grab the dress again, he took handfuls of the skirt and pulled. In a split second she was naked. Or almost. The tiniest pair of red undies covered only the essentials.

Mia took the poleaxed expression on Dylan's face as a good sign. "Are you window shopping?" she asked politely. He sat frozen, his gaze fixed on her underwear. The intensity of his gaze made her damp in a very intimate spot. Surely he couldn't tell.

Dylan cleared his throat. "Let's not ruin the dress."

He held her hand gallantly as she stepped out of it and tossed it toward a chair, not bothering to see if it landed properly. At the moment she was more interested in breaking Dylan free of his trance. Since he appeared to be stunned, she sat down beside him. "You've seen me naked before," she teased.

"Only once." He ran a hand from the middle of her thigh to her knee. His darker skin against hers made her shiver.

"I don't mean to criticize," she said, resting her head against his shoulder, "but there's a good chance Cora will be waking up soon. Do you mind if we speed this up?" She reached over and began unbuttoning his shirt with her right hand. Truthfully, she wouldn't mind if he made love to her with his tux on. Dylan was a younger, more handsome James Bond.

Or maybe she was a tad prejudiced.

Finally, he snapped out of it. His hand covered hers. "Stretch out on the bed, Mia."

It was an order. She took it as such, feeling ridiculously turned on by his air of authority. As she scooted toward the headboard, trying to act as if being mostly naked in front of a handsome man was the norm for her, Dylan stood with his hands on his hips and tracked her every move.

When she was settled, he tugged at his bowtie, beginning an unapologetic striptease entirely for her benefit. At least she assumed that was his intention. Maybe he just didn't like being rushed.

First he toed off his shoes and stripped off his socks. His trousers were next. The black silk boxers he wore did little to disguise his masculinity. His thrusting erection pushed out the fabric. His excitement was evident in the small wet spot near his waist.

He left the underwear in place and reached for the studs on his shirt. Instead of scattering them across the rug, he removed each one with painstaking slowness and dropped them into a glass dish on the dresser.

"Take the shirt off," she pleaded. If Cora woke up at this exact moment, Mia would die of frustration.

Dylan complied in silence, his eyes flashing, his face flushed.

When he was down to his one last item of clothing, she held out her hand. "Hurry. I can't wait anymore."

At last he showed some evidence of the impatience she was experiencing. He strode to the bed and came down beside her on one knee. "It was worth the trouble tonight of getting into a tux for the chance to see you in that dress. But without it, I think you're even more beautiful."

Before she could respond, he gathered her into his arms and rolled with her. Now she was on top with his silky drawers massaging her female bits. Shivers of anticipation raced up and down her spine. She rested her hands on his hard chest. Tonight he had looked every inch the wealthy, sophisticated Kavanagh.

Yet here, in the intimacy of her room and her bed, Dylan's true essence shone through. He could play the part of a civilized man about town when required. But the real Dylan, the bad boy she had met in high school, was this wild-eyed, feral male. Undomesticated. Determined to get what he wanted, no matter the cost.

She wasn't resisting. Why would she? Leaning down, supporting herself with one palm braced on his warm shoulder, she traced his jawline with her fingers, feeling the late-day stubble. "Your family loves you very much," she said. "And Liam and Aidan trust your opinions. I watched them tonight. They respect and admire you."

His smile was lopsided. "Not that I mind being buttered up, but what's your point?"

She felt his hands caress her butt. Did she really want to carry on a rational conversation at this particular juncture? "Never mind," she muttered. "It will keep." She wriggled her bottom, making Dylan groan.

Without second-guessing herself, she slid down in the bed and settled between his thighs. Licking gently, she dampened the silk that covered his sac. Dylan's back arched off the bed.

Panting, he fisted his hands in her hair. "I have a condom in my billfold," he croaked.

"You won't be needing that just yet."

Dylan's ragged curse ended in a moan as she gently bit his shaft through his boxers. She loved feeling him like this. His fiancée must have been insane to walk away from a man like Dylan.

It was clear his patience was at an end when he put his hands under her arms and dragged her upward for a hot, punishing kiss. "You're a heartless tease," he accused.

"All the better to seduce you, my dear."

He went still. "Is that who I am? A notch on your bedpost?"

"What does that mean?" Irritated, she pulled away.

He lay there like a great cat, his tawny skin radiating heat as he stared at her with an unreadable gaze. "You move in academic circles with men whose intellects are equal to yours. Is what we're doing here your walk on the wild side?"

She scowled, the impulse to slap him almost winning. "That's insulting to both of us. I thought we were having fun. Clearly I was wrong." Furious, she scrambled away from him, intent on fleeing.

But Dylan had other ideas. One strong hand grasped her ankle and pulled her back. He sat up, gripping her shoulders and shaking her gently. "I needed to know the truth, Mia."

Tears stung her eyes, but she blinked them back. "Why?"

His jaw worked. "I've been used before. I didn't particularly enjoy it."

"Well, I *am* using you," she cried. "Though maybe not in the way you're thinking. You're housing and feeding my daughter and me. You're paying me to do a job that any one of a dozen people in Silver Glen could have handled easily. So what does that make *me?* I've hit rock bottom. If I wanted to make love to you, it sure as hell had nothing to do with scoring some imaginary coup."

Their faces were mere inches apart, his breath warm on her cheek. She could see his long, thick lashes and the way they framed his beautiful, intense eyes.

He kissed her lazily. "Fair enough. I should have known you couldn't resist my animal magnetism."

Resting her forearms on his shoulders, she linked her hands behind his neck and played with his hair. "Modesty isn't one of your strong suits, is it?"

"I'm cursed with being irresistible to women."

His tongue-in-cheek humor restored her equilibrium. "Thank God you have me to take you down a peg or two. Otherwise, your head would be too big to get through the door."

"Hold that thought."

He rolled away long enough to get rid of his boxers and to grab protection. Though the banter was lighthearted, his expression was anything but. Standing beside the bed, he rolled latex over his straining shaft.

When he returned, settling on his knees in front of her, it was clear that the time for talking was past. He touched her intimately, checking her readiness. She was mortifyingly wet. Wanting Dylan was a living, breathing ache.

She rested her forehead against his shoulder. "I need you," she whispered.

Lowering her carefully onto her back, he moved over

her with purpose, fitting the head of his erection to her center and pushing with a firm thrust. She inhaled sharply, her mind spinning in a dozen directions.

The confidence of his possession was warranted. His knowledge of a woman's body guaranteed satisfaction. Mia realized he was bringing her to the brink in record time. She savored the physical connection, convinced that Dylan was the only man who ever had or ever would be able to touch her so deeply, so well.

The room was quiet, save for the sounds of his exertion. Whatever veneer of polish he had donned for the evening with his family was stripped away, incinerated in the heat of their coupling. She wrapped her legs around his waist. "Don't stop," she begged, spiraling upward toward an invisible peak.

"Never."

It was a futile request and an unrealistic answer. The force of their need reduced them to the most basic human level. She bit his neck, marking him as hers. His skin was damp with sweat. Her mouth was dry.

Suddenly, he cried out, his big body shuddering atop hers. What sent her over the edge was the realization that for this one moment in time, Dylan wanted her and needed her.

For now, it was enough.

Fourteen

Sometime in the wee hours of the morning, a sound woke Dylan. He lay still for a moment, processing the fact that he was not in his own bed. Then everything came rushing back. His sex stirred reflexively, stimulated by the memories.

The sound came again. He reared up on one elbow long enough to observe the monitor. Cora was stirring.

Stealthily, he slid out of bed, anxious to catch the baby before she awakened Mia.

Cora gave him an adorable toothless smile when he bent over her crib. "Hey, sweet cheeks." The way she looked at him made it clear that she already recognized the man in the house. When he picked her up and snuggled her, the baby smell entranced him. He realized in an instant that he had fallen in love with Cora. The sensation that gripped his chest was a simple, entirely natural emotion, but a profound one.

As he changed her diaper, she kicked her feet and cooed. Blowing a raspberry on her chubby tummy, he felt his heart turn over. She was so sweet and perfect. And she deserved a father.

The knowledge made him uncomfortable. He knew his limitations. What would it be like if he ever had a child of his own, and Dylan were unable to help with homework? Or even worse, what if the kid took after him?

Cora would be smart. He knew it. But Cora and Mia were a package. If he couldn't keep Mia, the baby wasn't his either. Wrapping the infant in a thin cotton blanket against the chill of the air-conditioning, he carried her into the bedroom and sat down on Mia's side of the bed. Touching her hip through the covers, he shook he gently. "Someone wants her mama," he said quietly.

Mia sat up, shoving the hair from her face. She was nude. The realization seemed to take her by surprise, because she flushed and scrambled for the safety of the bathroom.

Dylan kissed the baby's cheek. "Don't worry. She'll be back."

When Mia returned moments later, she was covered neck to toe in a thin black robe made of a soft knit that clung to her body. With her hair tumbled down around her shoulders, she looked like a sexually sated woman. She settled herself back in bed without looking at Dylan and reached for the baby. "You should have woken me up. Cora isn't your responsibility."

He stood for a moment, watching as the baby rooted for a nipple. "I love your daughter," he said flatly. "Nothing about caring for her is a chore."

Pissed for no good reason, he returned to his side of the bed and climbed under the covers, sprawling on his back. With one arm flung across his face, he listened to Cora's enthusiastic nursing. Occasionally, Mia murmured to her daughter. Although the tenor of the words was soft and affectionate, he couldn't actually make out what Mia said.

He was almost asleep when she addressed *him*.

Perhaps Cora was nodding off already, because Mia's words were a whisper. "When Cora gets in school, will you think less of her if she has learning difficulties?"

The out-of-nowhere question jerked him from the edge of slumber. "Of course not."

"So you won't think she's stupid or slow?"

Suddenly, he saw where this was going. "No," he said. "I won't."

He didn't need any further explanation to get what Mia was trying to tell him. He had worn the hair shirt of his academic failures stubbornly, unable to see past his youthful struggles. The truth was, he wasn't that high-school boy anymore. Sure, he still had trouble with numbers and letters, and he always would. But what did that matter?

Suddenly, the ridiculous irony of their situation slapped him in the face. Mia had used an "average" sperm donor so she wouldn't have a child as smart as she was. Dylan was unwilling to father a child who might struggle in school as he had. Unwittingly, he and Mia were trying to play God.

Neither of them had asked to be born with a high IQ or a reading disorder. They had both played the hands they'd been dealt. It was long past time to move on.

He'd used his frustrating studies as a yardstick to measure his success, but Mia was right. He had a lot to be proud of. The Silver Dollar drew customers from miles around and was a stopping-off point for those who wanted to explore the town. His family was close and supportive. He had a wide circle of friends and a house he'd designed from the ground up, a place of respite and peace at the end of the day.

Everything a man could want or need was his. Except for a wife. And a baby. Mia and Cora fit the bill more perfectly than any two people he could have conjured up in his imagination. There were obstacles. He'd be the first to admit it. But he loved Mia. Her job and her talent had kept him from admitting it. Now he acknowledged the truth.

He had believed he wasn't good enough for her. But maybe love was the one ability that trumped all the rest. He could offer Mia things she had never found with other men. And by God, he was going to make her believe it. The joyous possibilities swelled in his chest, though he tempered his enthusiasm, unwilling to tip his hand too soon.

His heart thudded in his chest. Was he really contemplating such an enormous change in his life?

As Mia shifted Cora to her other breast with a smile for her infant daughter, he knew that his answer was yes. Mia brought something unique to his home and to his life. Excitement, yes. But also a deep sense of satisfaction. When he was with her, he felt at peace. Which was odd, because until Mia and Cora arrived in Silver Glen, Dylan would have sworn that his life was perfect as it was.

Imagining his house without them, even after such a short time, was unthinkable. Here in Mia's bed, he realized that what he had shared with his ex-fiancée had been ephemeral at best. It was the difference between a flesh-and-blood woman and a hologram. Tara had been a chameleon, playing a part even when the cameras weren't rolling.

Mia was exactly the opposite. She was real and grounded and complete. Even with his eyes closed, he knew the moment when she got up to carry Cora back to her crib. Moments later the covers rustled as she climbed back in bed, this time staying far to her side of the mattress.

Despite the late hour and their need for sleep, a stronger need drove him. In the dark he donned a condom and then took her arm and urged her closer, meeting her in the middle of the bed. Mia came willingly. She was naked again—soft and warm and so intensely feminine in his arms. He was beginning to learn the touches that pleased her, the little catches of breath that told him he had found a sensitive spot.

Though his hunger for her was as fierce as it had been in the beginning, he didn't mount her at first. Instead, he reveled in the feel of her body pressed against him. Her legs tangled with his. Her hands pulled his head down for a kiss that was equal parts passion and play.

"You amaze me," he muttered.

"It's the testosterone talking." She slid her fingers into his hair, making him shiver. "I'm a rookie. Maybe it's beginner's luck."

Though she turned his rough praise into a joke, he had never been more serious. Parting her thighs with his hand, he moved between her legs and entered her slowly. Someone sighed. Maybe her. Maybe him. This time, there was no rush.

In the darkness, he could pretend this was all that mattered. This heady rush of physical bliss. This feeling that he was in control of his domain. That all was right with the world.

Mia came before he did, her orgasm a gentle rolling wave. He picked up the pace of his thrusts and followed her, welcoming the now familiar physical release that racked him and turned him inside out.

In the aftermath, he heard her breathing settle into an even cadence. In moments she would be asleep.

"Mia." He whispered near her ear, his lips brushing her temple.

"Hmm?" She was tucked into his embrace with her bottom nestled against his groin. It was time to yield to slumber, not to talk, but this couldn't wait.

"When the apartment over the Silver Dollar has been repaired, I don't want you and Cora to move. I want you to stay here."

He couldn't miss the way her body stiffened.

"Why?" she asked.

Because I like having you under my roof and in my bed.

That kind of declaration was a lot to throw at a woman in the middle of the night, so he backpedaled. "I think it would be better for Cora to have some continuity. She's already moved once, and she seems to like it here. Besides, I have a yard for her to play in."

"She's only three months old, Dylan. We'll leave Silver Glen before she even starts walking."

"I care about you," he said baldly, his hands shaking. "And about Cora. My house is still a healthier atmosphere for a baby than a cramped apartment over a bar. Promise me you'll think about it."

Her head pillowed on his arm, she yawned. "I care about you, too, Dylan. So I'll consider it. I promise. Go to sleep now. We can talk about this tomorrow."

When Mia woke up the next morning, Dylan was gone. Again. But this time, she knew he had spent the night in her bed. Shortly before dawn, he'd made love to her one last time.

It was anybody's guess as to where he was at the moment.

After pulling on clean undies and her robe, she went to fetch Cora, her limbs protesting every step. Much of her body was pleasantly sore, but any discomfort she experienced was offset by an almost palpable sense of well-being. She felt satiated and smug.

Dylan had told her he cared about her. It was a lot from a man who guarded himself so carefully. And she had been brave enough to reciprocate without worrying about getting hurt.

Cora was not a great conversationalist, but Mia engaged her anyway. "Dylan wants us to stay, little one. He loves you and he likes me. So we're going to enjoy the moment. Okay with you?" She took the baby's chortle as a sign of agreement.

Glancing at her watch, she decided to prevail on Gertie's good nature once again. She found the older woman occupying her customary morning post, frying bacon and scrambling eggs. "Good morning, Gertie."

"I suppose it is," Gertie said with a grin. "Did the baby sleep?"

"She did. One brief feeding in the middle of the night, but that was it, thank goodness."

The housekeeper set a plate on the table and motioned to Mia. "Eat it while it's hot." Mia, with the baby on her lap, wolfed down a double serving of both bacon *and* eggs and topped it off with one of Gertie's homemade biscuits and jam. It was embarrassing how hungry she was. Normally a cup of yogurt and some coffee would see her through the morning, but after last night's sexual excess, she was starving.

When Gertie finished up the last of the bacon and set it on a paper towel to drain, Mia suddenly realized that Dylan might not have eaten yet. Casually, she took a sip of her orange juice and fished for information. "Did Dylan head into town already?"

Gertie shook her head. "Nope. He's out back getting the boys started."

"The boys?"

"He gives jobs to boys in the foster-care system. Mostly yard work and the like. And he tells them if he ever catches them spending their paychecks on drugs, he'll tear them limb from limb."

"And they believe him?"

"Oh, yes. Mr. Dylan can be fierce when he needs to be. Everyone sees him as this laid-back, good-natured fellow, but he's got strong opinions and strong beliefs about right and wrong. Look how he brought you and the baby here to his house. He could have settled you in a motel room somewhere, but that wouldn't have been right. That boy's moral compass points due north. I know his mama raised her sons to be responsible, but Dylan takes it a step farther. He's a gentleman and a provider. He'll always look out for the weak and the helpless and the ones who've been given hard knocks."

As Mia finished her breakfast, she felt some of her euphoria winnow away. In the middle of the night when Dylan had asked her to stay longer than originally planned, her heart had flipped in her chest. Mentally, she had heard the word *care* as *love*. Dylan wanted to get closer to her. He wanted to pursue their burgeoning relationship, sexually and otherwise.

Now, in the cold light of day, and with Gertie's passionate analysis of Dylan's personality, it seemed more than likely that Dylan's invitation had been the result of altruism. Her mood deflated like a cheap balloon. She gave herself a mental pep talk. Nothing had changed. Cora and Mia still had a home. Mia had a job.

Best of all, Mia was sharing Dylan's bed for the moment. She had never expected more than that. So why was she now feeling disappointed and low?

Wiping her mouth with an elegant cloth napkin, she gave Gertie a beseeching smile. "Would you mind playing with her for twenty minutes while I grab a quick shower?"

"You know the answer to that." Gertie took the baby with alacrity. "Go do what you need to do. Me and this little lady will entertain each other."

Mia crossed the house toward the wing that housed her suite and Dylan's. As she passed his doorway, an unwelcome thought occurred. When Gertie went to tidy her boss's room and make his bed, she would see that the bed hadn't been slept in. The woman was smart enough to put two and two together. Surely she would guess that Dylan had been in another bed. Very close by.

Stealthily, Mia opened Dylan's door. She had never been inside. The furnishings and decor were equally as luxurious as hers, but the colors were more masculine.

Lots of navy and burgundy. Rapidly, she went to the huge bed and threw back the covers, twisting them until they looked like the remnants of a good night's sleep.

One by one, she plumped the pillows. She even knocked one onto the floor for good measure. Satisfied that she had done her best, she turned to leave and ran smack into the bed's owner.

"Dylan," she squeaked, feeling as guilty as if he had caught her raiding his safe.

The flash of white teeth in his broad grin added further color to her hot cheeks. "Whatcha doin', little Mia?" He crossed his arms over his chest. Since he was blocking her only exit, his stance surely wasn't coincidental.

"I, uh…" Well, shoot, she might as well fess up. "I didn't want Gertie to know you hadn't slept in your bed."

His lips twitched, but he didn't laugh. "I'm a grown man," he said, his voice deceptively mild considering the predatory gleam in his eyes. "Gertie doesn't weigh in on my sleep habits."

Before she could defend herself with additional rational explanations, Dylan reached out and stripped her out of the thin robe she wore.

She shrieked and batted at his hands. "Are you nuts? We're not alone."

With a calm she couldn't emulate, he turned and locked his door. "Gertie took the baby for a walk. I want you again, Mia."

The even tenor of his words didn't match the hot, intent gaze that took in every inch of her body. She didn't know why she was embarrassed. He had seen it all last night. Had touched it and kissed it and…

He cut short her mental gyrations by scooping her into his arms. But he didn't walk toward the bed. Instead, he pushed her against the nearest wall. Her legs went around his waist automatically. "Dylan, we can't." It was a weak protest at best, and he took it as such.

"A quickie, Mia. You've heard the term, I'm sure." Without letting her fall, he unbuckled his belt, unzipped his pants and freed his stiff erection. After one-handedly rolling on a condom, he bit her earlobe. "Hang on, honey. This is going to be hard and fast."

Before she could utter a word, he reached between her legs, thrust aside the thin cotton crotch of her undies and pushed inside her, all the way to the hilt.

Beyond the window, Mia could hear the voices of the young men working in the yard. Birds sang. A lawnmower roared. But in Dylan's beautifully appointed bedroom, there was no talking. He took her roughly, urgently, as if it had been months instead of hours since they had mated. His breath smelled of coffee. He tasted like bacon and orange marmalade. His big, tough body held her aloft easily.

She hadn't been prepared for this. No foreplay. No wooing. Which made it all the more mortifying when she climaxed wildly, even before Dylan had finished. The culmination of her pleasure galvanized him. Ramming into her with low groans, he jerked and cursed when his own release found him moments later.

Mia knew her bottom would be sore tomorrow from being pummeled against the wall. But she couldn't seem to care. The novelty of having a man go insane with lust in her presence was a powerful analgesic.

Dylan cleared his throat. "Should I apologize?" he asked, the words rueful.

She pressed her hand over his wildly beating heart. "I don't know. Maybe you should do it again so I can be sure."

Fifteen

Dylan was in over his head. In high school, as a popular kid with lots of money, getting girls had never been a problem. Fortunately, he'd had the good sense to use appropriate protection. But teenage sex and sex in his early twenties had been more about physical release than about bonding with any particular female.

He considered himself a generous lover. None of his partners had ever complained, not even Tara, who had appeared to enjoy his bed but not enough to stay. By the time he met her, he'd been old enough to actually consider settling down. She had flattered his ego. And he had been suckered into the fantasy.

But he had been naive. Fortunately, his broken engagement no longer gave him sleepless nights. He'd made a mistake. And he was lucky it hadn't taken him as far as the altar. Tara was firmly in the past.

Mia, on the other hand, managed to combine the past and the present in one confusing amalgam of nostalgia and sexual hunger.

Instead of releasing her, he carried her to his bathroom, knowing she would want to freshen up before she sneaked across the hall to the safety of her own bedroom. When he set her on her feet, he managed a smile, even though he was in no way sanguine about had just happened.

To be honest, he was pretty much a vanilla guy when

it came to sex. He liked sex. A lot. And often was always better than not at all. But Mia had done something to him. She'd made him feel a gnawing hunger that was not exactly comfortable. In fact, his response to her was pretty damned alarming. How could a meek, quiet, unassuming female turn him inside out and make him doubt everything he'd ever known about himself?

"Mia," he said, unable to keep quiet. "Are you going to stay? For now?"

At the moment, she clutched her robe to her chest with white-knuckled fingers. What she didn't know was that in the mirror he could see the outline of her cute heart-shaped butt through the thin fabric. Clenching his fists to keep from reaching for her again, he leaned against the doorframe. "I'd like an answer please."

When she smiled at him, his legs went weak. "Yes, Dylan. For now."

He cleared his throat, concealing the rush of jubilation evoked by her quiet agreement. "Good." He paused. "It's a gorgeous day outside. What if we get Gertie to fix us a picnic?"

"Cora, too?"

"Of course. She's part of the package."

"That would be nice."

Mia's eyes were huge. He noticed her gaze drop briefly to his pants where his fly was still open. Calmly, he tucked in his shirt, adjusted the rest of his clothing and hoped she didn't notice that he was still semierect.

"I'll go talk to her now," he said. "Let me know when you're ready."

"But we just ate breakfast."

"I'll throw in a tour of the house before we go. And there are things in the woods I want you to see."

"Sounds like the script for a horror movie."

He laughed out loud. Considering that he had to spend

the better part of the next three days dealing with construction headaches down at the Silver Dollar, he knew he deserved this outing. Mia's company was icing on the cake and then some.

Mia was grateful when Dylan disappeared. After one disbelieving look in the mirror, she straightened her hair, carefully fastened the sash of her robe and then returned to her own room to shower and dress. Since Dylan had given her a heads-up, she packed a diaper bag for Cora, and then chose for herself an outfit that was comfortable and suited to the outdoors.

The amber knit top and faded jeans were around-the-house clothing, but after she put her hair in a ponytail and slicked some lip gloss across her mouth, she didn't look half bad. Her canvas espadrilles were made more for style than for walking in the great outdoors, but they would do.

By the time she made it back to the kitchen, her twenty minutes had mushroomed to thirty-five. Since she couldn't explain why she was late, she decided it was better not to say anything at all.

Gertie and Cora were just coming in the back door when Mia found them. The baby threw out her arms when she saw her mama.

Mia took her, holding her tight. It never ceased to amaze her that her love for this little girl grew every day. "Come here, angel. Were you good for Miss Gertie?"

"Best baby I ever saw. Mr. Dylan asked me to put together a picnic. Any special requests?"

Mia shook her head. "Everything you make is wonderful. I've been avoiding spicy food since I'm nursing, but other than that, the menu is wide-open as far as I'm concerned."

Dylan joined them, his presence making the large

kitchen seem to shrink. "While Gertie is organizing our picnic, why don't I show you the upstairs?"

She didn't confess that she had already snooped. "Sounds good to me."

The guest rooms on the second floor were exquisite. "I had help with the furnishings and decor," Dylan confessed.

Each one was different and beautiful in its own way. "You must enjoy having company," she said.

"I do. Several of the guys I went to high school with have moved away. It's fun to host them and their families when they come back for visits to Silver Glen."

"And single women?" Mia gave him a wry look, knowing the answer to that one.

But Dylan surprised her. "If you mean girlfriends, the answer is no. I've never had a lover here."

"Not even Tara?" She raised an eyebrow.

"I lived in a condo in town when I was engaged to Tara. It was after we broke up that I built this place. It's my personal space. My retreat, I guess you'd call it."

"And yet you brought Cora and me here."

He shrugged. "No choice really."

"There's always a choice in life. You could have put us up in a hotel. Why didn't you?"

"I owed you something. For the past. And besides, Cora wormed her way into my heart."

"And me?"

His gaze settled on her mouth, hungry...wanting. "Let's just say that what I feel for you now is a wee bit different than it was in high school. C'mon," he said, taking her arm. His fingers were warm against her skin. She was so attuned to his touch that she felt little sizzles and sparks fizz through her bloodstream. It was impossible to be so close to him and not remember other things. More private things.

He led her to a door at the end of the hall.

"Another bedroom?" she asked.

"Nope. This is the attic access. Let me carry Cora. The steps are steep."

She trusted him implicitly with her daughter. And she was glad he had offered his help. The stairs were indeed slanted sharply upward.

When they reached the top, Dylan flipped a light switch. The cavernous, unfinished space smelled of wood shavings and dust. Cobwebs caught the light. "I'm not sure what we're looking at," she said. If this were a romantic tryst, he wouldn't have brought a baby along.

Handing Cora back to her, he cranked a large handle. Gradually, a section of the roof began to open. Now, with the sunlight pouring in, she saw a large telescope against the far wall. "It's a makeshift observatory," he said, clearly enthused about his revelation. "I come up here on clear nights and look at the stars. That's why I bought this property. We're far enough away from town to escape the light pollution."

"Where did you get the telescope? And how did you learn to use it?"

"I took a class online. Ordered the parts. Put it together."

"Dylan." The exasperation in her voice got through to him.

"What?" He seemed genuinely perplexed.

"I don't want to hear another damn word about how smart I am or how dumb you are. Are we clear?"

Dylan shrugged, grinning. "Yes, ma'am."

Poor Cora seemed baffled by her mother's rant.

Mia felt better for having that off her chest, but she realized that yelling at the man she was falling for probably wasn't the smartest tack to take.

Before she could apologize for her vehemence, an unexpected crack of thunder made all three of them jump.

A large summer storm cloud had come out of nowhere, it seemed, and suddenly the sky above was gray and roiling. The wind picked up, and they felt the first drops of rain.

Dylan manned the crank with all his might, closing the gap just in time to prevent the attic from being soaked. It was quieter suddenly, and awkward.

He put his hands in his back pockets. She saw his chest rise and fall. Sometimes she forgot how handsome he was. Looking at him now, she tried to see him through a stranger's eyes. Some people would write him off as a simple guy with a gift for gab and a charming smile. But there was so much more to Dylan. In that instant, she knew that her feelings were far more involved than was wise. She wished she knew what he was thinking. "I guess that's it for our picnic," she said.

"We could have it in the living room in front of the fireplace. I'm sure Gertie can rustle up an old blanket for us. Cora would like that, wouldn't she?"

"Of course."

Dylan busied himself carrying things from the kitchen to the living room, but he reeled mentally. Mia had read him the riot act upstairs in the attic. And she seemed so adamant that she was right. Had he really been so clueless about his own abilities? Had he allowed an unspoken competition with his older brother to make him feel inadequate?

As he settled onto the quilt with Mia and Cora, he had to smile. Awash in contentment, he listened as the storm raged in full fury. Rain lashed the windows in wind-driven sheets. Gertie, watching the radar, had decided to make a run for home half an hour ago, hoping to miss the worst of the weather. She didn't live far. Dylan was sure she had made it without much trouble, but he sent a text just in case and was reassured when she replied that she was home safe and sound.

Mia had said very little during their informal meal. In fact, she had addressed most of her attention toward Cora. Unfortunately for Mia, the baby was fast succumbing to sleep. Dylan, without asking, tucked sofa pillows around her so she wouldn't roll into anything hurtful as she slept.

When he was done, he crouched beside Mia and stroked her cheek. "Has the cat got your tongue?"

Her abashed look was adorable. "I shrieked at you like a fish wife," she said, her expression remorseful. "I'm sorry."

He drew her down onto the quilt, leaning against the low wall in front of the hearth and putting her head in his lap. "I'm actually flattered. And I'll concede, you may have a point."

After that, they were quiet, content to listen to the storm outside and the crackle of the fire close by. He combed his fingers through her hair, wondering if he would always remember this day as a turning point in his life. He knew what he wanted now. Mia. For always. And Cora. And maybe—when he'd had time to get used to the idea—a second kid.

There was still the matter of Mia's work. To be honest, he couldn't imagine ever leaving Silver Glen. But when it came down to it, he was more sure every moment that he would choose Mia and Cora over most anything else he could think of.

He touched her cheek. "What are you thinking about?

When she looked up at him, he could swear he saw something in her eyes that reflected what was in his heart. For a long time he thought she wasn't going to answer him. But finally, she spoke.

"I was thinking about how lucky I was to come to Silver Glen and run into you again. My life was in chaos, but you were so calm and reassuring. For the first time I began to think that Cora and I were going to make it."

"Of course you were going to make it. You're a bright, capable woman. But everyone needs help once in a while."

She sat up. "Is that the only reason we're together? Because you like helping damsels in distress?"

He cupped her face in his hands. "It was my pleasure to do whatever I could for you and Cora. But no. We're together because of a magnetic attraction. You must have learned about that in science class."

Nibbling his fingers, she smiled wryly. "So you're calling this thing between us *opposites attract?*"

He kissed her softly and released her, unwilling to let things get out of hand with the baby nearby. "We're not opposites at all, Mia. Not where it really counts. We both value family. And roots. You wanted that connection badly enough to have a baby on your own."

Desire shimmered between them. They were enclosed in an intimate cocoon courtesy of the storm and the fire and the memories of last night and this morning.

Mia cocked her head, her expression reflecting his own physical need. "Cora is asleep."

He felt his neck heat. "We can't leave her here. And if we try to move her, she might wake up."

"I was thinking about how comfortable your sofa is."

His eyes darted to the furniture in question. He swallowed hard. "Really?" It was not a question about the couch.

Mia understood. "Really."

He helped her to her feet and held her hand as they crossed the thick carpet to the long, leather-covered divan. In hushed silence, they undressed each other. Shirts and pants. Socks and shoes. Unlike the night that cloaked activities in secret, this was the middle of the afternoon.

There was no hiding, metaphorical or otherwise. Mia's

gaze held his steadily, though he could see remnants of her innate shyness. When he knelt and drew her last piece of clothing down her legs, she stepped out of the lacy panties and stood before him bare as the day she was born.

He shed his boxers and felt a rush of heat scald his spine when Mia immediately took his shaft in her hands and stroked him from root to tip. He saw wonder in her eyes, the same wonder he felt. How could two such different people find common ground in such a primeval way?

The bare leather sofa seemed cold to the touch, so he grabbed a soft mohair afghan and spread it across the cushions. "Ladies first," he said.

When she stretched out and propped her foot on the back of the couch, the bottom fell out of his stomach at the sheer eroticism of the view. After rapidly taking care of protection, he came down on top of her, bracing himself on one arm to spare her his weight. Thunder still boomed overhead, rattling panes of glass in the windows. Mia had been silent through it all.

"I need this," he croaked, almost beyond speech. "I need you."

Her small, winsome smile warmed him from the inside out. "Then we're both going to get what we want."

He wanted to ask her to stay forever. To walk away from her old life. But that seemed incredibly selfish. So he tried to show her with his body that she was special to him. Ignoring the blistering urge to mate, he paid homage to her quiet beauty. Lingering kisses at her throat. Sharper nips at her collarbone.

Soon, though, Mia was not content to be passive. She found his mouth and kissed him recklessly. "I won't break, Dylan. And I don't want to wait. Let me feel you inside me."

It was an invitation he couldn't refuse. Bending her knee to gain access, he positioned himself. "I want to go on record as saying that I'm working under adverse conditions."

He watched as Mia stifled her giggle, biting her lip. "Duly noted," she whispered.

When he entered her, they went from amusement to awe. Eyes open, locked on hers, he moved inside her, feeling his world shift on its axis. Nothing in his life had ever felt so right, so natural. "Mia…" He had no clue what he was trying to say.

She held his gaze bravely, her arms linked around his neck. "I know, Dylan. I know."

How long it lasted, he couldn't say. A minute. An hour. A handful of seconds. Everything faded away. At last, even looking at her became too much of an effort. He closed his eyes, concentrating. Her sex gripped his, making him sweat.

The sofa creaked beneath the force of his movements. Wooly fibers scratched his legs. Sliding his hand beneath Mia's butt, he lifted her into his thrusts, hearing the choked inarticulate cries that told him she was close.

So sweet…she was so damned sweet and sexy.

Without warning, something inside him snapped. Wildly he plunged into her, straining for the goal and yet trying to hold back an inescapable tide. "Mia, Mia," he groaned.

The end, when it came, was swift, incredible and draining.

As he collapsed on top of her, he heard her whisper something, but his heart beat too loudly in his ears for him to hear.

Sixteen

Mia found herself in a predicament for which none of her studies had prepared her. She was in love with a man who clung stubbornly to the idea that she was only passing through. And for the life of her, she couldn't tell him he was wrong, though more and more every day, she wanted to. What Dylan offered was unbearably sweet. But it would mean giving up a great deal. And her sacrifice was predicated on the assumption that he wanted her for the long haul.

His weight was a pleasant burden. She honestly could not tell if he was asleep or not, but the momentary quiet gave her time to think. In her estimation, the sex they had shared was more than just momentarily satisfying. Their physical intimacy seemed born of a deeper connection.

Dylan's tenderness made her believe he cared even more than he had admitted to her.

But was she deceiving herself?

Moments later, Dylan stirred, lifting off her and standing up. The eye-level view of his sex was disconcerting.

He pulled her to her feet, tucking her against his chest. "We need to talk, Mia." His big body was warm and hard, making her feel both safe and aroused at the same time, a dangerous combination.

Her heart stuttered. "About what?"

"You. Me. Us."

"Okay." Her face was buried in his chest. To look at him would have taken more courage than she had at the moment. Her hands rested decorously at his waist, but she badly wanted to stroke his firm buttocks. The tone of his voice could have meant anything, but considering the way his erection nudged her abdomen, she had to hope that this *talk* was going to be a good thing.

Chilled suddenly, and more than a little embarrassed about their nudity in broad daylight, she stepped back, folding her arms across her breasts. "I need to clean up and get dressed. Cora will want to eat soon. Patience isn't her strong suit."

Dylan stood with his feet braced, shoulders squared, as he covered her from head to toe with a hot gaze. His smile made her toes curl. "It's probably for the best. Otherwise we might spend the whole day screwing our brains out."

"Dylan!"

He held up his hands. "Sorry. I'm weak and you're irresistible."

"No, I'm not." His praise made her heart sing, but she tried to keep her feet firmly planted on the ground.

"I'll be the judge of that." He glanced at the clock on the mantel. "If you don't mind being alone here with Cora, I really should run into town and see if the storm did any damage to the building. The insurance company had a tarp installed over the roof, but I don't know if it held in the wind."

"We'll be fine."

"I want to take you to dinner up at the hotel tonight. Table for two. Very private. So we can talk about your future. Our future."

She shivered inwardly, hoping for a miracle. "I'd like that. But what about Cora?"

"I'm pretty sure Zoe would love to babysit for a couple of hours, but I'll call her as I drive into town and check."

Mia picked up her clothes and held them in front of her. Dylan appeared entirely comfortable in his nakedness and in no hurry to rush off. She was not quite so sanguine. So she changed the subject. "At some point today or tomorrow morning I need you to glance at the forms I filled out for your quarterly tax report. I haven't submitted it yet because I wanted you to take a look and see if it's okay."

"I'm sure it's fine, but if it will make you feel better…"

"Thanks."

He took pity on her physical paralysis. "Go get dressed. I'll make sure Cora's okay until you get back."

As Dylan watched her walk away, he enjoyed the rear view. Making love to Mia was a revelation. She had more passion hidden beneath her quiet, reserved personality that anyone he had ever met. Tonight he would tell her he loved her and feel her out about the possibility of staying in Silver Glen permanently.

He was not fooling himself. There was a better-than-even chance that his relationship might not make it to September. Autumn in the Carolina mountains was spectacular. By then the bar would be up and running, and he would have something to distract him from the pain if Mia decided she couldn't stay.

And it would be pain. He already knew that. Hopefully, he was prepared for it.

He dressed rapidly and picked up Cora as she cried out. The baby looked up at him with eyes that were so much like her mother's. For a moment, Dylan felt sympathy for the anonymous man who would never know this precious child.

Being a father was about more than planting a seed. It meant sharing sleepless nights, dealing with croup and strep throat, and reading up on ways to care for diaper rash. *Daddy* was a full-time job, but one with enormous benefits. Being with Cora had changed him...or at least opened his eyes. He would do anything for that kid.

During tonight's dinner, he would lay out his plan. If Mia was on the same page, perhaps during the next few months they could decide if it was possible to mesh their lives.

When Mia reappeared, his heart donkey-kicked him in the chest. He spoke gruffly to cover the emotion that threatened to choke him. "I'm leaving now." He handed over the warm bundle of baby fat and drooling smiles. "Unless you hear otherwise, we'll plan on leaving at six."

Mia bounced Cora on her shoulder. The kid was working up to a major screaming fit. "I'll be ready."

Her smile reached all the way down to his toes.

"Good. I'll look forward to it."

In his truck, away from the temptation that was Mia, he wondered if he had it in him to watch a woman walk away from him a second time. Tara's defection had hurt his pride, but whenever it came time for Mia to leave, he'd be in danger of getting down on the floor to beg.

His damaged business served as a welcome distraction even now. Fortunately, the Silver Dollar was in good shape. Water had seeped in around one of the ground-floor doors, but since repairs hadn't begun, it was no big deal.

He grabbed a cup of coffee from a shop near his business and took a moment to call Zoe, who was delighted to be tapped as a babysitter. When he finished his drink, he walked down one of the side streets, gazing in each window. Silver Glen boasted numerous unique shops.

He paused in front of an antique store. There in the window was a collection of silver charms. One caught his eye. A book. The tiny piece of silver seemed to encapsulate the very thing that had brought Mia into his life in the beginning. On a whim, he went inside and bought the charm and a bracelet to match.

On the way home, his excitement mounted. Dinner with a beautiful woman. The possibility of sharing her bed later tonight. It didn't get much better than that.

When he entered the house, it was strangely quiet. He grabbed a water bottle out of the fridge and only then spotted the note on the kitchen table.

Dylan—

Cora and I are napping. Don't let us sleep past four-thirty. I'll need time to get ready.

Mia

He tucked the note in his shirt pocket, grinning. Neither he nor Mia had gotten much sleep last night. To keep himself from climbing into bed *with* her, he decided that now was as good a time as any to look over the tax stuff she wanted him to see.

His office was neat as a pin…far tidier than he ever managed to keep it. Gertie was banned from this room. The housekeeper rearranged his stacks and made it impossible for him to find things.

The laptop he'd given Mia was on the desk where she left it…and it was turned on. She must have gotten up abruptly to tend to Cora. He used the touch pad to wake things up and saw immediately that Mia's email was on the screen.

His first impulse was to click out of it. He wasn't the kind of man who snooped in other people's stuff. But even with only a brief glance, one word jumped off the screen. *Interview.* His gut tightened as he sat down to read the rest, unable to help himself.

The sender had merely replied to a message from Mia, so Dylan was able to scroll down and see what she had written. It sounded like she had sent more of these letters, all indicating her availability and asking about possible job openings.

Even as his stomach tightened, he told himself it made perfect sense. Mia hadn't kept any secrets from him. Of course she had been looking for future employment. Still, the email felt like a betrayal. An illogical response on his part, but true.

The original email had an attachment. He clicked on the word *résumé* and hit Print. Pages began spitting out of his printer. Gathering them up, he sat down in a chair and started to read…slowly, as always.

Any dreams he had begun to weave about keeping Mia in Silver Glen disintegrated into something that resembled the ashes of a hot fire. Mia had earned not one, but *two* PhDs from prestigious universities. Her work history was impressive, but what he found the most daunting were her research and writing credits.

Over two pages of the résumé were devoted to lists of Mia's articles published in academic journals, as well as papers she had presented at scientific conferences all over the U.S. and around the world.

He had fooled himself into thinking of Mia as a simple, down-to-earth mother of a new baby. Helping Mia and Cora had made him feel like a man. He liked having them look to him for support.

But the truth was far less cozy. He'd been right in the first place. Mia didn't belong in Silver Glen. And she would never belong to him. Even if she wanted him physically.

Calmly, he fed the pages into a shredder. Then he went to the living room and sat down to wait.

* * *

Mia had only napped forty-five minutes, but she awoke feeling refreshed and energetic. A peep in at Cora told her the baby still slept. If Mia was lucky, she might have time to pick out an outfit before her daughter demanded attention.

The impulse to dance around the room made her sheepish. Yes, she was going to have dinner with her lover. And yes, he wanted to talk to her…in private. But that could mean anything.

Her nap had left her mouth feeling cottony, so she headed to the kitchen for a glass of the iced tea Gertie kept on hand round the clock. When she was halfway across the living room, she stopped short, her hand to her chest. "Dylan. You startled me. I didn't expect you back so soon. Is everything at the Silver Dollar okay?"

"Everything at the saloon is fine. No change." He sat sprawled in an armchair, a beer in his right hand and his legs stretched out in front of him. He wasn't smiling. And he didn't look the least bit amorous.

Gradually, a feeling of alarm squashed Mia's euphoria. "What happened, then? You look…" She trailed off, unable to decide what was wrong with the picture.

The fingers of his left hand drummed on the arm of the chair. That slight movement was the only visible sign that he was upset. "I changed my mind about dinner," he said.

She sank into a seat opposite him, her heart at her feet. "I see."

"I doubt you do." Fatigue and bitterness nuanced his words.

"Then why don't you explain?"

He reached into the pocket of his pants and pulled out a folded check. Tossing it on the coffee table beside a small white box, he grimaced. "I hired you in good faith. So I've written that for six months' pay. It should be enough to help you and Cora make a new start in Raleigh. The other thing is a little gift that reminded me of you."

When she bit down hard on her lower lip, she tasted the rusty tang of blood. "I don't understand. I thought you wanted me here. I thought you wanted *me*."

His gaze was bleak. "What I want doesn't matter. You have a job offer. I saw the email. When I went to look at the tax forms." He stopped. She saw the muscles in his throat work. "I need you to leave, Mia. You don't belong here. Go home. Go back to the life you were meant for. Take what you need in the short-term and when you have an address, let me know and I'll ship the rest."

She rose to her feet, frantic. "I don't want to leave. I don't know what's happened, but please don't do this."

For a moment, she thought her plea had gotten through to him. His left hand curled into a fist, and his right hand gripped the beer bottle white-knuckled.

Long seconds ticked by.

Then, with every ounce of expression wiped from his face, he stood up, his gaze landing anywhere but on her. "I'm sleeping up at the hotel tonight. I'd like you to be gone by noon tomorrow. If you need Gertie's help in packing, her number's in the kitchen. Goodbye, Mia."

The six weeks that followed were some of the worst of Mia's life, harder even than when she had welcomed a newborn into her home. The drive back to Raleigh was a blur she barely remembered. Fortunately, Cora had been a doll, napping peacefully for most of the trip.

After one night in a chain motel, Mia hit rock-bottom. She didn't have the luxury of tearing Dylan's check into tiny pieces. If it had been only her, she would have slept in her car before she would have accepted his money. But she had Cora to think of, Cora to protect. Sometimes a parent had to make hard choices.

Once Mia took Dylan's check to the bank, the train was set in motion. With what was left in her checking and savings accounts, and with the generous termination settlement Dylan had given her, there was enough to put down deposits on a nice apartment.

For the moment, Cora slept on the carpet beside her mother. Mia purchased a sleeping bag for herself. Eventually she would get some things out of storage, but for now she was hiding out. Since she had already talked to her friends and told them she was staying in Silver Glen for a while, how could she explain her unexpected return?

From her phone, she emailed the department head who had offered an interview and told him a family situation had put her plans on hold. After that, all she did was play with her daughter and weep. The crying jags ended after the first week. It wasn't good for the baby to see her mother so unhappy. Mia decided that by living only in the present, she could pretend that everything was normal.

She lost weight. Only the prospect of her milk drying up induced her to eat at all. Nursing Cora was a lifeline. It kept her sane. Made her feel whole. She had to take in enough calories to keep feeding her daughter.

Sometimes, if it wasn't too hot, they went for a walk in the park. She had brought Cora's stroller with her from Dylan's house. Amongst other families pushing infants along the paths, she could almost pretend that she was going to be okay.

But at night, when Cora slept, dreams of Dylan kept Mia awake. Ironically, now that she would not have minded Cora's company in the middle of the night, the baby slept from eight in the evening until eight the next morning.

At the end of the second week, Dylan texted her and asked where to send her things. In a panic, she went to the phone store and had her number changed. Even that minimal contact with the man in Silver Glen, the man she loved who had broken her heart, threatened her fragile composure.

Her entire world had imploded, and she didn't know what to do. On the basis of one stupid email, Dylan had decided that Mia needed to go back to her career. But that wasn't his decision to make. Yes, she loved her work, and yes, it was important. But did that trump love? Why couldn't Dylan fight for her? Why couldn't he let her make her own decisions?

In truth, though, she couldn't see a clear answer. Short of Dylan moving to Raleigh—and that seemed wrong on many levels—she didn't see a solution. If Dylan's feelings for her had been stronger, she might have decided to put her career on hold. But even that seemed like a poor choice.

By the time August rolled toward a steamy end, heading for the Labor Day weekend and the official end of summer, Mia had managed to reach deep inside herself and draw on reserves of strength she hadn't known existed. For her child's sake, she had to pick up the pieces of her life.

Cora was growing rapidly and needed new clothes. One blistering afternoon after naptime, Mia loaded the baby into the car and found a mall, one in a part of town she had never frequented. She still couldn't bear the thought of running into anyone she knew.

By the time she wrestled the stroller out of the trunk, lifted Cora out of her car seat, and trudged across the hot pavement into the mall, she felt dizzy and sick. Instead of heading to a department store, she made her way to the food court. All she could think about was buying a large, icy-cold soda.

As she rummaged in her purse for her billfold, she staggered, putting out her hand and grabbing for support. The young man behind the counter stared. "You okay, ma'am?"

Mia licked her lips, trying to breathe. Yellow spots danced in front of her eyes. "Yes," she whispered. "No problem." And then her world went black....

Seventeen

Dylan was frantic. When Mia didn't respond to his text, he hired a private-detective agency to find her…to make sure she and the baby were okay. But everywhere they looked they hit a dead end. It was as if Mia had disappeared from the face of the earth.

She cashed his check. That knowledge gave him a tiny bit of comfort. At least he didn't have to worry that Mia and Cora were destitute. But when he tried to have her phone calls traced, he knew she had deliberately changed her number.

In the intervening weeks, as he missed Mia and Cora with a raw pain that kept him awake at night, he realized he had given up without a fight. And that was not like him. He had been wrong to make them leave. He began to think of solutions, and if none of those panned out, he was ready to pack up and move to Raleigh.

Desperation drove him to extreme measures. Though it was immoral if not downright illegal, he found a tech guru who was willing to hack into the computer Mia had used in Dylan's office. The man tapped into her email account, but there was only one outgoing email. A note informing the sender that she would not be interviewing for a job, the job Dylan had seen earlier.

If Mia wasn't trying to find a job, then what in the hell was she doing? He even checked hospitals throughout the

Raleigh/Durham area in case either Mia or Cora was ill or injured.

The computer geek had showed him how to access the email himself. Every morning and every evening, Dylan sat with the laptop, praying for something, anything. But apparently, Mia was not using her email at all.

His break came in an unexpected way. One morning, an email from her bank popped up with the heading "address change." Without compunction, he opened it, jotted down the information and ran to his bedroom to pack a bag. Six hours later, he parked in front of a nondescript block of apartments.

With his heart pounding and his chest tight, he searched for the numbers that identified the units. There it was.

When Mia opened the door, her face went pale with shock. "What are you doing here?" Animosity crackled in every syllable.

"I came to apologize," he said. "May I come in?"

In case she decided to be obstructive, he didn't wait for an answer, but instead, eased his way past her into the tiny efficiency apartment. He stopped short. Now it was his turn to be shocked. The space was virtually empty. A camp chair sat in the living room in front of him. A portable crib and a sleeping bag occupied the central section of the carpeted floor. There were no other items of furniture. No television, no sofa, no bed.

Dylan's net worth amounted to over three million dollars. Yet, the woman he loved was sleeping on the floor every night. Guilt for what he had done to her sickened him. Fury raged in his chest for his own stupidity. He had to convince Mia that he was sorry. That he was wrong to send her away. That he loved her too much to let her go. He had a feeling his negotiation skills were going to be tested to the limit.

Projecting a calm he didn't feel, he walked past Mia's

single chair and lowered himself to the floor, his back against a wall. "We need to talk."

She glared at him. "The last time you said that it was a prelude to kicking me out of your house."

Swallowing hard, he took the hit without trying to justify his actions. "Please, Mia. Let me say what I came to say." She looked ill, and that worried him more than anything.

"If that's what it takes to get rid of you, fine." Instead of taking the chair, she copied his pose, leaning against the adjacent wall.

Cora was asleep, so he kept his voice low. "I'm sorry for being an arrogant, insensitive jerk. It was presumptuous of me to think I knew what was best for you, for your life, for Cora."

"And what brought about this monumental change of heart?" Now he could see the grief in her gaze. Grief that could and should be laid firmly at his door.

"You left." He said it bluntly, willing her to understand. "And?"

"And I realized how much I loved you. Well," he said, backtracking, "I was pretty sure about that *before* you left. But my empty house sealed the deal. I also realized that I had tried to play God with your future. As if you were not smart enough to choose your own path. And when you think about it, that makes me look pretty stupid."

"You're not stupid." Her response was automatic.

She'd said those same three words to him more than a decade ago and again when she returned to Silver Glen. The trouble was, he hadn't been able to hear them.

"Let's just say that I'm willing to learn from my mistakes."

"Okay. You're forgiven. Please leave."

"Not so fast," he said, stung by her rejection, though he undoubtedly deserved it. "I want a do-over."

"I don't know what that means."

As he studied her face, he was struck by the way her cheekbones stood out and by the dark smudges beneath her eyes. "You look terrible," he blurted out.

"Is that your idea of a do-over?"

For the first time he saw a glimmer of amusement on her face. "Sorry," he muttered. "I've been worried as hell about you."

"I'm not your responsibility."

They seemed to be going in circles. "Mia." He stopped, searched his heart, and did the best he could. He'd made a lot of mistakes in his life, but none he wanted to fix more than this one. "I didn't give you a choice before. I didn't ask what *you* wanted. That's why I'm here now. I need to know what *you* want. What will make *you* happy." He gave the tiny apartment a disparaging glance. "Surely not this place."

"I've moved on, Dylan. I'm making a new start. I'm not the same woman you booted out of your life eight weeks ago."

"Have you been sick?" He had to know.

She shrugged. "In a manner of speaking. When I left Silver Glen, I had a severe relapse into postpartum depression. But don't worry," she said quickly. "I'm under a doctor's care, and I'm going to be fine. I have three job interviews in the next two weeks. Cora and I are back on our feet."

"But are you happy?"

It hadn't escaped his notice that he'd told her he loved her and she never even acknowledged his declaration.

She looked down at her lap where her hands twisted and clenched. "I'm content. I think happiness is a bit of a myth. I'm focusing on Cora and her well-being. That's what matters to me now."

"Happiness is *not* a myth. It's real. And I'll ask you

again. What do *you* want, Mia? If I hadn't been such a jackass, what would have made you happy in Silver Glen?"

She had never said she loved him, but she had hinted at it. Why wouldn't she express that emotion now? Had he hurt her too badly for her to ever trust him again?

"Please go, Dylan." Her face was the color of skim milk.

He scooted across the distance that separated them and sat beside her, hip to hip. "You're wearing the bracelet I gave you." He toyed with the book charm, his fingertips brushing the back of her hand.

"It entertains the baby."

He ignored her ridiculous explanation. "I want to marry you, Mia."

He felt her body jerk, but she didn't say a word. So he forged ahead doggedly. "I may as well spell it out, so you know where I stand. But keep in mind that all of this is subject to your approval…to *your* wants and needs."

Needing badly to connect with her, he took her hand in his, clasping her fingers and resting their linked hands on his thigh. She didn't pull away. So maybe there was still hope. "My family has the means to build a research facility in Silver Glen. We could bring in top-notch scientists from all over the world. You could run the whole thing, or we could outfit a lab just for you and the projects that are important to you. I can hire a manager for the Silver Dollar so I'll be free to keep Cora while you work. I'd like to adopt her if it's okay with you." He ran out of steam, his heart sinking to the soles of his feet. Mia had all the animation of a block of wood, not exactly the kind of response a man looks for when he proposes.

Finally, when he began to feel foolish and depressed all at the same time, Mia stood up to pace. She paused on the far side of the room. "I appreciate your apology and your proposal…or all of your proposals," she said quietly. "But I have to say no."

Was it possible for a man to feel his heart shatter?

Swallowing the lump of regret and grief in his throat, he stood as well. "Why, Mia? Why do you have to say no?" In his bed and in his arms, he could have sworn that she felt something for him.

She rubbed her temples with her fingertips, her posture defeated. "I'm pregnant, Dylan."

Mia's emotions were all over the map. When all the color leached from Dylan's face, he slid down the wall, his butt thumping the ground. "How? Is it another man?"

Rolling her eyes, she shook her head. "Now you *are* being stupid. Of course not. Do you remember that night when we made love half-asleep? Actually, it was toward morning. Neither of us thought to use protection."

She saw the moment when he remembered. Some expression crossed his face, one she couldn't discern. "I don't know what to say." His words were raspy as if he could barely speak.

"It isn't your fault. We were both in that bed. And you've made it abundantly clear that you don't intend to father any children. You'll have access, of course, if you want it."

"If I want it?" He parroted the words, clearly in shock.

"I know this is a lot to absorb, but your life won't change. You don't have to worry about anything. I can handle this."

He shook his head as if trying to dismiss the remnants of a bad dream. When he rose to his feet a second time, alarm skittered down her spine. His black scowl promised retribution. "Are you insane? Of course I want my child!"

She refused to be frightened by his bluster. They had to clear this up once and for all. "But what if your son or daughter takes after you? What if your child has dyslexia?

Or bad eyesight? Or a heart murmur? Or isn't coordinated? What if he or she does poorly in school?"

He put his hand over her mouth and drew her close. "You've made your point, Mia." His lopsided smile broadened with dawning wonder. "My God, a baby." He touched her flat belly with reverence. "We're going to be parents. Cora will have a sibling." He kissed her hard. A possessive mating of teeth and tongues and ragged breath that took the starch out of her knees.

Mia's eyes stung with tears when they separated, her throat tight. "I love you, Dylan, very much. But I have to be sure where you stand. You can't kick us to the curb every time I get an award or receive recognition for my work. I have to know that our relationship is one of equals."

He understood what she was saying. And he wasn't foolish enough to think everything would be easy. But none of that was critical in the end. "I'm so proud of you, Mia. I'll always be proud of you. But what matters to me now is far more important than your brain. I see the love in your heart. For Cora. For me. I want to be the man who makes *you* proud. Your friend. Your lover. Cora's father. I love you, Mia. For always."

She searched his face with a gaze full of hesitant wonder. "You really mean it, don't you? You understand."

"It's taken me a while," he said quietly. "But yes. I do."

She flung herself against him, her arms tightening around his neck in a stranglehold. "I adore you, Dylan Kavanagh."

Stroking her hair, he propped his chin on top of her head. "Pretty soon, word's going to get out about us and it will be pretty clear that *I'm* the smart one for snapping you up."

"You're such a flatterer. But I like it."

He pulled back and took her hands in his. "We'll get

married this weekend," he said. "My family knows every-one in Silver Glen. We can do it at the hotel, or a church if you'd prefer. Zoe can help you find a dress…."

Mia put a hand over *his* mouth. "This isn't going to be easy for you, is it? Letting me make decisions?"

He nipped her fingers with his teeth. "We'll probably argue a lot. And have wild, incredible makeup sex. I love you, Mia, more than you'll ever understand, even with that genius brain of yours."

He went still as she cupped his cheeks in her hands and searched his eyes for the truth. What she saw must have reassured her, because when she spoke, the words were confident and strong. "I want to spend time with our children before they start school. It's important to me. But with what you're suggesting about the lab, I can work from home, or utilize a flex schedule."

Dylan sobered. "*Our* children." The reality was sink-ing in at last. He and Mia had built a family. The rush of exhilaration weakened his knees. "Then you will have your wish. And in that case…" He stepped back enough to take her hands.

"Yes?"

He paused, swallowing hard. "I'd like to go back to school and finish a degree. With your help."

Mia hadn't known she could love him any more. "Will you believe me when I say it doesn't matter to me? I love you, Dylan Kavanagh. And I always will."

"Not for you," he said quietly, his eyes alight with hap-piness. "For me. For Cora. And for this one." He placed both of his hands on her stomach. "I have a feeling I'm going to have more than one genius on my hands, and I need to be able to keep up."

She laid her head against his chest, feeling the wonderfully steady beat of his heart. "You're going to be a wonderful father."

"And lover," he reminded helpfully.

"That, too."

Dylan glanced around the small room that had been her hideout for long, miserable weeks. "I think we're done here, Mia, my love. Let's take Cora and go home. You're both mine now. For keeps."

* * * * *

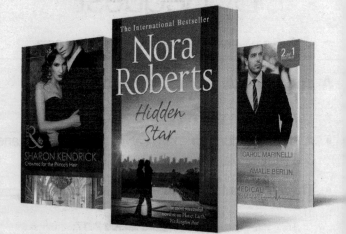

MILLS & BOON®

Congratulations
Carol Marinelli
on your 100th Mills & Boon book!

Read on for an exclusive extract

How did she walk away? Lydia wondered.

How did she go over and kiss that sulky mouth and say goodbye when really she wanted to climb back into bed?

But rather than reveal her thoughts she flicked that internal default switch which had been permanently set to 'polite'.

'Thank you so much for last night.'

'I haven't finished being your tour guide yet.'

He stretched out his arm and held out his hand but Lydia didn't go over. She did not want to let in hope, so she just stood there as Raul spoke.

'It would be remiss of me to let you go home without seeing Venice as it should be seen.'

'Venice?'

'I'm heading there today. Why don't you come with me? Fly home tomorrow instead.'

There was another night between now and then, and Lydia knew that even while he offered her an extension he made it clear there was a cut-off.

Time added on for good behaviour.

And Raul's version of 'good behaviour' was that there would

be no tears or drama as she walked away. Lydia knew that. If she were to accept his offer then she had to remember that.

'I'd like that.' The calm of her voice belied the trembling she felt inside. 'It sounds wonderful.'

'Only if you're sure?' Raul added.

'Of course.'

But how could she be sure of anything now she had set foot in Raul's world?

He made her dizzy.

Disorientated.

Not just her head, but every cell in her body seemed to be spinning as he hauled himself from the bed and unlike Lydia, with her sheet-covered dash to the bathroom, his body was hers to view.

And that blasted default switch was stuck, because Lydia did the right thing and averted her eyes.

Yet he didn't walk past. Instead Raul walked right over to her and stood in front of her.

She could feel the heat—not just from his naked body but her own—and it felt as if her dress might disintegrate.

He put his fingers on her chin, tilted her head so that she met his eyes, and it killed that he did not kiss her, nor drag her back to his bed. Instead he checked again. 'Are you sure?'

'Of course,' Lydia said, and tried to make light of it. 'I never say no to a free trip.'

It was a joke but it put her in an unflattering light. She was about to correct herself, to say that it hadn't come out as she had meant, but then she saw his slight smile and it spelt approval.

A gold-digger he could handle, Lydia realised.

Her emerging feelings for him—perhaps not.

At every turn her world changed, and she fought for a semblance of control. Fought to convince not just Raul but herself that she could handle this.